For Sam and Oscar
xx

Art & Soul

Claire Huston

I

Published by Goldcrest Books International Ltd
www.goldcrestbooks.com
publish@goldcrestbooks.com

ISBN: 978-1-911505-65-5
eISBN: 978-1-911505-66-2

JUNE

Chapter 1

The security gates were wide open. Hoping against all sense this was a sign Charlie was expecting her, Becky drove in and parked the unfamiliar car by the porch. She yawned, rubbed her eyes and sat back to collect her thoughts while admiring the imposing beauty of the Old Station House. Even she, who would happily admit to knowing nothing about Victorian architecture, could appreciate the original features: looped terracotta ridge tiles, steep gables topped by spiked finials, meticulously carved white bargeboards and three massive brick chimney stacks.

With so little notice, and a screaming toddler to contend with, her research the previous evening had been rushed and scrappy. When she finally got to bed, her ethics kept her awake. Charlie had clearly been drunk when he called her and left a message. She should return his call and give him the chance to withdraw his invitation. But then, from what his sister had said, he needed help and wouldn't ask for it when sober.

That morning, as she made herself a vat of black coffee, Dylan strapped in his highchair with more breakfast in his hair than in his stomach, the latest gas bill dropped through the letterbox and silenced her qualms. Placing the envelope in the neat pile next to the toaster, Becky decided a conscience was another item on the growing list of things she couldn't afford.

She got out of the car, tucked two strands of fine mousy hair behind her ears, adjusted her glasses and knocked on the door. Calm and composed, calm and composed, was her silent mantra. The key to a first meeting was to appear confident; the client needed her to be. Nevertheless, the fluttering in her chest reminded her just how out of practice she was and her empty stomach growled. Great. Exactly what she needed.

She was raising her hand to knock again when Charlie opened the door and stunned her into momentary paralysis. Oh dear God. Why hadn't Lauren warned her about this?

His facial hair was rampant, tufted and piebald. Above that undergrowth, dirty brown hair, with patches of grey at the temples, rambled down past his shoulders. Worn, faded jeans and a paint-stained T-shirt completed the crazy castaway look. But his eyes were of more immediate concern. They brought to mind those of a chocolate-brown Labrador she had once seen tied up outside the supermarket in the chill rain waiting for its owner to return.

She smiled. Calm and composed. Calm and composed. Kill Lauren later.

'Mr Handren? I'm Rebecca Watson.'

He blinked but showed no sign of recognition.

'Your sister, Lauren, emailed me. She gave you my number and then you called and left me a message last night. Around midnight.' She searched the visible parts of his face for any reaction. 'You asked me to come here after lunch. I wasn't sure when that was. I hope I haven't interrupted anything.'

He opened and closed his mouth but all that came out was an incoherent stutter.

'I'm sorry, you are Mr Handren, aren't you?' She gave him a tight-lipped smile. 'Please don't tell me I'm in the wrong place.'

His startled expression softened. 'No. I mean, yes. You're in the right place.'

'Great!' Becky pressed on. 'So can I come in or are we going to chat out here?'

'Look, sorry.' He shook his head. 'I think I made a mistake, that is, I called you by mistake.'

Becky refused to be so easily dismissed. The gas bill was no longer alone at the front of her mind. It was jostling for pole position with the boiler, which was grumbling and likely to take strike action soon. And this brown-eyed castaway needed help. She had to get through the door.

Charlie fiddled with the security chain. Becky decided it was time to push the point.

'You meant to call someone else at midnight and invite them here today?'

'No. I mean …' He faltered and scratched his beard. 'I shouldn't have called you. Sorry. It was late and I'd been … you know, I'd been thinking … and drinking.' The tips of his ears turned pink. 'I guess I wasn't thinking that clearly.'

Her lips twitched. Nearly there.

'Mr Handren,' she said, peering at him over the top of her glasses. 'I spent an hour this morning persuading my cranky best friend to look after my son and lend me her car so I could get here. I hardly slept last night because he's teething. So I am begging you to let me in. I promise it'll take under an hour and if you're still not convinced I can help then you'll never have to see or hear from me again.'

She watched as he blinked and swallowed. She needed a clincher.

'And if nothing else, you can tell your sister you talked to me and get her off your back.'

Charlie scratched his cheek, snorted, and opened the door. Becky hurried past him before he could change his mind.

To the left, the old station waiting room was now a bright study. To the right, the ground floor of the two-storey part of the house had been opened up to form a large living room. Beyond it lay the other single-storey section of the building: a spacious kitchen-diner. All the rooms were bathed in afternoon sunlight which streamed through windows at the rear of the house. In the study and dining area French doors opened to the back garden. The lush green lawn was bordered by rose bushes, purple foxglove spires and bursts of yellow marigolds. Charlie might not invest much time in maintaining his personal appearance, but his home was idyllic.

As she followed him into the kitchen, Becky compared his house to her own IKEA shoebox. Charlie interrupted her covetous thoughts.

'Tea? Coffee?'

'Water, please. From the tap is fine.'

Charlie left Becky standing on the other side of the breakfast bar. Opening and closing doors, he shuffled between cupboards, his shoulders hunched. When he found the glasses, his hands shook as he carried two of them to the sink.

Hoping to calm his nerves and hers, Becky started with a compliment. 'Your home is beautiful. It must have been a lot of work.'

Water sloshed over the rim as he thrust the glass towards her. Drops pooled on the countertop and he stared at them as if they were something he'd never seen before.

'A lot of dealing with bloody lawyers, I remember. My wife managed all the renovations.'

She nodded, glancing at the gold band on his left ring finger which glinted as he worried it with his thumb.

'I suppose doing any work on a listed building is a challenge and particularly on one that's been left to fall down.' She smiled but only received a grunt in reply. Time to get down to business. 'I guess you have some questions for me?' she said.

He went back to the sink and filled the other glass, moving his shoulders to shake out the tension. 'I might, if I understood what it is you do.'

'Ah. Well, I suppose the simplest explanation is that I'm a very hands-on life coach. But to really understand what I do, it's probably best to explain the process I usually follow.' She pointed towards the dining table. 'Do you mind if we sit down?'

'Of course not. Sorry.'

Good manners, in Becky's opinion, were sadly undervalued and vanishing. So as Charlie rushed to the table and pulled out a chair for her, he went up several notches in her estimation. Perhaps her first impression had been harsh.

She jammed her knees together and, keeping her back straight, lowered herself to the seat in what she prayed was a ladylike movement.

Her host retrieved his drink and took the seat at the head of the table. Becky took a sip of water to buy herself a few more seconds to compose her thoughts and avoid Charlie's expectant stare. His dark eyes and long black lashes were his most prominent features, although they had the advantage of not being obscured by hair.

Maybe sensing she needed some encouragement, Charlie said, 'Your process?'

Grateful for the prompt, Becky launched into her opening pitch.

'When I first meet a potential client—so you, in this case—we talk about you and your life at the moment. Once I have a good idea of what needs to be done, I go away and come up with a proposal for what I think we can do to improve your current situation.'

She watched for a reaction. His features remained inscrutable under the fuzz. At least he wasn't smirking or rolling his eyes.

'I'll also tell you how long it will take and what my fee will be. Then you can accept, negotiate or reject the proposal. If you reject it, that's it: I charge you nothing. Everything you've told me stays between us and I won't contact you again.'

He continued to stare at her, perhaps waiting for her to say more, or maybe preparing to dismiss her already?

Becky wrung her hands under the table, trying to keep her fidgeting out of sight. That had to be the worst explanation she had ever given. About anything. She wouldn't blame him if he told her to get stuffed and get out.

But when his reply finally came, his tone was unexpectedly playful. 'And if I say yes? I sign a contract in blood and the devil gets my soul when you've granted all my wishes?'

The tension in her neck eased. 'I prefer ink, but I'll take blood if you insist. I'm a modern Mephistopheles. I don't want my Faustus's soul, just fair payment.'

At the corners of his lips was a movement Becky interpreted as a mouth-shrug, rather than a smile. 'Is striking these Faustian bargains your full-time job?'

'It was. I finished my last commission a couple of weeks before I had my son, he'll be two in September, and you would be my first client since he was born. But before Dylan came along I'd been doing this eight years. I also do some events work.'

'Events work?'

Becky stifled a sigh and the urge to tell him she thought of her current employment as putting out fires for people too posh to piss on them themselves. Instead she said, 'Crisis management, that sort of thing.'

He nodded. 'So, what do you need from me? I expect my sister has already told you everything she thinks she knows.'

'She's told me a bit, but I need to hear things from you. How about we start with your routine? What do you do on a typical day?'

'I get up at seven. I take Phoebe, my daughter, to school and sometimes go shopping. Maybe a run after lunch, and the gym about three times a week. Then cleaning, washing, gardening … I collect Phoebe from school, make dinner and three nights a week I teach a class at the adult education college.'

Becky glanced at the patchwork of stains on his faded T-shirt. 'And I guess in there somewhere you paint?'

Charlie rubbed his left thumb across the dried black smear on his right knuckles and sighed. 'Every day. I try.'

'And what do you do at the weekends?'

He shrugged. 'More of the same.'

'Your daughter will be eighteen in October?'

'Uh-huh.'

'And she doesn't drive herself to school?'

'Sometimes, when I don't need the car.'

'This coming academic year will be her last year at school?'

He nodded.

'Is she planning to go to university?'

He rubbed his brow line. 'I don't know. She might prefer art college.'

'She's an artist too?'

'She's good. She'd be better if she practised.'

Becky tapped her index finger on the table. She had been warned he would be less than receptive, but Charlie's monotone mumbling was testing her mask of composure and her conversation skills. What did she have to do to get more than eight words out of him?

'Your sister mentioned your wife left about six years ago. Does your daughter hear from her?'

His eyes narrowed and he pressed his lips together. A flush appeared around the edge of the beard and he scratched his cheek, raking his nails through the thick hair. 'She sends birthday cards.' He coughed, but failed to dispel the sudden venom in his tone. 'Christmas too, last year.'

Becky swallowed a sigh. While part of her was delighted to have provoked any display of feeling from Charlie, angering him at this early stage would be stupid. She needed to retreat to less sensitive ground. What had Lauren said about a home studio? His pride and joy, an inner sanctum?

'I believe you have a studio here. Is it upstairs?'

Charlie's lips curled and he snorted, holding back a laugh. 'It's outside.'

If you could make someone laugh, you were halfway to getting them to like you. Sensing progress, she pushed on.

'May I see it?'

He tilted his head to one side and fixed her with a disconcerting stare. It seemed to absorb every surface detail while slipping under her skin to seek out her secrets. Was this a professional habit or an attempt at intimidation? Well, if it were the latter, he was out of luck.

Charlie blinked first. 'All right,' he said, rising and beckoning for her to follow him out into the garden. 'Come with me. I'll show you.'

Chapter 2

Charlie waited for Becky to step out onto the concrete band which had once been the northbound platform.

Even with his eyes narrowed against the bright sunlight, Charlie noted with pride how the garden was at its best in early summer. The air was still. Birds were singing in the sycamore trees and bees hummed among the sweet pinks of the border roses. And next to him, shading her eyes with her hand as she scrutinised every inch of it, was Rebecca Watson. An unwanted intruder, dark against the view.

This was mostly Lauren's fault. She was the one who had found this life-fixer character and foisted her number onto him. Although he had to take the blame for calling her and letting her into the house. God, he was pathetic! He'd allowed embarrassment and guilt to push him into being accommodating. And now he was taking her to the studio! What was he thinking?

As he closed the door after Becky, Charlie entertained a fleeting fantasy in which he hopped back inside, turned the key in the lock, and left his sister's spy to find her own way out of the grounds.

'Is that your studio?'

Her right hand still hovering over her eyes, Becky was using her left to point towards the large red brick building to the south, close to the perimeter wall.

'Yes.'

Without wasting energy on extending an invitation, he made off towards the building. If the woman wanted to see his studio she could bloody well keep up. 'It was the engine shed and workshop,' he said, glancing at Becky who had caught up and was trotting along next to him. 'We kept as much of the original walls as we could. We bricked in the windows on the long sides, which are about fifty feet long. We also restored the two sets of large wooden doors in both of the short ends of the shed. And the roof is new.'

They paused as they reached the nearest end of the building. An ordinary-sized door nestled within the giant frame of the original wooden gates.

'We'll go through the small door on the south side.' He set off down the small strip of shade along the east side of the studio.

'Why can't we use the door here?'

He rolled his eyes. Without turning back, he raised his voice and arm to beckon. 'Come on!'

Moments later she was back at his elbow. 'What did you do to the roof?'

'It had all but fallen in. We took what was left away and put up a roof with two slopes. At first the sides go up steeply.' He held his hands up, palms facing, and tilted his fingers together. 'Then the pitch changes and the slope is much flatter until the two sides meet at the apex.' He let his fingers drop until the tips touched.

'Why?'

He unlocked and opened the door. With his hand resting on the handle he turned back to her. 'You'll see,' he said and stepped inside.

Not many people had been inside the studio, but the happy few had been impressed. Two-thirds of the building formed a single open space. Currently furthest from Charlie and Becky, the height of the final third was divided in two by a mezzanine platform, which gave access to a floating gangway running along the long sides of the studio. Panels of grey-tinted glass acted as a safety barrier, reducing the risk of anyone taking a ten-foot drop to the floor. Sunlight poured through skylights in the higher roof panels and a series of windows in the north wall above the platform.

Charlie watched as Becky drifted like a sleepwalker to the middle of the building. She paused alongside his battered brown leather sofa and tilted her head back to examine the upper galleries. God alone knew what Lauren had told this woman. She had blabbed about Mel leaving and had probably laid it on thick: my brother, the sad, desperate loser.

Becky wandered to her right, stopping by the old card catalogue. She lifted her fingers towards one of the brass drawer handles and Charlie winced in anticipation of her touch. The large oak chest had been another of Mel's projects. A university somewhere in the south-west was digitalising its records and the beautiful piece of furniture had been bound for the scrap heap when Mel swooped in to save it. She spent the best part of a month sanding, varnishing and telling Charlie how much trouble he'd be in if he got paint on it. Hours crouching in a fine layer of wood dust, her dark hair pulled back in a high ponytail, smiling to herself as she worked. The memory was sharp and bright, and he was surprised by how much it stung.

In his pocket, his phone vibrated and a muffled voice shouted, 'Dad! You've got a message!'

Charlie swore and rooted out his phone. 'My daughter. Messing around with my phone again. She thinks she's funny.'

'Don't worry. My son can already work my mobile better than me.' Becky pulled her phone out of her pocket. 'This is more photo album than phone anyway. I must have hundreds of pictures of Dylan.' She beamed as she cradled the screen and scrolled. 'There's a brilliant one from last week here somewhere. I'll show you …'

'No. You don't have to.' He held up a hand and shook his head.

Her smile faded. 'Oh. 'Kay.' She put her phone back in her pocket and spun away from him, giving the top of the card catalogue a light pat before returning to her inspection of the building.

Charlie frowned. Had he been rude? He didn't want to offend her, but nor did he want to extend her visit by spending hours looking at photos of her kid.

Charlie sighed, turned the phone to silent and read the message.

Is she there? How's it going?

Bloody Lauren and her meddling. It must be the middle of the night in Auckland, but apparently nothing, not even thousands of miles, could stop his big sister sticking her big nose into his business. He huffed and tapped his phone against his chin, pondering how to deal with the female conspiracy moving against him. Of his various options, his first instinct seemed best: be civil to this alleged miracle worker while saying as little as possible. Hopefully she would take the hint and leave sooner rather than later.

Becky was still strolling about, pausing occasionally to glance upwards and tuck dark blonde wisps behind her ears. The rest of her fine, straight hair was drawn back in a short ponytail so loose Charlie half expected it to slip free of the black band resting against her nape. As she turned into the light from the windows above the mezzanine, he studied her high forehead, even brows and straight nose. Taken together with her bright hooded eyes and slightly prominent chin, she reminded him of one of Botticelli's subjects. A classic beauty, just not in this century. Her clothes were a good choice for her shape too. A fitted blouse in striking French ultramarine flattered her proportions and kept drawing his gaze away from her black trousers, which gave definition to her long, powerful legs.

Her wide eyes and parted lips suggested she was suitably dazzled by his sanctuary, although this gave him little satisfaction. As she strolled over to the bank of grey metal shelving and perused his jumble of folders, books and magazines, he worried she was making herself too much at home. Besides, he would have preferred to show off an active, chaotic space featuring work in progress. Instead, all his benches and trolleys were tucked against the walls and the painting supplies they carried had been used little recently.

'What do you think?' he asked.

Becky glanced up from the books. 'It's ... Wow!' She winced. 'I'm sorry. It's just so bright and big.' This time she cringed. 'Again. I'm sorry. I think I'm in shock. I'm usually fairly articulate. Honest.'

He waved a dismissive hand. 'Don't worry. You're right. It's a large space.'

'And warm, although so white.'

'Because it's not white.'

'Is this one of those things where a bridal dress isn't white, it's ivory or eggshell?'

'Exactly. This is a warmer white than pure brilliant white. And the wood floors and the underfloor heating stop it feeling cold.'

'What are these?' She pointed to the left where small canvases covered the wall.

'They're some things for my classes. Sometimes I ask students to make copies. It's a way to understand and practise different techniques.'

'And these are all yours?'

He nodded. He wasn't proud of them, but they were passable. 'Do you recognise any of them?'

'I think you can be sure nearly everyone would recognise these.' She swept her hand past replicas of some of the most famous paintings in the world, including *The Last Supper* and *Guernica*.

'In that case, do you have any favourites?'

She scanned the whole collection. 'The two by Monet. I like the Impressionists and especially the water lilies series. I like the colours and they're peaceful.'

Charlie nodded again. Another honest answer. Her tastes were predictably mainstream. And she wouldn't win any awards for art criticism. How could this woman revive his career when she knew less about art than the elderly ladies in his evening classes?

His phone vibrated. Another message from Lauren.

She's there now, isn't she?! What do you think?

Charlie was halfway through composing a reply when Becky, who had returned her attention to the gallery of copies, said, 'Now this isn't a copy, is it?' She pointed to a pencil portrait of a girl with long wavy hair and a crooked, cheeky smile. 'She's cute.'

Charlie let his hands drop to his sides. The resulting sting at the back of his neck made him realise his shoulders had been in danger of grazing his ears.

'That's Phoebe when she was four. It was so difficult to get her to sit. She kept jumping off the stool to see what I was doing.' He moved towards the sofa and indicated a spot on the floor. 'Right there. Like it was yesterday.'

'One minute she's playing with dolls and the next it's driving and boyfriends.'

His fist tightened, making the phone dig into his palm. 'Phoebe doesn't have a boyfriend.'

'Oh no? Well, plenty of time for that later,' she said, putting her hands behind her back. 'And you? Is there anyone special?'

A sudden tickle in his throat made him cough. He had a nasty feeling his sister was about to give him another reason to wish her dead. He coughed again and did his best to make his reply sound casual. 'Not really.'

'Oh. It's just that Lauren said you'd mentioned a woman you'd met a few times.' She reached towards the workbench, sweeping her hand over the bristles of the brushes crammed into a large ceramic pot. Charlie winced. 'That is, you'd met her a few times and mentioned her a few times too. Lauren thinks she's a gallerist or a curator here in South Compton?'

As Becky's fingers danced over to the pencil pot, almost knocking over a bottle of solvent, Charlie was prepared to do anything to get rid of her, including telling her things that were none of her damn business. Civil and concise, he reminded himself, then muttered, 'Um, yes. I think I mentioned the manager of the Coulson Gallery in town.' Becky's fingers froze and she turned to face him, returning her hands to her sides. Charlie sighed and continued, 'I met her at a few shows. We talked. And, I suppose … I wouldn't object to seeing her again.'

'Do you know her name?'

'Rachel Stone.'

Becky nodded and Charlie returned his attention to his phone, hoping she would also move on.

His reply to Lauren was still unfinished when Becky interrupted again. 'What's back there?' She pointed to the other end of the studio where a white wall closed off the area under the mezzanine platform.

'A couple of storage areas and a washroom.'

'And upstairs?'

'More space for storage and display. Currently empty.'

His phone buzzed yet again. Lauren had resent her previous message.

'I'm sorry, do you mind if I deal with this?' He held up his phone and shook it, wishing it were Lauren's neck.

'No, of course not. Don't worry about me, I'll carry on looking round.'

Waiting until she had her back to him, Charlie entered the final few characters and pressed 'send'.

She's here. Pleasant enough, but art philistine. How is she supposed to help?

He sighed and closed his eyes, only to snap them open moments later. What was that noise?

Becky had returned to the shelves and was running her fingers along the spines of the books. Utterly absorbed in her investigation, she was muttering to herself, her lips moving quickly as she paused to pick up and straighten a few of the collapsed volumes. Charlie raised his eyebrows and sent Lauren an addendum to his previous message.

And she's possibly crazy.

The reply came in seconds.

Good. Essential if she's to put up with you. L.

Closely followed by:

And don't be a condescending arty twat. Lxxx

Charlie had only a few seconds to process his sister's comments when the muttering stopped and Becky said, 'How long have you been working on that?' She pointed across the studio to a large white canvas propped against the wall.

His stomach clenched. He gaped at Becky with a renewed interest. 'A while,' he said, stuffing his phone into his back pocket.

'Too long, I'm guessing.' She walked towards the canvas and inspected it for a moment. 'You've painted over this a few times, right?'

Charlie was impressed. To the unobservant, the canvas appeared white. But as the light played across its surface, textures and tones emerged which revealed its previous use.

He nodded. 'Five times in the past two years.' He rubbed his brow. 'I have an idea. But I can't … it's … it's another thing to get the idea there.' He jabbed a finger towards the canvas.

'Hmn. You should probably get rid of it.' She gave him a teasing half smile. 'It'll start talking to you if you don't.'

Charlie's pulse quickened. Just last night, after more than a few drinks, he'd been convinced the damn thing was whispering. Taunting him, repeating the words of the critics: 'uninspired', 'derivative', 'weak'. But she couldn't know about that, could she?

'You need a fresh start.' She stepped forward and laid a hand on his arm, forcing him to meet her eye. 'Why not give it to your students to use? And, in the meantime, please put it in storage.'

Now scarcely a foot away, he had a clear view of her forget-me-not-blue eyes, which brimmed with concern. Holding her gaze and taking a deep breath, he noticed a fresh, clean scent. Rose? Lavender?

As her cool hand slid from his arm, leaving a patch of gooseflesh behind, he almost wavered in his resolve to consign the last half hour to memory as quickly as possible.

'I've taken up quite enough of your time,' she said, making for the door. 'I'll leave you to get on with your day.'

He strode forward to open the door for her and they stepped out into the sunshine together. Charlie smiled as he shook her hand, trying to hide his relief. At last she was leaving, although she dawdled for another minute to say something about putting together a proposal and having another meeting next week.

He watched Becky stroll across the lawn. When she disappeared into the kitchen, he backed into the studio, threw himself onto the sofa, and let out a sound somewhere between a growl and a groan. The ordeal was over. He just had to pray he'd done enough to get Lauren off his back and to never have to see Rebecca Watson again.

Chapter 3

Walking back towards the house, Becky once again felt as if she had stumbled into the glossy pages of *Homes & Gardens*. It was easy to imagine the station in use: an engine and its carriages sitting next to the house, puffing steam into the blue sky. She smiled: Dylan would love that. Trains were a new obsession and modern electric-powered locomotives were little fun compared to the roaring dragons of the steam age.

The smile faded from her lips as she neared the kitchen doors. Meeting with Charlie has gone about as well as she had expected. Lauren had warned her about her brother's reticence, if not his appearance. But at least if this all came to nothing, she would have had a glimpse inside a couple of buildings many others had failed to access.

Becky sighed and willed herself not to give up hope. Charlie was far from becoming her new best friend but, if Lauren was right, the person she really needed to convince was waiting for her inside. She pressed a hand to her stomach to settle her butterflies and opened the door.

Phoebe was standing by the sink. Hearing the door, the teenager looked up from her phone, smiled and came forward to shake Becky's hand.

Becky glanced at the flaking black varnish on the girl's chewed fingernails. Some were barely more than stumps. 'Sorry I'm late,' she said.

'Don't worry, I just got in,' said Phoebe. 'Anyway, it's great. Dad actually spoke to you. And he let you in the studio. No one gets in there. Aunt Lauren and I were betting on whether he'd slam the front door in your face.'

'He may have let me in, but I don't think he was delighted about it.'

'Oh. Then we should probably go up to my room,' said Phoebe, ushering Becky out of the kitchen, 'in case Dad comes back in.' She paused at the entrance to the living room. 'And I guess that means he didn't offer you the guided tour?'

'I don't mind,' said Becky. 'I bet you've had a few who'd like one though.'

Phoebe smiled and the same dimple Becky had seen in the portrait out in the studio appeared to the left of the girl's mouth. 'Too many. When Compton Hall reopened all the tour buses used to stop outside. Then Dad found some tourists in the back garden, trampling the flowers and taking photos ...'

'And he was less than impressed?'

'He went mental.' Phoebe led Becky to the foot of the stairs. 'That's when we got the gates installed.'

The thick wool carpet failed to muffle Phoebe's heavy tread as she bounded up the stairs two at a time. A more cautious climber, Becky trailed behind, wondering how someone barefoot and so slender could make such a racket.

The girl was wearing a white oversized T-shirt and black leggings which, instead of disguising her waiflike frame, only made her seem more fragile. Becky had to remind herself the reedy figure in front of her was the gatekeeper and a formidable potential ally.

Unlike the rooms downstairs, and with the exception of an enormous mahogany wardrobe which could easily have been a gateway to Narnia, Phoebe's bedroom had no period features. The walls were covered in posters of singers, bands and film stars and the rest of the furniture was boxy and unremarkable.

Blinking through a mist of bubblegummy body spray, Becky arrived in the doorway as the teenager bounced onto the bed and hooked a foot up under herself. 'That seat's comfy,' Phoebe said, gesturing to the padded office chair tucked under a desk covered in books.

On her way to the chair, Becky stopped to scrutinise the large photo collage hanging above the bed. In among snaps of friends, parties and holidays were several pictures of a woman in her mid-forties with long chestnut hair.

Becky pointed at the familiar dark eyes. 'Is that your Aunt Lauren? She looks like your dad.'

'Yeah. Those were taken when she came to visit with my uncle and cousins two years ago. I'd like to see them all the time, but New Zealand isn't really a short trip. Then again, if she did live round here, Dad would probably lock himself in the studio for good.'

'Yes, I get the feeling they don't always see eye-to-eye.'

Phoebe smirked. 'Yeah. They fall out. The last time they didn't speak for over a month. Dad's always telling me how lucky I am to be an only child.'

An only child herself, Becky could only wonder if having siblings would have softened the blow of Phoebe's mother's departure or made things worse. Glancing towards the bed, she noticed a photograph in a silver frame on the nightstand in which mother and daughter were enjoying the sunshine in the garden, laughing and hugging. Clearly that had been a good day. And, Becky guessed, a few years before an eleven-year-old Phoebe's worries about her mother's health would cause the girl to lose her appetite and have recurring nightmares.

Becky was reluctant to disturb the smile on the teenager's face, but if she were going to be able to help, she had to know more about what she was getting into. 'Your aunt said you were eleven when your mother left?'

As expected, Phoebe's smile vanished. She nodded.

'What did your dad do?'

The girl picked at her nail varnish. 'At first he pretended it wasn't happening. We ate takeaways for a week like it was a holiday and she'd be back any minute. Eventually he realised he was going to have to take charge, do all the housework, take me to school, come with me to dancing and clothes shopping.' She gave a short laugh. 'He's done his best …'

'But?'

'Dad …' Her voice disappeared into a sigh. 'Dad's OK, he just doesn't understand stuff.'

Becky smiled; she had forgotten how useless parents seemed at this age. 'Do you think there's any chance your mum and dad might …?'

'Get back together?' Phoebe shook her head. 'My birthday cards are the only time we've heard from her.

Although last Christmas she sent a card too.' Her cheeks reddened and she moved on to picking the varnish on her toenails. 'She put her address in London inside. Dad and I have been arguing because I think we should contact her. Aunt Lauren agrees with me and so she fights with Dad too.' She shrugged. 'I think it's stupid. They haven't seen each other for six years, but Dad still wears his ring. They need to sort things out. Move on.'

Becky nodded. She was impressed by the maturity of the teenager's answers, but sensed it was time to lighten the mood before Phoebe got through all the varnish and started removing layers of nail. She pointed at the collage again. 'That's an impressive cake.'

'The Disney castle one? It was for my thirteenth birthday. Dad made it.'

'Huh.' Becky walked over to the desk, reasoning that if Charlie did give up on painting, he could always become a baker. She smiled at the idea and gestured to a collection of sketches pinned on the noticeboard next to the desk. 'Are you thinking about pursuing art? Your dad thinks you could.'

Phoebe snorted. 'He'd like me to. But I'm not that talented, particularly not with painting and drawing. I like photography, but I can do it as a hobby.'

'When you're a successful …'

'Lawyer.'

'Oh!'

The girl's answer came the moment Becky had moved to sit down. To Phoebe, it must have looked as if shock had knocked her off her feet.

'Your dad doesn't know about this, does he?'

Phoebe shrugged, and in the sudden firm set of the girl's mouth Becky saw something of her father's stubbornness. 'He hasn't asked.'

'Hmn.' Becky added improving father-daughter communication to her Charlie task list. 'And you're sure you want to join one of the most beloved professions in the world?'

'I know. "Kill all the lawyers", right?'

Henry VI, Part II, thought Becky, unable to stop herself. She rubbed her hand over her mouth. Thank God she hadn't blurted it out. The girl had to like her, not think she was weird.

'Maybe not all of them.'

Although fairly sure Charlie wouldn't be thrilled with her career choice, Becky wasn't about to put the girl off a good profession which came with steady work and financial security. If only she'd had the sense to become a lawyer.

'Do you think you can help my dad?' Phoebe lifted her hair and let it fall through her fingers. A few strands dropped forward, giving her a temporary fringe which highlighted her freckles and the concern in her eyes.

'Yes,' said Becky, hoping to convince herself as much as Phoebe. The girl's smudged eyeliner was only slightly darker than the shadows beneath it. Poor kid. She had worried enough about her mother to make herself ill and now she had fretting about her dad to keep her awake at night. 'I've had more difficult cases.'

'Really?' Phoebe brushed the hair out of her eyes and returned to picking her nails. 'Like what?'

'Businesses bordering on bankruptcy, collapsed marriages, runaway kids, various addictions ... Real life coaches help their clients fix their own problems. The people I work with need someone to do some of the fixing for them.' She rolled her eyes at her continued inability to make her job sound convincing. 'Basically I sort stuff out however I think best and apologise later.'

'Good.' Phoebe nodded. 'But can you get him painting again?'

It was Becky's turn to be surprised. 'He's stopped completely?'

'I don't think he's managed anything the past couple of weeks. It's been really bad since the *New Aesthetics* article came out last month.'

She got up and stood by the door, her head tilted towards the stairs. Apparently satisfied they were still alone in the house, Phoebe closed the door, lifted her mattress and retrieved a magazine.

'Page twelve,' said Phoebe. 'Although the bit about Dad is towards the end. It's mostly about the Comptons. You know, the usual stuff about the Whitehalls coming here and South Compton becoming a haven for Britain's famous artists.'

Becky flicked through the pages and recognised postcard shots of Compton High Street, images of several local galleries, and paintings by Sheila and George Whitehall. There was also a black-and-white photograph of the Whitehalls in their studio dated 1852.

Phoebe dropped back onto the bed and continued, 'But then the writer's tried to be clever. He's contrasted the new interest in the artistic history of the area and the success of its galleries with Dad's problems.'

As Becky scanned the final paragraphs of the article she realised Phoebe was avoiding speaking the harsh truth: this was a hatchet job. The author's first mention of Charlie was promising: how serendipitous that one of the nation's most successful contemporary artists had made the fertile artistic region of the Comptons his home! A brief round-up of the first two decades of Charlie's career followed, charting his growing critical and commercial success. But then, five years ago, a show in New York, expected to be his best yet, was a disappointment. Two more solo exhibitions had followed, each more derivative and dull than the last. And in the last two years Handren's work had only appeared in group shows, where it was overlooked at best and derided at worst.

'The end of that paragraph is the worst,' Phoebe said, wrapping her arms around herself, drawing the T-shirt close to her thin frame. 'He basically calls Dad a recluse and hints he might be losing it. Aunt Lauren says we're lucky they used a photo of Dad from a few years ago and not one from the past few months.'

'If it's not too personal a question ...' Becky winced, no one said that unless they were about to ask too personal a question. 'When did your dad start on his current ... *look*?'

'You mean what Aunt Lauren calls "beardie-weirdie chic"?' She rolled her eyes. 'It was before Christmas. Soon after the last time he exhibited anything.'

'I'm guessing that didn't go well.'

'It was only one painting and it didn't sell. And it didn't get a mention in the reviews either. Although compared to that'—she jabbed at the magazine—'I think I'd prefer to be ignored. Read the last sentence of that paragraph.'

Becky dragged her finger down the page and read aloud, 'While the reinvigorated Compton region continues to thrive and sparkle, the increasingly insipid work of its current artist-in-residence appears to have doomed him to obscurity.'

'And now that's in Dad's head. Or part of it. I don't think he read the full article.' Phoebe shuffled to the edge of the bed and dropped her feet to the floor. 'I mean, he was pretty pissed off when he saw they gave his age as fifty-four in the opening line.'

'Ouch.' Becky cringed in sympathy. According to Lauren, her brother wasn't coping well with the idea of turning fifty the following year. With her own fortieth birthday approaching more swiftly than she would have liked, Becky could imagine the pain of being saddled with five unwelcome extra years.

'I know, right?' Phoebe flicked her hair again. 'I hoped he wouldn't see the worst bits. But the local press picked up on them and we get the paper delivered ...' She scowled and, for a moment, the look in her eyes was so fierce Becky was certain those responsible for writing and printing the article should fear for their lives.

'But anyone who knows Dad will know they've twisted everything.' She got to her feet. 'Come with me. There's something you should have.'

Becky trailed Phoebe down to the study, marvelling again at how fast the girl moved on such spindly legs. As the teenager checked her father remained outside and began to scour the bookshelves, Becky wondered if Lauren's concerns about whether her niece was eating properly were well founded.

The décor of the room further emphasised the fragility of the teenager's frame. Open-mouthed, Becky took in the pair of open-fronted bookcases framing the fireplace and the other set covering the opposite wall. The custom-made shelving, in rich golden oak, stood on carved plinths and heaved with books. And Becky hadn't thought it possible to be any more jealous of Charlie's home.

'Here it is!' Phoebe prised a book off a shelf by the hearth and offered it to Becky.

Becky read from the cover, '*John Charles Handren* by Melanie Bradley.'

'It came out when I was eight. That was when Dad was about as big as he got.'

'Your mum literally wrote the book on your dad?'

'Mum and Dad met because she did an article on him for the student newspaper. Later she worked as an arts correspondent. She covered different shows and wrote exhibition catalogues too. Take it, it might help.'

'Thanks,' Becky said, cradling the book. She stroked the cover, preparing to broach what was often the most sensitive aspect of a potential client's situation: money. Lauren's frustration with her brother had been clear when explaining her brother's lack of concern that his meagre teaching salary would barely cover the bills once his dwindling savings ran dry. His paintings had always sold, leaving him free to focus on his art and forget about the money it generated.

She cleared her throat. 'Sorry, I have to ask: your aunt said there might be some money worries?'

Phoebe nibbled her nails. 'This place is almost paid off and his teaching brings in a bit, but for the last few years we've been living off savings. I'm going to uni soon and he wants to cover my tuition and living costs. If I can't talk him out of it and he doesn't start painting pieces people want to buy, he might have to sell the house.'

Phoebe's voice faltered and her eyes glistened. 'My parents fell in love with this place. I was born here. His studio would get converted into flats or torn down.' She sniffed, crossed her arms and shivered. 'Things may be bad now, but that would be the end. He'd never get over it.'

Becky sidled over to the large oak desk under the window and whipped a tissue from the box. 'Here,' she said, offering the tissue to Phoebe as the first tears fell onto the girl's freckled cheeks.

Becky perched on the arm of the sofa and tried to appear reassuring as Phoebe mumbled a thank you and blotted away her tears. She was doing her best to keep her confident façade in place, but sitting up straight and fighting the urge to chew her bottom lip were becoming painful. As much as she needed the work, perhaps this was finally the job that was too much for her. And letting this girl think she could solve all her problems was unfair.

Right. It was definitely time for Plan A: wait until Phoebe stopped crying and remind her Charlie hadn't shown any interest in hiring her yet and the teenager shouldn't pin all her hopes on Becky's only human powers of persuasion.

Phoebe finished drying her face and brought the last of her tears under control with an almighty sniff. 'I'm so glad you're here, Ms Watson.' Phoebe beamed, her eyes shining with hope rather than tears. 'We so need your help.'

'Er, yes. About that—'

'Seriously, I know you can sort this out.' Phoebe grabbed Becky's hand and gazed up at her, blinking her long lashes stuck together with tears. 'You're our last hope, Ms Watson. You can fix everything and take care of Dad, can't you?'

Becky squeezed Phoebe's hand and forced her lips into a smile. 'Of course. Don't worry. We're in this together now, everything will be fine.'

❧

Back in her car, Becky slumped forward and let her head thud against the steering wheel. So much for Plan A: time for Plan B. Whatever the hell that was.

JULY

Chapter 4

Becky didn't have the money to take Dylan to the baby yoga-signing-music classes on offer in South Compton. But Wednesday mornings were reserved for a trip to the local leisure centre pool. Dylan wasn't yet two years old, so the excursions involved less swimming and more splashing, but the walk there and back was excellent exercise. Or that was what Becky told herself as she pushed the buggy up the steep hill on the other side of the river. A few minutes from the town centre, she paused to catch her breath, swear and kick the back tyre of a car parked across the pavement. It was the fourth one that morning and, once again, she would be forced to take the buggy and its precious cargo into the road to continue her journey. She kicked the tyre again for good measure; after all, physical expressions of pavement rage counted as exercise too.

Their route home usually included a stop at Sweet's Cakes, where Becky would reward herself and Dylan for their hard work. The bakery and cake shop was on a busy street in the town centre and popular with tourist parties. When Becky approached—red-faced, drained and longing for a sugar fix—a large group of foreign visitors was gathered around the glass frontage, blocking access to the door. Becky shoved the buggy through the first two rows, bashing them and their Compton Hall gift bags with her hips until she could see the window and what had them so entranced. The latest display featured a cake castle with turrets, drawbridge and moat. The windows in its highest tower contained sugary stained glass. Delicious gargoyles perched on the ramparts, gurning down at a verdant field of fondant where a knight on his white steed was facing a dragon with spun-sugar wings.

The displays inside were equally impressive. A high shelf ran around the interior, decorated with the owner's creations. Flowers were this month's theme. Multi-tiered confections dripping in fondant roses, lilies and hydrangea covered the shelf and, if it weren't for the large glass display case bursting with cakes, biscuits and muffins by the till and the racks of bread covering the wall behind it, a first-time visitor could have believed they had inadvertently wandered into a florist's. The smell was also a giveaway; permanent background scents of chocolate and vanilla were accompanied by a rotation of coffee, cinnamon and freshly baked bread.

The owner of the shop was behind the counter stacking vanilla cupcakes onto a blue-and-white porcelain stand. A short, stout woman in her mid-thirties, she glanced up as Becky entered and gasped. 'Dear God Almighty. That's a woman who needs cake if I ever saw one.'

Becky didn't have the energy to smile. 'Thanks, Ronnie. I love you too.'

Ronnie grinned and gestured to the far corner of the room. 'Take a seat. I'll bring it over in a minute.'

Becky had barely parked the buggy and made sure the now-snoozing Dylan was comfortable when Ronnie reappeared, carrying two large pieces of chocolate fudge cake.

'Your favourite.' She set the cake on the table quickly, making the dessert forks rattle against the china. 'The interns are in charge and tea's on its way. Now,' she said, taking a seat next to Becky, 'what the hell's happened to you? Why are you all red and sweaty?'

Becky bit her tongue. It would be nice if, just once, her best friend could be as sweet and flowery as her cakes. Anyway, Ronnie dyed her hair crimson. Who was she to describe anyone else as 'red'? 'It's Wednesday. We've been swimming.'

'Huh.' Ronnie raised a thin eyebrow. The pencil line was dark brown, almost black. Becky sometimes wondered if she'd considered using red to match her hair. 'A load of hassle if you ask me. But I suppose it knackered him out,' Ronnie said, pointing at Dylan who had started to snore. 'And you won't have to share your cake.'

'Only you would begrudge a toddler some of your cake.'

'Don't you believe it.' Ronnie grinned. 'Not having to share cake is the only excuse my mother will accept for me not having popped out a grandsprog yet.'

'How is your mum? And Mike? And his mother?'

'Ugh.' Ronnie shook her head. 'Don't get me started.'

Ronnie had recently moved in with her boyfriend, Mike, and their relationship was going through a number of inevitable adjustments. They had been together for three years and Ronnie had yet to see eye-to-eye with Mike's mother. He now refused to take sides in their disagreements, a policy of strict neutrality adopted after he had made the mistake of defending his mother's point of view, and Ronnie retaliated by dumping him.

'Anyway,' said Ronnie. 'You'll be more interested to hear I have the gossip you were after.' She lowered her voice. 'Rachel Stone: forty-five, single, never married, no kids. There are some rumours she's been involved with the new gallery owner. Apparently he's fit as you like, but I can't find anyone to confirm that. Yet.'

'And she's definitely Stone as in—'

'Only child of Barbara Stone. Does that make things worse or better?'

Becky sighed. 'Probably a bit of both.'

The Stone family had been in the art trade for over a hundred and fifty years and owned four establishments on two continents. They had the means to open many more, but the clan's current matriarch, Barbara Stone, had declared four galleries to be enough. Any more would have meant skirting perilously close to the vulgar status of a chain.

The family were entrenched in the higher levels of Compton society. When not supervising the business, Barbara Stone busied herself running the region's art society. Her presidential duties included managing the organisation of the society's New Year charity ball, which was held in the grandeur of the nearby stately home: Compton Hall. It was notoriously difficult to get a ticket for the annual event because Barbara and her minions could not be swayed by wealth alone. If anyone who could afford a one-thousand-pound ticket were able to buy one, they would be up to their antique pearl necklaces in hoi polloi.

Becky swallowed her bite of cake and asked, 'How long has Rachel been managing the Coulson?'

'She moved there about six months ago. She'd been working her way up through the family business at the Berlin, New York and London branches. Apparently she thought she was ready to come back to South Compton and step into the top job at Stone HQ but her mother had other ideas. So she defected to the Coulson where the owner lets her do what she likes.'

Becky ate her cake while listening to Ronnie and marvelling at the talents of her favourite gossiphound. What was her secret? It had to be cake. All that sugar was more powerful than truth serum.

'Thanks, Ron. Let me know if you hear anything else that could be useful.'

'OK, boss.' Ronnie gave a mock salute, sunlight reflecting off the silver rings which adorned every one of her fingers. 'Why do you want to know about this woman anyway?'

Damn. That was the problem with a gossiphound: you couldn't restrict her nose to the areas you wanted her to investigate.

'I told you already. If I get the green light for the new project then she could be important.'

'Ah,' said Ronnie in a tone Becky didn't like at all. It dripped intrigue and lechery. Hell, it was a verbal wink. 'The artist fancies her, does he? No wonder you wanted to know if she's attached.'

Damn and blast. 'Ron, you know I'm not supposed to talk to you about this stuff.'

'Oh come on. Who am I going to tell? Besides, you're not working for him yet. Client confidentiality doesn't kick in until he's hired you and that sort of thing is public domain anyway.'

'It's not a secret. I'm just not sure about it yet. He played it down, but his sister said he's raved about Rachel each time he's met her. Lauren said he described Rachel as "very pretty" and that's Charlie's way of saying she's a goddess.'

'Well OK then. Why didn't you say?' Ronnie took a large bite of cake and mumbled through it. 'You got a lot of work this weekend?'

'Yeah, but my parents are watching Dylan so you're off the hook.'

'That's not why I asked. Look at you!' Ronnie waved her fork at the dark circles under Becky's eyes, causing Becky to sway back in self-defence. 'You need a break.'

'I need a well-paid project. I'll rest later. And in the meantime,' she said, digging her fork into the last piece of her cake, 'I'll eat sugar in lieu of sleep.'

Ronnie watched as Becky chewed and swallowed. 'All right,' she said. 'But you know what I think.'

'Ron—'

'Don't pin all your hopes on this project coming through. Go into events work properly. You're great with weddings, better than half the people who organise them already. It's regular work, you'd make more money and could afford a childminder. And then,' she said, winking, 'you could find some time to try online dating.'

Becky brushed a few stray hairs from Dylan's forehead. 'I barely have time for the one man in my life. I don't think I can find the energy to deal with another.'

Ronnie tapped her rings against her cup. 'Of course, you could have time and money to spare if you made that bastard responsible for his son.'

'No.' Becky slammed her fork down, making the table shake. Ronnie talked a lot of sense, but she wasn't right about everything. 'Thanks for the cake and the gossip. We'd better be going.'

Chapter 5

By Thursday evening Becky had a rough outline for her proposal and was on top of things. Her parents had arrived earlier that day and were staying until Tuesday, allowing her to focus on an upcoming weekend wedding marathon and use Monday to finish her presentation for Charlie.

She had also finished his biography and had a good understanding of Charlie's pre-slump career: twenty years of success which had paid for a wonderful home and stuffed an increasingly threadbare financial cushion.

At around ten thirty she sent an optimistic update to Lauren, cleared the draining board and decided to get an early night.

As she locked the back door, raindrops rapped at the kitchen window. She shivered, then shrugged. If it had to rain, better it tipped it down during the night than tomorrow or at the weekend. Three dry weddings in three days was a challenge, but three muddy and gloomy events would be a trial. More reason to get to bed. Though days of constant rain were unlikely, a good night's sleep would leave her better prepared to tackle the issues that came with dark skies.

She was locking the front door when her phone rang. Throwing herself towards it, she fumbled to silence the ringer. Breathing a string of curses, she hurried into the kitchen, eased the door into its frame and accepted the call.

～

Twenty minutes later, Becky drove her parents' car through the gates at the Old Station House.

The drive from her home in Great Compton, a 1960s commuter village, to the leafy and palatial suburbs of South Compton had done nothing to lighten her mood. Pulling up behind Charlie's gleaming car, she ground her teeth. He drove a bloody Merc of all things and yet his life was supposedly unbearable. The seats were probably kitted out with massaging bum warmers. He should try getting everywhere on foot with a toddler in tow because he couldn't afford to run a car any more.

She tugged the keys out of the ignition and sighed. She had loved her little car. It had stuck with her for eight years and never let her down. But three months ago she was forced to sell it, the latest victim of belt tightening.

Her brooding irritation balanced on a quivering layer of work-related anxiety. In a few short hours she would be insuring a fourth-of-July-themed wedding against disaster. If it stopped raining, the evening celebrations would include a fireworks display organised by a party of groomsmen who had no previous experience with controlled explosives. Becky would have to act fast to prevent minor burns and other stupidity-induced injuries, particularly if she were unable to dissuade the bridal party from putting sparklers in the bouquets.

Becky was raising her knuckles to knock when Phoebe opened the door and threw her arms around her neck.

'I'm so glad you're here! Thank you for coming!'

Slipping into mummy autopilot, Becky patted the girl on the back and cooed reassuring monosyllables, using her free hand to close the door. As she uncurled Phoebe's trembling fingers, she silently pummelled Charlie with every expletive she could call to mind and a few colourful terms she coined for the occasion.

'It's going to be fine.' She took both of Phoebe's hands in her own. 'Come on, you better show me what we're dealing with.'

A few minutes later they ducked into the studio, shaking the worst of the downpour from their hair and coats. Charlie was visible from the doorway. Slouched on the sofa with his head back, he looked like a sleeping bear, although Becky wasn't sure bears could snore that loudly. An almost empty bottle of whisky sat on the small table next to the sofa.

She clenched her fists as she noted the presence of the not-truly-blank canvas, sitting exactly where she had last seen it. Rather than follow her advice, Charlie had made another attempt at getting his ideas out onto the material. The faint terracotta streak in the centre of the canvas suggested he had failed once again and wiped his efforts away with the red-stained rag which was lying across his knees. Becky took the upended trolley and the resulting mess of tubes and pots on the floor as further signs of vented frustration. Charlie had lashed out before passing out.

'He's honestly not an alcoholic,' Phoebe said, glancing towards the sofa and biting her nails. 'He sometimes has a drink in the evenings. But I've never seen him drunk until a couple of weeks ago, after the article came out. Last Sunday was the worst night so far. I think that was when he called you.'

Becky nodded and Phoebe continued.

'Tonight at eight-ish I went down to get some water and he was in the study looking through old photo albums. I think the wedding album was one of them. He'd already had a couple of glasses. At about half eight I heard him go out and then I saw lights in the studio—'

Becky decided to skip to the end. 'And when you called me you'd gone out to check on him and he was like this.'

'I couldn't leave him out here and …' Phoebe hunched her shoulders, her voice dropping to a whisper. 'I didn't know who else to call.'

Becky sighed. Whatever Phoebe might have been able to do on her own, there was small chance a skinny child on the verge of tears could have dragged a well-built, six-foot-two man back to the house across the moonless, muddy garden.

'Go into the house and make some industrial-strength coffee,' said Becky, patting Phoebe on the arm. 'We'll be in shortly.'

The slam of the heavy door failed to rouse Charlie or even disrupt the steady drag-whistle of his snoring. Becky sighed again and waited a minute to make sure Phoebe wouldn't return before approaching her father.

Standing in front of Charlie, she steadied herself on the arm of the sofa as she leant forward, called his name and shook him. He grunted and twitched, but otherwise showed no signs of waking.

Becky straightened up, frustrated but also relieved to be putting some distance between herself and the fumes on Charlie's breath. She picked up the stained rag from Charlie's lap using her thumb and forefinger and flicked it towards the canvas. Good. At least she wouldn't stain her coat while dealing with the drunken idiot.

As she rubbed a small smear of paint from her nail, her gaze fell to the side table and the single photo album next to the whisky bottle. Her natural curiosity got the better of her and she twisted away from Charlie to flick through the pages. She had assumed it was the wedding album Phoebe had mentioned, but instead she found a collection of family photos, most of them either featuring Phoebe alone or with her mother. Becky ran a hand over her mouth and adjusted her assumptions: the sorrows he was trying to drown appeared to go beyond pining for his absent wife.

She turned back to Charlie, whose snoring was now making her nerves jangle in time with the hairs on his upper lip. Enough, Becky decided and kicked his ankle.

Charlie woke up with an excessive amount of snorting and sniffing which Becky suspected was a reflex action common to all those roused from a self-induced stupor.

'Mr Handren! It's Rebecca Watson. I was here the other day.'

'Who?'

'Rebecca Watson.' She raised her voice and over-pronounced each syllable.

'Ahhhh!' His head bobbled up and down. 'Lauren's professional life fixer. She thinks I need help. None of her damn business.' He shook his head as violently as he'd nodded it. 'Life fixer! Ha! None of *her* damn business either. And what kind of a job is that anyway?'

He beckoned for her to come closer. 'Funny girl that one,' he said in a low slur, circling a finger beside his head. He giggled, then bent forward and confided in a stage whisper, 'She's got a great pair of legs though.'

Becky inhaled slowly through her nose. At another time, she might have found this amusing. But not tonight.

'She's also *me*, Mr Handren. I need you to get up. OK?'

Charlie made an attempt at rolling to a stand, but gave up halfway and slumped back to sitting. He lifted his arms and let them smack down onto the sofa.

'She's going to leave, y'know. Like her mother.' His head dropped onto the backrest. 'Can't paint. Can't do anything. It's all derivative and dull. S'what everyone's saying. Might as well sit here and rot into ob … obshurrity.'

He huffed and rubbed his eyes while Becky wondered how she was supposed to respond to his drunken ramblings.

She was toying with the idea of dumping a bucket of freezing water over his hairy head, when he looked up at her and blinked rapidly. He narrowed his eyes and stared as if she had just manifested before him. Then, moving faster than she would have thought him capable, he grabbed her arm and yanked her towards him.

'I didn't offer you a drink. Would you like me to give you one?'

Horrified, Becky felt his other hand crawl round her waist and creep downwards as he leered up at her through bloodshot eyes and, slurring, said, 'What do you say? Care to join me?'

The anger which had been winding into a coil since Becky received Phoebe's call slithered down her arm; she whipped her hand back and swung it forward, slapping him with a satisfying snap.

It felt fantastic. Stingy, but fantastic.

Unfortunately, elation was brief. Slapping potential clients wasn't exactly an orthodox way of winning their business.

Becky raised her throbbing palm to her mouth. Oh, good God Almighty. She could say goodbye to the perfect new project and chunky commission cheque. She'd have to branch out from crisis management at events to organising the damn things. In the Comptons. That would mean even less time for Dylan and when she did see him she would be cranky and cross. The people would be awful and she'd be working directly with migraine-inducing brides. And then there would be children's parties. With clowns and creepy magicians.

She shuddered and scanned Charlie's dazed and reddened face, wondering if an apology would penetrate the alcoholic fog.

But the smack appeared to have bounced off its target leaving no lasting impression. Charlie rolled his head back to centre, his features settling back into the pre-slap leer.

He laughed. 'That's a no, then?'

Becky balled up her fists but clamped them to her sides. Violence, while sure to be therapeutic, was not the answer. She cleared her throat; perhaps her bark would be more effective than her bite.

'For God's sake, snap out of it!'

The leer vanished. Encouraged, she leant towards him and lowered her voice to a vicious hiss.

'You may be feeling sorry for yourself right now, but the truth is your only real problem is you. You're sitting here getting drunk on expensive whisky in your glorified Wendy house—which is bigger than my home by the way—you've barely a mortgage to pay and stacks of cash in the bank.'

She rolled on, letting her prejudice and resentment of South Compton's elitist art set mingle with more justified criticism.

'You drive a Mercedes and make, or made, your living from paintings which look like the masterpiece my toddler produced the time he tipped his poster paints over the living room rug. You're acting like a privileged, pathetic, selfish fool who's one drink away from becoming a total cliché.'

Open-mouthed, Charlie was watching her with an unfocussed, glassy stare. She couldn't tell if her words were penetrating his hairy armour and thick skull, but she was buzzing and couldn't stop.

'Stop wallowing and get up!'

As if her words had been delivered via cattle prod, Charlie jerked out of the seat and jolted to standing. He swayed, but Becky swooped forward to drape his arm over her shoulders and used his momentum to help them stagger out of the studio back into the rain.

Having propped Charlie against the wall, she locked up. The locks were stiff and by the time she pulled him to standing his clothes were soaked. If they were lucky he wouldn't develop a nasty cold. Or flu. Or some other harmless but disgusting, grotty illness.

Her lips twitched as she put a hand around his waist to steady him and began to edge across the sodden lawn.

Clouds covered the moon, making the trek back to the house more treacherous. Becky's glasses were rendered useless by the cold raindrops sheeting towards them, forcing her to squint in the direction of the kitchen lights.

Every dragged footstep sprayed sucking, slippery mud over her feet and legs. Meanwhile, Charlie got heavier as more of his torso relaxed against her shoulder.

His mouth was only inches from her ear, allowing her to hear him over the patter of the rain as he chuckled quietly and said, 'You *are* strong. I noticed that before. Sturdy.'

Becky dug her nails into his waist and hoped it hurt. Either the alcohol had rendered him oblivious to her fury or he had a death wish.

When they arrived at the house, she gritted her teeth and made no effort to prevent him falling as she shoved him through the kitchen door. But, with the rolling balance of a lucky drunk, Charlie steadied himself on the table and dropped into a chair.

Phoebe was waiting for them with the coffee and a large towel. Becky acknowledged this display of forward thinking with a nod, draped the towel around Charlie and told the startled teenager to go to bed.

She took the chair opposite Charlie, fixed him with her hardest stare and spoke slowly. 'Mr Handren, I need you to listen to me.'

Charlie stared at her vacantly over the top of his coffee cup. He was steady and followed her hand movements as she calmed down to her normal, benign bossiness.

'You've done a good job raising your daughter. It can't have been easy to suddenly find yourself in charge of an eleven-year-old girl, but you rolled up your sleeves and did what had to be done. Without complaining and without a team of hired help to pick up the slack.'

Charlie didn't move other than to blink, and with each blink his eyes stayed closed a little longer. It was time to get to the point.

'But. Being a good parent isn't just about the cooking and cleaning and ferrying them to after-school activities. It's not only about how much you do or how much you care; it's also about who you are. And at this point you are a black hole sucking the happiness out of this home. This is where your daughter lives. Make it a place she wants to stay and come back to.'

She ran her hands behind her water-smeared glasses and rubbed her eyes. It wasn't the best motivational speech ever given, but it would have to do.

The rest of her instructions were practical: he was going to drink a glass of water and eat toast, followed by another glass of water and two painkillers. Tomorrow he would get up at seven, shower, brush his teeth thoroughly, dress, come downstairs, eat more toast and drink more water. He would make Phoebe breakfast. He would apologise to her and tell her he would never be drinking alone at home again. And he would mean it.

'Finally, and this is very important.' She reached across the table, pinched Charlie's chin between her thumb and forefinger, and tilted his head back until their eyes met. 'You are going to quit feeling sorry for yourself and count your blessings instead.'

Becky released him and pushed to standing. Sighing heavily, she skirted round the table and put her hand on Charlie's shoulder. As she helped him stand, cool raindrops dripped from his hair onto her hand and the surge of adrenaline which had been carrying her dried up. She closed her eyes. Nothing more could be done tonight. Or undone. She would just have to go home, scape off the dirt and wait to find out how much damage being a goodish Samaritan had done to her career.

Chapter 6

A weekend fighting fiascos had one significant upside: it didn't give Becky much time to think about whether she had scuppered her chances of working with Charlie.

After Thursday night's washout, it had stayed mercifully dry all Friday, and Saturday turned out to be another glorious day. Becky doubted she was the only one giving thanks for the unspoiled blue sky. The bride was so highly strung, a single wisp of cloud could have sent her into meltdown and it was Becky's job to do anything and everything to prevent that happening.

Fortunately, her task was made easier by being on familiar turf. South Compton Country Club's grand driveway, rose gardens, manicured lawns and large banqueting hall made it a popular wedding venue and Becky knew the grounds and building inside out. By South Compton standards, the Rose–Hartley reception was an average-sized affair with merely two hundred and fifty guests. They were easily accommodated in the shade of the terrace and the sunshine of the lawns, where the sound of croquet mallets connecting mingled with the strains of a string quartet, the clinking of crystalware and the hum of conversation.

Scanning the crowd, Becky wondered at the most expensive display of millinery outside Royal Ascot. Every female head was adorned with feathers, lace or flowers. The riot of colour was distracting, although this was to her advantage, making it easier for her to blend into the shadows and observe Amber Hartley, née Rose, as she flounced about in her ivory dress, bossing her friends and family and bullying the staff. Her treatment of one of her bridesmaids was particularly harsh. Clarice Barry, the bride's cousin, was expected to respond cheerfully to commands issued as if she were an unloved dog and laugh at insults. Becky fumed in silence as Amber—an emaciated matchstick with a sharp, joyless face—told her petite cousin, with gorgeous blonde curls and a rosebud mouth, that she was chubby, unattractive and could do with skipping her helping of wedding cake. The other bridesmaids tittered at Amber's jokes, confident of their appearance in elegant blush, rose and coral sheaths. Clarice's dress was an unflattering fuchsia tent and Becky was sure the bride had taken extra trouble when choosing it.

At the wedding breakfast, Clarice was exiled to the very end of the top table and had to listen to speeches which included hilarious tales of Amber's childhood pranks, including the time the scamp had shaved off Clarice's eyebrows. Apparently the school photos that year were simply a hoot!

How Clarice was sticking it out was beyond Becky, particularly as she didn't appear to be drinking. At the centre of the table, the new Mrs Hartley cackled and quaffed champagne. As she lowered her drink, the bride winked at Clarice, then twisted to haul the groom into a sloppy kiss. The bridesmaid blinked and gripped the edge of the table. From Clarice's reaction, Becky guessed this was yet another piece of spiteful provocation.

Without taking her eyes off the bridesmaid, Becky pulled her phone from her pocket. It was only the tenth time she'd looked at it that afternoon, and she was pleased with how she had restrained her irrational need to check for missed calls from her parents. Dylan was fine. She was worrying about nothing. The worst call she could expect would be from Ronnie, ranting at her for not being in the car park at six o'clock on the dot.

Shaking her head, she dialled a number and glanced towards the best man as she listened to the tone. After far too long a wait, the chinless idiot retrieved his phone from his suit jacket. His eyebrows shot up and he leapt out of his seat, gesturing to one of his equally clueless friends.

Meanwhile, at the other end of the table, Clarice was still glaring at Amber. Her look of patient suffering had morphed into one Becky recognised all too well: the cold determination of a woman hell-bent on revenge. Clarice snapped her gaze away from her cousin, grabbed a teaspoon and pushed herself to standing. Surveying the guest-infested waters below, her hand trembled next to the rim of the nearest glass, ready to strike. She took a breath and—

'Ladies and gentlemen!'

The best man's voice thundered from the PA system, making Clarice jump and drop the spoon.

'It's time for the cutting of the cake!'

Under a dazzle of camera flashes, the happy couple clasped hands and frolicked to the other side of the room. Clarice blinked against the pulsating glare, put one hand over her belly and swayed.

Before she could faint, Becky had an arm around her waist. 'You're all right,' she whispered. 'I've got you. Just breathe.' A few deep breaths returned colour to Clarice's face and Becky felt confident enough to move her. 'Let's go somewhere quiet and get you a nice cup of tea.'

Becky helped Clarice down off the dais and through a door hidden behind an excessive floral arrangement. A series of narrow corridors led to the swing doors of the kitchens where the catering staff were preparing to serve the pre-sliced cake. Several trolleys were covered in plates carrying equally sized rectangles of cappuccino swirl with chocolate frosting. On the stainless-steel countertop to her right, Becky noticed the distinctive pink-and-white stripes of an empty Sweet's Cakes box and made a mental note to tell Ronnie how impressed the caterer had been with the new design.

Clarice squeezed Becky's hand and lowered her head. The lighting in the kitchen was harsh fluorescent and the air smelled of roasted meat and poached vegetables, hardly an ideal environment for someone in a delicate state. The bridesmaid needed a seat.

Lucinda, the head of the catering team, was standing next to the trolleys completing her inspection. Becky coughed and Lucinda looked up. 'Hello, Becky. On time as always.' She tipped her head to the left. 'I've set up the quiet corner. You won't be bothered.'

Becky beamed and grabbed the empty cake box with her free hand. 'You're a godsend.'

Lucinda smiled and turned back to the waiting service trolleys. 'No problem at all. I know you'll return the favour.'

The quiet corner was to the left of the main food preparation area. The space was mostly occupied by three tall double-doored fridges which filled the air with a low drone of white noise. In front of the fridges, two high-backed wooden chairs were waiting. Between them, an upturned blue plastic crate served as a table, laid with a pair of cups, saucers and spoons.

Becky lowered Clarice into a chair, put the cake box on the floor by her feet and took the other seat. 'Sorry it's not much of a footstool,' she said, gesturing towards the box. 'But it's probably a good idea for you to put your feet up. And here ...' While Clarice put her dainty, silver-sandaled feet onto the box, Becky picked up the cup and saucer nearest the bridesmaid and prayed Lucinda had remembered to add sugar. 'Try to drink some of this. It should help you feel better.'

Clarice's fingers trembled as she raised the steaming tea to her lips and took a cautious sip. The drink appeared to have an instant restorative effect: her shoulders dropped and her hands stopped shaking.

The bridesmaid sipped her tea daintily, sneaking glances at Becky over the rim of her cup. Meanwhile, Becky gulped her own drink and prepared for the inevitable question.

'Who are you?'

Clarice's voice contained a tremor, even though her hands were steady. Becky decided to approach with caution. 'I'm Rebecca Watson. I'm a member of the wedding staff.'

'No, you're not.' Clarice set her cup back on the table and shook her head, sending her golden curls swinging. 'You're not with the event organiser. I know that lot. And what you're wearing is similar to the waitresses' uniform,' she said, pointing to Becky's white blouse and black skirt, 'but it's not the same.'

'You're right, but I am working here today. I guess I'm a … sort of professional fairy godmother.' Becky chose to ignore Clarice's raised eyebrows. She lifted a silver spoon from the makeshift table, stirred her tea and continued, 'And I think if you've ever needed a fairy godmother, it's now.'

Clarice lowered her gaze to her lap and picked at the silver embroidery on her skirt. She took a deep breath, lifted her chin and regarded Becky over the pointed tip of her nose.

'I'm sure I don't know what you mean.'

Becky stopped stirring. 'You are pregnant? And the groom is the father?'

Clarice gasped. Her hand flew to her mouth and the colour drained from her face.

'Don't worry,' said Becky. 'It isn't obvious. I've been watching you all afternoon and I wasn't sure until a few seconds ago. I'm not going to tell anyone, I promise.'

Clarice looked over her shoulder, probably searching for the nearest exit. 'Why have you brought me in here?' Her voice rose to a squeak. 'Who are you?'

Becky put the spoon back on the crate next to her cup. She glanced towards the main area of the kitchen where the catering staff could be heard wheeling out the last of the cake. Leaning towards Clarice, she dropped her voice, 'When I'm not granting wishes, I offer a kind of insurance certain people like to contract for events. It's my job to make sure everything goes smoothly. I can offer total discretion in dealing with delicate matters. Matters my clients don't want their event coordinators to know about.'

Clarice's neat eyebrows contracted into a frown. 'You got them to cut the cake early? To stop me making a scene?'

'Yes, I'm sorry. I doubt it's any consolation right now, but announcing it out there wouldn't have helped.' The corner of her mouth flickered upwards. 'Personally, I think the look on the bride's face would have been a treat, but in the long run you know you would have come out of it worse.'

Clarice dropped her head into her hands and groaned. 'Who hired you?'

'The groom. But he doesn't know about the pregnancy,' Becky said as Clarice's head snapped up, eyes wide with alarm. 'He wanted me to stop anything from sending Amber supernova. But he also mentioned you and he were an item when he met Amber. And when he talked about you he was shifty, like he was hiding something, then you've been green around the gills all day, and finally your glasses of untouched booze at dinner … I put one and one together and got three.'

A tear fell onto Clarice's dress, staining the evil fuchsia a pleasant magenta. Becky produced a tissue from her sleeve and passed it over.

'Amber's vile,' Clarice said between sobs. 'The wedding's been on and off. It was during one of the "offs" when he and I …'

Becky nodded. 'She's a nasty piece of work. For starters she made you wear that dress and …' She shuddered. 'She doesn't eat cake. Not even chocolate.'

A snort and a sly smile replaced the sobbing. 'That's because if she let so much as a sliver past her lips it would double her weight.'

'I know! She'd look like a snake when it swallows a mouse.'

Clarice snorted again and blinked back the remaining tears.

'Have you thought what you're going to do?' Becky asked.

Clarice shook her head. 'If I keep the baby then my parents will make me go away and give it up. If I refuse to have it adopted then I'd never be able to come back here. I'd have to leave my job and I'd be all alone. And either way I'll have ruined things with Steve.' Tears welled up again. 'My boyfriend. We've only been seeing each other a couple of months, but it was going so well.' Her bottom lip wobbled. 'I love him.'

Becky passed Clarice another tissue and waited for her to dry the latest bout of tears. 'Ms Barry.' Becky laid her hand lightly on top of Clarice's. 'Whatever you decide to do, I know it's not going to be easy. But—'

'No. You don't know that.' Clarice snatched her hand away and swiped at her tears with the sodden tissue. 'You can't know the first thing about what I'm going through.' She sniffed. 'Unless by some miracle you're also a single mother who got knocked up by her cousin's fiancé?'

Becky shrugged. 'Well, he wasn't my cousin's fiancé, but otherwise, yes. Actually, I went one better because my Prince Charming turned out to be already married.'

Clarice's lips parted, her frown vanishing as her jaw dropped. 'You're joking?'

'Nope.' Becky smiled. 'And, if you'll let me, I'd like to help you. I have a fair deal of experience solving other people's problems and getting them what they want. I think you deserve that kind of help. Sure, you made a mistake. But who hasn't?'

Clarice drained the last drop from her cup and stared into its depths, as if hoping to find a better future spelled out in the tea leaves.

Becky's phone buzzed. She glanced at the screen and frowned.

'Is everything all right?' asked Clarice.

'Yes … It's just … A friend is doing me a favour and I'm … You know what, it's not important.' She stood and offered Clarice a hand up. 'I think you've done brilliantly to get through today. But why don't you sneak off now and put your feet up?' In her pocket, her phone started to vibrate again. Ronnie must be livid. 'I'll call you a taxi. Please go home and get out of that dress. If it'll help, burn it.'

Clarice giggled and Becky smiled. If you could make someone laugh, you were halfway to getting them to like you.

'Here's my phone number.' Becky slid a piece of paper into Clarice's hand. 'Give me a call in the next few days. How about I take you out for more tea and some cake? I know the perfect place. And there's not much a good cup of tea can't fix. Trust me.'

Chapter 7

On Monday, as the sun woke her by warming her face, Becky smiled and rolled away from the light onto the cool, smooth side of the pillow. She listened to the latch click downstairs and Dylan's laughter as he was lifted into the car. His grandparents, who knew no fear, were taking him to an early soft play session at the leisure centre. She marvelled at their foolhardiness: the South Compton mothers at those things were often toxic, at best tetchy. And the children of the worst ones were biters.

Sighing at the blissful prospect of a rare lie-in, she stretched her feet down to the bottom of the mattress and pulled the duvet over her neck, right up to her earlobe. She would drop Lauren an email later to see whether Charlie was applying for a restraining order against her. But for now she would treat herself to one hour of quality dozing.

Cocooned in a marshmallow of freshly washed bedding—her mum was an angel—she smiled again and relaxed deeper into the wall-to-wall peace and heavenly aroma of warm buttered toast.

The doorbell shrilled.

Becky groaned and flung the duvet away. She guessed even angels forgot things occasionally, including their copy of the house keys.

She blundered downstairs, shoved her feet in the general direction of her slippers, missed and stubbed her big toe on the skirting board. Her howl of pain and subsequent swearing were partly covered by a more persistent ring of the doorbell. Becky swiped at the door latch, praying she'd be able to hand over the keys and take her stinging toe back to bed in under a minute.

But rather than her parents, Becky found Phoebe shuffling on the doorstep, bouncing out of her turquoise ballet pumps.

'Hi!' Phoebe said, lifting her fingers in an unnecessary wave.

'Morning.' Becky squinted in the sunlight and adjusted her grey flannel robe to cover the cartoon bears on her pyjamas. She lifted a hand to her hair. If she'd known anyone other than her parents would be at the door she'd have paused to drag a comb through it.

As Phoebe glanced down at her nightwear and fluffy slippers Becky fought the desire to run back into the house and hide under the duvet. This was why she hated surprises. Success in her job meant appearing unflappable. And while she couldn't read Phoebe's mind, she guessed squealing, swearing and appearing in front of a potential client in pyjamas decorated with bears holding hearts proclaiming 'I love you Mum', suggested 'crazy lady hanging in there' more than 'composed professional'.

Phoebe bit her lip. 'Sorry, I didn't get you up, did I? Don't kids jump on their parents' heads at dawn or something?'

'Usually. But his grandparents are taking care of him today. I was working all weekend.'

'Oh.' She glanced down at Becky's feet again. 'Good thing I didn't manage to persuade Dad to come along!'

Becky imagined her face was as grey as her dressing gown and her eyes shot through with a colour similar to that rising in Phoebe's cheeks. Right at this moment she couldn't be gladder Charlie hadn't been talked into joining his daughter's impromptu visit. He likely already thought she was an interfering witch; no need to reinforce the belief by appearing hag-like. 'Hmn. I'd say you're right about that.' She opened the door a little wider. 'Is everything OK? Do you want to come in?'

'No, no, everything's fine. I can't stay long, I have to get to school.' She motioned behind her to where Charlie's car was parked on the street. 'Dad sent me.'

What? Becky raised her eyebrows.

'Er, actually, he told me to call you.' She took a nip at her thumbnail. 'But I thought I'd drop by. I wanted to thank you again for helping me.'

Ah. That sounded plausible. 'You're welcome. Was your dad all right on Friday?'

'He was!' She beamed. 'I didn't think I'd see him 'til I got home from school, but he was waiting for me when I came downstairs, not looking too rough either. He was showered and dressed and he made me breakfast.'

Becky nodded, pleased Charlie had taken notice of her instructions.

'And then,' Phoebe said, 'he apologised. He felt bad for forcing me to … How did he put it?' She frowned, nudging her dad's words down into her mouth. 'Oh yeah, "ask for the help of a virtual stranger". And he's been in a good mood all weekend, and he went out for a really long run yesterday.'

'Is that unusual?'

'He runs all the time. But the mood is a big change. I heard him humming yesterday. And not any of the usual slash-your-wrists, depressing music he runs to either. It was something, you know, upbeat.'

'And he told you to call me?' Phoebe's large eyes shone as she nodded and Becky was pleased the teenager was already feeling the benefits of Charlie's change in mood. No one so young should have to spend most of their time worrying about their parents. But Becky was also concerned the girl was putting too much faith in her ability to help her dad. He hadn't hired her yet, after all.

'I suggested,' Phoebe continued, 'since you'd been so brilliant on Thursday, coming over in the rain and so late to help me when you were a virtual stranger and had no real reason to help, and you had a really mad weekend of work coming up you should have been resting for, that given all that he should hear you out. Your proposal to help him, I mean. And Aunt Lauren agreed with me and said it was the least he could do. And Dad said, "Fine," and so we said, "No time like the present." So could you come over tomorrow afternoon?'

Phoebe dragged in a breath and Becky closed her mouth. While prone to ramble at alarming speed, the girl was clearly persuasive. Becky wanted nothing more than to help her, but tomorrow afternoon wouldn't work. 'I'm sorry, but my parents are leaving tomorrow morning and it's too short notice to find anyone to look after Dylan—'

'Don't worry! Dad said that might be an issue, so I said I'd look after him. If it's OK with you. If you like, I can drive over here and pick you both up and then you can leave him with me in the house while you're talking to Dad. I've babysat some of my friends' brothers and sisters before, and you'll only be in the garden.'

Well, hadn't she just thought of everything? Becky nodded, impressed, although wouldn't it be too much of an imposition? And what if Dylan had an accident?

Perhaps sensing she was wavering, Phoebe jumped back in. 'And I did first-aid training with the Scouts too!'

Becky smiled. She should have known: like her, someone who had been trained to 'Be Prepared'. But there was still a niggle scratching at her conscience. Once again it seemed Charlie had been coerced into dealing with her.

'You're sure *your dad* wants to see me?'

'Definitely.' Phoebe grinned. 'You'll see. It'll be totally different from last week. He'll be nicer. He's promised.'

Chapter 8

The next day, as arranged, Becky found Charlie waiting for her in the studio, sitting in the same place she had found him on Thursday night.

A quick glance around the building and at its owner confirmed Phoebe had been right: things were different. The not-truly-blank canvas had finally gone, all trolleys were standing and the floor was free of paint supplies. Charlie had tied his clean hair back into a tight bundle, his clothes were stain free and she suspected he might have attempted to comb the facial growth.

As the door closed, he sprang to his feet and extended a hand in greeting. 'Hello, again.' Shaking her hand, he made eye contact for just long enough to say, 'I think, from now on, you should call me Charlie.'

'Not John?' she asked, remembering the book about his work that Phoebe had shown her.

'John is my dad. My family and friends call me Charlie, from my middle name.'

That was it: the apogee of the apology. She had been classed along with his nearest and dearest, confirming her suspicion he didn't remember the slap. Perhaps they would be able to start with a clean slate after all. And, in that spirit, she decided it was time to cut him some slack.

'In that case, I'm Becky.'

She noticed a shudder in his moustache and, guessing a smile lay behind it, she smiled in return.

Charlie reached towards the clutch of presentation boards wedged under her arm. 'Let me take those for you.'

Assuming Charlie would appreciate something other than her to look at while she delivered her proposal, the previous evening Becky had robbed Dylan's craft supplies to cobble together some pieces of paper and card. A few years ago the idea of going into a pitch without a thoroughly rehearsed PowerPoint would have horrified her, but now she wondered if it had ever been necessary. Besides, Charlie didn't strike her as the type who found computer graphics or a laser pointer impressive. And once a potential client had tried to grope you, and you'd given him a slap and a good telling-off in return, attempting to put a professional gloss back on the relationship seemed futile.

'Thank you.' She pointed at the vacant easel in front of the sofa. 'If you could set them on there that would be great.'

He hurried over and fumbled the boards into place. When he turned back to face her, she was reminded of the hangdog, Labrador expression she had noticed on their first meeting, although now he appeared eager for a reward.

'Thanks. If you'd like to take a seat, I'll try to keep this brief. The presentation is in three sections. Please save your questions for the end of each of those sections.'

She paused to gauge his reaction so far, but his face and posture betrayed nothing. He sat upright with his arms relaxed at his sides and his feet planted in line with his knees.

Becky tucked her hair behind her ears and made a mental note: Charlie was never going to be a great conversationalist and if they were going to work together she would have to learn to read his non-verbal cues. And that would be easier if she could convince him to lose the whiskers. But she was jumping ahead. She had to get the job first.

~

Charlie relaxed back into the sofa as Becky outlined her three main goals and how they would be achieved.

At least she was keeping it mercifully short. And, as she had claimed the first time they'd met, she was articulate. Though not as articulate as the other night when she'd called his behaviour privileged, pathetic and selfish. And he doubted anything she could say would be as articulate as that tremendous slap. Just thinking about it made his cheek sting. He was lucky she hadn't punched him. Her right hook was probably a jawbreaker.

Becky turned over to the third board and Charlie scanned its contents. Thank God she hadn't brought some awful computer thing. Staring at screens always made his eyes ache, while her neat, rounded script was reassuringly solid.

As she spoke, Charlie did as instructed and kept his questions to himself. But he failed to control his fidgeting and, as she whipped away the third board to reveal a summary of her objectives, his frown had grown so deep he had a pain between his eyes.

Surrounded by a border of hand-drawn stars, Becky's three main points sat before him:

1. *Kick-start career to ensure financial security (for Phoebe too). How? A solo comeback exhibition in a prominent local gallery for a new collection. Guaranteed success.*

2. *Tackle love life: Rachel Stone?*

3. *Improve family relations: Phoebe and Lauren.*

He had been wrong. Becky wasn't crazy; she was totally insane.

She brought her speech to a close and clasped her hands behind her back. 'Understandably, you have questions,' she said. 'If you're not sure where to start, pick one of them at random.'

'OK.' He sat back and put his fingertips together. 'Assuming you can get me this solo exhibition. When would it be?'

'Ideally the first Thursday of the new year.'

Charlie bit the inside of his cheek. She had no idea of how unrealistic her timescales were. 'I used to have one solo show a year, max.'

'Yes, but you often had a couple of group shows too. And you were prolific for some of those solo shows. In one in Sydney you exhibited almost fifty pieces.'

Oh. Maybe she had done her research after all.

She continued, 'And for this show I was thinking of more like twenty to twenty-five. I think it's doable.'

He groaned and dropped his head back against the sofa, then raised it and let it thump down.

Becky sighed and took a seat next to him. Charlie stared up at the skylights and muttered, 'Impossible, totally impossible.'

'No, it's not, Charlie.'

It was the first time she had called him by his first name. It was a little odd but, somehow, it sounded right.

He rolled his head towards her. She smiled and used two fingers to tap him on the knee. 'It'll be a lot of hard work, but not impossible.'

He pushed himself upright and raised his voice as he said, 'And are you going to produce these paintings? Have you forgotten I only paint dull and uninspired pieces?'

'Now that,' said Becky, raising a finger, 'is a matter of opinion, not fact. I, for one, believe you can do this. Phoebe and Lauren do too.' She shrugged and tilted her head from side to side. 'Maybe not tomorrow, granted. But we'll get there.' Becky jumped up and flicked over to the next board. 'Which brings me to the next section: the commitments I need from you if this is going to work, and what you can expect from me.'

Once she got past number one—provide the art for the show—the rest of her requirements were straightforward and involved him sticking to his existing routines, including exercising and teaching. However, the final stipulation was considered so important it had its own board.

Tapping the two words in capital letters in the centre, she said, 'And now for the hard part.'

'*Now* for the hard part?'

'Yes.' She smiled at his disbelief. 'I need you to *trust me*.' She underlined the words on the board with her finger as she said them. 'Sometimes I'll only tell you what you need to know. Other times you won't know anything about things I've done until you experience the results. But I'll always act in your best interests and I'll never lie to you. And as far as everyone else is concerned, I'll be working with you on your show as your agent or publicist or whatever title you want to give me. The rest will be as confidential as you decide.'

Charlie sighed and rested his chin on his hand. So he actually got to make some decisions in all this, did he? That was big of her. Then again, he'd made all the decisions in his life over the past six years and that hadn't got him far.

It was pie-in-the-sky madness. But could it hurt to let her try? The last week had been one of the most eventful for years. If nothing else, having Rebecca Watson around might prove a welcome break from the emptiness of a life without inspiration. Not to mention that Lauren and Phoebe would be delighted.

❧

Becky was exhausted. She had expected some resistance, but Charlie was doing a decent impression of an immovable object.

'And finally,' she said, as Charlie sighed and rested his chin on his hand, 'this won't be easy. My experience is that clients find my meddling annoying. But we've worked things out and they've all been happy with the results.'

She dropped her arms to her sides. Not the most professional presentation, but she guessed Charlie would appreciate its brevity rather than being appalled by her handwriting.

Charlie turned his attention from the wall to the easel and narrowed his eyes. 'And, if I were to agree to this plan of yours, what would it cost me? Because you've said my soul isn't of interest.'

Becky was relieved to see her audience and his sense of humour were still with her. 'You're right. Which brings me to the last section of the presentation.' She flipped to the final board. 'You would give me twenty per cent of the gross sales from your exhibition. And I expect there will be some expenses along the way.'

'Hmn. I won't be left with much if you take twenty, the gallery takes forty—'

'They'll take twenty as well.'

'Huh. You seem very sure about that.'

Becky resisted the urge to smile. 'Trust me.'

He tilted his head and crossed his arms. 'Do I have to start that already?'

She mirrored his body language and volleyed his smart question with one of her own. 'That depends. Are you hiring me?'

She could see him weighing his options, although, from what her sources told her, he had few. In the days since Becky had come to Phoebe's rescue, Charlie's daughter and sister had waged a war of attrition against his scepticism and reluctance, slowly twisting his arm until he agreed to give Becky's proposal a hearing. And now he had complied with their first demand, Charlie had to know the women in his life were unlikely to give him any peace until he hired Becky. Moreover, as she worked on a commission basis, the fallout from turning down her proposal was certain to be worse than giving her a chance. He had nothing to lose.

'Ah … What the hell!'

He pushed himself to standing and extended his hand. Becky grasped it and, smiling, said, 'That's your way of saying you'd like to hire me, right?'

'Yes. Sorry. You'll notice I'm not good with words. Although …' He kicked the sofa. 'I haven't been that great with paint lately either.'

'Think positive, Charlie. This is a new start. It's all going to be—'

Her phone buzzed. Apologising, Becky fished it out of her pocket and scanned the message. Oh crap. Was that today? She glanced at her watch; she could make it, but she would have to leave immediately.

'If you're wondering what happens next,' she said, gathering up the boards, 'it tends to seem anticlimactic at first. I'll be busy for a few weeks getting your exhibition venue sorted, but I'll be in touch and probably meddling too.'

She looked at her watch again. Twenty minutes. It would be enough time if Phoebe could drop her and Dylan at the clinic. She couldn't miss the appointment: Clarice would be in a state anyway, and if Becky were late she might find her under a waiting room seat, curled—appropriately enough—in the foetal position.

'I'm sorry to run away like this, but I promised to go with a friend to the doctor.'

'Nothing serious, I hope?'

'Well, yes and no.' She winced. 'I'm sorry, you may have to get used to that sort of answer.'

He escorted her to the door and held it open as they said goodbye. Becky clung to the boards and added a skip to her step as she made her way across the garden, not caring if Charlie were watching.

Her mind was in a whirl. Apart from the potential to earn her enough to pay off her mortgage—a delirium-inducing prospect in itself—one project tended to lead to another. This might be her last chance to avoid twenty-five more years of frustrating, make-do work and worries about how she would find the money to give Dylan the best future.

She had to make this one a success.

Chapter 9

Charlie was in a self-congratulatory mood the morning after Becky's latest visit. Although still sceptical of Becky's abilities, hiring her had brought him a shower of praise from Phoebe and Lauren. They were excited by the possibilities Becky represented and their enthusiasm was infectious.

Not bothering with a shower or breakfast, he threw on an old grey T-shirt, running shorts and well-worn trainers, and started the morning run which had been part of his daily routine for over five years.

Outside the air was warm and clear, further bolstering Charlie's positive mindset. Humming to himself, he slotted his mobile and keys into his armband, adjusted his headphones and began to trot down Station Avenue. In the distance, one of his neighbours was having their grass cut. The steady buzz of a lawnmower and a fresh, spirit-lifting scent drifted over him as he made progress through the shade cast by the beech trees in the Avenue's central verge.

At the end of the street he turned on his music and quickened his pace.

Two minutes of frantic button-pushing later he ripped the phone from his arm. A quick inspection confirmed his suspicions: someone had messed with his music. Over fifty albums had vanished, replaced by one playlist in which none of the two dozen tracks were labelled.

Unwilling to run without a soundtrack, and driven by the remnants of his sunny state of mind, he put his indignation to one side, repositioned the armband, pressed 'play' and set off.

⌒

As Charlie settled into his run, on the other side of town Becky was helping Dylan down the step into the back garden. She opened his sandbox and waited to see whether he was in the mood for outdoor play. On a good day the simple plastic shell with a few toys could keep him amused for long enough for her to get some work done. Today she was in luck. Dylan clapped, grabbed his spade and settled into some major excavation work. This left her free to sit at the garden table and study the seating chart for this weekend's wedding. From the notes she had taken during her meeting with the groom, she saw subtle changes were needed to avoid reigniting a dormant feud between the two sides of the bride's family.

She was close to finishing when the doorbell rang. Becky checked her watch and smiled. Phoebe certainly knew her dad's routines; she had predicted his arrival time to the minute. She positioned her pens to prevent any papers taking flight and scooped up Dylan who giggled and squirmed as she tickled him.

'Come on, poppet. Charlie's here,' she said as they made for the front door, arriving just as the ringing was replaced by some aggressive knocking. 'Coming!' she shouted, struggling to hold Dylan while hunting for the keys. On the other side of the door, Charlie was muttering and pacing. The words 'Bloody woman, who does she think she is?' were the most distinctive. Becky fiddled with the keys and decided to wait thirty seconds before venturing outside.

When she finally eased the door open, Charlie had given up pacing and was leaning against the wall next to the front window, lowering his heels to the ground and gasping as he stretched. Becky was wondering how best to interrupt when Dylan laughed and Charlie looked up.

'Morning, Charlie,' Becky said, hoisting the toddler higher up her hip and adjusting his sun hat to better shade his eyes. 'Dylan, this is Charlie. Say "hello".'

'Bee!' chirped Dylan.

'Don't be offended,' she said. '"Bee" is his word for "hello" and "goodbye".'

She was the first to admit her bias, but Becky defied anyone to stay angry when faced with her son's undeniable cuteness. Fluttering under the brim of his hat, two circles of long dark lashes framed Dylan's eyes which sparkled above a pair of rosy, chubby cheeks. He regarded Charlie quizzically and reached for his beard.

Becky drew back, putting Charlie's facial hair out of harm's way. 'Come in, come in. You must want some water.' She took a few steps inside. 'If you close the door after you I can put this beastie down. He tries to make a break for it if I leave it open. Come through.'

She led him straight into the living room of her skinny end-of-terrace. The stairs were immediately in front of them, although getting up them would have involved vaulting over Dylan's buggy.

Becky made her way to the kitchen, trying to picture her home through Charlie's eyes. Her smooth magnolia walls must seem insipid compared to the colours, textures and motifs of the reproduction Victorian wallpaper in the Old Station House. Colour in Becky's house was provided by Dylan's bright and often garish toys which littered every visible surface. At least she'd had the chance to clean last night. Mess was acceptable; dirt was not.

When Charlie entered the kitchen, his water was waiting for him. He drank it down in a series of long chugs, then said, 'Thank you,' as he put the glass down next to the sink.

Dylan had found his way back to the sandbox and chattered nonsense while stuffing all his toys into a bucket. As they watched him through the window, Becky observed Charlie out of the corner of her eye. She had anticipated this visit when she asked Phoebe to acquire her dad's phone, report on his choice of workout soundtrack, and then change it. Medicine was often unpleasant, especially when administered unexpectedly and by a relative stranger.

'I imagine you're here about The Sunshine Mix?'

Leaning on the countertop, Charlie snorted. 'So that's what you call what you, and I assume Phoebe, have done to my music?'

Becky laughed.

He crossed his arms. 'It's not funny.'

'Oh come on. It is.' She gave his shoulder a small shove before whipping her hand away from the sweat-drenched cotton. 'You'd agree if you could see how grumpy you look.'

Charlie glanced down at his stance and uncrossed his arms.

'Your music is safe. Phoebe backed it up. Lighten up,' she said with a smile. 'If a bit of Katrina and the Waves and Beach Boys is going to upset you like this, I don't know what's going to happen once I start digging about in your finances and love life.'

Charlie's eyebrows shot up and Becky had to swallow another chuckle. It was impossible to take him seriously in his current state. Sweat glistened in his excessive hair and the uncovered parts of his face were flushed. Although she was slightly distracted from her amusement by the intriguing contrast between the unkempt bushiness above his shoulders and the impressive solidity of the muscles visible through the soaked grey T-shirt. It was such a startling mismatch. Like coming across an impressive oak four-poster bed, only to be disappointed by a lumpy mattress and missing pillows.

She patted him on the arm. 'You'll get used to it.'

Despite her reassurance, Charlie's scowl lingered until Dylan came back into the kitchen with a ball and started to bash it against his legs.

'Bol, bol!'

Becky picked up the ball and offered it to Charlie. 'A rough translation would be: "Excuse me, good sir, would you care to play with me?"'

Charlie took the ball, crouched down to Dylan's level and threw it into the living room. Dylan chortled and, arms waving wildly, set off after it. There was a ghost of a smile on Charlie's face as he stood up. 'Well, I suppose it is difficult to hate "Mr Blue Sky".'

'Indeed. And, while I don't wish to criticise your taste in music, you were listening to some truly depressing stuff.'

Dylan returned and, as Charlie threw the ball once more, Becky decided to make the most of her client's visit to mend some fences.

'Look, we were going to head into town soon.' She pointed towards the living room and a stack of books on the coffee table. 'We have books to return to the library. Why don't we go to Sweet's and I'll treat you to a slice of the best cake in town?'

In her experience, there were few people who could stay peeved with someone who was offering them free cake.

Charlie glanced at her and gave a small shrug. 'Sounds fair.'

She pointed at his top. 'You're welcome to shower here and I can run your things through the quick wash and dry.'

'No, don't worry. I can shower and change at the gym.'

'You have a change of clothes at your gym?'

'Yeah, in my locker. And they give you towels.'

'Where on earth do you go to the gym?'

'Tyler's.'

Tyler's was the most exclusive gym and spa in town. It was the sort of place where hand dryers and paper towels were rejected in favour of Egyptian cotton flannels which disappeared into a marble-lined chute after a single use. Becky suspected the monthly membership fee was more than her mortgage payment.

She shook her head. 'Yet another example of how dreadful your life is, Charlie.'

'Hmn?' He was absorbed in making Dylan's day by continuing the game of throw-fetch and joining in with the toddler's exuberant clapping.

Becky smiled and shrugged the chip off her shoulder. Anyone who made her son that happy could go to whatever gym they wanted.

She waited until Dylan was busy fetching and tapped Charlie on the back. 'We'll meet at Sweet's in an hour. I can introduce you to Ronnie. She's looking forward to meeting you.'

Chapter 10

Sweet's Cakes was starting to empty of the morning coffee break traffic when Charlie arrived. He paused under the shade of the candy-striped awning to admire the window display which was as spectacular as always: a sea battle between a pirate galleon and a navy ship, complete with exploding cannons, swashbuckling on the decks and marzipan crew climbing the rigging. The Jolly Roger seemed to flap and snap in the breeze as sharks circled both ships, rising out of a frothy sea of blue icing.

Inside the shop, Ronnie looked up from her tea, spotted Charlie and expressed her first impression with her usual subtlety. 'A man with a beard which can only be described as "disturbing" is staring at the window display. Please tell me that's him because I don't want to think there's another Wild Man of Borneo wannabe on the loose in Compton.'

'Yep, that's him.'

'Holy crap! What have you got yourself into this time?'

'Ron—'

'And an artist! Ugh! They're all useless. Trust me. I dated a few of the losers in art college.'

Becky waved to attract Charlie's attention and turned back to Ronnie. 'Despite what some of his recent, less than sober behaviour might suggest, he's one of the good guys.' Charlie opened the door and Becky hissed a final warning at her friend. 'So be nice!'

'I'm always nice,' she said, extending her hand towards Charlie at an angle which left it unclear as to whether he was supposed to shake it or kiss it. Charlie eyed it warily and Becky sympathised. One of Ronnie's rings was topped by a large silver thistle design which looked like it could draw blood.

'I'm Ronnie, Becky's best friend. Good to meet you.'

Charlie wrapped his fingers around her rings and shook her hand. 'I'm Charlie. Nice to meet you too.'

Becky silently noted his choice of name as she popped more cake into Dylan's gaping jaws. She gestured towards Ronnie and said to Charlie, 'Ronnie owns this place.'

Charlie took another look at Ronnie. 'You're Sharon Sweet?'

'The one and only.'

Charlie gestured to the window. 'Your displays are amazing. You're the best artist in town.'

Becky watched with amusement as Ronnie grew two inches past her usual five foot nothing under the sunny light of Charlie's sincere adoration and then tried to be modest.

'I do my best,' she said. 'And I suppose the interns have to take some credit for the displays.'

She moved to retake her seat, but Charlie got there first and pulled out her chair. Ronnie paused, her eyebrows raised, but recovered quickly, sitting down and nodding at Charlie as he pushed her seat towards the table as if he had been her butler for years.

'I've always wanted to meet you,' he said to Ronnie as he took the last chair at the table. 'There was a castle, a couple of weeks ago.' He gestured towards the window. 'It had stained glass. How did you do that?'

Ronnie opened her mouth to answer, but Becky cut in. 'Charlie. The next time Ronnie's putting together the display, why don't you come down here and help?'

Charlie's mouth formed a large O in an expression most commonly seen on the face of children on Christmas morning.

The women exchanged glances. Ronnie received the telepathic message from her friend and getting to her feet, said, 'Sure. Why not?' She winked at him. 'And if you think my creations look good, wait until you try some. I'll be back in a minute.'

Charlie watched her disappear behind the counter. He drummed his fingers on the table and frowned.

'Everything OK, Charlie?' Becky asked.

'Yeah, great. I just ... You know Sharon Sweet! How did that happen?'

'Um, well, about a year after I moved down here from London I was working a wedding and, twenty-four hours before the ceremony, the bride decides she hates the cake and must have a new one.'

'That's insane.'

Becky shrugged. 'That's the Comptons. Anyway, Ronnie was working in a bakery over in Wolston and she was the only one who would help me. She made the most amazing cake and the bride loved it. Unfortunately, she sneakily used her boss's kitchen to make it and he fired her.'

Charlie raised his eyebrows. 'Isn't this story supposed to be about how you became friends?'

'Of course it is,' said Ronnie, reappearing at their table carrying a tray laden with tea and various slices of cake. 'I'd been making cakes on the side for months and getting the boot was the best thing that ever happened to me. I hated working for those twats and had been meaning to start up my own place for ages. Becky helped me sort all that stuff out—'

'By "that stuff" she means small, inconsequential things like drawing up a business plan, getting a loan, finding premises, getting renovations at cost, sourcing second-hand equipment—'

Ronnie sat down and held a hand up in front of Becky's face. 'The poor bloke asked for a story, not a sermon.' She sighed and turned to Charlie. 'I opened this place a year later.'

Becky raised her teacup towards her friend. 'And she's never looked back.'

Ronnie grinned, touched her cup to Becky's and took a swig of scalding tea.

Charlie shook his head. 'I guess there's no better way to start a friendship than with someone getting fired.'

'There certainly are worse ways,' said Ronnie darkly, taking the largest plate off the tray and sliding it in front of Charlie. She was treating him to one of her tasting platters, usually reserved for clients visiting to discuss a large commission. The six dainty slices were each inspired by a flavour of ice cream, from raspberry ripple to mint choc chip.

As Charlie investigated the handwritten labels beneath each slice, Becky was distracted by a far less appetising prospect. She sniffed in Dylan's direction and wrinkled her nose. 'Excuse us,' she said, lifting Dylan out of his buggy and rustling in the nappy bag for essential supplies. 'We're off to change someone's stinky bum.'

❧

As soon as the door to the customer toilets closed, Ronnie tapped Charlie on the back of the hand. 'So what do you think of Becky's plan for you?'

Dragging his senses away from the cakes in front of him, Charlie was caught off guard. He was never comfortable talking to people he had just met and he didn't want to talk about Becky behind her back. Plus he didn't know how much Ronnie knew or was supposed to know.

But, good God, her stare could cut through lead.

'Um. She seems confident about it.'

Ronnie grabbed Charlie's arm and squeezed. 'I know right now you think she's some bossy cow who's full of shit. But I warn you …' She narrowed her eyes and wagged a finger at him. 'I know Becky and you shouldn't underestimate her. Yeah, you'll probably want to kill her at some point, but she'll make your dreams come true. Even if she has to go to hell and back to do it.'

Chapter 11

The oak door was solid and forbidding. Ignoring her trembling fingers, Becky laid her palm flat against it and closed her eyes. Beyond it was just another room in South Compton Country Club. A venue she had worked so many times it was practically her office. Nothing to be scared of.

She wiped her clammy hand on her skirt, balled it into a fist and knocked on the door.

'Enter,' boomed a voice from within.

Becky inhaled, pushed back her shoulders and stepped over the threshold.

The oak continued on the other side of the door. Dark panelling covered the walls, broken by the fireplace on the wall opposite her. A fire burned high in the grate despite the sweltering heat outside and, for the first time, Becky was pleased she'd switched her comfortable trousers and boots for a skirt and strappy sandals. Her heels were low, but sank into the deep-pile carpet as she approached the two high-backed chairs facing the fire. A discarded newspaper lying next to the chair on the left and a pair of black patent shoe tips in front of it were the only signs the room was occupied.

Unsure how to proceed, Becky cleared her throat.

A hand appeared on the arm of the chair, a silver pocket watch resting beneath its short, pudgy fingers. 'Right on time,' the voice said, its owner punctuating the comment by snapping the watch closed. 'An excellent start. Do take a seat, Ms Watson.'

The tickle in her throat was now real. She coughed again and did her best to glide through the carpet, which sucked at her unfamiliar heels like a bog. Reaching the chair without falling over was an achievement and Becky sank onto the paisley upholstery with relief.

Unlike her, Lloyd Blake was clearly in his element. Snugly tucked into his armchair, a crystal brandy snifter cupped in his left hand, he eyed her, unblinking, the reflected firelight dancing across the toes of his shoes. Lloyd had been a club patron for forty years and was once an admired host and honoured guest of the Comptons' most dazzling high-society soirées. From the whispers Clarice had been able to gather, Becky knew exhibition openings had been Lloyd's particular favourite. And looking at him now, with his thick silver quiff, piercing blue eyes, crisp-cut suit and gold signet ring, she could imagine him standing in the centre of rooms lined with beautiful art and people, watching as the suns and stars of Compton society danced to his tune.

But that was years ago, before disgrace and downfall.

Lloyd sipped his drink and studied her over the rim of the glass. She wondered if she should speak first, but somehow that didn't feel right. If you willingly enter the dragon's lair, best to wait to see how it will react, rather than poke it. That said, his gaze was far from reptilian. In fact, it seemed amused and warm. She adjusted her glasses to stop her hands twitching and caught sight of the dry skin on her knuckles. Lloyd was sure to have noticed; she bet most of the women he dealt with had silky hands and fresh manicures. But then they didn't change their children's nappies, scrub floors or mishandle hot pans.

She folded her hands in her lap, palms upwards. Lloyd watched the movement and smiled. 'It's wonderful to finally meet you, Ms Watson.'

'Likewise, Mr Blake.'

'Of course, I'd heard of your work and hoped our paths might cross one day. But when your friend suggested a meeting … Delightful girl. Clarry, Clara …?

'Clarice.'

'That's it.' He snapped his fingers. 'Hugh Barry's girl. Cornered me at one of her aunt's ghastly socials. Although she did rescue me from having to be civil to that dreadful cousin of hers, so I owed her. And here you are.' He placed his drink on the table. 'So, down to business. You have a proposition for me in connection with John Handren, I believe. Although I suppose you call him Charlie.'

Becky's mouth went dry. Used to working in the shadows, it was unsettling to come across anyone who knew about her work at all, let alone the details. And, while she was more comfortable using subtlety to get her way, this was one occasion when she guessed it would be best to get straight to the point.

'I want Mr Handren to have a solo exhibition of his new works in a South Compton gallery—a good one—in the new year,' she said. 'And I would like you to use your influence to help get him the show.'

The fingers of Lloyd's right hand clasped the arm of the chair, but his face remained immobile. It was a big ask. But Becky had hoped he'd be flattered. After all, no one had appreciated this man's talents for twenty years, when once he had been surrounded by acolytes keen to benefit from his support.

Lloyd Blake had appeared in South Compton in the late 1980s, sidling in on the back of a rumour, apparently self-sown, that he was a possible heir to the extinct earldom. The gossip opened doors, but it was his charm and intelligence which earned him the respect of the more rarefied tiers of local society, and his wealth won over any who were reluctant to subscribe to his fan club.

Working his way up the pecking order, he'd entered into business with several gallery owners. And his star rose until an aggrieved former associate put it about that Lloyd's claim to the earldom was a farce and he had, in fact, built his fortune in property development. Why, the man was little more than a common builder!

Feeling duped by an upstart fraud, Compton's great and good turned their chipped shoulders away from him. Yet they didn't dare turn their faces for fear he would fashion a dagger out of the dirt he had quietly compiled on each and every one of them and use it to stab them in the back.

So he stayed on in the area he had made his home, occupying a strange limbo where he was neither shunned nor welcomed, but met with an icy civility. Nevertheless, Becky understood a few calls from him could still move mountains. But even then her request was ambitious.

The timescale was daunting, Charlie was damaged goods thanks to the ridiculous article in *New Aesthetics*, and would any gallery owner be happy to speak to her—an unknown—even if she had an introduction from Lloyd? Just how much power did he still have?

Becky started as Lloyd broke out of his reverie to chuckle. 'That's quite the favour, young lady.' He steepled his fingertips. 'And why should I use what influence I have to help you and Mr Handren? I have no need for more money. How do you propose to tempt me into taking part in your scheme?'

Had the fire got hotter? Becky fidgeted as she felt sweat forming on her brow. This was the tricky bit. She wished she had a stunning inducement to offer, but she was basing her hopes on one of the Comptons' oldest rumours and pop psychology. Word was that he was on the verge of retirement. She imagined Lloyd, who had spent a lifetime plotting and manoeuvring, controlling every aspect of his empire, would be dreading letting go. A shark doesn't stop swimming willingly, even if Clarice said he had some young protégé ready to take over. And then there was the more sentimental appeal of her plan: the chance to recover a long-lost love. If he had ever loved her. That was a matter of some debate.

Another bead of sweat inched its way down her neck. She was either about to get the help she needed to make dreams come true or offend a man who could snap his fingers and stop her from working in the Comptons ever again. She thought of Charlie slumped on the couch in his studio, Phoebe's doe-eyed worry and Dylan's beautiful face, and prayed what she was about to say would go down well.

'First, by helping us you will be back at the centre of Compton's art set,' she said. 'Second, my plan would allow you to greatly upset Barbara Stone before delighting her in equal measure.' She leant towards him and lowered her voice, inviting him to mirror her movements. 'And finally, I think you would enjoy taking part in my plan immensely.' Job done, she sat back. There was nothing left to do but to wait and see whether he would come on board or throw her over.

Lloyd took a gulp of brandy. He eased himself out of the chair, paced over to the fireplace and rested one hand on the mantelpiece. She couldn't be sure, but for a moment Becky thought his fingers had been trembling.

'Barbara Stone, you say?'

'The one and only,' said Becky.

'And how would we upset a woman who is as immoveable as her name suggests?'

Becky exhaled. Questions were good. Questions meant he was considering it. 'Mr Handren's show will be at the Coulson.' She let the penny hang for a beat, then fired the shot to knock it out of the air. 'Rachel Stone is the Coulson's latest manager.'

Lloyd's shoulders began to shake. Becky braced herself for an explosive tirade, but was surprised when he threw his head back and roared with laughter.

She smiled. He was halfway to liking her already.

When the guffaws had subsided into a few genteel coughs, he returned to his seat and perched on its edge so his knees were almost touching hers.

'My dear, I see you and I are of a kind.'

'How so?'

'You are a born schemer.'

Becky frowned. 'I prefer to say I excel at project planning and management.'

He waved a dismissive hand. 'Let's not fall out over semantics. It was a compliment. Back to the matter in hand.' He winked at her. 'Tell me, how shall I be delighting the Supreme Commander of the South Compton Art Society?'

Ah, yes. Another sticking point. Becky cringed as she said, 'Do you mind if I tell you when we have the show?'

The impressive white eyebrows lifted. But surprise was better than outrage. She had known he wouldn't like to be shut out of the finer details, but she had to keep his interest. And how was she going to do that if she showed all her cards now?

Lloyd stood again and slipped behind his chair. His fingers trailed over the embroidered upholstery as he replied, 'Ms Watson, you found your way to me.' He extended his hands to take in his lair. 'You have intrigued me. And most importantly, you have not made the mistake of underestimating me.' He thumped his hands down on the back of the chair. 'So I will help you.'

Becky stayed silent, rightly anticipating there was more to come.

'However, I warn you not to disappoint or try to trick me.' He stared her straight in the eye. 'Because I can make sure you never work another event in this area again.' He came out from behind the chair and extended his hand. 'Do we have a deal, Ms Watson?'

She stood and smoothed her skirt before clasping his hand. In his eye was an infectious spark of excitement which chased away the last of her jitters. She smiled and placed her free hand on his arm.

'Please, call me Becky.'

Chapter 12

Getting involved with Lloyd Blake was a necessary risk. Becky knew the limits of her powers as a Mephistopheles and landing Charlie a solo show, in a specific Compton gallery and at such short notice, would be impossible without Lloyd's help.

It had been Clarice who suggested bringing him into the plan. Sitting in the doctor's waiting room and fizzing with the excitement of her new project, Becky confided that John Handren had hired her to act as his agent. Clarice was delighted and happy to help by spilling everything she knew about the people involved in the Compton art world, including the Stone family and Lloyd Blake. All Becky had to do was listen carefully. When it came to gossip, who would have guessed the girl was the upper-class Ronnie?

Becky was pleased with how her meeting with Lloyd had gone, especially since she had found his appearance— the staggering white hair, crafty blue eyes and chunky ring—unsettling. She would have been more comfortable if he had been stroking a fluffy white cat; at least then she would have known he was a villain.

Glad to have escaped his lair and confident he had matters in hand, she settled back to wait a month or so to hear from him again. So it came as a jolt when he contacted her only a week after their first rendezvous to announce he had readied the Compton art world for her grand entrance. By various ways and means—Becky didn't ask for details—every gallery owner and manager in the district had heard John C. Handren was looking for a special venue for his comeback show. Of course, as the man was an eccentric recluse, no one could say which venue would be given the chance to host the exhibition, but every gallery in the area was waiting for a call.

❧

Becky went to the Stone Gallery on Wednesday morning where she was greeted by a grinning attendant. 'Of course, you're Mr Handren's agent. We're expecting you.' The woman nodded, sending her oversized chandelier earrings swinging. 'Please wait here while I let Mrs Stone know you've arrived.'

'Mrs Stone?'

'Yes.' She lowered her voice. 'She came in today especially.'

Bloody hell, thought Becky. Clarice hadn't exaggerated the extent of Lloyd's influence.

While a one-to-one meeting with Barbara Stone was sure to help the plan, it did little to calm the squirming in Becky's stomach. The claustrophobic décor didn't help either. The floors were an inlaid patchwork of treacle-coloured mahogany. Similarly dark wainscoting covered the lower half of the walls, while the upper half was a bottle green. Lighting was restricted to a few ceiling pendants and wall lamps above the pictures.

Unwilling to wander aimlessly through the gloom, Becky inspected the painting nearest to her, a bland still life featuring some wilting freesias. Most of the other paintings on display were small watercolour landscapes, dwarfed by ornate golden frames.

Even straining her imagination, she couldn't see Charlie's large bright canvasses in the space. They wouldn't fit in, physically or stylistically.

A door opened behind her and Becky turned to receive her host.

While Barbara Stone was well-preserved for her age, she was also proof Botox could only do so much. Her brow was frozen smooth, but many years of smoking and disdainful pouting had produced a thick barcode of creases along her upper lip. 'Ms Watson. Such a pleasure,' she said, shaking Becky's hand using her fingertips.

Liar, thought Becky, as she watched Barbara withdraw her hand and trail her fingers down the skirt of her pink Chanel suit. Becky wouldn't have chosen pink for her; a green or blue would have better complemented the warmer red tones in her hair. Such a shame too that Barbara's welcoming smile was not as bright as her appearance: a sincere beam would have helped her upper lip no end.

Insincere pleasantries completed, Barbara made a convincing pitch as to why the Stone was the natural home for Charlie's comeback show. All things considered, with its illustrious history of supporting local talent, where else could do justice to the work of a resident, if slightly tarnished, star and restore his career to its former glory?

Becky was a patient audience, and her responses were non-committal, though not discouraging. Barbara had to believe this show was hers and, as she tried to persuade Becky her gallery was the only venue which had the right to this exhibition, she was also convincing herself.

'I'm pleased to be able to say my husband was one of the first collectors to appreciate Mr Handren's talent, over twenty years ago,' Barbara said, lifting her hand to pat her hair. 'Naturally, once those in the know recognised the value of his work, his success was guaranteed.'

Becky was surprised by this compliment for the late Peter Stone. According to Clarice, the Stones' was a marriage of mutual inconvenience and the fatal car accident ten years ago had saved Barbara the hassle and ignominy of a divorce.

By the end of their twenty minutes together, although Becky made a point of saying she had other galleries to visit, Mrs Stone was sure Mr Handren's January show would be the event of the season and an unparalleled triumph for her family business. Her certainty radiated from her, a pompous glee so potent it nearly melted her forehead into movement.

❧

Becky spent Thursday in a number of smaller galleries. Being polite to people who regarded her as unfit to lick their shoes left her exhausted and pleased her next meeting would be her last.

Her keenness to be done with it all caused her to arrive at the Coulson early on Friday morning. As she had hoped, Charlie's crush was busy talking to some customers, leaving Becky free to appraise both her and the gallery.

And it didn't take Becky long to see that Rachel Stone was a gifted salesperson. Entranced, her audience followed the graceful movements of her fingers as she explained the form and significance of the lumpy sculpture next to them. Her taupe jersey dress clung to her like a second skin revealing not a single flaw in her svelte shape and she wore her four-inch heels as if they were natural extensions of her slender legs. Her voice was gentle and conspiratorial, drawing her customers closer to her glossy dark hair and brown Disney princess eyes. Becky sighed: damn but Charlie aimed high! Right up at a face that could probably launch a couple of thousand ships.

She shivered and stared out through the floor-to-ceiling glass panes which formed the storefront. On the street, a group of flushed, sweaty tourists trekked past in shorts, T-shirts and sandals. While they were enjoying another warm July day, Becky felt as if she were trapped in a snow globe. Under the frosty glare of abundant strip lighting, the whitewashed floorboards and the blank ivory walls glowed. The blasting air conditioning dispersed an aseptic, dentist's waiting room smell, making Becky hanker for the Stone Gallery's faint odour of cigars and Chanel.

She meandered between the current exhibits—a series of bronze abstract sculptures balancing on plinths—waiting until Rachel had completed her sale before approaching her. The gallery manager did an excellent job of being delighted to receive her, though Becky noticed some familiar lip pursing. However, unlike her mother, Rachel's scepticism was also directed towards the potential success of Charlie's exhibition.

'Mr Handren could be seen as something of a toxic asset these days. After that unfortunate business with *New Aesthetics*.'

'I understand,' said Becky. 'But everyone's career has less successful periods. And Mr Handren is confident his new work is his best yet.'

Rachel frowned and Becky hoped the woman couldn't detect her outright lies. 'Hmn. Even if that were the case, I don't see Mr Handren's work as a natural fit for the Coulson.' Rachel trailed her immaculately painted nails down her neck, leaving faint red marks on her alabaster skin. 'I don't expect you understand our project and vision, but we've been trying to champion new, young talent.'

Becky noted the use of the royal 'we' while Rachel outlined her personal agenda for the Coulson, which Becky would have summarised as 'to be as different as possible to what my mother does at the Stone'.

'I'm no art expert,' Becky said. 'I leave that to people like you.'

As Rachel preened in response to what she interpreted as flattery, Becky decided it was time to go in for the death blow.

'And, of course, someone like Barbara Stone. Such a knowledgeable woman. Any relation?'

Her best clueless expression elicited the desired response from Rachel: another lemon-sucking lip pucker and a reply which was almost a growl. 'My mother.'

Becky widened her eyes. 'Ohhh. How silly of me! I should have seen that.'

'You've met my mother?'

'A couple of days ago. She's convinced the Stone is the ideal setting for Mr Handren's new work. Her gallery has such a long and illustrious history of supporting local talent. What better place to host Mr Handren's comeback and most successful show yet? After all, as you say, here at the Coulson you usually display works by younger artists.'

She left it there. Having scattered her words like breadcrumbs, she had to hope Rachel would follow.

Rachel scratched her neck again and Becky gave her a verbal nudge. 'Your mother even suggested she would curate the show herself.'

Rachel clasped her hands behind her back. Her reply was slow and careful. 'But the Coulson would be far more suited to Mr Handren's style. The Stone, while a great traditional gallery,' she conceded, 'wouldn't be my first choice.'

'Mr Handren himself expressed that opinion. He also mentioned you. I believe he's met you on several occasions and been impressed by your knowledge and approach.'

Rachel smiled, straightened and brushed a perfect wave of hair off her shoulder. 'How kind. I only remember having met him once, but I'm glad I made an impression.'

'He also had his doubts as to whether the Stone was the natural home for his work. Perhaps it's too abstract—'

'Non-figurative.'

'Sorry?'

Rachel raised her voice and pronounced each syllable. 'Non-figurative. You must know some artists regard "abstract" as a pejorative term?'

Becky blinked. There was that patronising tone again. For all her sinuous charm, there was something sharp and spiky about Rachel. Besides, Becky couldn't imagine Charlie giving two hoots what anyone called his work.

'Right. Well, as I said, I'm no expert. But Mrs Stone was very convincing and offered to drop her gallery's commission to thirty per cent.'

Rachel frowned. 'I don't usually deal with such matters. You would need to speak to the owner regarding commissions.' She flicked her pink tongue over her lower lip. 'Thirty per cent, you say?'

A voice from the other side of the gallery cut in, saving Rachel the indignity of having to deal with anything as vulgar as money. 'Then the Coulson will charge twenty-five.'

The speaker, while as tall as Charlie, had the wiry build of a long-distance runner. Becky guessed he was in his mid-thirties and his suit had cost a hundred times that. Taken together with the confidence of his oily swagger, she concluded this was the gallery's owner, Virgil Locke.

He sidled over to Rachel and stood close to her, perhaps too close, leading Becky to give more credence to the rumour about their romantic involvement.

Becky shook his hand as she marvelled at his green eyes and gleaming teeth. The symmetry of his features made him seem slightly unreal, as if he had been baked by the gods themselves, trimmed from golden clay using a cookie cutter labelled: 'Improbably handsome mortal. Use sparingly and with extreme caution'.

And yet there was something familiar about him.

'A pleasure to meet you, Ms Watson,' he said.

As he released her hand, Becky fought the urge to wipe it on her jacket. Black marks were stacking up against him:

he oozed arrogance, he had interrupted her conversation with Rachel and, now he was in sharp focus, he reminded her of Dylan's father. Another incredibly attractive, confident bastard.

His grin slipped and he narrowed his eyes. 'Haven't we met?'

Becky blinked. 'I don't think so.'

'Hang on … it'll come to me.' Virgil tapped his index finger against his lips. 'Ah! I have it now: Amber Rose's wedding. A couple of weekends ago. Hideous woman but the food was superb. Were you a fellow guest?'

Oh please, thought Becky, pressing a hand to her stomach. Not now. The Coulson was the lynchpin of the project. If she had to answer questions about her other line of work then the whole plan would go to hell in a handcart.

She adjusted her glasses, hoping they would be as effective a disguise for her as they were for Clark Kent. 'I'm sure I would remember if we had met, Mr Locke.'

His grin returned. 'I would hope so.' He glanced at Rachel and continued, 'But I interrupted you ladies talking about an exhibition. All I have to add is that if Ms Stone here believes our little gallery is the place for Mr Handren's show, then it must be. I won't take no for an answer.'

Ugh! That smugness again. If giving the show to the Coulson hadn't been so central to the plan, Becky would have enjoyed telling him she'd decided on the Stone.

'Well, in that case, I'm sure you'd be happy with fifteen per cent,' she said.

The grin didn't falter, although his eyes went cold. 'I see you are as shrewd as you are beautiful, Ms Watson.'

Becky wanted to laugh, but restricted her reaction to a raised eyebrow. Did that sort of line work on anyone?

'Twenty per cent.' He raised an eyebrow to match hers. 'And dinner.'

'Excuse me?'

She glanced at Rachel to see if her surprise was shared, but she hadn't moved. The skin over her high cheekbones was pale, her arms were locked across her chest and her dark eyes were downcast.

Virgil drew himself up and cleared his throat. 'I'd very much like to take you to dinner.'

Becky wondered whether the offer sounded chivalrous, rather than creepy, in his head. Worst of all, she suspected the demand, disguised as an invitation, was intended to wound Rachel in some way. On the other hand, although reluctant to include her personal time in any bargain, she had spent more time with worse people. Plus, if his invitation did upset Rachel, it might make her more receptive to Charlie's advances. And if Ronnie found out she'd turned down a date with a man this good-looking there'd be hell to pay.

'Done.' She nodded. 'But I choose where and when.'

He beamed. Appearing to remember Rachel was standing next to him, he placed a hand on her arm to bring her back into the conversation. 'Splendid. Now, I'm sure Ms Stone will take care of the contract and all those other trifling details.' He chuckled. 'She's in charge after all; I just own the place. Isn't that right?'

Rachel raised her head enough to glance at him and give a curt nod, but Virgil reacted as if her response had been enthusiastic. 'Excellent!' he said, glancing at his Rolex.

'It's been a pleasure, but sadly I must ask you to excuse me.' He pulled his sleeve over the watch, adjusted the cuff and strolled away, leaving a subtle scent of sandalwood and musk behind. Becky began to turn her back to him when he glanced over his shoulder and said, 'I hope to see more of you soon, Ms Watson,' then disappeared through a door at the end of the gallery.

As the door clicked shut and the smell of Virgil's cologne faded, Rachel took a deep breath in through her nose. She raised her chin and stared in the direction of Virgil's departure. The colour had returned to her cheeks, her eyes were bright and tone clipped as she said, 'Let's go to my office to talk terms, shall we?'

Becky shuffled after Rachel's aggressive strutting towards a door next to the reception desk. 'Does Mr Locke often get involved in exhibitions?' asked Becky.

Rachel opened the door and gestured for Becky to pass through. She sniffed. 'I run the gallery. Mr Locke has always preferred the role of silent partner.'

'Until now?'

Rachel looked Becky square in the eye. Prior to Virgil's appearance, Rachel had glanced at her with light contempt, but now her stare was intense and dark. 'Yes, well. He can be fickle in his interests,' she said. 'I suppose something about this show has caught his attention.' She wrinkled her nose and looked Becky up and down. 'At least for the time being.'

Chapter 13

After making a calm and dignified exit from the Coulson, Becky ducked around the nearest corner and did a mini victory shuffle. She grinned at her reflection in a nearby shop window, tucked her hair behind her ears and strode off in the direction of the Old Station House.

When she arrived, she banged on the door until her impatience brought Charlie running. Unable to hold it in, she blurted out the news when the door was only half open.

'You have your show! The Coulson. Opening the eighth of January and running for four weeks.' She suppressed the urge to rerun her victory dance and took a breath before delivering a mock-casual flourish. 'Oh, and their commission will be twenty per cent.'

Charlie's jaw dropped, but otherwise he appeared to have turned to stone. Pressing her back against the doorframe, Becky edged past him into the living room and waited for him to react.

'But ... the Coulson ... isn't that ... that's ... that's Rachel's gallery!'

'Well, yes, Charlie. That's sort of the point. Now you have a reason to talk to her.'

He closed the door and stood in the hall for a moment, his fingers gripping the latch. He glanced at Becky, said, 'Huh,' then plodded past her and sank onto the sofa.

Becky continued, 'Because you'll have to chat about the exhibition, how you want to use the space, what you're painting, the catalogue, publicity ...' She bit her lip. Perched on the edge of the sofa, Charlie had hunched forward and was staring at the wall behind the television. His right hand covered his mouth, the top finger tapping a regular rhythm on his upper lip. And though bright sunlight streamed through the windows on both sides of the room, the area around him seemed gloomy and crawling with shadows.

Becky folded her arms. Getting Charlie to join her in a victory dance was definitely out of the question. She should have expected as much. But a little enthusiasm would have been nice. In fact, any reaction would have been preferable to his withdrawal into his own head, no doubt full of worries about putting on an exhibition when he still wasn't painting. That would be the next thing to fix.

She would have to snap him out of it. Time for another distraction.

'I have to go up and talk to Phoebe about some babysitting, but first I'm going to give you some homework.'

Charlie moved his hand to uncover his mouth, leaving his chin resting in his palm. 'Homework?'

'I need you to start thinking about what you're going to write in your first email to Rachel. Now don't panic,' she said, as Charlie's eyes bulged, 'it'll be nothing complicated. "Hello" and "maybe you could send me the paperwork I need to sign", et cetera. I'll help you. I just need you to think about it. This weekend's very busy for me but we'll get together and send it next week. OK?'

She waited for Charlie to acknowledge her last comments, but he seemed to have vacated his body, leaving it staring open-mouthed at the floor. Deciding to give him time to process, she nipped upstairs to have a quick chat with Phoebe and left five minutes later, easing the front door shut behind her.

❧

Charlie remained unaware of her departure and the arrival of dusk until Phoebe came to tell him she was going out to dinner with friends.

In the kitchen he dug about in the freezer, though he had no appetite. His stomach felt as though it were full of smouldering coals, releasing a heat which was drying his throat and building up pressure in his head. He was unsure which terrified him more: having to fill a gallery with paintings or speak to Rachel. Probably the latter. He and Mel had been married for nineteen years, if you counted the last six, and they had been together for six years before their wedding. He couldn't remember exactly how their relationship had started, how or if he had wooed her, what he had said or done. And now Becky was pushing him towards Rachel and well beyond his comfort zone.

He had never found it easy to talk to anyone, and women, especially attractive women, were a particular problem. Yes, he had chatted to Rachel on previous occasions, but always in the safety of a group. If he were ever alone with her, he wouldn't have the first clue what to say.

A sharp squeal came from the hinges as he slammed the freezer door closed. Damn Becky and her successful meddling! 'Email Rachel, Charlie'. 'It's easy, Charlie'. Why did she assume everything was so bloody easy? He already had enough problems with paint. The last thing he needed was writer's block.

AUGUST

Chapter 14

When Becky had accepted bookings for every weekend in August, her priority had been maximising income during the highly lucrative, but equally short, peak of the wedding season. How she was going to get the work done had seemed comparatively trivial. But now, as she goggled at her bursting agenda, she wished she could go back in time and stop herself from being so stupid.

Charlie's continued lack of inspiration was the other big work-related worry. For once entirely stumped, Becky turned to Lauren for advice. But while Charlie's sister was eager to provide insight into her brother's character, her only suggestion regarding ending Charlie's creative slump was patience. This squared with the rest of her comments about painting as his preferred means of self-expression. It had always irked her that her brother could swiftly translate his thoughts and feelings onto a canvas and display it to the world, while getting him to talk about the same thoughts and feelings was a painfully slow process.

She found that nagging, like the dripping of water on stone over millennia, eventually penetrated Charlie's stubborn silences. Similarly, if Becky were able to wait a little longer, perhaps the pressure of the upcoming show would jolt Charlie into a return to production?

She also suggested Becky turn her attention to Phoebe while she was waiting. Lauren was worried her niece was ambling through her summer and wondered whether Becky could find her something to do other than reading. And after sleeping on it, Becky came up with an idea which could allay Lauren's concerns and solve some of her own more immediate problems.

She invited Phoebe to visit the next afternoon and, as they played with Dylan in the garden, Becky interrogated the teenager about her previous employment.

'Nothing? Not a Saturday job or paper round?' Becky asked, as Phoebe tipped out another bucket of sand, much to Dylan's delight.

Sitting in the sunshine next to the sandpit, Phoebe's hair glistened as she shook her head. 'I thought about it, but I've had a lot of reading.'

Becky sighed and reassured herself that the proposal she was about to make wasn't ridiculous. She had overstretched herself and needed help. And student labour had always worked for Ronnie.

'How would you like to work for me until the end of the year? It'd be work experience, so no salary, but I'd cover your expenses. It would also mean working a few Friday nights and weekends, and I'd need your help with your dad's show too.'

Phoebe wrinkled her nose and Becky couldn't blame her. She'd made the job sound about as appetising as one of Dylan's mud pies. Something else was needed to improve the sale.

'And, as my former intern, I think I'd be able to get you work experience next summer with a law firm in London. I know a few lawyers who owe me a favour.'

Dylan destroyed the castle with the gleeful cackle which accompanied anything falling or being knocked down.

Phoebe swayed her head, then nodded. 'OK. What exactly do you do?'

Becky grinned. She had seen the girl's initiative and persuasiveness first hand. If she turned out to be as useful at work as she was with Dylan, this internship could be the answer to her prayers. And she might even take up Phoebe's repeated offer to watch Dylan while she went to the hairdresser's for the first time in over a year.

'I'll explain the events stuff as we go. It's never the same from one to the next. But, in the meantime, I have another job for you: the publicity for your dad's exhibition.'

'Don't the gallery take care of that?'

'Their main concern is promoting the gallery. We want to promote your dad and his work. That's why we are going to let Ms Stone and her winged monkeys get word out about the show while we make people care about Charlie and his art.'

Phoebe nodded. 'My mum could have helped with all this. She knew everything about Dad and his paintings, and she could talk about it much better than Dad. Although that's not hard.' She gave Becky a small smile. 'I'll see if I can get some friends to help, especially with the online stuff.'

With Phoebe and Lauren rhapsodising about the internship, Charlie kept his qualms to himself. He would have liked to know more about what Phoebe's role involved, but his daughter gave vague responses, telling him the demands placed on her changed from one job to the next.

However, the teenager was keen to tell him about a work trip to London she and Becky were planning for an afternoon at the end of the first week of August. It wouldn't be a child-friendly journey, and Phoebe had been tasked with finding a babysitter for Dylan. One with experience of looking after small children. Someone mature. Trustworthy. Now where could she find someone like that?

Charlie imagined Becky had been expecting Phoebe to produce one of her classmates, and was amused by her shocked expression when presented with a man nearing fifty.

As he closed the car door and took in Becky's face, Charlie's lips curled into a smirk. 'What? Not who you were expecting?'

'He has experience,' said Phoebe. 'And he was free at short notice.'

'Fine.' Becky pressed her lips together and beckoned to Charlie. 'Come in and I'll show you the important stuff.'

Why was she so stressed out? He didn't remember looking after Phoebe being that difficult. Then again, he wasn't sure he remembered looking after her at all. As Becky bombarded him with information about when Dylan should be waking up, snack time, his favourite toys, emergency numbers and lastly, and most dreadfully, nappy changing, his confidence in his babysitting abilities started to drain away.

Becky accelerated as she neared the end of her informative ramble, encouraged by Phoebe's frantic watch-tapping. 'If all else fails, take him to the park, he loves the slides.' She grabbed her handbag. 'But if you do that, then take his red sun hat and pack water. Oh, and if anyone asks who you are, it'd probably be best to say you're his uncle or something. It'll stop you getting the third degree.'

Charlie frowned and scratched his neck. 'Is that necessary?'

Becky's stare drilled into him. 'Your choice. You could always say you're his dad.'

He held up his hands. 'Uncle's good.'

'Good.' She snatched her keys from the mantelpiece and swept Phoebe towards the door. 'Remember to check his nappy regularly. We should be back by seven.'

'Becky?'

'Yes?' Becky was flushed as she whirled back to face him.

'Phoebe says you're going to London to meet a potential client?'

'Um. Yes. You could say that.'

'Becky! We're going to miss the train!' shouted Phoebe from the driveway.

'I'm sorry, Charlie. We have to go. Phoebe will tell you all about it later. And call me, or Phoebe, if there's anything you're not sure about.'

When they returned a few hours later, Charlie had developed a healthier respect for Becky and indeed anyone who looked after small children. The time had flown by, leaving him both exhausted and strangely energised. His face was also sore from Dylan's curious tugging at his beard, to which Charlie had responded by crossing his eyes and yelping, eliciting giggles every time.

❧

By the second week of August, Charlie was still to be struck by inspiration. Lauren might have had time to adopt a 'slow and steady' approach to all Charlie-related problems, but Becky needed him to fill a gallery at the start of January and couldn't leave the matter to natural processes of erosion. She needed the advice of a jackhammer. And fortunately her favourite jackhammer also provided cake.

So Becky left Dylan with Phoebe and made a late afternoon trip to Sweet's to indulge in some therapeutic moaning. 'I don't know, Ron. I'm good with practical things, but how do you inspire someone?' She pouted and stirred her tea. 'And *he* isn't helping. Every time I feel we're making progress I look up and there he is, with his stubborn, grumpy head stuck in a big barrel of doom.'

Ronnie laughed and signalled to one of the interns to bring them more carrot cake. 'No one is happier than me you've finally realised he needs a swift kick up the backside. But let's come back to that.' She took the cake from the waiting flunkey, giving no acknowledgment or thanks for the speed at which they'd produced it, and slid Becky's plate across to her. 'Did you say you have somebody working for you?'

Becky nodded.

'Wow. We are talking about another person, right? Or have you found a way to clone yourself?'

Puzzled by Ronnie's surprise, Becky replaced her cup in its saucer and said, 'I think Phoebe qualifies as another person. Don't you?'

'Absolutely. I just can't believe you're willingly handing off work to anyone else. Particularly someone so young. And inexperienced. Someone who could easily screw up at any—'

Becky held up a hand. Ronnie's words were making her skin itch and she didn't need her friend to list the worries she was doing her best to ignore. 'I will be supervising all her work, obviously. Until she gets the hang of things.'

Ronnie smiled. 'Thank God for that. I was starting to worry you'd hit your head. Or you're an alien imposter.'

Becky drummed her fingers on the table, refusing to get drawn into an assassination of her own character. So she liked to keep on top of things. Why was that so terrible? And why was Ronnie's chaotic approach to life and work so much better? 'Can we get back to Charlie not painting, please?'

'Why don't you take it a little easier? You look tired already, and there are months before the finish line.'

Done with her personality, Ronnie had moved onto her appearance. Becky wondered if there was any part of her Ronnie couldn't find fault with. 'I'm fine,' she said, although her words came out as more snarl than statement.

'OK, OK,' said Ronnie. 'I should know better by know than to argue with a Taurean. Appropriately bullish and stubborn, the lot of you.'

Becky sighed. When Ronnie wheeled out astrology to make her point there truly was no arguing with her. Instead, Becky tried to give her a mighty 'that's enough' stare. Thankfully, it seemed to work.

'Look, I'd say anyone who hasn't left the Comptons for a few years is in love with their rut,' Ronnie said. 'You're going to have to drag him out of it. Get him and his hair out of here for the day. Why not take him up to London? See if that doesn't improve his mood.'

Becky's irritation with her friend vanished. For all her hard edges, Ronnie was simply brilliant. 'That's not a bad idea.'

'Gee, thanks.'

'But will it be enough to get him painting?'

'Doubt it.' The only things Ronnie couldn't sugarcoat were her opinions. 'You'll have to get him there and then hit him with something spectacular. You must be owed a few favours from your old clients. Cash them in. Blow the grumpy bastard's mind.'

Becky laughed. 'Brilliant, Ron. While you're on a roll, can you give me a hint as to what "something spectacular" might be?'

Ronnie took a few moments to think about it, but drew a blank. 'Sorry. I don't think a cake-based solution will help. Besides, I can't do all your work for you. Speaking of which …' She got up and turned towards the kitchen. 'I have twelve lemon drizzle cakes to sort. Duty calls.'

'OK. Thanks,' said Becky. 'Oh! Do you still need my help for your birthday party?'

'Yeah, thanks,' Ronnie said. 'And if you're still working for him when you get back from London, invite the artist.' She paused to point at Becky. The barrel of a shotgun would have been less intimidating. 'Make sure he knows attendance is mandatory.'

Chapter 15

Shortly after lunchtime the following Thursday, Becky and Dylan met Charlie at Compton Station. Becky was pleased to see Phoebe had followed her instructions to the letter: the flip-flops, ripped jeans and stained T-shirt had been left at home and Charlie was wearing smart trousers, shoes and a clean polo shirt.

'Thanks again for coming with us, Charlie.' Becky smiled as she wheeled Dylan towards the lift. 'It seemed like a waste of this good weather not to go up to London. If only for the afternoon.'

'I'm still not sure I won't be in the way.'

Becky pressed the button to call the lift. 'Not at all. Like I said, this is the first time I've taken Dylan to London and I feel much better with two of us to outnumber him.' She pressed the button again. 'And, as this will be Dylan's first time in an art gallery, who better to come with us than an artist and art teacher?'

Charlie's brow was furrowed as they stepped into the lift. He didn't seem to be looking forward to the trip as much as Becky had hoped. He certainly hadn't been easy to persuade.

'To be honest, he'll probably have more fun terrorising the pigeons in Trafalgar Square,' she said, glancing down at Dylan. 'But it's like you said: it's never too early to start taking kids to galleries.'

Charlie scratched his beard as the doors closed. 'I think we took Phoebe for her first visit to the National Gallery when she was about Dylan's age. And I haven't been there in a while …'

The lift doors opened and they strolled onto the platform. 'There you go then. This is great. And what's better,' she said, standing back as the express service to Waterloo approached the station, 'is that Dylan will probably sleep the whole way there.'

Once inside the train, the carriage was quiet, and Becky paced the aisle with Dylan in her arms, sending him to sleep using the usual medley of lullabies and the soothing motion of the train.

When he was snoring gently, Becky eased the toddler into his buggy and parked it next to her seat. She sat to face Charlie who was staring out the window and wearing his trademark 'slightly cross' expression.

'Why don't you wear your glasses, Charlie?' asked Becky, testing a hunch she'd had for a while.

The creases in his forehead slackened as he shifted his focus to her. 'Is it that obvious I'm blind without them?'

'Not really. But I've needed glasses since I was fifteen and my mum used to tell me off for frowning like that.' She pointed at his forehead. 'Why don't you wear yours?'

'I've never found any that suit me. I wear them when I drive and watch TV. And I do have some contacts, but I don't get on with them.'

'I don't either. I don't blink enough, my eyes dry out and then they sting. I'd rather wear glasses.'

'But glasses suit you.' He shifted in his seat and the frown returned. 'They make me look like my dad.'

Becky considered Charlie's face, imagining it bespectacled and de-haired. In fact, even if the hair remained they would add a much-needed solid element to balance the chaos. 'I think you'd suit them.'

Charlie's facial hair twitched and she hoped a small smile had been the cause.

'How did watching Dylan at the weekend go?' she asked. 'Sorry I didn't ask before, but by the time I get in I'm so tired I'm running essential functions only.'

Following the success of Charlie's midweek babysitting debut, Becky had gratefully accepted his offer to come over on Friday afternoon and Saturday evening while she and Phoebe were working.

'Fine,' he said. 'He sleeps well.'

'He does now. The first year he didn't sleep more than a few hours at a time. It was a good thing I wasn't working because I wouldn't have been much use to anyone.'

'You didn't go back to work for a year?'

'Yeah. I made quite a lot of money on my last two projects and so I gave myself a year's maternity leave. I should've gone back sooner though.'

'Why?'

'Partly because it was so hard to leave him. And also because of work. Each project was a stepping stone to the next. While working for one client, my next would usually be someone they knew. But after taking a year off, everyone had forgotten about me. I called all my previous clients and they said they'd recommend me if they could, but it came to nothing. I was glad to have the events work to fall back on.'

Charlie nodded and glanced at Dylan. 'Would you like more children?'

'I thought I'd have at least two, but I guess that wasn't meant to be. How about you?'

'I always wanted a big family. Mel did too. But then with how Phoebe's birth affected her … I guess it wasn't meant to be either.' He ran his hand over his hair. 'If you don't mind my asking, where's Dylan's dad?'

'That's a short and sordid story.'

She paused to give him a chance to change the subject. However, his interest appeared to be genuine, so she continued, 'I met him at an event I was working. Not in the Comptons, thank God. He came up to me, which caught me off guard because guests never see me.' She smiled as she remembered. 'He walked right up to me as if there was no one else there. And we chatted for a while. He was friendly. And handsome. Too handsome.' Sighing, she closed her eyes. 'A week later, he called me and we went to dinner. Eventually we were seeing each other a couple of times a week. Then, in February, about six months after we met, I was working an anniversary party.' She paused. This was the hard part. Her mouth dry, she ran a heavy tongue along the back of her teeth and swallowed. 'I was speaking to this lovely woman. She wanted to tell me the hosts were singing my praises. She was so beautiful: long dark hair, big violet eyes. We chatted about her job, her kids, blah, blah, blah, and then she said, "Have you met my husband?"'

Charlie flinched and sucked in air through his teeth.

'And there,' Becky said, 'standing next to his lovely wife, was Dylan's dad. He pretended he didn't know me and I must have been in shock because I went along with it. Like a complete idiot. I made an excuse to leave and I ran. I never contacted him again and he hasn't tried to reach me. I was two months pregnant at the time.' She ran a hand through her hair. 'And do you know the worst part? He didn't look guilty or embarrassed. Nothing. As if every day of the week he was introduced to one of his gullible mistresses by his gorgeous wife!'

But that wasn't the worst part. Far worse was the damage his deception had done to Becky's confidence in her own judgement. A great deal of her career success was built on her ability to jump to the right conclusion, to make educated assumptions, to read people and between the lines. How could she not have seen he was married?

Outside the carriage the fields shot past, gradually giving way to an urban landscape. Staring out the window, Becky continued her journey back through her recent past.

'I was thirty-seven and I knew it could be my one chance to have a baby.' She shrugged. 'So I went ahead with it. But I didn't want him to be involved in any way. He's either a psycho or just an ordinary stone-cold bastard. And I don't want him anywhere near my son.'

Charlie propped an elbow on the window ledge and ran a hand over his mouth. 'You didn't consider making him take responsibility, at least financially?'

'When money's been tight, I've considered it. But only for a second. If he pays, he gets a say, and he's not having that. And as for his wife …' She shook her head. 'I don't think I have the right to possibly ruin her and her kids' lives just to make a man I despise acknowledge my existence.'

Charlie nodded. He stared out the window and, behind his hand, muttered something which sounded like, 'total wanker', but Becky dismissed this as her brain colluding with her ears to hear what she wanted.

When he dropped his hand away from his mouth and returned his gaze to her face, his final pronouncement on the matter was delivered in a clear and definite tone. 'His loss. Dylan's a great kid.'

Chapter 16

Arriving into Waterloo station only ten minutes behind schedule, they decided to make the most of the sunshine by completing the journey to the gallery on foot.

Charlie would have liked to stroll to their destination, pause to admire the view from Waterloo Bridge and enjoy the art deco architecture on the Strand. But as they crossed the Thames, the gaggles of tourists became densely packed and more concerned with getting a good photo than ensuring their own safety. Their thoughtlessness forced Becky to perform several tricky swerves to pass them without letting the buggy fall into the road and under a double-decker bus. While Charlie saw the increase in obstacles as a reason to slow down, Becky accelerated. As she barrelled towards Charing Cross, her glare burned holes in the crowds and her cheeks glowed an ominous shade of red. Charlie lengthened his stride to keep up, but was happy to drop back from her side and follow at a safe distance. Becky's momentum was probably the only thing preventing her from snatching a selfie stick out of its owner's hand and shoving it somewhere only a doctor could retrieve it.

Perhaps sensing her mood, the pigeons in Trafalgar Square took flight before she reached them, leaving a clear channel between the fountains to the columned and domed façade of the building that dominated the square. Planning to offer her a break from driving, Charlie pulled level with Becky and glanced at her face. The angry flush had gone and her stare was friendlier: more likely to stun than kill. But she was still muttering to herself and he decided it would be best to say nothing and leave her to lead the charge.

It came as a relief when they were finally inside the gallery's central rooms. A safe distance from Crazy Becky rage triggers, the buggy's wheels rolled unimpeded over the wooden floors, under the glazed ceiling and between masterpieces. But Becky seemed immune to her surroundings and didn't pause to admire Constable's glowering skies or the glossy flanks of Stubbs's racehorse; instead she made a beeline for the double doors at the end of the room. Not wishing to fall behind and risk irritating her further, Charlie could only throw wistful glances at the walls and hope he would have more time to view the paintings later.

Becky pulled up in front of the doors. They were closed and two black panels behind the glass obscured the view of the space beyond. A sign apologised for the lack of public access and reassured the reader the room's closure was merely a temporary necessity.

She glanced at her watch, then down at Dylan. 'It's three oh four.'

Charlie peeled his attention from the Turner to his right. 'So?'

'First,' she said, pointing down at Dylan, 'he is likely to wake up any minute. And second—'

She was interrupted by a click and a subtle creak as one of the doors opened.

'Quick, inside!' She pushed Charlie through.

A po-faced security guard stood in front of them. His features were so meticulously motionless that Charlie imagined his family had always been in the profession, the craft of being a sullen blank passed down from father to son. He stared past them as he approached, his gaze locked on a point above their heads.

'Hello.' Becky smiled and extended her hand.

The guard didn't move his hand or his eyes.

Undeterred, she asked, 'Ten minutes 'til your colleague comes on shift?'

He gave a curt nod. 'Get out before.' He shoved past them and through the door.

Charming, thought Charlie.

From the way Becky was glaring at the guard's back, he guessed her thoughts were similar, but she didn't seem to have time to make comments about absent manners. 'This way,' she said, moving deeper into the room.

As he made to follow, he scanned their surroundings. His feet froze and his eyes bulged as he glanced from one corner of the room to another.

Standing between the red wallpapered walls was a series of tall temporary dividers. Beams from the afternoon sun fell through the skylights, throwing shadows across the irregularly placed white walls which were arranged to form a small borderless maze. Immediately visible were a number of paintings, including a Picasso, a Chagall and a Manet.

She tapped his shoulder. 'Come on, Charlie. I know it's impressive, but what we came to see is on the other side of that wall.'

He blinked. What the hell was going on? 'Why is no one in here?'

'The exhibition doesn't open for another week. They're still waiting to receive a couple more paintings,' she said, tugging at his sleeve.

'There is no way we should be alone in here.'

'Shhh! I know. That's why we don't have much time and need to keep quiet. We should get out before Dylan wakes up.'

'But what if someone comes in?'

'Then we're tourists who took a wrong turn.'

Charlie made a strangled gargling noise and turned to look at the exit.

'It's not like we're going to steal or deface anything!' she said.

He reluctantly accepted she was right, but despite her encouragement his legs had taken on a leaden-jelly consistency. Unable to do anything other than gawp at her, he cringed inwardly. He must look ridiculous. Like a wimpy teenager scared to join the cool kids smoking behind the bike sheds.

She gave an exasperated growl, grabbed his hand and dragged him around the first wall, where he found himself face to face with the *Starry Night*. He'd seen it in Paris, years ago. Back then he had been jostled by tourists and irritated by pompous guides who droned on about Van Gogh as if they had known him personally. He'd been an undergraduate and unable to fully appreciate the variety and richness of the blues the artist had seen in the darkness, accentuated by the dancing lights on the Rhone. The peacefulness of the scene was a perfect backdrop for the two lovers in the corner of the canvas, and so different to the dizzying movement in Van Gogh's other *Starry Night*, painted a few months later. He'd seen that one too, in New York …

Becky touched his arm to rouse him. Her tone was gentle but insistent. 'I love this picture and could look at it all afternoon too. But we need to keep moving.'

He shuffled after her like a reluctant dog on a tight leash, his head swivelling back to keep the painting in view.

When they turned the corner at the end of the second divider, Becky said, 'We're here.'

In front of them was another white partition. Between Dali's melting clocks and the sharp suit and bowler hat of Magritte's faceless man was a small canvas covered in a diffusion of red and orange cumulus clouds punctuated by a sunburst of aquamarine. The vertical lines in the lower half of the picture suggested a body of water. Perhaps it was a sunrise or sunset, but it was impossible to say which. Most of the colours were moody and threatening, although the final feeling was one of harmony and balance. Any conflict between the various tones and forms was resolved within the borders of the canvas.

Charlie stalked towards the painting as if it were a wild animal he was afraid to startle. Impossible. It was buried somewhere in the Royal Academy of Arts. How the hell did it get on a wall between a Dali and a Magritte?

His mouth was open and he didn't snap it shut until he was close enough for the picture to come into focus without the aid of his glasses.

Next to the lower left corner of the canvas was a label:

```
John C. Handren
A Most Rare Vision, c. 1989
Oil on canvas
```

He crouched to examine the lower right corner of the painting, where the artist had signed his work in familiar black letters.

Behind him, Becky was getting impatient. The tap-tap of shoe on floorboard made that evident enough. 'It's one of yours,' she said. 'Honest.'

How? he wondered. How had she done this? One of his earliest works hanging between masterpieces! It was something he'd never dreamed he'd see. His imagination would never dare aim so high, which was the only reason he knew he was awake.

He managed some nonsensical stammering in Becky's direction while gesticulating towards the picture.

'A Klimt will fill the space in the exhibition,' she said, thankfully making sense out of his gibbering. 'Your painting is keeping it warm this morning.'

Blinking, Charlie turned back to the wall.

'You have five more minutes.' She laid a hand on his shoulder. 'Try to take it in. And, if you've seen enough, you can go back to the Van Gogh. I'll see you back at the door. Five minutes.'

When Charlie joined her, there were mere seconds left until the next guard was due to arrive. Possibly sensing her rocketing stress levels, Dylan began to squirm and squawk. Chewing her lip, she hustled Charlie through the door. Then, using the buggy like a snowplough, she pushed her way into the middle of a large clump of tourists who were absorbed in contemplating the painting in front of them, their audio guides rendering them deaf and blind to the rest of their surroundings. From her hiding place in the middle of the oblivious flock, Becky stood on tiptoe and watched the new, but equally stone-faced, guard arrive and petrify into his post.

She exhaled. Everything had gone to plan.

However, just in case, she decided to put some space between them and the scene of their misdemeanour. As she strode forward and round to the right, Charlie shadowed her, his gaze fixed on the buggy's wheels.

He didn't speak again until they had spent a good ten minutes among the Impressionists. This was more than enough time for Dylan to work out he could climb onto the wooden bench in the centre of the room unaided and stand on it before Mummy made him sit down.

With a mighty headache brewing, Becky found herself getting short-tempered with Dylan and his antics. In the short breaks between her son's attempts to injure himself, she threw cold glances at Charlie's back. Unmoving as other visitors bustled past him, Charlie was standing in front of Monet's *Irises*, staring at the painting with his hands clasped behind his back, infuriatingly unaware of Becky and her indignation.

He hadn't asked her how she had done it. Nor had he made any comment, positive or negative. What was wrong with him? This was supposed to have been 'something spectacular'. She had expected surprise, but had hoped for more from him than silence. And, if she were honest, she had also done it to show off. But now she felt like a conjurer whose audience refused to applaud, even when she had pulled an elephant out of a top hat.

Next to her on the bench, Dylan took advantage of her lapse in concentration to sprint towards the metal rail designed to keep people a respectful distance from the art.

Before Becky could get to her feet, Charlie pounced. He grabbed Dylan round the waist and lifted him back from the wall. The toddler wriggled and reached for Becky, who accepted him from Charlie with a sigh and a tight-lipped smile. The parcel passed, Charlie went back to staring at the canvas.

The headache was pressing at the backs of her eyes. Perhaps this was it. All those favours she had called in to get a daub on a wall for a sneaky ten minutes and he had hardly noticed!

She let her gaze settle on the three paintings showing scenes from Monet's gardens.

'Have you been to Monet's gardens at Giverny?' she asked, merely to see if he were ever going to speak again.

'No.' He didn't take his eyes off the wall. 'But I always thought I'd go one spring.'

Dylan grabbed for her earring and she batted his hand away. Maybe she needed to bring the conversation back to his work and its one feature she knew something about.

'And do you particularly like *A Midsummer Night's Dream*?'

'Hmn?'

'The title of your painting. It's from *A Midsummer Night's Dream*.'

'Oh.' He turned his shoulders towards her and frowned. 'Some of Mel's friends were in a student production. I think it was the third or maybe second time we went out.'

'It must have gone well. For it to lead to a painting, I mean.'

'No, not really.' He shook his head. 'We had a fight. I don't remember what about.'

She probably did something amazing for you—Becky thought—and you were a sullen, ungrateful sod in return.

'Becky?' Their arms touched as Charlie sidled closer.

'Yes?' She resisted the urge to shrug him off. Perhaps he was finally about to say thank you.

Charlie tilted his head towards her and dropped his voice. 'You couldn't get me into the Tate Modern, then?'

She gasped and swung round to glare at him, but his reaction to her death stare was a burst of laughter. His face came alive; a broad smile and shining eyes creating more of an impression than the rampant hair.

His laughter was so surprising it took her a while to catch up with the joke. She used her free hand to punch him on the shoulder and hissed, 'You bas—', before modifying her language for Dylan's benefit. 'You can bloody well do some work and get in there yourself!'

Dylan copied Charlie's laughter and clapped. The heaviness in the atmosphere lifted and Becky joined their giggling.

'Let's get out of here. Dylan will need a snack soon and I could do with a cup of tea. You are most definitely buying.'

A few minutes into the return train journey, Charlie rested his head against the window and closed his eyes. Dylan scrambled on and off seats, giving Becky few opportunities to glance in Charlie's direction. When she did, apart from the occasional fleeting smile, the only other body movements she noticed were caused by the train lurching over points.

However, as they pulled into South Compton, Charlie opened his eyes and shuffled to the middle of his seat. He cleared his throat and scratched his beard. Below the cover of a deep frown, his gaze darted between Becky, the view, and various points inside the carriage.

The fidgeting persisted once they were on the platform. As they strolled towards the lift, he eased his hands into his pockets and then snatched them out, swinging his hand forward to punch the call button.

Becky stared at the illuminated arrow and balled her fists. To her left, she heard Charlie sigh and take another deep breath. 'Becky,' he said, 'thank you for today. I'm sorry if my reaction wasn't very ...'

'Effusive? Enthusiastic? Excited?' She spat her words towards the lift doors. 'Any other word of your choice beginning with *E*?'

The lift arrived and Becky whirled Dylan inside while the doors were still moving. Charlie followed them and, reaching across Becky to press the button to take them down to the entrance hall, said, 'Putting things into words isn't my thing.'

She rolled her eyes as the doors closed and was opening her mouth to reply when Charlie stepped forward and wrapped her in a hug.

Crushed against his chest, Becky steadied herself by clutching his shoulders, leaving her forearms pressed against his solid biceps.

He released her slightly from the initial embrace, but held her close enough so he could lower his lips to her ear. 'Thank you,' he whispered.

The lift arrived at the ground floor and Becky jumped as the doors opened. Charlie stepped back and extended a hand in the direction of the exit. 'Women and children first.'

Becky raced ahead. She parked the buggy next to the ticket machines and stooped to rummage in the nappy bag. While digging for Dylan's sun hat with one hand, she used the other to rub her right ear, which tingled and burned from its brief contact with Charlie's lips. That damn moustache and bloody beard. The sooner they went, the better.

The crackly announcement of the next departure from platform one must have covered Charlie's approaching footsteps, but it didn't matter: she knew he was behind her. There was something so still about his presence that to Becky, someone who existed in constant scrambling motion, standing next to Charlie was like wandering into the eye of a storm, the one calm spot in the centre of chaos.

Keeping her back to him, she fussed unnecessarily with Dylan's hat and rubbed her right ear again, all while trying to ignore the left side of her face, which was inexplicably as hot and sensitive as the right.

As they said their goodbyes, Becky remembered to pass on an invitation to Ronnie's birthday party a week on Saturday. Charlie accepted at her third time of asking, after she made it plain that upsetting Ronnie would be bad for his health. It wasn't until a couple of days later, in a rare quiet moment, that she wondered whether his initial hesitancy had come from the mistaken impression she had been asking him to be her plus one.

Chapter 17

A week after his trip to London, Charlie went to bed late after spending hours drafting his latest email to Rachel. Following some of her suggestions, he had taken delivery of several new materials that afternoon and he wanted to thank her for her ideas.

Sleep did not come easily, and when it did he dreamt he was back in his studio. It was entirely empty, expect for the vacant easel and a workbench carrying his pot of brushes. An uncanny silence permeated the space; the normal background hum of birdsong and trees shifting in the breeze was eerily absent.

The south door opened and the lady entered. She was surrounded by golden light and the scent of a summer rainstorm. Her clothing consisted of nothing more than a large white shirt. The cuffs hung past her fingertips and the tail to the backs of her knees. She glided towards Charlie but said nothing, nor did she acknowledge him in any other way. Her expression was unreadable, neither friendly nor hostile. In each hand she carried a can of paint and when she was within arm's reach she put them down and stepped back towards the easel.

Charlie looked down at the tins. They were open. He glanced up at her, waiting for instructions, but none were forthcoming.

With no specific goal in mind, Charlie picked up a two-inch brush and crouched to dip it into the first colour, a deep Prussian blue. He stood and edged forward, extending the brush in front of him. She shut her eyes and showed no reaction as he ran a line of paint down her shirt from the right edge of the collar to the cuff. He applied a firm, even pressure, using a long smooth stroke from her collarbone to her wrist.

Feeling more confident, Charlie seized another brush and repeated the movement on her left side, using the second colour, a vibrant emerald green. This time, when he reached the cuff, he stepped back to review his work.

She opened her eyes. Their colour was dazzling, a searing infinity of sublime shades and tones which forced Charlie to turn away and use his arms to shield his face.

When he turned back, she was gone and the easel held a painting.

∽

The next day Charlie went out to the studio early and got to work. By late evening he was satisfied he had reproduced the painting in his dream and perhaps bettered it.

The hairs on the back of his neck tingled as if reacting to the stare of an unseen guest. He laughed and clapped his hands together. The muse had returned.

Chapter 18

Becky reserved the fourth Saturday in August for Ronnie's thirty-sixth birthday party. Delighted her dad was also going, Phoebe volunteered to babysit Dylan from late in the afternoon, allowing Becky to get to Ronnie's early to help set up.

As the women prepared the kitchen for the hungry hordes, Ronnie expressed her dissatisfaction with Charlie's physical display of gratitude from the previous week. 'I don't care if he's not good at putting his feelings into words,' she snapped. 'He should try harder.'

Becky shook her head as she tipped crisps into a bowl. That was Ronnie, Sweet in nothing else but name. 'To be fair, from what I've seen so far, I'm guessing a hug is his equivalent of a handwritten thank you on expensive paper. You know he managed to propose to his wife without saying anything.'

Ronnie had been about to fill an ice-cube tray. She dropped it in the sink. '*What?*'

'He gave her a painting for her birthday called *The Proposal* and when she turned round he was waiting on one knee with the ring. She said yes. Job done.'

'Ugh! I suppose that is romantic, if that's your thing. But I say it's just another example of him being useless.' She carried on with the ice cubes. 'Anyway, how do you know this stuff? Because I'm guessing you're not having long heart-to-hearts with Mr Hairy.'

'Phoebe told me. She's an information goldmine as well as a brilliant babysitter. Dylan loves her and he loves Charlie too. Actually, I think Dylan's delighted to be able to get away with saying "ee" to refer to the three of you. Now all that's left is to convince Mike to let us call him Mikey.'

Ronnie's lips curled and her eyes glittered. 'If he doesn't soon get the hang of putting the toilet seat down I may start calling him that. I sometimes wonder if the useless artists wouldn't have been easier to suffer. You'd think you'd be on safe ground with an accountant. But then I suppose I should have seen it coming: he does have an artistic side, with his photography and all.'

Photography was one of Mike's passions, in addition to sport and Ronnie. He was skilled, and Becky had used him as a backup a couple of times when she feared the official wedding photographer might forget to put the memory card in the camera.

Ronnie changed the subject. 'How is Phoebe doing at work?'

'She's been great. Something about her being so young makes people trust her. They don't question anything she says and she's getting the hang of staging distractions.'

'And how are things going with the great artist and his penfriend?'

'Fine. I had to help him with the first couple of messages, but now he's flying solo. And her ideas are definitely inspiring him. I went over there a couple of days ago and he'd had a tonne of painting supplies delivered.'

'Has he told Rachel he isn't painting yet?'

'No. But he thinks she won't be expecting him to deliver anything months in advance.'

Ronnie snorted. 'I bet she won't. She knows artists are useless.' She put a large supply of plastic cups next to the booze. 'And what were Lady Stone's fantastic ideas?'

'Charlie was vague, but something to do with switching to acrylics and using colour as a theme.'

'I guess those aren't bad. Damn! Are you sure they were hers?'

'Don't be mean,' said Becky. 'She may not be the most loveable person, but she does know about art. And Charlie likes her. That's the main thing.'

'Speaking of love interests …' Ronnie dropped another stack of cups on the countertop and nudged Becky. 'Has "Mr Fit and I Know It" been in touch to fix a date for your dinner?'

Becky arranged the cups into neat columns, ignoring Ronnie's leer. 'No. And don't get your hopes up. I will not be going to dinner with Virgil Locke.'

'Why not? I know his name's ridiculous. Poor bloke was probably named after some ancient relative, but that's hardly his fault. Anyway, he's loaded. And if he's as gorgeous as you say—'

'You weren't there. It was creepy.' She shuddered. 'Anyway, he's probably forgotten about it already and I'm not about to jog his memory.'

✎

When the first guests arrived, Becky and Ronnie were still busy with the food. Mike was put in charge of answering the door and ushering visitors towards the kitchen and birthday girl.

When the initial wave had passed, Ronnie returned to their previous conversation. 'Any idea when Charlie and Lady Stone might meet in person? Although you'll have to convince him to spend some quality time with a barber first. I can't imagine she'll go for his current look.'

Becky slid another pizza out of the oven and passed it to Ronnie to cut. 'I've told you. He'll shave off the hair shirt when he's ready.'

Becky had a theory, one of many, that Charlie's recent scissor-dodging was an outward sign of grief and unhappiness. All the pictures of him taken during his years of professional and personal success showed a hairless face topped by a short-cropped scalp.

Ronnie was sceptical. 'I don't know. I still think you'll have to drug him to get a blade near that face.'

A few minutes later, while in the middle of more pizza shuffling, Becky heard Charlie's voice in the hallway. Mike had been given strict instructions: he was to look after Charlie all evening, show him around and introduce him to the least frightening guests. Becky had also suggested plying Charlie with a little alcohol might help ease him into what anyone might find a daunting social situation. Fortunately, Mike was the ideal person for this job. Ronnie was always complaining how he picked up friends with greater ease than most kids got nits. He would go to the pub for the afternoon and the next day he was going to the football with five guys Ronnie had never seen before. Apparently this was one of the several drawbacks of dating a Sagittarius.

Becky was wondering if the astrological issues in Ronnie's relationship stemmed more from her egomaniacal leonine qualities than anything to do with Mike, when her friend suddenly broke into a fit of coughing. Dismissing this as more non-urgent attention-seeking, Becky kept her eyes on the task in hand. She had just closed the oven door when she felt a sharp poke in her ribs.

'What?' said Becky, spinning round to glare at her friend.

Behind Ronnie, Charlie and Mike were at the bar. Although she was without her glasses, Becky could see Charlie was treating them to a proper view of his strong jawline and even lips. The facial hair hadn't gone, but it was restricted to a short, well-groomed beard and moustache. His hair was once again tied back and he had found a blue shirt to wear with respectable jeans.

'Hello,' said Charlie. He gave them a small wave.

'Hi,' chorused Becky and Ronnie, trying to suppress giggles.

Charlie nodded at Ronnie. 'Happy birthday.' He turned his head towards Becky. 'Nice dress,' he said, addressing the comment to her shoes.

'Thanks,' both women said, Becky quietly pleased she had let Phoebe bully her into changing into a knee-length dress which hadn't been maternity wear.

Ronnie turned her back to them and went over to the sink where her shoulders continued to shake, accompanied by the occasional muffled snort.

Mike handed Charlie a beer and gestured towards the garden. 'Come on, mate,' he said. 'Too many cooks and all that. I have to introduce you to some people.'

At some time around ten, a guest arrived bearing a karaoke machine. He claimed Mike knew all about it and had offered to help set it up. The birthday girl harrumphed and dispatched Becky to locate Mike. Unable to find him on the ground floor, she headed upstairs to the spare room which had recently become home to Mike's photographic paraphernalia.

Charlie and Mike had their backs to her as she reached the open doorway. They made an odd couple. Mike always seemed to tower over Ronnie, making Becky forget he was also below average height and shorter than her. Charlie loomed half a foot above him, his broad frame a dark shadow next to Mike with his short fair hair and designer stubble.

Mike had laid some of his large portfolio folders out for inspection on his desk. Becky raised an eyebrow: of all the pages Mike could have chosen to display, these appeared to be filled with pictures of busty bridesmaids.

Staying on topic, Mike asked, 'I take it you're not seeing anyone at the moment, Charlie?'

'Not at the moment.'

Becky was about to interrupt and rescue Charlie from what she guessed was an uncomfortable line of questioning, when Mike said, 'What about Becky? She's single.'

Charlie shrugged and pointed back towards the portfolio. 'Do you only do weddings?'

Mike nudged him. 'Come on. Becky's not a bad-looking girl. Great legs.'

Charlie gave Mike a stiff smile, then turned back to the portfolio. He didn't look up as he delivered his reply. 'She is not really my type.'

146

'Oh? Why's that then?'

Charlie rubbed the back of his neck. 'She's a bit pushy.'

Mike laughed. 'You know, I've never thought of her as pushy. But I guess that's what people like you pay her for. And then again, I live with Ronnie. By choice.'

Becky coughed. As they turned round, she crossed her arms.

'Hi, Becky!' said Mike. 'How are you?'

She waited long enough for them to have a good, skin-crawling think about how much of their conversation she had heard. Then she turned towards Mike, refusing to make eye contact with Charlie, and said, 'Someone's here with a karaoke machine. Ronnie says they need your help.'

'Fantastic! I'll do that now!' He gave her two trembling thumbs up. 'Er, you won't mention what I just said to Ronnie, will you? I mean—'

'Go,' said Becky, pointing towards the stairs.

'Right! Thanks!' said Mike and scrambled past her. Charlie followed close behind, his gaze fixed on the floor.

Becky watched their retreat and chided herself for letting Charlie's opinion irritate her. It was her own fault for eavesdropping. And Mike was right: if Charlie thought she was pushy then it was a sign she was doing her job. Besides, it definitely was for the best that he had no interest in her whatsoever. Definitely. The very last thing she needed was the added complication of a boss who fancied her.

✎

By eleven the karaoke was in full flow. The sounds filtering through to the kitchen weren't all bad, although occasionally Becky wished she could develop selective hearing.

About half an hour later, she noticed the kitchen was emptying of guests. 'Where's everyone going?' she asked Ronnie.

'Front room. Sounds like Mike's doing his epic rock version of "Total Eclipse of the Heart". That's always good value.'

'But who's singing with him?'

'Pete? Or Brian.' She stopped by the door to listen. 'Doesn't sound like those guys, though. I suppose it could be—ouch! What are you doing?' she said as Becky grabbed her wrist and dragged her to the lounge.

An area had been cleared to form a stage. Charlie and Mike were absorbed in the song, belting out the lyrics with boozy confidence. Microphone in one hand and a beer bottle in the other, they took turns to sing a line. They closed their eyes as they tackled the chorus and Mike added dramatic flair by falling to his knees for the finale. Rapturous applause covered the final chords and Charlie and Mike celebrated with a high-five and man hug.

Grinning and whooping with the rest of the audience, Becky joined the general plea for an encore. Alcohol certainly brought out parts of Charlie which stayed buried while he was sober. She had no desire to see the return of the gloomy letch she had slapped back in July, but she had no objection to this cheerful, sociable drunkenness, and it was high time Charlie had some fun and forgot about work.

As he passed the microphone over to the next wannabe rock star, Charlie looked years younger than the stern, silent man she was used to dealing with. And the impromptu duet was evidence the party had achieved another of her aims: Mike and Charlie were on their way to becoming firm friends.

Chapter 19

Becky's next meeting with Charlie was the following Monday. Ronnie had given him permission to assist in the construction of the latest window extravaganza at Sweet's, and Becky took advantage of the opportunity to check in with her client on neutral territory, free of any association with his painter's block.

Ronnie had shut the shop for the afternoon so she and her team could give their undivided attention to replacing the window decorations and changing the summer in-store displays for autumnal designs. When Becky and Dylan arrived they were all busy in the kitchens, although Charlie managed to escape to open the door and show them to a table in the corner where her tea and cake were waiting.

'Tell me, Charlie,' she said as she sank onto the chair he had pulled out for her. 'Is Bonnie Tyler your regular karaoke choice or was that Mike's idea?'

'Honestly?' He took the seat opposite her. 'It was that or "All by Myself".' He grimaced. 'The Celine Dion version.'

'Ah. Devil and deep blue sea. I understand. Anyway, you can sing. I think you got away with it.'

The sugary scent from the slice of cake Charlie had chosen for her was divine. She took a small bite and asked, 'Is chocolate your favourite or did Ronnie have this left over?'

He opened his mouth, then closed it and looked over his shoulder.

Becky laughed. 'She's still in the kitchen. But if you're about to say anything bad about her cake, I'd keep your voice down, just in case.'

He leant forward, close enough for her to notice the light dusting of icing sugar in his hair and smell hints of vanilla and cinnamon. He tapped the back of her hand with the tip of his index finger and said, 'Honestly, the best cake I ever had was at school. The canteen made this dense plain sponge in huge tins. It was covered in white icing and coloured sprinkles and served in big, right-angled triangles.' He smiled, his eyes drifting up and to the left. 'It was soft and fluffy and slightly synthetic-tasting. It was great.'

Becky mirrored his smile and, as Ronnie emerged from the kitchen, said, 'Don't worry. Your secret's safe with me.'

'Aha!' said Ronnie. 'He's got round to telling you he's painting, has he?'

Becky choked on her cake. Waving away offers of backslapping, she took a sip of tea and raised her eyebrows at Charlie.

'He told Mike yesterday at the rugby.' Ronnie rested her hands on Charlie's shoulders and gave them a hard squeeze. 'He's being inspired in his sleep, isn't that right, Charlie?'

Charlie's gaze wandered towards the exit, then down to the floor, where Dylan was busy running a plastic car up the table leg.

'You could say that,' he said, rising from his chair. 'I should get back to the kit—'

Ronnie pushed down on his shoulders, shoving him back into his seat. 'I'll give Becky the short version, shall I?' Ronnie smirked as Charlie squirmed under her hands. 'Last Thursday night he dreams some woman comes into his studio. She's in the buff, except for a big white shirt. He paints the shirt a while. She vanishes but then there's a painting in her place. Next day he reproduces the painting.'

Becky blinked. It sounded weird. But if Charlie was finding productive inspiration in his sleep then she'd volunteer to make him cocoa and sing lullabies.

'That's one painting down!' she said.

'Um, actually it's two.' Charlie squirmed some more. 'I painted another yesterday. They're small and I'm still not completely happy with them, but I've made a start.'

'Exactly!' Becky beamed at Charlie's newfound, glass-half-full thinking. 'This is great. I'm so pleased for you.'

'Yeah, whatever,' said Ronnie, taking the chair between Charlie and Becky. 'Let's get back to the dream. I want details. Does this mystery woman have long dark hair, big brown eyes and bear an uncanny resemblance to a certain local gallery manager?'

'Ronnie!' Becky kicked her in the shin.

Blushing to the tip of his nose, Charlie twisted free of Ronnie's hands and sprang to his feet. 'I should go and see how they're getting on with the display.'

Giving Ronnie her sternest glare, Becky spoke quickly before Charlie could complete his escape. 'Maybe I can come by and see what you've been working on. When are you back to teaching?'

'Second week of September. I have Monday, Tuesday and Wednesday evenings this year. Come by whenever you like.'

'OK. Thanks,' she said, waving at his back as he ducked into the safety of the kitchen.

The second the kitchen door closed, Ronnie got back to business. Rubbing her shin, she said, 'I told you he and Mike would be best mates in minutes.'

'Well, you seem happy to have him around.'

'True. And I'd say your project is on track. You were right about Rachel inspiring him and now he's painting. You just need to keep an eye on him and make sure he doesn't stuff it up.'

Becky agreed. The peak wedding season was drawing to a close and she was looking forward to a change in pace. Charlie had finally connected with his muse and, as long as he stayed positive, she was confident things could only get better.

That said, it didn't come as a complete surprise when he fired her a few days later.

SEPTEMBER

Chapter 20

September arrived on a Monday. It was before eight when Phoebe rammed a slice of toast between her teeth and slipped into her flip-flops. Charlie admired her determination to enjoy the final days of her summer holidays as he watched her shout goodbye over her shoulder and race out the house to join her friends for some retail therapy in Barnsby.

Charlie had barely noticed Phoebe's recent comings and goings. In the last week of August he finished two more paintings, took care of Dylan on Friday and Saturday and found time to flick through his course syllabus. So he was looking forward to a quiet day when the postwoman knocked on the door and asked him to sign for a delivery. Turning the A4 white envelope over in his hands, Charlie hummed and bounded into the study for a letter opener.

As he skimmed the envelope's contents, the happy tune died on his lips.

Melanie Bradley, wife of John Charles Handren, was applying for a divorce from the aforementioned spouse.

Her solicitor, Mr William Gregson, asked Charlie to decide whether he wanted to contest her application and be so kind as to complete and return the enclosed forms accordingly.

Charlie folded onto the nearest sofa and stared into the garden. Outside the last breeze of summer was worrying the trees and birds were stabbing the lawn. Inside the only movement was his wedding band, which glittered as he twisted it back and forth.

When Phoebe came home for lunch he didn't tell her about the letter. It was proof he had failed. Although he had known divorce would probably happen one day, a small part of him had always hoped he could fix his family.

He smiled and nodded robotically as Phoebe talked, pushing his lunch around his plate until she finished and went upstairs. Then he wandered out to the studio to brood without having to mask his disorientation and swelling anger.

He couldn't claim to be in love with Mel any more and he had made his peace with her absence long ago. But surely he deserved more consideration than this? Six years with barely a word from her. After nineteen years of marriage, was a phone call too much to ask?

Amazingly the world continued to turn, the sun set and rose, and Charlie still didn't know how he felt about the small pile of papers sitting in the study when the phone rang shortly before midday on Tuesday.

'Hello?'

'Charlie?'

Be careful what you wish for, he thought. Yesterday he had wanted to talk to her, but now she had got in touch his throat was closing up, strangling any attempt he made to speak.

'I see you're still talkative. That hasn't changed,' Mel said, and Charlie remembered how she had always tried to cover her nerves with sarcasm. At least he wasn't the only one finding this difficult.

'Hi. I got the letter from your solicitor. I assume that's why you're calling.' He covered the mouthpiece and cringed, squeezing his eyes shut and taking in a whistling breath through gritted teeth.

'Yeah, um, that was mostly why. But I think we should talk and I want to explain some things and say sorry.'

'No rush. Only been six years.'

'I know. It was Phoebe and Becky coming to see me which gave me the push I needed to do this. I shouldn't have left it this long, but after talking to them I realised I've been holding on to you unfairly …'

Mel kept talking, but Charlie wasn't listening. His world, which had been increasingly rosy of late, was covered in a red mist. He gripped the phone so tightly his knuckles went white.

'Mel,' he said, 'I'm glad you're well. You'll be hearing from my solicitor about the divorce. Bye.'

He punched the button to hang up and threw the phone behind him as he made for the car.

Becky had just got Dylan down for his afternoon nap when she heard the banging on her front door. She ran downstairs, cursing and shushing the unexpected visitor.

Opening the door, she found Charlie attempting to pace a trench into the doorstep. The crease between his

155

eyebrows was so deep and immobile she knew this wasn't a casual social call. The vein in his right temple was also throbbing, another red flashing light on the dashboard of Charlie's mood.

'Where's Dylan?' he demanded.

'Asleep upstairs. What's going on?'

He stopped pacing, but didn't raise his head to look at her. His voice was quiet, its tone flat and dead. 'You're fired.'

He stalked down the drive.

'Wait!' Grabbing her keys, Becky ran out of the house. She swung herself in front of him, blocking his path, and held up her hands. 'What happened?'

'I'm surprised you don't know. Seeing as you have more control over my life than I do.'

Oh great, she thought. This conversation. Already.

'OK, you're upset.' She tried to catch his eye, but he was looking everywhere but her face. 'Why don't we talk about this inside?'

'No!' His nostrils flaring, he raked his fingers through his hair. 'I've just been talking to my wife. You remember my wife? She tells me you met recently. So I guess I can give you credit for the divorce petition I received yesterday.'

'Ah. Let me explain—'

'No.' He pushed past her, strode to his car, yanked the door open and threw himself in. 'You had no right. And to drag Phoebe along with you …' He grimaced and shook his head. 'That is unforgiveable. Let me know if I owe you for any expenses, but otherwise I never want to hear from you again. And stay away from my daughter.'

As his car disappeared under the railway bridge, the adrenaline which had carried Becky through the past few minutes ebbed away. Blood thudding in her ears, she slumped against the garden wall and let her head hang forward.

The tears came quickly, but frantic blinking kept most of them in check. Becky closed her eyes, swiped at her damp cheeks and swore. Everything had been going so well! Just when she was on her way to forming a solid working relationship with Charlie. It was only a few days since she'd congratulated herself on getting more smiles than frowns from him.

She straightened up and turned towards the house. Her gaze drifted to the upstairs window and Dylan's curtains. She raised her hand to the back of her neck to rub the collection of tight knots there. It was like trying to massage concrete. Sighing heavily, she removed her glasses and ran her fingers over her itchy eyes.

Of course, this was all her own stupid fault. And with Charlie in such a righteous rage, and the ever-present pressure from the encroaching financial black hole, she wouldn't be able to trust in time and chance to bring him round.

Back inside, she hunted her phone out from under a mound of toys and called Phoebe. Then she sent an email to Lauren for good measure.

Chapter 21

Becky's next wedding was on the second Saturday of September in the nearby town of Wolston, where the Old Grange Hotel and Spa had the honour of hosting both the ceremony and reception.

While it was half the size of the Compton Country Club, the Grange was almost three hundred years older and offered a nostalgic charm the bigger venue couldn't buy. And while the Watkins–Jefferson wedding, with its a hundred and sixty guests, was a small affair by local standards, Becky guessed the spend per head easily outstripped anything she had seen that year.

Phoebe and Becky arrived half an hour before kick-off to complete their final checks. Roaming between the glittering silver and crystalware in the dining room, they stopped at every table to adjust the settings and centrepieces.

'It's been nearly two weeks,' said Becky.

'Don't worry. He'll get over it.'

Phoebe fiddled with the chairs, moving each one an unnecessary half an inch to the left. 'Does he know you're here today?' Becky asked.

The girl didn't look up and her response was barely audible. 'Sort of.'

'Phoebe! No more lies, remember. That's what got us into this mess in the first place.'

Phoebe shrugged and tapped her growing and freshly varnished nails on the back of the nearest chair. 'He won't find out. I've hardly seen him, he's spending so much time in the studio.'

'And you wouldn't be avoiding him at all?'

'No! I've been busy. The teachers haven't exactly eased us in gently this year. I've got a million tonnes of homework.'

Becky glared at Phoebe over the top of her glasses.

'All right,' Phoebe said. 'Maybe I've been dodging him a bit. But he's doing it to us too!' She crossed her arms and stuck out her bottom lip. 'He's ignoring all Aunt Lauren's messages and he keeps vanishing when I come into the room. I think he knows he won't be able to stop himself asking about Mum. He's probably dying to ask. But now he's gone all huffy and he won't back down.'

Moving the chair in front of her a quarter of an inch back to the right, Becky sighed. The past two weeks had been hard going. She'd done her best to roll on with work and Charlie's project as if nothing had happened, but she was haunted by worry laced with guilt. For all the tricky situations she worked her way into and out of, she preferred approaching problems with a sprinkling of stealth. Out-and-out confrontations always left her feeling off-kilter, often because they involved accepting she was at fault. Sometimes. Partially.

She glanced at the teenager and envied how unperturbed she appeared to be by her father's ongoing disengagement. 'You're not filling me with hope.'

Phoebe slipped an arm around her shoulders and squeezed. 'It'll be fine. We won't let him dump you, I promise.'

She frowned at Phoebe's choice of words, but wasn't given much time to dwell on them.

'I can still come with you to the Coulson next week, can't I?' said Phoebe. 'When you go to see Rachel?' She dropped her chin and gazed up at Becky, batting her eyelashes. 'Please?'

Becky raised an eyebrow. It was that puppy-eyed look which had persuaded her to go with Phoebe to London and started all this trouble. The girl better hope one day it would be as effective on juries and judges. 'Of course you can. But tell your dad this time. And please talk to him about our trip to see your mum.'

'No probs, thanks. Ooo! The cake's here!' She pointed to the other side of the room, where one of Ronnie's interns was staggering through the doors carrying a large box. 'I'll go help unpack it!'

Watching Phoebe bounce away, Becky shook her head. She hadn't been sure whether to cancel the trip to see Rachel, but if Lauren and Phoebe were right about Charlie then it was important she continue with the plan as if she and her client were still speaking.

Phase one of the reception inspection complete, she moved to the top table and made a few changes as she put her thoughts in order. He was painting, that was the main thing. Her next job was to make sure the paintings sold well. And she would need Lloyd to help her with that.

But that was a task for next month. In the meantime, her biggest concern was keeping Rachel happy and the Coulson on board. She hummed as she left a packet of painkillers on the mother of the groom's seat. Apart from one close shave when Virgil Locke showed up, everything connected with that aspect of the plan was on track, particularly now the gallery owner had vanished, leaving the organisation of the exhibition in Rachel's smooth hands.

'Ms Watson, what a marvellous surprise!'

She raised her gaze slowly, following the familiar silky voice over to the other side of the table. Her lips parted. The gods were laughing at her. How could he be here? His name wasn't on the seating chart or she would have taken the necessary precautions.

She pressed her lips together and forced a smile. 'Hello, Mr Locke. Bride or groom?'

Virgil Locke was resplendent in a grey, double-breasted suit. It was unfair to compare him and Charlie, but the contrast was so great Becky couldn't help it. How did he get such a close shave? Or perhaps he'd had his facial hair lasered off; he struck her as someone who believed beauty was pain. He employed Rachel after all.

'Bride,' he said. 'A second cousin. Lovely girl. A particular favourite of my uncle.'

This small but sincere display of affection was unexpected, reminding her she shouldn't prejudge him. It wasn't his fault he reminded her of Dylan's dad.

Virgil looked her up and down. In her unofficial uniform of black shoes, black tights, black skirt, white blouse and black cardigan, Becky knew she could easily be mistaken for a member of the catering team. It was the same outfit she had been wearing at Amber's wedding when Virgil had done something none of the other guests had managed: he'd noticed her.

'And you're here to pursue your more regular line of work?' he asked.

'More regular compared to …?'

'Compared to representing reclusive artists.'

He was staring at her with his usual confidence, smiling broadly to reveal his long white incisors. Becky could see him as a vampire: it would explain a lot.

As he appeared to know more about her than she did about him and showed no sign of disapproving of her having two jobs, there was no point in trying to lie or make herself invisible. 'I was hired by the groom to make sure his and your cousin's wedding goes as planned.'

'Good,' he said. 'I'm glad to see Nigel isn't as dopey as he looks.'

'You don't get on with the groom?'

'He's all right. He may not be the sharpest or best-looking chap on the planet, but he worships the ground Georgie walks on, so he's OK by me.'

Becky examined his face, weighing up whether to involve him in her next task. His desire to see his cousin happy seemed genuine, and he clearly knew something about subterfuge. Ah, what the hell. She could use the help and it would be great to have him onside.

'Mr Locke, would you mind missing the start of the ceremony to help me deal with an unwelcome guest?'

'Not at all.' He beamed. 'This sounds positively underhand. How intriguing!'

'And do you have any other cousins who might like to help? Ideally they would be big, strong and know the meaning of discretion.'

'I have a good few to choose from. Where and when do you need us?'

❧

Becky met Virgil five minutes later in the lobby. She briefed him on the plan and then strode off, leaving him to hurry after her down a series of corridors.

'Let me see if I've got this straight,' he said. 'Georgie's ex-boyfriend is going to stop the ceremony?'

'Well, he's planning to. Whether he would have gone through with it or not, we'll never know.'

'Because your assistant is going to lure him to our current destination?'

'Lure is a bit strong. She'll tell him the bride has asked to see him. He'll fill in the rest himself. He'll assume she's come to her senses and wants to run back to him.'

They stopped in front of an unmarked door. Becky unlocked it and stepped inside. Virgil followed. Two wooden chairs were all the furniture in the room. The door they had used was the sole entrance and exit.

'But what if this chap loves Georgie?' he asked.

Becky picked up one of the chairs and moved it to face the door. Her tone was flat and lifeless as she said, 'Then he should have told her that at some point during the four years he was stringing her along, cheating on her and making her feel worthless, while all the time basking in her adoration like the selfish snake he is.' She paused to take a breath and place the other chair facing the first. 'If he loved her, he wouldn't be here, invited or uninvited. And he certainly wouldn't come here to interrupt the ceremony and ruin the happiest day of her life.'

Not waiting to be asked, Virgil occupied a seat and tugged at his shirtsleeves, revealing his diamond cufflinks. 'So he's a selfish prick who's incapable of putting anyone else's happiness before his own?'

Becky looked at Virgil with a new respect. 'Exactly.'

He rubbed his hands together. 'Do we get to tie him up and throw him into the boot of a car?'

'Sadly, no. We'll keep him here until the ceremony is over. Then you and your cousins will escort him from the premises using the back door. Make him understand, gently but with a fair degree of menace, you'll be looking out for him the rest of the day. If you'd like to add it'd be best if he stayed away from Georgina for the rest of his miserable life, I wouldn't be against it.'

Virgil jumped up and began to pace. He unbuttoned his jacket and thrust his hands in his pockets. 'And you do this all the time? How exciting!'

'Not really. No one ever objects during wedding ceremonies. It only happens in movies.'

'Maybe that's because there are countless Ms Watsons all over the place bundling potential objectors into cars.'

She laughed. 'I take it your day job doesn't involve this sort of thing?'

'God, no!' Virgil stopped pacing. 'Well, maybe a smidgeon of intrigue. Sometimes. But we have lawyers for all that.' He frowned. 'My life was far more exciting when I was in New York, and even Berlin had its moments. But since coming back to London the old man's been working me hard.'

'The old man?'

'My uncle. He's grooming me to take over the family empire.'

'That doesn't sound dull.'

'It's mostly property management. Some events—'

'Shhh!' Becky held up her hand and tilted her head towards the corridor.

'God, sorry, I suppose I was boring on—'

'No! They're here!'

Phoebe's voice, raised to warn them of her approach, was outside the door. Becky waved Virgil into the corner and tried to compose herself. Unaccustomed to an audience, and especially one as observant as Virgil, she was more self-conscious than usual. However, despite her misgivings, he didn't allow a single detail of the following scene to escape his notice, took instruction well and performed his part to perfection.

～

Later that afternoon, when the reception had passed off without any interference, Virgil spotted Becky in a corner of the dining hall and sidled over.

'Ms Watson, please tell me all is well and you'll be going home soon for a rest. Working several jobs at once can be exhausting and I'm sure none of us want to see you laid low by illness.'

Becky only moved her eyes and mouth as she replied. 'I will.'

With a glance, Virgil absorbed and copied the trick. He manoeuvred until they were standing shoulder to shoulder and became another muttering statue. 'I have to admit, I am a little disappointed, Ms Watson. I honestly wouldn't have minded seeing you in action again.'

Becky dipped her head a fraction.

'I'll leave you to get on,' he said. 'Although I wanted to apologise for being so indiscreet as to almost blow your cover when we first met at the gallery. And second for not taking the trouble to find out more about you before we became acquainted.'

She swallowed the sudden tickle in her throat and kept her gaze glued on the far corner of the room.

'I admit I'm out of my depth when it comes to gallery matters,' he said. 'I haven't given our visitors the attention they deserve. And I fear I have been particularly lax with those visitors who are perhaps most deserving of my attention.'

Out of the corner of her eye she could see he was glancing towards her. She nodded again.

'I wanted to remind you I'm still waiting to hear about where and when we're having dinner. But please take your time. I'm a patient man.' He touched the small of her back. The light pressure, instead of making her flesh creep, produced a not unpleasant tingling in the area under the pads of his fingers. 'I wouldn't like to think my invitation and the manner of its delivery had given irreversible offence.'

He was a couple of steps away when she called him back. 'Mr Locke?'

'Yes, Ms Watson?'

'Please. Call me Becky.'

He nodded and strolled away, whistling a merry tune. When Becky was sure he couldn't see her face, she treated herself to a smile.

Chapter 22

It was nearly another week before Becky saw Charlie again.

To ensure he arrived after Dylan was in bed, Phoebe pushed Charlie out of the house shortly after eight and sent Becky a warning message the second his car had left the drive. Ten minutes later, Becky was scrubbing the kitchen sink and listening to the rain spitting against the window when she heard the sheepish tapping on her front door. Oh dear, she thought, not without some glee. He'd be getting wet out there.

She flicking the kettle on, gave the sink another squirt of citrus cleaning spray and resumed scrubbing.

The rain started to fall in earnest. Becky dropped the scouring pad and grabbed two towels from the hooks by the sink. So as not to reward him for flying off the handle and three week of stubborn sullenness, Lauren and Becky had told her not to be too nice to Charlie, but the man did have the moral high ground and she wasn't going to let him catch pneumonia.

She trotted to the front door, drying her hands as she went. Nerves tickled the sides of her stomach as she remembered their last encounter and it was a comfort to find a far calmer version of Charlie on the doorstep.

'Hello,' she said, ushering him across the threshold and handing him the second towel. 'Leave your shoes and coat by the door, and come through. Kettle's boiled.'

When he entered the kitchen, Charlie put the towel and a rain-spattered plastic bag down on the counter, then leant against the fridge while Becky made tea. His gaze followed her around the kitchen, watching her spin and sway, rarely doing one thing at a time. As she opened the cupboard to get teabags she dipped to open a drawer to retrieve a teaspoon. She twisted the top off the milk with her left hand as she held the kettle in her right and poured steaming water into the mugs, and then stirred the tea in one mug while pouring the milk into the other.

Routine complete, she placed his tea on the counter next to him. 'Sugar?'

'No. Thank you.'

'Sweet enough already. Like me.'

His lips curled as he wrapped his hands around his mug. With relief, she pushed on through the breaking ice. 'Guess how many sugars the great patisserie artist Ms Sharon Sweet takes?'

When Charlie looked up the small smile was still there. 'Two?'

'Good guess, but you have to remember this is Ronnie we're talking about. It's three. And on most days she could probably do with four.' Becky retrieved her own mug from next to the kettle and placed it by Charlie's. Resting her fingers on the counter to disguise their trembling, she knew she couldn't avoid the reason for his visit any longer. 'You're here,' she glanced up to catch Charlie's eye. 'So I guess Phoebe finally explained what happened?'

He nodded. 'She found and contacted her mum, arranged the meeting. She was going to go to London alone but then you found out and wouldn't let her go on her own.' He paused, dropped his gaze to his mug and mumbled, 'Thank you for that.' He cleared his throat and continued. 'She also said you told her she should tell me where she was going and why, and she made you promise not to tell me about it.'

'She's good at getting her way.'

'The makings of a good lawyer.'

'She told you about that too?'

'I know a lot more about Phoebe today than I did a few days ago.'

They settled into silence again, Becky taking comfort from the knowledge that this little drama, if nothing else, had brought Charlie and Phoebe closer.

She returned to the big unresolved issue. 'Have you decided what you're going to do?'

'About the divorce?' He shrugged in response to her nod. 'I guess I'll go along with whatever Mel wants. Our marriage was over long ago. Anyway, Phoebe says her mum's engaged and it would be hypocritical of me to get upset about that.'

Becky agreed. A man pursuing a raven-haired gallery manager in both the real world and his dreams could hardly claim to still be in love with a woman he hadn't seen or spoken to for six years.

'Is Mel's fiancé handling the divorce for her?' she asked.

'He is.'

'Then if you're not going to contest, I imagine you'll be a single man by Christmas. It's not often a solicitor is so motivated to work quickly.'

Her last comment drew another wry smile as he played with the handle of his mug, the back of his hand brushing against the plastic bag, making it crackle and drip.

'What's in the bag?'

'Oh, yeah.' He picked it up and slipped out a present wrapped in cartoon-dinosaur paper. 'Phoebe said it was Dylan's birthday yesterday. So, um, here.' He thrust the gift towards her.

Rarely surprised—and pleasant, touching surprises were the unicorns of surprises—Becky needed to take a moment before replying. 'Thanks. You didn't have to do that.'

'It's just a book. He had it from the library. It made him laugh.'

Becky was very glad she hadn't left him outside to catch pneumonia. It was a small gesture but, as she had to remind herself, what would be a throwaway comment or action from anyone else was often a significant message from Charlie, backed up with a great deal of thought and effort. 'That's really kind. He'll love it. Would you like some birthday cake?' She pointed at the pink-and-white cake box next to the sink. 'Ronnie's finest vanilla buttercream.'

'Sure. Thanks.'

'Why don't you take the tea into the front room? I'll be through in a minute.'

As she cut two slices from the remains of Dylan's teddy bear cake, Becky wondered if this was as close to an official rehiring as she was going to get. Perhaps if she could convince him to hang around for a while, the tea and cake would relax him into a climb down. Either that or she'd have to wait for him to paint her a picture entitled *Sorry I shouted at you. Let's start again?*

She joined him in the living room. 'Do you want to stay and watch a film? I usually watch something on Thursday nights because there's never anything decent on TV and I don't often have time at the weekends.'

'What film? Not some weepy girly costume thing?'

'I try to stick to light-hearted stuff. My weekend work comes with enough weepy girly costume things to last me.' Becky opened a cupboard next to the television and pointed at her DVD collection. 'You can choose,' she said, taking a seat. 'Are you ready for back-to-school next week?'

Charlie knelt in front of the films and appraised them. 'Ready for everything except Mrs Howard.'

'Who is?'

'An octogenarian who does her best to sexually harass me.'

Becky almost inhaled her tea. 'How?'

'She's pinched me a couple of times, but mostly she winks a lot and makes comments.'

'Ask her to stop.'

'That would involve being alone with her.'

Becky snorted.

'It's not funny.'

Picturing strapping, six-foot-two Charlie cowering behind his easel, a feisty old lady in hot pursuit, Becky's giggles intensified.

Charlie ignored her amusement and changed the subject. 'What's work like for you?'

'It usually slows down once we're out of the summer, but I think venues have started giving out my number. And I suspect the local wedding planners, although they look down their noses at me and would never admit it, are telling their clients about me too.' She shrugged. 'It makes sense. The invisible woman makes their events go perfectly and they get all the credit.'

He still had his back to her. She had forgotten the clock on the mantelpiece thudded like that. It boomed through the gap in conversation until Becky's impatience got the better of her. Time to be pushy.

'And I have this one client who is proving to be a bit of a pain. He seems to have ... what's the fashionable term for it? Oh yes, trust issues. In fact, I'm not sure if we're still working together.'

Charlie exhaled as he straightened up. He came over and sat on the other end of the sofa. 'He sounds like a complete arse to me. I don't know why you're bothering with him.'

'I guess I can understand where he was coming from.' She gazed into her mug and prepared herself for a painful moment of self-reproach. 'And ... I suppose I sometimes get carried away and take liberties.'

After he had given her the sack, slammed her car door and blazed away, she had tried to imagine herself in a similar situation. The closest she could come up with was how she might have felt if Charlie had sneaked Dylan off to see his father. She would have gone berserk.

'Besides, I'd be disappointed if I weren't fired at least once during a project.' She blew on her tea, then raised her gaze to meet his. 'So. We're OK?'

He gave her a lopsided smile and nodded. 'We're OK.'

She returned his smile and watched him take a sip of tea. His brow was smooth and his shoulders were relaxed. Thankfully, her posture began to mirror his, the nervous tension in her neck and jaw receding.

Burden of guilt lessened, her confidence returned and, after taking a gulp from her own mug, she broached another potentially difficult topic. 'In that case, I was hoping we could talk about Phoebe's birthday.'

Charlie put his mug back on the coffee table and raised his hands. 'Don't worry, Lauren's already prepared me for this. And I guess a party is the least I can do. Phoebe hasn't had the most exciting birthdays the past few years. Her mum was always much better at thinking up presents and sorting out parties.'

Becky grinned. She must thank Lauren later. Now she had a clear green light for the party, the enthusiasm for Charlie's project which had been smothered under worry the past three weeks flooded back, leaving her slightly light-headed. 'Did Lauren say anything about putting up a marquee in the garden and coupling it to the studio? We'd empty it first, of course. All your things would be safe. Then we can put the refreshments and DJ booth in there.'

'How many people are we talking about?'

'A few dozen. So we won't need many tables and chairs and only a bit of food. A dance floor will be the most important thing. Nothing too fancy.'

'I've already made the mistake of telling Phoebe she can have whatever she wants. Just let me know when I need to clear out and when I can get back to work.'

'No problem.'

That had been far easier than expected. What had happened to grumpy, resistant Charlie? Who was this likeable, laid-back imposter?

She pulled her legs up onto the sofa. 'How's work going?'

'Well …' He picked up his slice of cake. 'I sent Rachel some photos of my latest painting and she thought using more colours was a positive development. And then she suggested I use other materials, so I've been experimenting with charcoal and some pastel.'

'Yeah, she mentioned the photos when Phoebe, Dylan and I dropped in to see her on Tuesday. We wanted to check she has all the information she needs for the moment.'

Charlie stared at her. The cake chewing came to an abrupt stop.

'Phoebe didn't tell you, did she?' Becky stifled a curse. 'I promise I've told her to tell you everything from now on. I'm going to kill her.'

He swallowed. 'No, it's all right. She must have forgotten. But it's odd Rachel didn't mention it when we spoke this morning.'

'Hang on, 'ang on, 'ang on.' Shock made her swallow most of her consonants. 'You're *speaking*? When did that start?'

'Just on the phone,' he said, looking down at his plate. 'How did your visit go?'

'She lit up when talking about you. She was impressed with what you've done so far.'

Becky was running at maximum diplomacy. She omitted to mention Rachel had been even more pleased when Becky's dejected expression had allowed her to guess she was yet to see any of Charlie's new work. Rachel had patted Becky on the shoulder. Nothing to worry about, Ms Watson. She assumed Mr Handren had only favoured her with an exclusive preview because he wanted an opinion he could value from someone who knew about art.

Patronising bitch. As much as she tried to like her, there was something about Rachel that made Becky want to arch her back and hiss. The cool glances, snide comments and then—and this had made Becky bite her tongue more than once—the way Rachel spoke about Charlie as if she owned him.

'How did Phoebe and Dylan get on there?' asked Charlie. 'Does Rachel like children?'

'Not in her gallery, I think.'

Rachel had watched Phoebe chasing a chortling Dylan between the exhibits as if they were trailing filth behind them.

Unable to think of anything nice to say about the object of Charlie's desire, Becky took another sip and let the clock fill the silence for a while. But there was no getting away from her. 'She's keen to talk to you in person. You'll have to go to the gallery soon.'

'Hmn.' He returned his plate to the table and picked up his mug. 'I know. But there's no rush.' Frowning, he gestured towards the front door. 'Are we going to watch a film? Because if we are I have to get my glasses from the car.'

'Sure.' She got up. 'And while you're doing that I'll go up and find mine.'

Becky followed Charlie to the front door and found herself smiling at the prospect of their impromptu movie night. She missed the cinema. Not so much the films but the experience. There was something about sitting in a darkened room, sharing a story with other people. The contrast in dim and bright lights, the occasional whisper, the smell of popcorn ...

She paused, her foot on the bottom stair, and said, 'Charlie?'

He had already opened the door but turned back at the sound of his name. The movement made his ponytail swing. Becky narrowed her eyes at the offending hair and wished her glare alone could cut it off.

'Yes?'

She tipped her head in the direction of his car. 'I was thinking about home cinema snacks. Don't suppose you've got any chocolate out there, have you?'

Charlie sucked in air through his teeth and narrowed his eyes, making an exaggerated pretence of thinking it over. 'I'm sorry to say, I don't think so. No.'

'Ah well. Don't worry.' She gave him a consoling nudge. 'You can always redeem yourself next time.'

OCTOBER

Chapter 23

A week before Phoebe's party, Charlie took his daughter to the Old Grange Hotel and Spa for the first of her birthday treats. Or that was how the trip was sold to him, who thought he was in for a relaxing afternoon pottering about the pools while Phoebe enjoyed various baffling-sounding 'treatments' involving hot stones and Dead Sea mud. He had been surprised she didn't want to go for these mysteriously feminine experiences with a friend, but was secretly delighted she had chosen to spend time with her old dad, and so kept his misgivings to himself.

Five minutes inside the building and he was asking himself how, once again, his daughter had made him feel like a perfect idiot.

The coven had been plotting against him and it turned out that, in addition to an aromatherapy massage, *he* had appointments with a barber, manicurist and, after Phoebe talked him into it, a beautician who was ruthlessly effective with wax.

Although he would never admit it, the massage and manicure weren't too bad. Unfortunately, any relaxing effects were quickly erased by having what felt like strips of his skin torn off his lower back by a smiling torturer who insisted on tutting and telling him the hellish agony she was inflicting couldn't be all that bad.

He was still sore as the barber positioned him in front of a mirror and, seemingly unaware his client might have any feelings on the subject, proceeded to cheerfully outline his plans to update Charlie's 'tired' appearance.

Did he look tired? Not someone who enjoyed gazing at his own reflection, Charlie took a breath to steel himself and stared critically at the man in the glass. The dark circles under his eyes had been a feature nearly his whole life, although he supposed the beard did nothing to lighten the additional shadows which added a sullenness to his already grave expression.

Charlie flinched as the barber flicked his hair, all the while gabbling on about colour and cut. To his side, Phoebe looked on, smiling with her usual youthful enthusiasm.

He sighed. It was only hair. It would grow back. So why did the thought of losing it make him so uncomfortable?

'Dad? What do you think?'

Charlie gladly turned his attention from the mirror to his daughter. 'I suppose a trim is out of the question?'

'Oh, Dad.' Phoebe laid a hand on his shoulder. The worried frown he hated to see on her face was back. 'We can go, if you want.'

'But?'

'I think this is a good idea. For your exhibition and everything. It'd be nice to look your best.'

She had a point. Though he had tried to steer clear of gossip, some ill-advised Internet searches had turned up rumours of his increasingly 'reclusive' behaviour and 'aged' appearance.

'And Becky will be pleased,' said Phoebe. 'And Auntie Lauren too, obviously,' she rushed to add.

Charlie gave her a small smile. Impressing Becky was quite a feat; one to which few people could lay claim. And it went without saying that keeping Lauren from moaning at him for a few days would be a pleasant break.

The barber was patting the closed scissor blades against his palm, impatient to get hacking.

'I guess you're right,' said Charlie, his flat tone an echo of the leaden feeling in his stomach.

'Thanks, Dad.'

The relieved smile on his little girl's face was the final push he needed. 'OK. Let's do this.'

He closed his eyes and braced himself, trying not to tremble as the cold steel of the scissors grazed his neck.

Fortunately, the trauma of the spa visit was forgotten soon after he left the hotel. His head was strangely light and the wind chilled his cheeks. He shivered and burrowed into his thoughts, ignoring Phoebe on the drive home and then hurrying out to his studio.

While mixing colours and sketching, he gradually came to terms with his new look. He reflected that for all the time and money people spent on guarding and grooming their hair, they were just struggling to nurture something already dead. Maybe it was true: a good haircut was sometimes a crucial step in getting over a break-up of any kind.

～

Becky called Phoebe that evening.

'How did it go?'

'Fine. The spa and beauty salon are amazing. You should go sometime. I could watch Dylan for you.'

'Right. Sure. But how did it go with your dad?'

'He was upset about the ponytail but otherwise not much complaining. Wait, I'll send you a picture now.'

'Where is he?'

'Painting.'

'Checking he hasn't lost his superpowers along with the hair?'

'Something like that. And er …'

'Yes? What's wrong?'

'He was getting looks. From women. In fact, from all the women we walked past.'

'Well that's not a bad thing, is it?' she said. 'Admiring looks means it's not only us who thinks this is an improvement. And maybe it might make your dad happier about us pushing him into another big change?'

'Yeah, I suppose,' said Phoebe. 'As long as you don't mind.'

'Why would I mind?' Becky cleared her throat to get the squeak out of her voice. Why did Phoebe ask such odd questions? Charlie was a free agent, or would be once the divorce was sorted. It wasn't as if he had any interest in Becky outside of the project and Becky would never have anything other than a purely professional interest in her clients. No matter how obviously handsome they might be now. And besides … Becky checked herself. How had she wandered down this rabbit hole? Oh yes, strange women leering at Charlie. 'Did he notice?'

'He told me I was imagining it.'

Becky smiled, pleased the attention wasn't going to Charlie's head. 'He'll notice eventually.'

⤞

'Eventually' turned out to be during Charlie's Monday evening art class. Accustomed to being ignored by his chatty students, he was unsettled when the room fell silent shortly after his entrance. Whispering followed.

When he gave his opening lecture they all stared at him, nodding and smiling as he detailed Caravaggio's use of chiaroscuro, and giggling when he faced the whiteboard. In the break, instead of huddling into circles to cluck, many of the women nipped out to the bathroom and returned wearing freshly applied lipstick.

For the first time in three years he had to stay behind after class to deal with a string of questions and some determined eyelash batting. And, as the last lady gave him her phone number and flounced out of the room, he gave thanks Mrs Howard was on the Tuesday course. Perhaps leaving some stubble the next day might dampen the effect.

⤞

Becky expected to wait until Thursday to see and speak to the newly shorn Charlie. He was due at her place at about eight in the evening for their now regular movie-watching appointment. So his Wednesday morning phone call caught her on the hop, just as she was arriving at the pool.

'I need you to come with me to the Coulson this morning.'

'Does it have to be this morning?'

'Rachel called. She says it has to be today and eleven is the one time she can manage.'

'But I have swimming with Dylan.'

'You could go to the gallery after you finish. I'll meet you there.'

'I don't know, Charlie. Dylan got up at the crack of dawn and he's cranky, so swimming is probably going to be torture.' And I'll have to stand next to the perfect Ms Stone looking like a knackered old mare, she added to herself. One who hasn't showered since yesterday morning—what's the point in getting clean right before swimming?—and who didn't shower after swimming because her toddler screams if he has to go anywhere near a shower. And who has no make-up on. She glanced down at herself. Damn, the scuffed but comfy black boots, old maternity dress over jeans and her favourite threadbare coat. Crap.

'Please, Becky.'

She pictured the sad Labrador eyes and sighed. 'I'll see you there.'

⌐

Swimming, as it happened, was indeed torture. Dylan screamed and cried for most of the class, but stubbornly refused to kick because that would have been too much like swimming. The one blessing was that he exhausted himself and, safe from the elements under the buggy's plastic rain cover, was rocked to sleep as Becky half ran to the gallery.

She arrived at five past eleven, rain-beaten, windswept and prepared to kill for a cup of tea. She reversed into the Coulson, using her behind to open the door, and parked the buggy near the reception desk.

Although she hadn't made any effort to sneak in, her arrival went unnoticed. On the other side of the gallery, Rachel was talking Charlie around the latest exhibition: a collection of grey-and-white textured canvases which looked to Becky like the creations of a preschool class allowed to rampage with papier mâché and PVA glue.

Rachel was punctuating her explanations with a great deal of fidgeting, smiling and the occasional laugh. Charlie's smile was spread all over his infuriatingly chiselled, naked face.

Becky was wondering whether she could sneak out and head for Sweet's when Virgil appeared at her elbow, making her jump.

'Good morning, Becky. You're looking positively radiant.'

'Thank you, Virgil. But I wasn't expecting to work today or I'd have made more of an effort. We've come straight from swimming and I know I look "interesting" at best.'

'Don't be ridiculous. You're as fetching as always.'

Becky laid a hand on his arm and gave him a weak smile. His comments were slightly restorative, although she would have traded them for a cup of tea.

He bent forward to peer into the buggy. 'And this handsome young man must be Dylan.'

'Why am I not surprised you know his name?'

'I have excellent sources.'

'I bet you do. And, yes: that's Dylan. Thankfully asleep at the moment. And if I'm lucky he'll stay that way long enough for me to have a cup of tea.'

'Sounds like a plan. Would you mind if I joined you?'

Virgil looked over at the happy couple on the other side

of the room as Rachel burst into a fit of giggles and gave Charlie a playful shove. The gallery owner winced as if the small shove to Charlie had landed as a sharp punch in his own guts. Not for the first time, Becky wondered exactly what was going on between Rachel and Virgil and whether she could get Clarice to do some digging. But for now she would settle for getting them out of the building and to some tea and cake as quickly as possible.

She dropped her chin and muttered, 'Let's go before they—'

'Ms Watson!'

Rachel sailed towards them, her dark hair floating behind her, scattering a delicate scent of jasmine. Charlie trailed her, staring unashamedly at his muse, his pupils as large as dinner plates.

As he approached, Becky had to admit she understood why the 'new' Charlie had caused more than one passer-by to do a double take. His dark hair was short and neat. The facial hair had gone, revealing a strong jawline and letting his expressive brown eyes take centre stage. Eyes which were stubbornly fixed on Rachel.

Becky tried to tuck a pained expression behind her ears along with the most rebellious strands of her hair. But it was no use; she would have come off badly in a comparison with Rachel on a good day. Right now, next to such petite perfection, Becky felt like a blob. A dishevelled, chlorinated blob. And for a horrible second she was back at that party, standing next to her lover's beautiful wife. Seeing them side-by-side, no wonder Dylan's dad had disowned her.

Becky stood up straight and flicked her hands at the hem of her dress. Whatever she might say, Becky didn't have to let Rachel get to her. Although that thought was little comfort as her fingertips brushed against the mud splatter on the knee of her jeans. Why did she find it so hard to be polished and poised? She bet Rachel could have taken Dylan swimming and shown up at the gallery without a speck of dirt on her clothes, a face of expertly applied make-up and no desire at all to disappear through the cracks in the floorboards.

'Good morning, Ms Stone,' she said. 'I see you and Mr Handren have finally been reunited.'

'Yes! Finally,' she said, touching Charlie's arm in a gesture Becky thought entirely unnecessary. 'I had started to wonder if he was hiding from me.'

Charlie joined Rachel in a polite chuckle, his gaze never leaving her face. Meanwhile Rachel was using her doe-like eyes to scour Becky from top to toe. Releasing her hold on Charlie, she rubbed her smoothed and varnished hands together. 'I assume you walked here, Ms Watson? You must have been unfortunate with the weather, although I see you are dressed for the outdoors.' She paused to let her barbs sink in, then changed her target. She jabbed a dainty finger towards Dylan and sniffed. 'At least he's quiet today. A gallery is no place for children.'

Becky opened her mouth to defend her son, but Virgil interrupted.

'Becky and I are popping out for tea,' he said with an impressive degree of self-importance and an emphatic tug on his jacket's cuffs. 'We wouldn't want to get in the way of you two and your little plans.'

Becky could have kissed him. Rachel's mouth was twisted into a pucker only her mother could rival and his comments had also torn Charlie's stare away from his muse.

Charlie blinked at Becky, inspecting the mess passing for her hair and face. 'Becky, are you all right?' he said. 'You're all red.'

Thanks, Charlie, she thought. Couldn't have come up with 'radiant', could you?

'I rushed straight here from swimming.' She paused to narrow her eyes. 'I thought I might be needed.'

'Oh, yes.' Charlie suddenly found the floor fascinating. 'Right. Thanks.'

Rachel interrupted his inspection of the parquet by returning her hand to his arm. 'Yes, well, as Mr Locke says, we should get back to our *little* plans.' Her sneer melted into a smile as she turned her face to Charlie and led him away by the elbow. The image of the Labrador returned to Becky, but for far less flattering reasons.

Virgil seized the buggy and drove it out of the gallery, apparently not wanting to witness round two of Charlie and Rachel's courtship ritual. Becky followed, scurrying to keep up as he strode away from the gallery. She would have to talk to Clarice again. There was definitely something more going on with Virgil and Rachel than she'd understood.

As if wanting to confirm her suspicions, Virgil muttered his next words through clenched teeth. 'Your Mr Handren isn't quite the bearded recluse I was expecting.'

Becky trotted to catch up with him. 'You only missed out by a few days. Believe me.'

Virgil huffed and let Becky take control of the buggy. 'I suppose what he looks like is neither here nor there. And anyway,' he said, his smile reappearing, 'this is wonderful! I've finally got you to myself. Tea and brownies at Sweet's?'

Now they were out in the fresh air, Becky found it easy to return Virgil's smile. 'Perfect. And, speaking of Sweet's, that's reminded me about something I've been meaning to ask you.'

'Ask away.'

'I have a friend who wants to know: were you named after a relative?'

'No. I'm the only one in my family called Virgil.' He shrugged. 'My mother loved the classics, it's the only explanation I have.' His smile turned wolfish and he linked an arm through Becky's. 'But more importantly, does this mean you've been talking about me? More than once?'

She nudged him with her elbow, but didn't shake his arm off. 'Don't flatter yourself.'

'I wouldn't dream of it.' He winked. 'After all, today that rather seems to be your job.'

Chapter 24

The Saturday of Phoebe's party, Charlie arrived at Becky's in the middle of the afternoon to report for babysitting duty. From his stream of questions about the guest list, she guessed he felt uneasy about a group of unknown teenagers invading his home but had accepted it was better for everyone if he were out of the way.

Hoping to keep them both occupied, Becky asked Charlie to play with Dylan in his room so she would be free to dig through her wardrobe for a party outfit.

The wardrobe was one of the few items of furniture in her bedroom. Becky never found time to look in to accent wallpaper or feature walls, leaving a duvet cover strewn with small blue flowers and a pair of matching curtains straining to break up the monotony of the magnolia and white colour scheme. They were assisted by a large print of *The Japanese Bridge* on the wall above the bed. The blues and greens of Monet's garden brought a much-needed splash of colour to the room where the water lilies were bright stars on a bland backdrop.

The familiar sound of falling wooden bricks followed by giggling and thunderous footfall warned Becky that Dylan had sent another tower flying and was on his way, moments before he barrelled into her legs.

Charlie followed cautiously, pausing in the doorway and knocking.

'Come in!' Becky turned away from the wardrobe to face Charlie and gestured to her clothes. She was wearing black, as was her custom when working an event. But, unusually, she had opted for a short dress over thick dark tights. She was also wearing knee-high black boots. 'What do you think?'

In response to her question, Charlie blinked, then shrugged. Her heart sinking, Becky glanced at the mirror on the back of the door. Surely she didn't look that unremarkable?

She was about to rethink her entire outfit when Charlie stepped forward, lifted his hand to her right ear and cradled the silver pendant hanging there. Becky startled, but Charlie appeared unfazed, his warm fingers steady against her neck. Not daring to move, she breathed slowly, trying to slow her hammering heart.

Apparently oblivious to the shock he'd given her, Charlie's attention was fixed on her left ear. His gaze flicked to her face and away again. 'You're missing an earring,' he muttered, his fingers lightly tracing the side of her neck and lingering next to her chin before he withdrew his hand.

Becky blinked and cleared her throat. 'Yes, well, I'm under strict orders from your daughter to wear something "nicer than normal". And that includes jewellery, apparently. Which is giving me a bit of a problem.'

Keeping her tone light, she turned back to her jewellery box. She used one hand to rummage through the tangled mess of studs and necklaces and the other to rub the side of her neck which had suddenly developed an acute case of prickly heat. 'You know, one day they will discover a species of jewellery pixie. Preferred diet: one of every pair of my favourite earrings. Only known predator: the sock elf.'

She glanced down to where Charlie was crouched next to Dylan. Initially jubilant at seeing his lips turn up, disappointment followed when she noticed the smile didn't reach his eyes. Focusing on the jewellery, Becky bit down on the urge to fish further for a compliment or a laugh. He clearly wasn't in the mood and, as he followed Dylan out the door, she wondered if he was sulking because she too was being stingy with compliments.

The staff at the spa had done a fantastic job on Charlie, particularly whoever had been in charge of his hair. There was not a hint of grey to be seen. The close shave had taken years off him and, although there was little that could be done about the under-eye circles without surgical intervention, being able to see the rest of his face accentuated its positives.

Nevertheless, Becky was reluctant to tell Charlie how much his looks had improved. Firstly because she didn't want to inflate his ego. Secondly because she was still annoyed about his dragging her to the Coulson on Wednesday. And finally, it would be odd for her to bring it up now. She hadn't said anything at the gallery and, although she guessed the abundance of face stroking and head scratching while they were watching a film on Thursday evening was his way of asking for her opinion, she hadn't mentioned it then either. He could bloody well wait. When he gave her compliments, instead of shrugging or saying she was 'sturdy' and 'red', she would return the favour.

She gave a cry of triumph as she found the missing earring. Looping it into place, she grabbed her least distressed coat and skipped downstairs where she picked up her everything-and-the-kitchen-sink events bag and began to run down her mental checklist.

Charlie and Dylan had come downstairs while the earring hunt was still in progress and were huddled on the sofa reading the book Charlie had given him for his birthday.

'I think I've got everything. It'll all be over by half eleven and I'll try to be back by one. If you need anything, call me.'

'Becky …'

She already had her hand on the front door handle, but turned back to indulge some more of his last-minute fretting. What was it now? Did she have the name and addresses of all the boys attending? Had she run background checks on them? If necessary, would she help him chase after them with a shotgun and shovel?

Charlie waved a hand in the direction of her knees while staring at a spot on the wall above her right shoulder. 'You look nice,' he said, with no discernible expression in his voice or on his face.

The fingers gripping the door handle tingled where they had turned white. 'Nice' was hardly dazzling praise, but it could well be the understated Charlie equivalent of 'sublime'. She had her compliment; it would be churlish not to give in now.

Becky waved a non-numb finger vaguely in his direction and peered over the top of her glasses to look him square in the eye. 'So do you,' she said.

Not waiting to see his reaction, she opened the door and stepped out to the car.

Chapter 25

Ronnie arrived at the Old Station House shortly after six. Meeting her on the driveway, Becky helped carry the cake to the studio, whose large south doors had been thrown open to allow the marquee to be joined to the building.

Shaped as the number eighteen, Phoebe's choice of cake was a classic and a homage to those her mother used to make her when she was little. The idea had been Charlie's, who also suggested the jelly diamond and chocolate button decorations.

Ronnie had wrinkled her nose when first shown Charlie's sketch. Apparently it was 'simple', which was her way of saying it was boring and small. Although she had conceded that white chocolate with raspberry was a decent enough choice.

Charlie failed to specify dimensions, so Ronnie compensated for lack of difficulty with surplus enormity and went further off brief to add some sugar paste models around the cake. They represented some of Phoebe's interests, including a pile of books, a camera and dancing shoes.

Becky watched as her friend put the last model next to the cake, gave a small nod of satisfaction and stepped back to scrutinise the studio.

'What's the verdict?' asked Becky. 'Is it a worthy frame for one of your masterpieces?'

Ronnie glanced at Becky, then shrugged. 'It's OK, I suppose.' She started to pack the empty model containers into the cake box, clicking each lid into place with a vigorous snap and a twitch of her nose. Wondering whose neck she was visualising breaking, Becky opened her mouth to ask, when Ronnie said, 'You know you're doing it again, don't you?'

Ugh! Becky closed her eyes to stop them rolling out of her head. 'Not this again!'

'Yes, again! Because this happens every time. You get too involved. You spend too much time with these people. They're not your friends, Becks. They're not your family. When you've made their lives better they'll wave you off, all grateful and "oh how can we ever repay you", but in a few weeks they'll forget you because they'll be busy living their marvellously improved lives.'

Becky slid her fingers behind the legs of her glasses to rub her temples. How many times did she have to listen to this speech? 'You've said this before, but it's always been fine. They move on. I move onto a new project. Everyone's happy.'

'Maybe.' Ronnie crossed her arms. 'But that was before you had Dylan.'

Becky loved Ronnie. God knows you'd have to if you were going to put up with her prickliness, mood swings and downright rudeness. And Becky always preferred to think of her best friend as sensitive, dynamic and forthright. But Dylan was a line Ronnie knew better than to cross and she was edging perilously close to it.

Becky raised a finger and then curled it down into a fist. 'Where are you going with this, Ron?'

Ronnie dropped her voice, probably sensing a cautious approach would be best. 'Where's Dylan now, Becks? He's with Charlie. And he's with Charlie at least twice a week, and if not then he's with Phoebe. In January, when the exhibition's opened and you're surplus to requirements, do you think Rachel's going to be delighted with Charlie being a regular babysitter for your son? Will Dylan understand why his new babysitters don't come round any more? And then there's your Thursday night thing ...'

'I've already told you. Nothing's going on. Phoebe drops him off. We watch a film, eat popcorn and sit at opposite ends of the sofa being thoroughly middle-aged and curmudgeonly. Phoebe picks him up. The craziest it gets is drinking a glass of wine or a beer.'

Ronnie held up her hands. 'Don't get your knickers in a knot. I'm not saying you're shagging him. I'm just saying, he's not your friend and certainly not your boyfriend. And at some point he'll act more like an employer than a friend and you'll be disappointed. He's already fired you once. Just ...' She put a hand on Becky's arm. 'Try not to get too sucked in. Please?'

Becky pulled away and turned to the table to give the cake board an unnecessary adjustment. She was too tired to have this fight now. It was easier to nod and let Ronnie rant.

'How's it all going, anyway?' Ronnie asked, her tone softening. 'I know filling the gallery isn't going to be a problem, but will the paintings sell well? It's been a while since all the kerfuffle over that article. Do you think there's still enough interest in him and his work out there?'

It was uncanny how Ronnie could put her finger on the main items on Becky's mental list of 'things keeping me awake at night' and poke them until sore. She worried about Dylan constantly; she worried this project was too ambitious, that it would be a monumental disaster that would leave Charlie, Phoebe, Dylan and herself worse off than ever.

She took a deep breath and avoided Ronnie's eye as she said, 'Everything's under control'.

'Has he paid you for organising all this?' Ronnie flicking an accusatory finger towards the marquee and the bar. 'He didn't pay for the cake, I know that much.'

Becky took another deep breath. If Ronnie carried on like this she was sure to start hyperventilating. 'Lauren and Mel have covered the supplier costs. And the cake is my present to Phoebe. I did offer to pay you, remember?'

'I don't want *your* money.'

'OK, then!' Becky placed a hand on the table to steady herself, taking a moment to remove the edge from her voice and try for a change of subject. 'And thanks again for the cake. It's great. Those models must have taken ages.'

'You're welcome. Who did the photos?' Ronnie pointed towards an area to the right of the doorway, near the DJ booth. A large canvas had been set up on an easel and decorated with photos of Phoebe taken over the last eighteen years.

Becky smiled. At last, a topic with no negative side. 'It was my idea. Lauren sent a few photos but Charlie did all the work of getting them printed and put together.'

'Huh.' Ronnie narrowed her eyes, scanning the pictures. 'I don't see Charlie in any of the pictures past when Phoebe was a little girl.'

Calm and controlled be damned. Becky had listened to Ronnie's carping long enough, and there was no way she was letting her go after Charlie. 'Jesus Christ, Ronnie! What is with you? If he's not there it's because he was behind the camera. Somebody has to take the picture. Not all of us want to be centre stage.'

She turned away and used a container which had strayed under the table as an excuse to duck out of Ronnie's view and vent some grumpy mumbling at the floor. Closing her eyes, she counted to ten while trying to figure out what was behind Ronnie's latest barrage of sunshine and joy. They often disagreed, but Ronnie didn't often go on the attack. Something else had to be getting to her.

Becky straightened up, bringing the box with her. 'How is cohabiting going?' she asked.

Ronnie ran her hand through her hair. 'Better. The toilet seat is down ninety per cent of the time and we've sorted out sharing the bathroom. Mike also bought me a tablet so I can watch TV when he wants to watch the football. We're getting there.'

'Good. I'm sure Mike's doing his best. God knows I couldn't live with you.' She gave Ronnie a sly smile. 'I'd end up clubbing you to death after finding you'd put empty After Eight wrappers back in the box.'

Ronnie returned the smile as Becky nudged her in the ribs. They never could stay annoyed with each other for long. And Becky was keen to bury the hatchet if it meant she could bury some of her worries along with it and instead get to the bottom of whatever was causing her friend to lash out.

Ronnie tossed the last container in the box. 'Did you know Mike and Charlie now go to the gym together, as well as their weekend rugby dates?'

'Dates, plural? I knew they'd been to a friendly back in August. And Charlie's mentioned the odd game now the season's under way. But the gym too? Doesn't Charlie go to Tyler's?'

'Not any more. Mike convinced him it was a waste of money when the leisure centre has everything he needs.'

'So he quit Tyler's? Do they let you do that?'

Ronnie laughed. 'They do, and he did, but only after he took Mike there as his guest a couple of times. Mike's not stupid, even if he looks it.'

'And now they're gym buddies?'

Ronnie folded her arms and sagged, deflating like a day-old balloon. 'Every Monday and Wednesday night after Charlie finishes at the college.' She sniffed as she slumped further. 'Mike's going to do a full audit of his finances.'

Ah. No wonder Charlie was in Ronnie's bad books. He dared take up Becky's time and now he'd moved onto Mike. Although Becky could take the heat off Charlie when it came to the audit. 'Sorry. You can blame that one on me. It was my idea. Charlie really needs someone to sort his accounts and Mike's the best. But then you already know that, right?'

Ronnie raised her gaze to meet Becky's and flashed her a weak smile.

'Cheer up.' Becky wrapped an arm around her shoulders. 'It's Saturday night and you'll have Mike all to yourself. In fact, I'm sure he's waiting for you at home with dinner prepared. It could be pizza.'

'Yeah, right.' Ronnie picked up the cake box and made to leave. 'I should be so lucky.'

Becky waited until she had waved Ronnie off before calling Mike to suggest a few simple ways he could make his world a sweeter place, starting with ordering pizza.

Chapter 26

At nine thirty, Lloyd Blake was decanted from his Rolls Royce into the Old Station House porch. He waved his driver off, skipped over the threshold and kissed Becky on both cheeks.

'Delightful to see you again, my dear. And such a treat to see inside a local landmark.'

'I'm afraid I'm not qualified to give you a tour.'

'Nonsense. Look at this spectacular fireplace. And the carving on the bannister rail and spindles is wonderful,' he said, striding into the living room.

Becky scurried to halt his progress. 'The caterers have taken over the kitchen.' She pointed towards the extension. 'So it would be best for us go out that way.'

She led him to the study and then out into the garden. Lloyd had recognised the Lucinda's catering logo and, on their way to the marquee, he quizzed her regarding all the companies she had persuaded to supply Phoebe's party.

'When did you start planning this particular soirée?'

'About four weeks ago. Luckily I know a few people who were willing to help me out at the last minute. It's only fifty guests and some finger food after all.'

'Don't sell yourself short. Your contacts are among the best and booked up months in advance. They either owe you more than you're letting on or your powers of persuasion are remarkable.'

Becky winked at him. 'I'd like to claim remarkable skills, but the truth is I know where the bodies are buried.'

'Excellent. Keep it that way and you'll go far.'

In the marquee entrance they paused to watch the guests. The teenagers sprang around the dance floor, darting between a kaleidoscope of lights. Their movements were energetic, bordering on acrobatic, but not one let their smartphone slip from their hand.

Despite all the bouncing about, the air in the tent was still and stifling. The sudden contrast to the crisp autumnal night outside was enough to make anyone half Lloyd's age dizzy, so Becky wasn't surprised when he gasped and raised a hand to his chest.

'Shall we go somewhere quieter?' shouted Becky over the din passing for music.

He nodded and followed her into the studio where, after a brief restorative visit to the bar, they entered the restricted area at the back of the building and climbed to the platform. The DJ's box was downstairs, but the speakers were inside the marquee, allowing Becky and Lloyd to talk rather than shout.

Though not a party guest, Lloyd had invested time in making sure he cut an impressive figure. A liberal application of wax made his white quiff gleam in the dim light and in contrast to his pitch-black suit.

Cupping a balloon glass in his right hand, he rested his elbows on the safety rail and peered down into the space below. 'It's impressive,' he said. 'But I imagine it's better in the daytime. The skylights are ideal. Having bricked up the east- and west-facing windows the light must be fairly constant throughout the day. Monet had a studio which was lit similarly, although he had paintings in his.'

'We thought it best to remove them. A few are in the storeroom beneath us and Ms Stone offered to take some into storage at the Coulson ahead of schedule.'

'Ah, of course, the lovely Ms Stone. I believe she and Mr Handren are getting along splendidly.' He chuckled at Becky's raised eyebrows. 'Come along, my dear. You had to know I would be keeping a discreet eye on you. Besides, not much happens in our little art community without my knowledge. My contacts tell me Mr Handren and Ms Stone's reunion was a roaring success and he has been back to the gallery at least once a week since.'

Becky turned her face to the shadows. The first tremors of panic she'd felt when Ronnie had been quizzing her earlier were settling in again, although this time they felt more like nausea. That day at the gallery hadn't been one of her best moments and, as much as she tried not to dwell on it, memories of her chlorinated 'redness' next to Rachel's styled composure, and the way Charlie had been staring at her as if Becky had ceased to exist ... Her stomach churned again. She glanced at Lloyd, who was pulling at this shirt collar and looking a little peaky too.

'Are you sure you're all right?' she asked. 'It's not as hot up here, but we could go and sit downstairs.'

Lloyd turned to rest his back on the safety rail. 'Nonsense. I'm fine.'

Becky raised her eyebrows again and Lloyd laughed. 'I see you can't kid a kidder.' He patted her arm. 'Some minor trouble with the old ticker.' He moved his hand to his chest. 'In fact, I would have been keeping a closer eye on you, but my doctors have turned positively rabid on me. Insisting I go in for a small procedure.'

Oh God! thought Becky, the flutters of panic sinking into dread. Nothing could happen to Lloyd. Not now.

Her worry must have shown on her face because Lloyd laughed again, although this time it quickly deteriorated into a wheezing cough. He held up a hand as she opened her mouth to suggest she find him a seat. 'Now, now. Nothing to worry yourself about. I won't let them near me until the middle of November and it's a trifling procedure. I won't let you down.'

'I am worried about *you* as well, you know,' Becky said, guilty that her first thought had been for her plans instead of Lloyd's health. For as much as his involvement worried her, she had grown fond of Lloyd and found his larger-than-life presence comforting. When this was all over, he was someone else she would miss.

'Bless you. But don't worry, I'm not putting it off just for you. I have to check my business affairs will be in good hands.' He took a sip of brandy. 'And speaking of plans and business, I'm here, as requested, and waiting to hear about phase two of your plan. Dazzle me.'

Becky took a deep breath. 'Have you ever been to Barbara Stone's New Year's ball?'

'At Compton Hall?' He tutted and shook his head.

'How would you like to have a seat at Barbara Stone's table this year?

'Is this some sort of joke?'

Lloyd glared at her and Becky could well understand his sudden pique. According to Clarice, it was common knowledge among local non-commoners that the New Year's ball was the one Compton society event impervious to Lloyd's advances. He had managed to buy, bribe or bully his way into every other important date on the calendar, but Barbara Stone had blocked all his attempts to get a ticket to the ball.

'No,' Becky shook her head. 'Please, just hear me out.'

Lloyd pursed his lips. 'Go on.'

'The ball is in aid of a different charity every year. The tickets cost a fortune but most of that money goes to pay for the event. The donation comes from the proceeds of the auction on the night.'

'Yes, yes.' He waved a dismissive hand. 'Barbara's friends donate a few mangy bits and pieces. Then the guests pay over the odds to acquire them because they're blotto and competing to look more flush than all the people they are pretending so hard to get on with.'

'Exactly. Last year, the vice president of the art society, Nancy Sheridan, managed to unearth a sketch by Sheila Whitehall which sold for fifty thousand. A large picture of Nancy featured in the *South Compton Gazette*. She was standing next to the representative from the local donkey sanctuary and clutching one of those large display cheques.'

'Barbara can't have liked that.'

'She was not amused. I would guess as Supreme Commander of the Art Society and the Ball Organising Committee she is keen to bring something to this year's auction that will trump anything else her friends might contribute.'

Lloyd swirled his drink, his gaze flickering over the churning liquid, and in the quick movement of his eyes Becky could see him following her train of thought, unravelling all her schemes in seconds.

His next question was tentative. 'Let us suppose I were to convince Mr Handren to donate one of his new pieces to the auction and let Barbara take the credit for the donation...' He paused to watch his brandy dance, encouraging its movement by circling his wrist. 'But would the painting go for over fifty thousand? Mr Handren's reputation has suffered quite a dent in recent years.'

'I think, between the two of us, we could manage it.'

'Hmn. Perhaps.' He tapped his signet ring against the glass while holding Becky's gaze. 'Are you absolutely certain about this, my dear? Once I contact Barbara, we'd be committed. This isn't just about some gallery space any more. We're talking about bending morality, if not the law, and putting a great deal of money on the line along with Mr Handren's career. And yours too for that matter.'

Becky closed her hand over Lloyd's, silencing the chime of gold against glass. 'This has to work,' she said, staring Lloyd straight in the eye, hoping she was holding his hand tightly enough he couldn't tell hers was shaking. 'And it will.'

Lloyd stared back at her. 'Fine,' he said and Becky removed her hand. 'Your word is all I need. However, in the spirit of belt and braces, would you object if I were to bring in a third man?'

Her instinct was to refuse. The more people involved in a plan the more opportunities for things to go wrong. But it wasn't as if this was Lloyd's first rodeo, and he hadn't let her down so far. 'Do you trust him?' she asked.

'Absolutely. He's family and runs several of my business concerns.'

Although it would mean adding another small item to the list of worries buzzing round her head, Becky knew she had to let Lloyd have his way. 'Then he's OK by me.'

Lloyd smiled. 'I'm sure you've foreseen Rachel Stone won't be too happy about this.'

'She should be. It'll be brilliant publicity for the exhibition.'

'But her mother will have robbed her of the big reveal. Mr Handren's new work will have been exposed before opening night.'

'Well, Rachel robbed her mother of the exhibition first. And I'd say giving Barbara the chance of getting back at her daughter will guarantee you a sympathetic hearing, don't you agree?'

The thin smile which had been slowly creeping over his face cracked into a grin. 'Do you know, my dear, I think this might actually work!'

Becky laughed. 'I should hope so! But, if you don't mind asking Barbara for something else, I'll need a few tickets for the ball,' she said. 'Including one for me.'

His eyes sparkled. 'I don't foresee any problems with that,' he said. 'In fact, I think I'll get a ticket for my nephew while I'm about it.' He nudged Becky. 'Kevin. He's about your age. Single, you know. Bright lad too. And I'll be handing over the business to him soon enough.'

'I'm sure he's incredibly eligible,' Becky said, choosing a diplomatic response while planning to avoid said nephew at all costs. She had enough on her plate without another distraction.

But Lloyd didn't seem to hear her reply. Staring down into the space below, his eyebrows were drawn together, wheels busy turning above them. 'I'll need to have a ponder before speaking to Barbara,' he said. 'This needs to be handled delicately if it's going to work.'

'Oh, come now. Is there anyone better than you at getting blood from a stone?'

He laughed. 'Very droll. But hopefully it won't come to blood.'

All signs of the fatigue he'd shown earlier now gone, he stood up straight and finished his remaining brandy in a gulp and gasp. He shifted his weight from foot to foot, like a large cat preparing to leap. 'I would ask you to dance,' he said, 'but I'm afraid I have no idea how to move to this particular type of noise.'

'Save me a dance for the ball instead.'

'I will …' he wagged a finger at her, '… as long as you save one for Kevin. I think you two would get along nicely.'

Becky replied with what she hoped was a non-committal nod. Just how many dinners and dances was she going to have to give away to get this job done?

'Excellent,' said Lloyd, passing her his empty glass. 'Now, if you don't mind, I think it's time I called my driver. I have a great deal of thinking to do before Monday when I'll make my first move. Let's see how long it takes me to capture the queen.'

Chapter 27

Becky got home from the party at a quarter to one.

She eased the door of the Mercedes into its frame and dragged her feet to the front door, struggling to keep her eyes open. Her bed was calling out to her and she was looking forward to falling into its downy arms and forgetting all about tipsy teenagers and her badgering best friend.

Aside from the ticking of the mantle clock, the only other sound inside the house was Charlie's slow, steady breathing. Asleep on the sofa, he was surrounded by a soft halo of light cast by the standing lamp in the corner.

Becky set the box containing three slices of birthday cake on the coffee table and eased off her coat and boots. She threw Charlie envious glances, but decided to let him sleep on a while: long enough to enjoy a cup of tea in interrogation-free peace.

She lifted a blanket from the back of the armchair, put one knee on the sofa, and bent forward to drape the cosy blue cloth over him. He didn't stir. His brow, so often furrowed when he was awake, was relaxed, and his lips were set in the smallest suggestion of a smile.

They really had done a terrific job at the spa, she thought, as she appraised his strong jaw and lightly tanned skin, imagining it soft and smooth to the touch.

Absorbed in her inspection, Becky moved closer and ran her fingertips down his cheek, then back through his hair. It was the one fault she could find: she would have cut it a little shorter.

☙

Cradled in the comfortable plush of Becky's sofa, Charlie was dreaming of his muse again. Now accustomed to her visits to the dream studio, he worked quickly and was bolder in applying colour to her shirt. Meanwhile she remained as inscrutable as ever and only made the smallest of movements.

He crouched to dip his hands in the tins of paint, but this time stayed low. Edging towards her on his knees he slid his fingers along the ridges between her toes and up her feet. He encircled her ankles, twisting his wrists to rub more olive green onto her skin. Pausing to refuel, he rose steadily, massaging colour into her calves and thighs with strong butterfly strokes.

As he worked, a spreading warmth tickled its way up his back. Glancing left and right, he found her hands resting on his shoulders. They were weightless but drew him towards her, lifting him to his feet.

When they were face-to-face, he made a proper study of her eyes. In along with the swirl of colour and clarity, there was a glimmer of something else: an invitation, a guiding spark.

Although he couldn't be sure he was right, he decided the risk was worth taking. Running his hands through her hair, he drew her towards him gently and touched his lips to hers.

The kiss obliterated their surroundings, uniting them in a moment of radiance. Transformed by her power, he could hear light and smell colour. Her lips tasted soft and felt sweet.

When the metallic brightness faded, Charlie opened his eyes. She was gone. However this time she had been particularly generous: the platform, upper galleries and the workspace below were filled with paintings. The walls were covered with completed canvases and easels boasting works of various sizes occupied every inch of floor space.

Approaching euphoria, Charlie spun until everything was a blur, stirred further by his rising laughter.

He dropped to the floor. Stretching out on his back, he giggled. There was a tickling sensation by his ear, as if an invisible hand were stroking his hair.

Intrigued, Charlie closed his eyes and followed the feeling out of the dream.

≈

Becky froze as Charlie stirred. She was practically lying on top of him, her fingers were in his hair and her face was a few inches from his.

He opened his eyes. Blinking, he turned his head towards her hand and his lips grazed her wrist. When he turned back, his eyes were narrowed under a puzzled frown.

Well this was awkward.

Her cheeks started to tingle. It wouldn't be long until

they burned. She would have to brazen this out. And quickly.

'Personally, I would have taken another inch off,' she said, ruffling the hair under her hand and springing to her feet.

To her relief, Charlie yawned. He sniffed and looked about him, as if he had expected to wake up somewhere else.

Capitalising on his drowsiness, she moved on to diverting his attention. 'Cup of tea? I brought leftovers.' She pointed at the cake box in front of them.

'Yes. Please.'

'Great!' she said, already on her way out of the room.

The kettle was boiling when Charlie stumbled into the kitchen and leant against the fridge, watching her juggle the tea things. 'How did the party go?'

'Fine.' She retrieved a teabag from the cupboard with her left hand while getting a spoon from the drawer with her right. 'At least, I think so. You'll have to ask Phoebe once she's heard her friends' morning-after opinions. There weren't any problems, anyway. I sent Phoebe to bed and locked up. By Monday afternoon all evidence of the party will have gone. And your studio will be ready for use by tomorrow lunchtime.'

'Good. I think I'm going to be very busy.'

'Oh? Inspiration been striking in your sleep again?' She tipped her head in the direction of the living room. 'I've always said how comfy that sofa is. If it had anything to do with it, I should charge you extra.'

Charlie cleared his throat and dropped his gaze, focusing on rearranging the letter magnets on the fridge.

Becky ignored his embarrassment and nudged him aside so she could put the milk back in its place, all while trying not to think about what he and dream-Rachel had been up to this time. Thank God he never wanted to talk about it.

Tea and cake in hand, they returned to the living room, where a card on the mantelpiece reminded Becky she had to ask Charlie a favour. She blew on her tea, waiting until he had enjoyed a bite of cake before she pounced. 'I know you said you're going to be busy, but could you take a break for a couple of hours next Friday afternoon? I'd need you to be here for about half two.'

Charlie swallowed and used his fingers to mop up crumbs from his plate. 'I have to meet Rachel at the gallery that morning. She has some more ideas she wants to talk to me about. But I should be free in the afternoon. What are we doing?'

'Helping out a friend. Do you own a suit and tie?'

Chapter 28

When Friday arrived, Charlie took a reluctant break from work to visit the Coulson. Rachel was as charming as always, but painting number fifteen was in progress and he was itching to go home and get on with it.

After squeezing in another hour in the studio before lunch, he dressed as directed and went to collect Becky and Dylan. The drive through South Compton was pleasant: there were few cars on the road and the sun was shining after four days of steady rain-soaked greyness.

As he parked the car, his passengers came out onto the doorstep. Taking Dylan from Becky, Charlie took charge of safely stowing him in the car. The child seat was a permanent fixture in the Mercedes now Phoebe had her own wheels. Her red-and-white Mini Cooper, a joint birthday present from Mel and Charlie, was delivered complete with a child seat: one of Charlie's better ideas given the amount of time Phoebe spent ferrying Becky and Dylan around.

Becky shivered as she got into the car, a warm cocoon sheltering them from the bite of the autumnal air outside. As she rubbed her hands together, Charlie redirected the heated airflow down to her feet.

'So where are we going?'

'Barnsby.' She blew into her hands. 'Head for the centre.'

❧

Although it was often infuriating, Becky sometimes found Charlie's reticence a welcome break from having to give, or avoid giving, explanations. As they left Great Compton and headed east on the Barnsby Road, she relaxed into the twenty-minute drive to the nearby county town.

They had negotiated a couple of the trickiest junctions on the route and reached the midway point in their journey before Becky realised she hadn't applied the imaginary brake once. Charlie steered the car calmly, projecting an aura of assured control. She also noticed his choice of music.

'I see you've made peace with our meddling with your playlists.' She gestured towards the stereo.

'There are a few things in The Eighties Mix I could live without.'

'You better not be talking about this,' she said, swaying along to Duran Duran. 'Or you can stop the car, and Dylan and I will walk.'

'No need.' He smiled. 'This is one of the better ones. And you'll be pleased to hear I like nearly all the soundtracks stuff.' He threw another smile at her, took a left turn, and glanced at her a second time. 'Becky?'

'Yes?'

'Do you have glitter on your face?'

'Oh sugar!' She pulled down the sun visor to look in the mirror as Dylan chuckled at her non-swearing. 'I hate greetings cards with glitter on.' She rubbed her cheek with her coat sleeve. 'You brush against the stuff once and your face sparkles for a week. It's worse than sand after the beach.'

'Nothing's worse than sand after the beach.'

'I know, right? And everyone always talks about going to the beach as if it's the Promised Land. I'd prefer to be by the pool.'

'Me too.'

They returned their eyes to the road and sat smiling to themselves, bathing in the enjoyable stew of mutual grumpiness which was also a regular feature of their Thursday movie nights. Over a bowl of popcorn they would share their lists of increasingly middle-aged things which ticked them off. Becky had come up with a few things which had made Charlie almost choke with laughter and Charlie's peeves had a snarly originality which made Becky smile every time she recalled them.

❦

Charlie followed Becky's directions to the centre of Barnsby and parked next to the post office. In an unspoken division of labour, he went to pay for the parking while Becky scooped Dylan and the nappy bag out of the car.

She had just got Dylan positioned on one hip to counterbalance the weight of the nappy bag, when Charlie stepped in. 'I'll take him. You lead the way.'

'Thanks.' As she handed Dylan over she looked Charlie up and down. 'You should have left your glasses on. You might miss something. I'd still have glitter on my face if you could drive without them.'

'I only need to see you two. Stay close and I'll be fine.'

Charlie smiled and held her gaze long enough for Becky to feel a flush creeping into her cheeks. She was glad when Dylan started squirming and Charlie had to look away to adjust his grip on the wriggling toddler. Not for the first time, she wondered how a man of so few words could leave her struggling to put her own thoughts together.

She cleared her throat. 'OK then. It's not far.'

They walked shoulder to shoulder down Barnsby High Street, Becky attempting to stop herself overthinking Charlie's last comment by staring at the shop window displays. Christmas had already come to most of them, held in check temporarily by the ghouls of Halloween.

At the end of the street was their destination: the town hall, an unfortunate child of a post-war era when the concrete Mayan temple was the ultimate in architecture. Having arrived early, they killed time in the lobby. Becky put down the bag and took off her coat. Compared to the sunny freshness outdoors, the environment inside was a greenhouse with condensation clinging to every windowpane.

They soon discovered that Dylan found the revolving door enchanting, and Charlie patiently accompanied him round and round the alternative carousel until the toddler slipped out of his coat to make a run for Becky. Dylan flung himself into his mum's arms and she swung him into the air, kissed him and fussed over his hair. Looking up, she caught Charlie's eye. 'We should get going,' she said. 'The lift's down there.'

Dylan bolted through the lift doors, rushing to the back to stare at himself in the mirror. Waiting until the doors were fully open, Charlie and Becky stepped in together.

'Which floor?'

'Third,' she said, sucking in her tummy as he reached across her to jab the button.

The doors closed and the lift rumbled into life.

Nearing the first floor, Becky sneaked a glance at Charlie. He was staring at the floor number display, running a finger around the inside of his collar. He shifted slightly and his arm brushed against hers. The hairs on her arms prickled. They hadn't been in such a small space together since August at the train station.

Charlie coughed and Becky whipped her gaze down to her shoes in case he should catch her peeking at him.

They reached the second floor.

He coughed again. 'That dress is nice.'

'Really?' She was wearing a short dress in her favourite bright blue. A swirl of white butterflies floated over its surface, dancing around its pinched waist and up to the high neckline. She looked up and into his eyes. 'Thanks. I wasn't sure about it. Ever since having Dylan I'm not sure anything looks good on me any more.' She gave his jacket cuff a tug. 'Your outfit's great. How are you coping with the noose?'

He raised his hand to the tie. 'I'm getting used to it.'

The doors opened onto the registry office's characterless waiting area. The one thing in its beige favour was a basket of miscellaneous toys in the corner. Dylan headed straight for the plastic phone, eager to start his important calls.

Becky looked at her watch and waved Charlie over to the seats. He took the chair next to hers and tapped his thumbs together while staring at the sheen of her shoes. 'Becky, I already have a good idea, but are you going to tell me what we're doing here?'

'Sorry for all the mystery, but I was sworn to secrecy.' She put a hand on his shoulder. 'Charlie, you are here to witness something which doesn't happen often enough: things turning out well for a good person.' She grinned as she launched into the whole story, keeping it as brief as possible.

When she had finished, he contemplated her for a few seconds and then said, 'You're beyond pleased about this, aren't you?'

'I cannot tell you how pleased I am. I deal with so many people I would secretly love to slap; days like today are a relief.'

'Ah. You don't slap all your clients, then?' His lips curled. 'Does that make me special?'

She blinked but kept her mouth shut. So he did remember! And after his brain had been so thoroughly marinated in whisky too. She dropped her gaze and played for time by fiddling with her watch, hoping they wouldn't have much longer to wait. While she would have liked to know if he could recall the words which had accompanied the slap, now wasn't the time to take the top off that can of worms.

Refusing to be goaded, she matched his teasing tone. 'Too right you are. I've said it before, but I should charge you extra.'

Becky was saved from having to get further into what was likely to be an awkward conversation by the arrival of the lift. With a jaunty *bing!* the doors opened, revealing the bride and groom. Seven months pregnant, Clarice was blooming in every sense. She swelled into her knee-length white gown, proudly presenting her bump under a sweetheart neckline. Towering protectively at her elbow, Steve was all lanky jitters, but beaming nonetheless.

The registrar showed them into the ceremony room, which would have held a congregation of forty. As it was, the two and a half witnesses stayed at the back until they were called to sign the register.

When proceedings were under way, Charlie edged closer to Becky. 'So she's managed to keep her pregnancy hidden from everyone back home, they get married, disappear, and then move back to the Comptons when the baby is old enough that few people will bother asking whether it was born in wedlock?'

Becky nodded. Charlie had grasped the basics.

'And he knows the baby isn't his, right?'

'Of course.'

When Clarice had decided to keep the baby, she thought her only option was to end her budding romance with Steve, breaking his heart with little explanation. But Becky suggested she try telling him the truth.

Steve had walked out when Clarice had confessed, saying he needed some time to think. Clarice feared the worst, but after a few days' absence he turned up on her doorstep with a stack of pregnancy manuals, a large box of chocolates and a ridiculous oversized teddy. Proving himself to be one of the most understanding men since Joseph, he told Clarice he was sure he'd come to love the baby just as much as its mother. This declaration instantly got him onto Becky's short list of favourite people.

'But I don't see why they have to sneak around,' said Charlie. 'This is the twenty-first century!'

'Not in certain circles. Anyway, it doesn't matter. They have each other. Escaping her family and their vipers' nest of friends will do her a lot of good and give the baby a great start in life.'

'But I don't understand how—'

'Shhh! This is the best bit.'

As the registrar pronounced Clarice Elizabeth Barry and Steven Daniel Wyatt husband and wife, Becky swallowed a lump in her throat and squeezed Charlie's hand.

∽

As Steve stepped forward to kiss Clarice, Charlie glanced at Becky. Without taking her eyes off the bride and groom, she slid her hand over his left knee and closed her fingers around his hand. Although slightly taken aback, Charlie smiled as she squeezed his fingers and moved his hand slightly to be able to return the pressure. His own wedding band caught the light as he relaxed his grip, and he couldn't help but think about his own wedding day, now a hazy memory. Mel had been so different then, so free of the doubts and fears that would gradually crush her spirit. She had laughed and danced with everyone until the venue manager had turned off the lights and thrown them out. That had only made her laugh more. And now she was getting ready to move on and do it all again with someone else. So maybe, he thought, as he glanced at Becky who was smiling and blinking to keep back tears, it was time to follow her example.

The bride and groom pulled apart. Charlie sighed, squeezed Becky's hand again and let go.

Chapter 29

Confetti throwing was banned in the vicinity of the joyless council building, so the wedding party skipped off to the park.

Becky and Dylan scattered paper petals over the new Mr and Mrs Wyatt while Charlie took pictures. A passer-by was persuaded to take a few photos of all five of them and then it was time for goodbyes.

While Charlie stepped aside to return a missed call, Becky went to shake Steve's hand but decided to grab him into a hug instead. Judging she had embarrassed him enough, she moved on to Clarice, who she embraced more carefully while making her swear to send updates and baby photos. She had planned to say more but cut it short before the recurring lump in her throat became too large to swallow.

Having waved the young newly-weds off to their brighter future, Charlie and Becky let Dylan run to the playground, following the toddler as he charged through piles of drying leaves, scattering them in miniature tornadoes of colour.

By the time they reached the slide and swings, the sky had clouded over and the falling sun was playing a teasing game of peek-a-boo. Becky slipped her arm through Charlie's, hoping to borrow some of his constant warmth. 'Thanks again for coming today, Charlie.'

'No problem. It was good.'

She looked at him out of the corner of her eye. He was absorbed in watching Dylan but at least he wasn't frowning. 'Do you think you'll marry again?'

'I doubt it. I only wanted to do it once.' He shivered and crossed his arms, pulling Becky closer with the movement. 'What about you?'

'No, I don't think so. I've been to enough weddings. And anyway, if it's death do us part then it's because we want to be together, not because we signed a contract and had a big party.'

Charlie's mouth twitched. 'Even if the contract was signed in blood and offered you his eternal soul?'

'Ah, well, that would be different.' She gave him a playful push and stepped forward to help Dylan up the slide. 'Maybe, under those circumstances, I would accept the deal. But the blood still seems over the top.'

Dylan flipped onto his belly and whizzed down the slide backwards. Charlie caught him and helped him to his feet.

'How are things going with Mel?' she asked, avoiding the 'd' word.

'We're expecting the decree nisi at the start of November.'

'That's quick!'

'Not really: we've got nothing to fight about. Phoebe is eighteen, Mel doesn't want the house or money, and she's about to get married.'

'So you could be divorced by Christmas?'

His lips curled, but the smile didn't reach his eyes. 'Looks like it. Isn't that what everyone asks Santa for?'

The sky clouded over and the light began to fade; they decided to head back to the car. As they walked, taking it in turns to hold Dylan's hand, Becky tried to come up with a way of banishing some of the gloom which had settled over them. 'How about we hold an extraordinary session of the smallest movie club in the south-east, tonight? I know you're busy, but you can choose the film and I have popcorn.'

'Um, actually, that call I missed when we were inside was from Rachel.' He rubbed the back of his neck. 'She needs me at the gallery as soon as possible.'

'Oh, right. Well that's good, isn't it?'

'I was planning to work, but she said it was important.'

As Charlie negotiated Dylan into his car seat, pulling faces to make the toddler laugh, Becky realised, from the outside, the three of them must look like a family. A happy family. She sighed, the lump in her throat returning; she would miss Charlie and Phoebe next year. So would Dylan. Her son already loved Charlie and Phoebe as much as they loved him. Opening the car door, she tried to focus on Dylan's cheerful laughter rather than the haunting spectre of life with a large Charlie-shaped hole punched clean through it.

❧

Back at Becky's, Charlie helped get Dylan out of the car and inside. 'See you soon,' he said as he opened the front door to leave.

'Charlie?'

'Yes?' He spun round on the doorstep as she came forward and leant on the doorframe.

'You know I'm a glass-half-full person, so obviously I'm optimistic about their chances, but do you think Clarice and Steve are going to be OK?'

Charlie pushed his glasses up to the bridge of his nose. What were anyone's chances of staying married these days? Didn't one in three marriages end in divorce? Or was it one in two?

He looked up at Becky and the ground shifted. The sight of her parted lips and wide eyes transported him back to the Christmas ten years ago when Phoebe had grasped his hand and asked if Father Christmas was real. Her rare belief in the magical was so fragile and beautiful, disillusioning her would have been like stamping on a butterfly.

'Charlie?'

'Yes,' he said. 'In fact,' he continued, encouraged by the sparkle he had brought to her eyes, 'I think they're going to be very happy.'

NOVEMBER

Chapter 30

November was a quiet month for Becky but, while her work slowed down, everyone else was busier than ever. Charlie was spending more and more time in his studio or at the gallery with Rachel, Phoebe was buried in exam revision and Ronnie was busy dusting a little sugar over the often-sour residents of the Comptons.

Becky enjoyed the extra time with Dylan while it lasted, knowing calm work phases were often suddenly interrupted by frenetic periods with too many clients demanding results yesterday. Her parents came to stay for a week, which involved shuffling the usual sleeping and bathroom arrangements, but was otherwise a relatively stress-free experience. Nevertheless, she was delighted when Lloyd called and gave her an excuse to get out of the house unaccompanied.

'Checkmate, my dear. You shall go to the ball.'

She punched the air. 'Fantastic! Tell me everything.'

'I would prefer not to discuss this further over the

telephone. Would you care to take tea with me tomorrow morning? At Sweet's Cakes?'

Becky frowned as she agreed to the meeting. Was his anti-phone paranoia further evidence of Lloyd's shady past or simply an excuse to go out for cake?

The choice of time and venue further unsettled and intrigued her. She had never seen Lloyd in a day-lit venue and wasn't certain he wouldn't burst into flames or melt. Secondly, Sweet's was somewhere she had always seen as a home from home, not the sort of place to meet a man who could well be a retired master villain.

⬮

Arriving at Sweet's early, Becky inspected the window display. The team's latest work was a series of wedding cakes. These included a stand covered in a hundred heart-shaped cakes, one for every guest, and a simple single tier which was the seat for cute edible models of the bride and groom in their wedding car, complete with 'Just Married' sign, balloons and tin cans. In an attempt to give the group a seasonal relevance, the backdrop had been painted a deep blue and starred with a drama of exploding fireworks.

Already unnerved by his choice of venue, Becky was troubled to find Lloyd and Ronnie sitting elbow to elbow, sharing a pot of Earl Grey and cackling like two old ladies in a crocheting circle who had spent all afternoon on the gin.

After some table banging and wheezing, Ronnie calmed down enough to say hello. Shaking her head at Lloyd, she gave him a peck on the cheek and made her way back to the kitchen.

Becky repositioned the seat Ronnie had occupied so she was a comfortable distance from Lloyd and sat down.

'Quite the ball of fire, your friend,' he said. 'Like her extraordinary hair. She has some wonderful stories too. I'm so glad she'll be coming to the ball.'

'She will?'

'Yes. During one of our recent conversations it occurred to Barbara that a cake from Sweet's was precisely what the event needed.'

'It occurred to her? Spontaneously?'

'She is nothing if not a ceaseless fountain of ideas.' He dabbed at the upturned corners of his mouth with a napkin. 'Although I had to apologise to Sharon for being unable to get her a full ticket, including the dinner. However, I hope she'll enjoy the dancing. She's already promised to save one for me.' He devoured the remnants of his slice of red velvet, chewing enthusiastically. 'Before you ask, Barbara was eventually as delighted as we imagined with the proposal and is looking forward to donating a decent-sized canvas.'

Becky nodded. 'And you have your seat at the top table?'

'On the left hand of the Supreme Commander herself. And I have secured four more tickets for you and Mr Handren to use as you wish. I'm sure he would like to take the lovely Ms Stone as his guest.'

'Thank you.'

Lloyd glowed with satisfaction. She asked herself if someone could explode as a result of being overly pleased with himself. But then this was Lloyd, and so implosion would be more likely: he wasn't one to make indiscreet messes.

She eyed his hair, then the gold ring. She had to ask. 'You don't own a cat do you?'

227

'No.' If he were perplexed by her non sequitur, he didn't show it. 'I'm not a cat person. I have a dog though; a beagle called Ariel. I've had him for years.'

Of course he had. What kind of sorcerer would he be otherwise?

Her Prospero finished his tea with a flourish and got to his feet. 'We'll talk nearer the event about the finer details, but I'll let you get on. You'll need to hurry if you want to talk to Mr Handren before the young Ms Stone does. She's not going to be too pleased about her mother getting her hands on one of her artist's paintings. And for nothing.'

Becky waved as Lloyd stepped out of the bakery and straight into his car, the door held open by a uniformed chauffeur. He was right. She should capitalise on Dylan being in safe hands and go to see Charlie straight away.

She got up, slung her bag over her shoulder and was about to follow Lloyd out the door when Ronnie called her back. With her usual lack of ceremony, she bundled Becky into a corner of the kitchen and said, 'Are you going to see Charlie now to fill him in?'

Becky sighed. Clearly Lloyd had told Ronnie more than she would have liked. 'Yes.'

'Good. Ask him to give Mike a call, will you? Mike hasn't seen him for a couple of weeks because the great artist is always working when he invites him out to play. I think the poor guy is starting to have withdrawal symptoms.'

'But doesn't that mean he has more time to spend with you?'

Ronnie waved a hand dismissively, forcing Becky to sway back to get clear of her chunky silver rings. 'Yes, yes, of course, and that's good. Although sometimes I think it's wise for a couple to spend time apart. Especially when they live together. In a small house. With one bathroom.'

Becky held up a hand. 'Say no more. I'll have a word.'

'And …'

Ronnie batted her eyelashes and smiled sweetly. Becky dreaded to think what was coming next. 'Yes?'

'Can you get Mike into the ball as well?' Ronnie chewed the next word and spat it out. 'Please?'

Unbelievable: from pushy to pleading in under thirty seconds. Becky guessed that was what Lloyd would call 'fiery'.

'I can't see the new year in without him, but I'm dying to go to the ball,' Ronnie said. 'And if anyone can get him in, you can.'

'OK. I'll try to come up with something. But I want a pile of takeaway cake boxes in return. You know how my mum likes to stockpile them.'

Ronnie squealed and pulled her into a constrictor hug. 'I knew you could do it. Thanks.'

Sliding back into pushy mode, she manhandled Becky out into the shop. 'Right. Now get over to Charlie's and let him know what's going on before he hears it from someone else.'

Chapter 31

The studio was a productive mess. Two paintings rested on easels close to the storage area wall. In the middle of the space, Charlie was working on a canvas over three foot in length and two in height. The painting was a mixture of brown and red shapes, as if a group of competitive quadrilaterals had got in a tangle playing Twister. There was also a large blank canvas on the floor to the right of Charlie's work area. It must have been over six feet long and four feet wide. Becky imagined Charlie adopting it as a mattress. Perhaps that was what a painter had to do to get a visit from his muse while he slept.

Charlie glanced round as she came in but didn't return her greeting. Instead he turned back to his workbench and the task in hand. He was wiping brushes on a rag, using sharp, jerky movements, as though he were trying to decapitate them. His exertions were accompanied by a series of sighs, each one containing more exasperation than the last.

She was too late.

'You've spoken to Rachel then?'

'Yes, Becky.' He threw the brush he'd been mauling onto the bench, causing two others to leap off to take their chances on the floor. He put his hands on his hips and glared at her. 'Rachel's upset she had to find out from the event organisers that one of my paintings is being donated to the art society ball.'

'But she's not upset with you, is she? You had nothing to do with it.'

'Yes. It became very clear, very quickly, that I have no clue what's going on with my work, which you feel you have the right to give away as you please!' He strode towards her, nostrils flaring. 'Rachel suggested I get a better handle on my staff and maybe she has a point.'

Becky crossed her arms over her chest. He was upset. Fine. It must have been disorientating to hear about the auction from Rachel. And probably embarrassing too. But she was not being called staff by him, especially not when he was parroting the snobby comments of an over-privileged Compton princess.

'Well, before you dismiss me to the servants' quarters,' she said, taking a step towards him and lifting her chin to look him in the eye, 'perhaps you would like to hear my side of the story?'

Charlie didn't back away. He was so close she could feel the angry heat of his breath. His eyes bulged and his lips had all but disappeared. If he hadn't been so obviously hurt, there would have been something comical about his expression and stance. A shorn grizzly bear with a sore head.

Becky held her ground. She refused to be intimidated by a man she had recently had to carry out of this building, particularly when he wasn't giving her a fair go. She narrowed her eyes. 'Or perhaps you don't want to hear what I have to say. Perhaps you'd prefer to assume I'm failing to act in your best interest. I'm sure that's what the lovely Ms Stone thinks and she is your inspiration, isn't she?'

Charlie turned pink. Then puce. A muscle in his jaw twitched and he snapped his gaze away from her and down to his hands, which he started to clean on the paint-stained rag.

She watched him clawing the scrap of cloth for a moment. Much more of that and he'd either rip it to shreds or take a layer of skin off. And they'd still be no closer to understanding each other.

'Ugh!' Becky closed her eyes and shook her head, disgusted at them both. This stand-off was ridiculous. Someone had to be the bigger man. Besides, as Ronnie never tired of telling her, she *was* staff. And it wasn't as if she hadn't foreseen this reaction if Rachel got to him first. 'This is stupid. Why don't we sit down for a few minutes and I'll tell you about it from the beginning?'

Relaxing out of his rigid warrior pose, Charlie retreated to the sofa as she launched into her defence.

'I'm sorry I didn't tell you about all this sooner, but I was waiting until I knew for certain it was happening. As soon as I did, I came here. But apparently the jungle drums travel faster than I can walk.'

Charlie snorted, and the corners of his mouth flickered. Taking this as a sign his mood was improving, Becky decided it was safe to perch next to him on the arm of the sofa.

'This is a great opportunity to generate interest in your show a week before it opens, particularly with the

Compton arty brigade and their friends. This auction pushes the bidders to be more generous, so we're practically guaranteed a terrific sale price which will set the bar for the rest of the exhibition.'

'Will I have to be there for the auction?'

'Yes. But that has a silver lining too,' she said, raising her voice over his groan of despair. 'You can ask Rachel to be your plus one. It's the perfect invitation: if you ask her and you think she's reluctant to be your date, you can always say you're asking because, as your curator, she should be there for the auction.'

Charlie seemed to have slipped into a trance. Unable to tell if it was a good 'dreaming of Rachel' reverie, or a bad 'Becky's pushing me into another nightmare' coma, she carried on. 'And, even if it isn't a date, going to the ball should cheer Rachel up about losing the painting because she'll get to share in the glory. And you'll get to spend more time with her socially. Two birds with one Stone!'

His lips definitely twitched that time.

'And if all that isn't enough for you, giving the painting to the ball will have earned you brownie points with Rachel's mother.'

He stirred, turning his head towards her. 'Her mother?'

'Did Rachel not mention her mother organises the ball? It's one of her activities as president of the art society.'

Charlie's jaw dropped. 'Barbara Stone is Rachel's mother?'

'Oh, didn't you know? Strange that's never come up while you and Rachel have been chatting.'

Becky turned away from his still-dangling jaw and hid a smug smile by wandering towards the painting in progress. She pretended to appreciate it while she reviewed what she had told Charlie. All of it was technically true. Of course, she hadn't mentioned that getting on Barbara's good side was likely to hinder rather than help his cause with Rachel, but she would try to get round the troll under that particular bridge when and if necessary.

'And,' she said, turning back to him, 'the proceeds of the auction go to the local hospice. You can't deny it's a good cause.'

Charlie threw his hands up. 'All right. Let's say I'm OK with this. What would I have to do?'

'Stand next to the painting while they take photos. Introduce the piece, mention your show, say how pleased you are to contribute to such a good cause …'

He looked as if he were about to be hit by a bus. 'I've never been good at public speaking. What if I can't think of what to say?'

'It'll be a few words and your audience will be fairly tanked by then. And I'll be there if you need a prompt.'

His shoulders and frown relaxed.

'I'm going to go.' She got to her feet. 'And, Charlie, I've said it before, but you need to trust me. I'm trying to help you.' She rested a hand on his shoulder. 'I guessed Rachel wouldn't be too happy about the auction, so it was best you didn't know about it so all the blame could go on me. Now you'll be able to tell her you've had a stern word with your staff, as she suggested, and then you can offer to take her to the ball to make it up to her.'

Charlie looked as if the oncoming bus had been joined by a train.

Becky continued, 'Just think about it. I've got to get going. This pushy serf has more people to piss off.'

Chapter 32

The third Saturday in November was the Spencer–Swift wedding. Becky arrived at the South Compton Country Club shortly after noon, having left the church while the confetti was still airborne. Her plan was to check the reception venue before it was cluttered with guests—one more small way of preventing unwanted surprises.

While perusing the seating chart, she noticed some last-minute changes. Her heartbeat lurched, and it wasn't until she tasted blood that she realised she was biting her lip. No matter how hard she tried to anticipate, not everything was within her power to control.

She licked her wounded lip. Achieving total invisibility today would be impossible. She would have to accept that and get on with the job.

As the first guests arrived, she placed a seat for herself at the back of the reception hall and crossed her fingers the day would continue smoothly. And it did. Right until three minutes and forty-two seconds into the father of the bride's speech, the moment Becky knew she had a problem to solve. From her limited viewpoint, she guessed Alan Spencer was still carrying ten prompt cards in addition to the one he had just put down on the table. And while mental arithmetic had never been her strong suit, she knew ten cards added up to too many minutes.

At many weddings an insanely overlong first speech wouldn't be a problem. However, this man was father to Tamara Spencer, a woman who had got everything her own way for the past thirty-one years and who, it was rumoured, needed to take horse tranquilisers to dial down from 'upset' to 'peeved'. And today she was a shimmering vision of jitters, contained in a corseted tank of satin.

Rising silently from her chair, Becky skimmed around the perimeter of the tables, stopping only to retrieve a serving tray and a small package.

The wedding coordinator and her legion had been at work in the large banqueting room at the club since seven o'clock that morning. Although it was early afternoon, four large crystal chandeliers dripped light over the tables, making sure the guests could appreciate the dishes placed before them and, more importantly, the money spent in embellishing the venue. Clusters of dwarf cherry trees had been huddled into the corners of the room and showered with pale pink bows and fairy lights. Forty round tables filled the remaining space. After the breakfast, a team of nuptial ninjas would deploy. Working in silence they would shift and shunt both furniture and guests to ready the room for the final stages of the celebrations.

Becky took up position a discreet distance behind the top table. Dressed like the rest of the catering staff and with a tray resting on the fingers of her left hand, she stilled herself and became invisible. That is, invisible to everyone except three of the guests, who watched what followed with amused curiosity.

Alan Spencer was building up to a punchline which, as he still had the good will of his audience, was sure to get a laugh. Becky stepped forward, dropped her lips to the best man's ear and whispered. As the laughter swelled, the best man rose to his feet, encouraged by a sharp prod to his lower back. A microphone appeared in his hands and another nudge indicated it was time to interject.

'Ladies and gentlemen, if you'll allow me.' His voice disappeared into the vacuum created by the attention of hundreds swerving towards him. He gave a nervous chuckle and continued, 'Alan, I'm sure everyone here today would like to thank you for hosting such a wonderful do. And I'm sure it'll come as no surprise that Alan has one further gift for the bride and her highly unworthy groom.'

A gift-wrapped box materialised in his left hand. The small parcel was wrapped in iridescent ivory paper and baby-pink ribbon, a perfect match to the event colour scheme.

'Tamara and Geoffrey. Alan gave this to me for safekeeping—a gamble which nearly backfired. But I'm sure we're all pleased I eventually recognised my cue and can hand this over safely. Right, Alan?'

Alan Spencer's flushed, puffy face betrayed his complete bafflement. He was still grasping his clutch of prompt cards and the navy ink was bleeding under his hot fingers.

A final nudge directed the best man to pass the box to Alan, in whose ink-stained hands it rested for a second before Tamara snatched it.

'It matches my colours and everything! Thank you, Daddy!' Whipping away the ribbon, she opened the box and seized the contents, letting the container fall where it would. But there was nothing sparkly inside and she was left staring slack jawed at the roll of paper nestling in her hand.

'My love, I think this is where I'm supposed to come in,' said the groom, laying a gentle hand on the bride's shoulder and taking the scroll out of her palm. Tamara sat down as Geoff opened the scroll, cleared his throat, and read,

'Tamara, our daughter, and now Geoff's wife,
We wish you joy in your married life.
And soon our couple, our bride and groom,
Will leave us for their honeymoon.
A voyage back to the start,
To Rome, where Geoff first won Tam's heart.
Once Miss Spencer, now Mrs Swift,
We hope you'll accept this parents' gift
And fly in first to arrive refreshed,
In an ocean paradise, heaven blessed.
In Polynesia your private cabin stands
Over a lagoon, its feet kissed by virgin sands.
As you look up at the stars and down to the fish,
Remember us and be happy; this is our only wish.'

A chorus of gooey cooing gave way to applause as the bride threw herself onto her father, who did well not to collapse under the impact of the satin tank.

After one last prompt, Geoffrey took the opportunity to segue into his own short speech, taking care to thank Alan again for the entirely unexpected honeymoon extension. And when thanking all relevant parties for their contributions to the success of the day, he glanced behind him, but the only thing there was a bouquet of pink roses.

Chapter 33

The rest of the speeches, cake cutting and first dance went off without a hitch.

Becky had stationed herself in the corner of the room next to the French windows and as distant as possible from the band stage. Standing next to the doors which led to the kitchens, she was camouflaged by the comings and goings of the catering staff.

The band was good and the music was still in its initial phase: pieces considered appropriate for older guests who would abandon the venue with various aching joints long before the 'you can't even hear the words' music was loosed.

She saw him approach out of the corner of her eye. There was no need to turn her head to get a better look: he was wearing his good aftershave, the one he wore every time he visited the Coulson.

'I liked the poem.'

'What can I say? It's great when a degree in English Literature finally proves useful,' she said, scanning the bar area for anyone who needed their drinks to be swapped for non-alcoholic options.

'Geoff hired you?'

'Yeah. How do you know him?'

'He was more a friend of Mel's. He and his first wife were at our wedding. I think he invited me to be polite.'

'And you weren't going to come but you changed your mind at the last minute?'

'I thought I wouldn't know anyone here, but then Rachel mentioned she was going to a wedding on Saturday and it turned out—'

'To be this one.'

She moved on to scanning the dance floor and the reduced seating area. Though she was wearing contact lenses, habit prevailed and she narrowed her eyes to get a sharper view of the two women in conversation next to the tea and coffee station. With their heads tilted towards each other, the similarities between them were striking, accentuated by their choice of dark green clothing and rigid postures.

Becky nudged Charlie and tilted her head in the direction of the pair. 'Has Rachel introduced you to her mother?'

Charlie blanched. 'No, not yet.'

As he muttered his reply, Rachel turned away from her mother and began her own survey of the room. While Becky used only her eyes, Rachel used her whole body, standing on tiptoes and swivelling like an owl on hot sand. When she found Charlie she tapped her mother on the arm and gestured in his direction.

Becky took a step back into the shadows as Rachel approached. 'Well, I think you're going to be given the honour right now. Good luck.'

'There you are!' Rachel grabbed Charlie's hand. 'There's someone who wants to meet you. Come along.'

Dragging his feet after Rachel, Charlie threw a glance at Becky over his shoulder and parted his lips, looking for all the world as if he were about to ask the way to the lifeboats. Then another sharp pull and bark from Rachel made him snap his head forward.

Left alone in the privacy of the darkness, Becky sighed and prepared to watch Rachel and Charlie's progress without distractions.

But she should have known she wasn't the only one at home in unseen places.

'Becky,' boomed a voice behind her. 'Another fine day's work.'

'Thank you, Lloyd. Bride or groom?'

'Groom. I did a few favours for his father a while back and he hasn't forgotten me.' He swirled his drink, making the ice cubes rattle around the glass. 'Unlike others.'

'And are you enjoying the party?'

'It's wonderful.' His praise seemed sincere, although resting on the unstable foundation of rocks covered in slippery Scotch. His cheeks were flushed, showing up a web of red spider veins, but his hair and clothes were as impeccably coiffed and brushed as ever.

'I've been chatting to Barbara. She's excited about the ball.'

Becky nodded but didn't take her eyes off the area by the tea table where Charlie was taking Barbara Stone's hand. When offered it, he had almost bowed.

'That little meeting is going well, wouldn't you say?' said Lloyd.

He was right. Barbara Stone was laughing at things Charlie said. In the right places.

'Between you, me and the gatepost,' he said, 'Mr Handren is precisely the type of man Barbara would have dreamt up for Rachel. And if the auction and new show are a success then I imagine she'll be bullying her daughter into setting a date.'

Becky clenched and unclenched her fists, mirroring the movements in her stomach.

'Although I'm not convinced the young lady's heart is set on him. What do you think?'

Not wanting to shock Lloyd with her thoughts concerning Rachel, she shrugged and started another scan of the room.

'My dear, I hope you won't mind this question, but are you and Mr Handren romantically involved?'

Bloody hell! Why did everyone think she was sleeping with Charlie? She answered through gritted teeth. 'No.'

He nodded. 'As I thought. I didn't think you would do anything so unprofessional. And that is wonderful news for Kevin, my nephew. He's here somewhere. I must see if I can find him and introduce you two.'

Just what she needed. Another reason to get out of here as quickly as possible.

She was struggling to come up with a polite response, when Lloyd noticed his glass was empty. Crunching an ice cube, he said, 'I'll let you get back to concentrating on the job in hand. We'll talk soon.'

Lloyd sashayed over to the bar and, rather than relax, Becky braced herself. She remembered the seating chart and knew visitations were guaranteed to come in threes.

Slinking into the still-warm space left by Lloyd, the third apparition didn't keep her waiting.

'Watching you in action again has been terrific. Old Al's speech was inspired. Everyone's buzzing about his hidden poetic talents. God, even he's starting to believe he wrote the thing.'

Virgil had also been taking advantage of the free bar. His customary swagger was a gunslinger strut. He made large hand gestures to accompany his statements and she worried he would give away her position if he didn't quit the amateur semaphore.

'And why shouldn't he?' he said. 'I'm sure you could have written better, but it had to be ropey enough we'd believe Alan could have written it, eh?' He dazzled her with one of his best Hollywood grins. 'I've had a chat with the groom and he is overjoyed. You, my dear, are an artist. It's such a shame your talents are wasted on people who don't truly appreciate them.'

Amen to that, she thought, but said, 'I get paid.'

'You deserve to be worshipped.' This pearl was wrapped in a cloud of gin-laced vapour which made her blink and lean away from him.

'Don't let me stop you.'

'I am not worthy.' He waved his hands up and down in a show of mock reverence.

Trotting out his best banter seemed to have left Virgil thirsty. He took a long sip of his drink and let his eyes wander away from Becky. The second time he lifted the glass to his lips it froze in mid-swing, his gaze locked on Rachel, Charlie and Barbara. He lowered his drink slowly and was absorbed in observing the group for a while before he noticed Becky was watching him.

He coughed and tried to act casual. 'What did you think of the first dance choice?'

'Mistake. But one many people make.'

'I couldn't agree more. If you pay attention to the lyrics it's a miserable song and the tune is a repetitive dirge.'

'It's not the worst choice.'

'It has to be.'

As if Virgil's disbelief was a signal, the overhead lights went out. Lit by a few table lamps and the banks of multicoloured bulbs either side of the DJ booth, the band shuffled off the stage. The thunder and lightning of the bride's first choice—'It's Raining Men'—covered their exit.

Virgil stared, open-mouthed, as scores of women materialised to occupy the dance floor, the jiggling mass made up of a series of formidable Amazonian groups.

With the decibel-ripping music providing plenty of cover, Becky decided now was as good a time as any to talk about the elephant in the room. Although in this case the elephant was a petite brunette in high heels with red soles.

'You know, I'm a terrible poet, but I do have an idea for a novel.'

'Oh? Do tell.'

Avoiding looking him in the eye, she brought her lips closer to his ear. 'Working his way up through the family firm, a young Englishman moves to New York where he falls for an older woman.'

Virgil didn't move, but his breathing hitched.

'Our hero follows her to Berlin and then London, where they become more than friends. At first, things are rosy, and she confides in him that while she masquerades as a gallery manager, she is actually a princess, heir to a kingdom of art.'

Virgil snorted. She ignored him and bowled on with the melodrama.

'Our heroine is crushed when her mother, the wicked queen, refuses to abdicate in her favour. Desperate to console her, the hero buys a gallery in the kingdom for her to reign over. She is delighted and their happiness is restored. But one day he comes home to find suitcases in the hall. He is now her boss and their romance is no longer appropriate. If any of the queen's cronies were to find out how she got her new position she would be a laughing stock. And so their love cannot be, but she hopes they can stay friends and excellent colleagues.'

She slipped into Rachel's voice for the last sentence, hoping to raise a smile.

'Their new arrangement takes its toll on both of them and our hero finds himself provoking her jealousy. And the appearance of a more suitable suitor has made things more of a mess. He's older than the heroine, a local of the kingdom and a wealthy painter of some renown.'

They watched Barbara Stone tip her head back, cackle and pat Charlie's arm. He was lucky she didn't tickle him under the chin and pat his head.

'And this new suitor is precisely the man the queen would want for her daughter. In the kingdom this man is a handsome prince and our hero, for all his success and beauty, is a frog.'

Becky followed Virgil's gaze over to Rachel, who had her arm linked through Charlie's and was quaffing champagne as if it were lemonade.

Virgil gripped Becky's elbow and turned her to face him. 'And what does the hero do next?'

'He doesn't give up. And, while waiting for the princess to see sense, he goes to dinner with another frog, although he only asked her out to annoy the princess. Which worked, by the way, I think she hates me.'

'I get that feeling too. Sorry.' His gaze flickered back to Rachel, who was emptying another glass. He sighed. 'The course of true love and all that, eh?'

'Never did run smooth. *A Midsummer Night's Dream*, act one, scene one.'

He raised his eyebrows. 'Showing off your hidden depths again?'

'You should be so lucky.' She winked at him. 'But I would be delighted if you would come with me to the art society's New Year's ball.'

His smile hardened into a grimace. 'That could be very complicated.'

'She's going with him,' Becky said, waving her hand towards Charlie.

'I don't think so. She's not interested in him in that way.'

His voice had cracked and he dropped his gaze to the floor. Becky stepped closer and put a hand on his shoulder. 'Please think about it. It's over six weeks away. If nothing else, I've heard it's a good party. I can dance.' She nudged him. 'And for you, I'll even wear a dress.'

Chapter 34

With Virgil gone, Becky dutifully turned her attention back to the room. Watching the bride and groom twisting and shouting with their friends while the older guests shuffled home, she could tell there would be no more trouble. She was finished for the day.

She looked at her phone for what had to be the hundredth time that evening. She knew this was irrational: Phoebe would have called if anything had gone wrong.

A deep voice, raised to cut through the music, said, 'She would have called you if there were a problem. And he'll have been in bed for the past couple of hours.'

'Reading my mind now, Charlie?' she shouted back.

He smiled instead of trying to compete with the ear-shredding noise coming from the disco. The music was also masking what appeared to be a heated discussion between Rachel and Virgil on the other side of the room. Squinting in their direction, Becky wished she could read lips, although the frantic gesticulating suggested they weren't having a pleasant chat about the centre arrangements.

Becky couldn't tell if Charlie was watching the same show but hoped she could distract him from it. 'Did you like the cake?'

'Delicious, as always.'

'Although you'd still prefer a slice of the synthetic school sponge?

'Some people can't be helped.'

'The new window display at Sweet's looks great.'

'Thanks. My idea.'

'I should have known.'

'Why?'

'Ronnie's a genius with cake. But the painted backdrop … not something she could make herself.'

The DJ lurched into a piece of music which was a ghastly, pounding din. She tapped Charlie on the shoulder and signalled to the door. He nodded and they made a quick exit.

The lobby was deserted and, with the noise in the banqueting hall trapped behind a forest of oak panelling, mercifully quiet. They wandered a short distance from the hall doors and stopped near the giant Christmas tree beside the reception desk. Becky guessed its early presence, over five weeks before Christmas, meant it was expensive and the club were getting their money's worth. The decorations alone must have cost hundreds: silver and mauve tinsel with matching globe baubles; strings of fairy lights fading on and off in a hypnotic glow; and at the base a pile of boxes wrapped in gold paper and silver bows. The overall effect was chillingly beautiful, but Becky would have preferred to see some red and green, or any sign the tree had been dressed by a person rather than a team of joyless robots.

Speaking of which.

'You met Barbara Stone and survived. Congratulations.'

He blinked a few times. 'She was friendlier than I'd been led to imagine.'

'It certainly looked like you were getting on.'

'I suppose so.' He frowned and scratched the back of his head. 'Anyway, you were talking to Mr Locke for a long time.'

'Oh? Was I?' She hadn't thought anyone had been watching her conversation with Virgil, let alone Charlie who'd had his hands full of Rachel and her mother for the duration. 'Yeah, well,' she said, 'Virgil can be very charming when he wants to be.'

'He was doing a good job of charming you. What were you talking about all that time?'

'This and that. Nothing important.' She moved so she could rest against the wall and out of the path of further questioning; her feet were starting to ache. 'For starters,' she said, 'he thinks the bride and groom made a terrible choice in their first dance song.'

'It could have been worse.' He rubbed his eyes and blinked again. 'Could have been "Every Breath You Take".'

'Exactly! I hate it when couples choose that one. What did you and Mel have?'

'"It Had to Be You".'

'Ah! Excellent choice.'

'Glad you approve. And what would Ms Watson, the great wedding expert, choose for herself?'

'Purely hypothetically—and not that I've had the chance to give it a lot of thought—but Louis Armstrong's version of "La Vie en Rose", or maybe Nat King Cole and "Let

There Be Love". I like the lyrics and they're both easy to dance to.'

'And does Mr Locke have a favourite?'

The question had a sharp and rusty edge. 'You don't like Virgil much, do you?' she said. 'What's that about?'

He shrugged. 'He upsets Rachel. I don't want him to start on you.'

She shook her head and took a step away from the wall so she could straighten his tie. 'Don't worry about me. I'm immune to good-looking scoundrels. I've been inoculated by prior exposure.' Satisfied with his tie, she moved onto his pocket square. 'More importantly, did you ask Rachel to the ball?'

The bemused smile he had been wearing while watching her improve his appearance twisted into a wince. 'No. Actually, I wanted to talk to you about that. I'm not convinced she'd be interested.'

Becky looked at him over the top of her glasses, before remembering she wasn't wearing them. 'Not interested?! We are talking about the woman who just introduced you to her mother and spent the past twenty minutes draped all over you?'

How much encouragement did he need? She never understood why clients were reluctant to grab the opportunities she put under their noses. Perhaps they wanted a silver platter too.

She gave his pocket a final pat. 'You don't have to ask her today. But don't leave it too long.' She leant back against the wall and glanced at her watch. 'I have to go soon: I told Phoebe I'd be home by eleven.'

'I'll give you a lift.'

'Don't worry. I brought Phoebe's car. Well done again on that one, by the way. You must be in the running for Dad of the Year.'

Charlie smiled and straightened up while Becky glanced at her watch again and shivered. Steely draughts were sneaking under the main doors and sweeping across the lobby. The heat she had built up while in the near-tropical conditions next door had worn off.

Before she could protest, Charlie had removed his jacket and draped it over her shoulders. He took her hands in his. 'You're freezing!'

'I'm fine. You know I'm always cold.'

He enclosed her right hand in both of his and tried to rub some heat into it. 'You haven't been wearing gloves when cleaning.' He tutted. 'Again.'

He was right. She never remembered or it was quicker not to bother. The result was dry, cracked skin between her fingers and over her knuckles, and finger pads she could use to scour pans.

'I know. My nails are terrible. I was cleaning the window casements and I scrubbed my hands with one of Dylan's old toothbrushes, but I couldn't get it all off. I swear this stuff is Jurassic. And don't ask me where that bruise came from because I don't know.' She shrugged. 'I guess it must have hurt at the time.'

She watched him at work, using gentle circular motions to mix some red into the blue tinge which had taken over her flesh. Trust Charlie to notice her hands were a mess.

'Anyway, yours are nearly as bad,' she said. 'You should use gloves when cleaning your brushes. Turpentine and washing-up liquid, or whatever it is you use, dries your skin something shocking. Look!' She grabbed both his hands and used her thumbs to point at his knuckles. 'Desperately in need of some love.'

To reinforce her point, she ran her thumbs along the cracked skin on the backs of his fingers. As she moved her hands, his wedding ring winked in the light. Why he was still wearing it?

Her thumb wandered unchecked and grazed the offending gold band, making Charlie flinch. She began to apologise but when she looked up the words evaporated as her mouth went dry.

Today truly was full of surprises.

Charlie was giving her a look she hadn't seen in almost three years. She imagined it was close to how she gazed at chocolate and a cup of tea at the end of a hard day.

For the first time, his warm brown eyes gave her an uncanny feeling, as though she was falling away from them even though they were getting closer.

He brushed his fingertips along her forearms and murmured her name.

The hairs on the back of her neck stood up to join those on her arms and her thoughts derailed, piling up in a smouldering heap. As he stepped closer she fought to get back on track. This would make things awkward. She worked for him and, although she would never admit it, she agreed with Rachel on something: romantic involvement with your boss was a bad idea.

Charlie raised his right hand and brushed a stray strand of hair away from her neck. His lips were a few inches from hers, and yet she still failed to react. This was absurd! He'd just been playing happy families with Rachel. What the hell was going on?

Don't look up, she told herself. Eyes forward. His tie. Focus on the tie. Not his arms. Not his strong arms and how great they look in that shirt. Argh! Focus, Becky. A gracious exit strategy. How hard could that be to come up with?

But her brain was being drowned in a surge of hormones and was far too busy imagining Charlie shirtless. Then shirtless and wearing his glasses. Oh God.

Desperate, she laid a hand on his chest, halting his advance. 'Um, sorry … but I'm … I don't feel too well. I think I should get some water.' She sidestepped towards the banqueting hall. 'Would you like some?'

Charlie stuffed his hands into his pockets and gave her an almost imperceptible nod. His mouth was set in a tight line and his eyes were downcast. The frown had returned.

She turned and all but ran from the room.

Chapter 35

The few feet back to the reception seemed to be on a steep incline and littered with broken glass. It was a relief to make it through the door and find an empty chair. Leaning forward, she rested her head in her hands and waited for her pulse to slow.

Once she trusted her legs to bear her weight, she made for the bar. Having removed Charlie's jacket, she folded it and draped it over the stool next to her.

She was stroking the soft material, running her fingertips around the collar, when the teenager masquerading as a barman asked, 'Champagne?'

Becky shook her head. 'Two glasses of water, please. And could you give me my bag? I put it back there earlier.'

'Sure,' he said, retrieving her handbag from under the bar. 'By the way, there's a woman over there who's been staring at you since you came in. Not in a good way.'

Becky followed his glance. In the corner, Rachel was propped against a table. Glaring at her. Their eyes met for a moment. Becky shivered. Rachel emptied her glass, slammed it down on the table and strode towards the exit.

'I guess she's finally had enough,' the bartender said as the lobby door swung closed. Winking at Becky, he left the glasses of water on the bar. 'Amazing she can still stand with the skinful she's had tonight.'

Becky gave him a weak smile as she hooked her bag onto her shoulder, folded Charlie's jacket over her arm and picked up the drinks. Having dragged her feet back across the room, she paused at the door to take a sip of water and think.

She had done the right thing. Assuming that Charlie had been about to kiss her, he would have regretted it. He was nervous about getting close to Rachel, uncertain about whether she would reject his invitation to the ball. So he had reached out to her because she was reliable, sturdy Becky. The red, flustered woman who came running to his aid at the drop of a nothing more than a phone call. Surely that woman would be flattered anyone would want to kiss her, never mind a handsome, renowned artist?

She had definitely done the right thing. Nevertheless, she cringed at her own clumsiness. Had she really used the swooning maiden excuse? Then again, what was the alternative? Looking up into those dark lonely eyes and saying, 'I'm sorry Charlie, I'd love you to carry me off in those fine strong arms of yours but, as I work for you, it would make things too damn weird'?

No. It had been the toe-curling but sensible option. The alternative ... Well, what would that have been like?

She bit her lip as a timid voice whispered: What if it wouldn't have been a mistake? What if he likes you? *You.* Yes, it seems unlikely, but it is possible, isn't it?

This time, rather than dismissing the idea, she inched towards it. Apart from the fact he was currently her boss, she couldn't see any other reason why their friendship couldn't develop into something more. And she wouldn't be working for him for much longer.

Her heart and mind racing, she used her back to open the door. Focusing her attention on not spilling the water, she didn't look up until the door had clicked shut behind her.

She was too late again.

In front of the glacial Christmas tree, Rachel was trying to consume Charlie. Her arms were wrapped around his neck and she was pressing her whole body into his. Becky couldn't tell if Charlie was pulling her towards him or holding her up. His hands were on her thighs, gripping her pencil skirt, which had ridden up above her knees, exposing a ladder in her tights. Charlie was characteristically silent, while Rachel sounded as though she was enjoying her meal.

Becky found herself at a total loss. She doubted there was an accepted protocol for this specific situation. Should she cough politely? Drop the drinks and scream? Vomit noisily all over the floor?

Her unlikely saviour was Virgil, who barrelled out of the hall, slamming the door against the wall. 'Ah, Becky!' he boomed, bouncing towards her. 'Have you seen …?'

His voice withered into a strangled croak as Rachel came up for air, startled by his entrance. She giggled and hid her face behind Charlie's tie. Meanwhile Charlie had his hands full keeping her vertical.

Virgil sniffed, tweaked his immaculate cuffs and turned his back on the couple. Taking Becky's hand, he lowered his voice and said, 'Becky, I would be delighted to accept your invitation for the ball.' He raised her hand to his lips. 'Thank you. I'm sure you'll excuse me.' Virgil stared dead ahead as he barged back into the hall. Hopefully the bartender had a bottle of gin going spare.

As the door slammed behind him, Becky closed her eyes and hoped she was on the verge of waking from a bad dream. But when she opened them she was greeted with the sight of Rachel teetering towards her. Charlie scampered along in her wake with his arms extended, ready to catch her, as if she were a child who'd recently had her training wheels removed.

'Ms Watson!' Rachel bellowed. 'You are everywhere! Do you work here too?' She pointed at the glasses of water in Becky's hands. 'Perhaps waitressing?' She giggled and jabbed a perfectly manicured finger at Becky's clothes. 'Or perhaps the cleaning staff?'

Charlie rolled his eyes and seized Rachel's elbow. Her response was to lay a hand on his chest, stroke him a few times and burst into giggles again. 'Pushy, pushy Ms Watson. Always hard at work. Although, I guess this scullery outfit is your idea of party wear!'

'Right, that's enough,' said Charlie as he manhandled her towards the door. 'Get your things. I'm taking you home.'

Rachel widened her eyes. 'Ooo! Lucky me!'

'Please. Get your things.' He gave her a final push into the reception.

Becky sipped her water while the lovers' tiff was in progress, then dumped the glasses on the floor by the wall. When she straightened up, Charlie had turned back to her and was running a hand down his face.

Trying to ignore the lipstick smeared around his mouth and his bedraggled tie, Becky put on her cheery voice. 'Well, you know for sure she likes you now, right?'

Charlie frowned and shook his head, blinking.

What was the matter with him? Maybe his first real kiss with his muse hadn't lived up to his imagination. She was fairly sure the Rachel in his dreams wasn't plastered and falling over. Or maybe he was upset they'd been interrupted?

Whatever was going on, Becky decided she'd had a lucky escape. The last thing she needed was to give Charlie and Rachel more reasons to laugh at the staff. Anyway, it was getting late and time to go home to the one man who would always love her. The drive would also give her twenty minutes for some cathartic, sweary ranting.

'I really should get going.' She pulled a tissue out of her bag, held it out to Charlie and circled a finger around her mouth. 'You might want to wipe that.' She pressed her lips together as Charlie grabbed the tissue. Taking the opportunity to have a good look at his face she realised what was different about his eyes. 'You're wearing contacts too!'

He blinked, opening and shutting his eyes slowly as he dragged the tissue over his top lip. 'They're murder. Itchy.'

'Mine too! I've left my glasses in the car so I can take these bloody things out as soon as I've left here.'

'I wish I'd thought of that. I'll have to wear mine until I get home. And that's going to be later than I'd hoped.'

Of course. He was taking Rachel home now.

She shuddered and got back on topic. 'But if you know they irritate you, why did you wear them?'

'Rachel said I should.'

Becky gave him a curt nod and handed over his jacket. Of course. Stupid question. 'Right. I'll let you get back to it. See you soon.'

As she crossed the lobby she heard Rachel cackling as she careered out of the hall and into Charlie's waiting arms. Her and all her bloody brilliant ideas.

Given the eventful day behind him, Charlie was expecting the muse to visit his dreams that night.

Her appearance was the same as ever. She was again wearing a white shirt and betrayed no emotion as she gazed past him towards an infinite horizon.

Charlie had carried the baggage of the day into the dream studio. He itched with irritability and impatience.

Lunging for a tin of paint, he threw its cobalt contents at her, then hurled the empty container to the other end of the building where it bounced off the wall with a satisfying clatter.

As the paint ran down her arms and dripped onto the floor, she smiled. Not a mischievous or meagre smirk, but a generous grin. She stepped forward and seized his hands, interlacing their fingers and letting the colour ooze between them.

All nerves gone, he kissed her with the fire which had built up during months of frustrating restraint. He found she was supple but irreducible; her soft skin was a thin cover for the flint beneath and she pushed back at Charlie with a strength greater than her size.

He had closed his eyes and expected her to be gone when he opened them; instead, a bed had materialised behind her and she drew him onto its inviting white sheets, staining them blue as she slid to the centre.

She encircled his waist with her legs and used her feet to encourage him towards her. His excitement increasing, he smoothed her hair from her face and kissed her again. Although sticky with paint, her fingers were deft, making quick work of his shirt buttons. Meanwhile, he skimmed his hand along her thigh, daring to venture beyond the shirt hem border.

Around them, the cool white air turned a damp and dewy red. Charlie's blood crackled with energy. Every nerve ending burned under her touch and, as the temperature continued to climb, he became aware of a single bead of sweat tickling its way down to the base of his spine.

In their first awkward moment, she was unable to open his fly. He took his eyes away from her long enough to complete the task and when he looked up she was gone.

Crouched on his hands and knees, Charlie roared. He pummelled the mattress until he was out of breath and dropped onto his back. He stared up at the skylights until his breathing slowed. He could still smell her scent: a subtle, fresh fragrance which rippled around him.

When the perfume had dispersed, he realised he was no longer lying on a bed. The material under his fingers was too taut and tough to be a sheet. Intrigued and suspicious, he rolled onto his knees.

She had given him another gift. If he could recreate the painting under him he knew he had the star piece of the exhibition. And, as his eyes adjusted to the gloom left by her departure, he saw the studio had been refilled with new pieces. They were lined up like soldiers ready for roll call; enough for years of exhibitions.

Elated, he fell back onto the canvas and relaxed into hours of sound sleep. He needed the rest: the next few weeks would be very productive.

Chapter 36

At the end of November, Becky had an appointment with Rachel at the Coulson. Without provocation, the curator had invited Becky to hear her plans for the exhibition.

'I can't believe you're there!' said Ronnie, her disapproval so loud Becky winced and put a safe distance between her mobile phone and her bruised eardrum. 'You do know this isn't some kind of apology, right?'

'You're probably right,' Becky said as she opened the door to the gallery. 'But you agree she knows about art. This could be a good opportunity to understand something about Charlie's work.'

'Fine. But don't let her bully you. How's it looking there, anyway?'

The Coulson was a work in progress. The part of the gallery nearest the front door was playing reluctant host to a few pieces by other artists. Meanwhile, the back had been screened off so Rachel could get a head start on arranging Charlie's work.

'Busy.'

'Any sign of Cruella de Vil?'

'Not yet.' Becky crept away from the door. 'But I should probably go—'

'Have you heard from Lloyd lately?'

'I thought you knew. He's in hospital.'

'What?!'

'Don't panic! Your latest admirer is fine. I spoke to him the other day. He said he was in for a "quick and trifling procedure".'

'Ms Watson!' Rachel's voice shrilled across the white silence of the room, making Becky jump.

'Oh, well that's all right then,' said Ronnie. 'He's promised to introduce me to the catering manager up at the Hall. See if we can't supply the tea shop with cake, scones, biscuits …'

'That's really great,' Becky said as the menacing click-clack of Rachel's stilettos approached. 'Look, I should go—'

Ronnie continued, 'And then maybe some events catering further down the line.'

'Ms Watson!' Rachel stepped out from behind the screen and, after giving Becky a disapproving head-to-toe glance, beckoned. 'You're finally here. Come along.'

Becky lowered the phone to her shoulder. 'Be right there,' she said, giving her host an apologetic smile. 'Don't worry,' she murmured into the phone. 'Lloyd said he was still looking forward to the ball and if he's promised you an introduction then I'm sure you'll get it.'

'When you're quite ready, Ms Watson,' said Rachel, punctuating her words with a haughty eyebrow raise, then vanishing behind the screen.

Becky closed her eyes and tightened her grip on the phone. No matter how much Rachel provoked her, no matter how much she'd love to throw the phone at the woman's annoyingly beautiful face, she had to go into this meeting with a positive attitude.

Oblivious to her discomfort, Ronnie rattled on, 'And Mike said to say thanks again for getting him the photography gig at the ball.'

'No problem. Look, sorry, but I have to go,' she whispered. 'It's time for an education.'

⸏

On the other side of the screen Rachel was contemplating a number of paintings which were sitting on the floor at irregular intervals, propped against the white walls.

Becky hid her surprise at how many paintings were already in Rachel's clutches. In addition to the nine she could see, she was informed there were another nine in the storeroom.

'Have you spent any time with the collection?' asked Rachel.

'Not as such.' She scanned the pictures on the floor and wished she could see them through Rachel's eyes. 'Is there a progression from the ones he painted first to his latest?'

'Yes! It's fascinating! Look!' Clicking over to the far corner, she beckoned for Becky to follow. 'What do you see here?'

The canvas was portrait orientation and about three by two feet. A series of brown curves flowed across it in horizontal sections, covering its surface.

She shrugged, drawing a long sigh from Rachel.

'If you had to describe the piece using one word, what would it be?'

She might as well be honest. 'Dull.'

'Hmn.' Rachel tapped a shiny red nail on her upper lip. 'It is a gloomy piece, although the darker shades provide for a higher contrast with these bright flecks which act as points of light, drawing the eye to the top of each element in the series of curved shapes.'

Becky narrowed her eyes to examine the blue highlights Rachel was attempting to spear with a crimson talon.

Rachel continued, 'And, if we consider "dull" in the sense of lacking variety, it's obvious the artist used a restricted colour palette. In fact, the first few paintings he produced are similar in his use of analogue colours. However, if we move over here …' Becky trotted after her, stopping in front of a landscape-orientated picture. 'You'll see changes. What comes to mind now?'

Becky put some effort into it. This one was more colourful with blocks of colour arranged in diagonal bands. In some bands the blocks grew in size from left to right, while for others it was right to left. Although the shapes had clear edges, this wasn't a case of someone carefully colouring inside the lines. The application of paint was messy and in places it must have hit the canvas at some speed because there were flecks of colour all over the place.

As it roved over its surface, her gaze was drawn to the centre of the image where a large block of light blue stood out in contrast to the darker colours around it. It also literally stood off the canvas because the paint had been applied in several thick layers.

Rachel listened to Becky's observations then exploded into her own commentary. 'Think about the first painting we saw and then look at this one again.' She moved her left hand in an energetic sawing motion. 'This diagonal arrangement of "blocks", as you call them, is far more dynamic. A horizontal arrangement creates a harmony, but one which is stable, steady and "dull". But here the artist is gaining confidence in his use of colour, tone and contrast. We also have fewer closed shapes; this work and the others like it are more immediate. There is more emotion, more passion here. The paint has been applied with considerable force. That shows confidence and a willingness to take risks. In the earlier works the strokes are smooth, cautious. However, in these later works we see the development of the theme. Look how the mere flecks of blue in the early picture have evolved into this central shape which leaps out at us.'

'Through his use of impasto.' Becky was pleased with this comment although she only knew what impasto was because Ronnie had explained it to her. Apparently Charlie's years of applying oil paints to canvases meant he was a wizard when it came to using a palette knife to apply buttercream to cakes.

'That's right,' said Rachel in a tone both surprised and patronising. 'But you're not impressed with the use of technique or the overall result.'

Becky chose her next words carefully, not wanting to sound as if she were dissing Charlie or his work. 'I suppose, like a lot of people, I find some of these paintings look like a jumble of colours and shapes. So it's easy to dismiss them as meaningless and something a child could have made.'

'Too many people dismiss non-figurative art.' Rachel was starting to bristle and Becky suspected 'too many people' was code for Barbara Stone. 'Personally, I have always found it fascinating because the artist is sharing part of himself, allowing to interact with his feelings and thoughts. And as he has gifted us with this opportunity, I think we should try to appreciate what he has shared rather than dismissing it as a series of unintelligible daubs.'

As Rachel returned to contemplating the painting, Becky had to concede it was much harder to dislike her when she was making sense and particularly when she was making sense in defence of Charlie. Finally warming to her hostess, Becky accepted Rachel's invitation to show her the latest arrival.

⮠

Rachel led Becky down the dim corridor to the storeroom.

As Rachel ushered her inside and towards Charlie's latest creation, Becky could feel the woman's gaze drilling into her back. She was obviously far from impressed with Becky's art appreciation skills. Perhaps there was more Becky could do to build bridges.

'I hope it's OK now, one of the paintings going to the ball auction?' Becky asked, glancing towards her host.

'It was an unwelcome surprise. However, I hope a successful and well-publicised sale will benefit us all.'

Her lips curved into a tight, cold smile and Becky felt her skin prickle. Although that could be less due to Rachel's stare and more to do with Becky's jacket. It was her smartest and she had left the house feeling good about it. But Rachel was dressed top to toe in cotton and linen, all without a single crease—the woman wasn't human—and it made Becky hyperaware that all her clothes contained some percentage of polyester and were likely highly flammable.

Perhaps it wasn't just the auction or a disdain for man-made fibres which had got under Rachel's skin? Maybe Virgil had something to do with it. Becky hadn't had the chance to ask him what their row at the wedding had been about and had no idea if he'd spoken to Rachel about her and Charlie's kiss.

Becky took a deep breath. The scene of those two grappling under the Christmas tree wasn't one she liked to recall, but she struggled to shake it or the accompanying hollowness.

Rachel stopped in front of another painting. 'This will be the star piece unless he comes up with something utterly remarkable in the next couple of weeks. What do you see here?'

Determined to be a better pupil, Becky focused all her attention on the canvas. She owed it to Charlie to understand his work and him a little better. And clearly it was incredibly important for her job too. It would be easier to keep up a front as his 'agent' if she could appear to know something about her client's work.

Prepared to do her best, she broke into a ramble. 'It's like there are two halves. The left side with that blue cloud which moves up and to the right. Then on the right there are those browny-yellow blocks, like bricks in a wall. They're expanding over to the left, towards the cloud. And then there's that unfinished line in the middle …' She pointed at the jagged red line which separated the two halves of the painting. It ran like a lightning bolt through the composition, starting at the bottom and petering out before it reached the top.

Rachel listened with her head tilted towards Becky, a smirk stealing onto her lips. Her next question was delivered in the same tone Becky used when asking Dylan if he needed to go pee pee. 'And what might it represent?'

Becky decided to cut her losses and let Rachel show off. 'Why don't you tell me?'

Rachel waved her hands as she explained. 'Paler colours are often used to depict the feminine. Bolder, darker colours are associated with masculinity and strength. We could see this as an interplay between the male on the right and the female on the left.'

'But I wouldn't say the male side of the painting is stronger,' Becky said. 'It's more passive than the left side and the red line is more over towards the right, as if the feminine side is pushing it over that way.'

'I don't disagree. In fact, what we have here are two elements in balance. The darker and more solid elements are more imposing, but the more ethereal and pale elements on the left are taking up more of the composition as a whole and are attractive to the eye because of the implied movement.'

Becky stepped back from the painting and removed her glasses. So if this painting represented a meeting of male and female, perhaps there was significance in its size? She supposed it was worth mentioning, if only to gain points with her reluctant teacher. 'Would I be right in saying that the canvas being the size of a single mattress is no coincidence?'

Rachel's eyebrows jumped. Aha! thought Becky. She'd seen something Rachel hadn't. Maybe she wasn't entirely useless at this interpretation business after all.

Rachel scanned the painting for a few moments before saying, 'How clever of you! A plausible inference.' She smirked again. 'Although I suppose it's an observation that would only come straight to the mind of some.'

What in the world was *that* supposed to mean? Did Rachel assume she was sleeping with Charlie? Was that her explanation for how Becky had her job despite knowing nothing about art? God! In that case Rachel probably thought she was sleeping with Virgil too. Putting it all together, it would certainly explain the gallery manager's unyielding frostiness. Someone who had ended a long-term relationship because it would be unprofessional to be romantically involved with their employer would despise another woman they believed was not only breaking an ethical code, but also capitalising on their sticking to it.

Best to be leaving as soon as possible. Becky had hoped coming to the gallery would improve her and Rachel's relationship, particularly now things had gone further between her and Charlie. But it would take a miracle for the woman to like her.

Putting her glasses back on and jabbing the bridge into place, Becky rushed on, hoping to bring the conversation to a close quickly, 'But if this painting represents a romantic meeting of some kind, why are they separated by the fat red line? And why is it broken?' She frowned. 'It's annoying.'

'I know. It conveys, brilliantly, the frustration of being separated from the object of desire or perhaps ...' Rachel paused, giving her final words emphasis. 'An encounter that was interrupted?'

Rachel smiled again, and this time there was a triumphant glitter in her eyes. Her gaze flicking between her host's face and the canvas, Becky cursed herself for being so slow. No wonder Rachel was so pleased with herself: the painting was about her. Or her and Charlie, getting interrupted under that lifeless Christmas tree.

Becky's cheeks burned and the hollowness returned to her stomach. Her brain refused to respond helpfully, instead giving the immediate options of covering her face with her hands or running from the room.

Fortunately, before she could go for either of her poor alternatives, Rachel lifted a delicate finger and stroked the edge of the painting. The simple action added to the fire in Becky's face, but it was an angry red. She was tired of letting this woman get to her. She was done.

Becky clasped her hands behind her back and pulled herself back on track. She opened her mouth to say goodbye, when Rachel cut in, 'I hope you weren't too mortified, happening upon John and me at Tamara's wedding.'

Becky balled her fingers into fists. Rachel leant towards her and dropped her voice to add, 'You shouldn't worry. John more than made it up to me when we got back to my place.'

If Rachel had been hoping to blindside Becky, she more than managed it. She had never considered the possibility Charlie and Rachel might have gone further than kissing. Rachel had been drunk and Charlie would never take advantage of someone in that state. He wouldn't.

Her mind whirred. Though part of her knew her jaw must be hanging open like a stunned fish, she couldn't drag her mind from unsavoury thoughts about what might have happened at Rachel's house long enough to attend to her face. Charlie would never. But then, what if Rachel had asked him to stay for a while? Suggested a few drinks? Had Charlie already been drinking at the wedding? Perhaps he wasn't as sober as he seemed? Rachel was beautiful, persuasive, and Charlie already liked her …

Becky flinched as Rachel touched her arm and recoiled faster than was entirely polite. Her hostess either didn't notice or care and, sickly smile still in place, pointed to the painting again. 'And for those not as in-the-know about the inspiration for this piece as you and me,' Rachel said, 'the artist has given a clue as to what the painting is about in the title: "Kiss Consume". It's from Shakespeare.'

Right, Becky thought, anger returning to replace her confusion. Rachel might be messing about with Charlie, but she wasn't about to let the woman dig her claws into Bill Shakespeare. Some things were sacred.

'Indeed it is,' Becky replied, teeth clenched. '*Romeo and Juliet*, act two, scene six. It's part of a warning to Romeo from the Friar that passionate encounters often burn themselves out like a mixture of fire and gunpowder, while long-lasting love is based on a more moderate, slow-growing affection.'

In her own disorientated state, it was a relief to see her words throw Rachel off balance. The curator blinked and the beyond irritating smile finally disappeared. 'You know Shakespeare?' Rachel asked.

Becky relaxed her shoulders. Finally, firm ground! 'Let's just say I also studied art but a different type to you.' She turned away from the painting. The urge to leave there and then was strong, but Rachel had invited her here for some sort of revenge. To make her feel stupid and small. Ronnie would kill her if she left without making a stand.

The higher ground was attractive, but Becky wasn't in the mood to take it. After all, she wasn't the only one with weak spots to be exploited.

'The New Year's ball should be exciting,' she said.

'Absolutely! I'm so glad John asked me to go with him.' Rachel giggled. 'I think he'd been building up the courage for a while.'

Becky responded with an equally fake laugh. 'Yes. I guess he was waiting for the right time to ask. Like Virgil.'

The giggling ceased. 'Sorry?'

'Oh, he hasn't mentioned it? We're having our outstanding dinner date at the ball. It should be lots of fun.' Becky smiled in a way she hoped suggested 'fun' involved letting Virgil ravish her on the dance floor. 'And don't worry, I'll leave my scullery maid's outfit at home.' She winked. 'I can always wear it for Virgil another time.'

Becky adjusted her jacket and glanced towards the door. 'This has been delightful, Rachel. Thank you so much for suggesting it and being incredibly generous with your valuable time.' Laying a hand on her shoulder and taking in Rachel's pale cheeks and wide eyes, Becky told herself Ronnie would make her feel OK about this later. Right now out-bitching Rachel didn't feel as great as she had thought it might.

Rachel gargled an inarticulate sound and her pale neck turned blotchy. Becky moved to leave before the urge to apologise became overwhelming. 'I'm sure you have work to do, so I won't keep you any further. And don't worry, I can show myself out.'

Chapter 37

The weekend after her encounter with Rachel, Becky took Dylan to visit his grandparents. Having forgotten to mention anything about Mike to Charlie when she had seen him on Thursday night, she decided to pop in for a chat on Sunday evening when returning the Mercedes to the Old Station House.

She left Dylan with Phoebe and hurried across the lawn, braving the icy wind. She let herself into the studio and perched on the arm of the sofa while she rubbed her hands together.

All the overhead lights were on and Charlie was also using a couple of standing spots directed towards his work area. The underfloor heating was keeping the building cosy. Becky shrugged off her coat and left a cake box on the small table next to her after finding a clear spot between a growing collection of mugs, most of which were full, their contents cold and untouched.

Charlie didn't turn around as she came in, so she slid down over the arm of the sofa and got comfortable.

She guessed he was putting the final touches on the painting. This phase involved more staring and fewer flicks of the brush than in the earlier stages of creation, which at times resembled an aerobic workout. She sat back, let her gaze settle on Charlie's movements and her mind wander.

Looking at him in profile, she noticed the lines to the side of his eye and the shadows under it. It was strange, but she never saw these things when talking to him. In fact, she often forgot the ten-year age gap between them. Anyway, she wasn't getting any younger. Sometimes she imagined Dylan as a mini Dorian Gray and she his portrait, withering and shrivelling as he grew stronger, chubbier and more beautiful.

As she followed the slow brush movements, she enjoyed what was a moment of peace at the end of a weekend full of niggles. While she understood her parents' concern for her and the state of her finances, when she had told them everything was fine—for the twenty-fourth time—she had hoped they'd drop it.

She'd had enough of lectures. Although, she conceded as she rubbed her neck, Rachel's might prove useful. Narrowing her eyes, she squinted at the painting in front of her on the easel and tried to appreciate it. She had no doubt Charlie knew what he was doing and was sure Rachel would gush that this was another masterclass in form, expression and technique. Yet Becky still wouldn't choose to hang any of Charlie's new paintings in her home. Given the choice she would stick with Monet, Renoir and Degas.

An enormous sneeze brought Becky's attention back to Charlie. Too caught up in his work to find a tissue, he was resorting to some disgusting sniffing.

Employing great restraint, she waited until he put his brush down before speaking. 'Charlie, you're not well. Sit down.' She thrust a tissue towards him. 'And use this for goodness' sake.'

He clutched at the tissue as he collapsed onto the sofa. 'Tank oo,' he said, blowing his nose and letting his head fall onto the backrest. 'It was worse before. I think this is the end of it.'

Becky put her hand on his forehead and noted the three days' worth of stubble. 'At least you haven't got a temperature. You were fine last Thursday night.'

'I woke up on Friday feeling like death. I spent most of Friday in bed and yesterday morning. But today's been better.'

'You should have called me.'

'You were going to your parents. Anyway, Phoebe said it was just man flu.'

'Well I'm glad you're feeling better. Mike's worried he hasn't seen much of you recently.'

'Which means Ronnie is worried that Mike's worried, right?'

'You're getting good at this. Keep it up.' She grinned and gave him a gentle push. 'And when you get a second, call Mike so Ronnie gets off my back.'

'Soon, I promise. I only have to finish these three.' He waved at the canvas on the easel and two more set back against the wall behind it.

'What's that one?' asked Becky, pointing to the small canvas behind the sofa which was covered in a cloth.

'Nothing. That is, I mean, it's not for the exhibition. It's something for my classes.'

Becky didn't follow up. If Rachel were to be believed and Charlie's stuttering was anything to go by, the covered painting was probably a nude portrait of the devious cow. She shivered and tapped Charlie on the back of his hand. He jumped as if she had tasered him. 'Sorry, were you falling asleep?'

'No, no, just thinking.'

Probably about Rachel. Was there no avoiding her? Ah well, if she couldn't beat her—and she had indulged in some enjoyable daydreams along those lines—she might as well join in.

'Rachel's excited about the exhibition,' Becky said. 'She gave me an interesting talk about the paintings. I may have actually learnt something. And I didn't realise you'd done so many.'

'Those three will make twenty-two, including the one going to the ball auction.' He kept his eyes shut and pointed in front of him again. 'They're practically finished. Another couple of hours and that's it for this show.'

'Wow! What will you do with yourself?'

'I have to help Rachel plan the gallery layout and Ronnie with a Christmas cake spectacular.'

'I was kidding, Charlie. You should take a break. Get better. You've pulled off something you said was impossible a few months ago so why don't you put your feet up? I'm sure Rachel and Ronnie can manage. And once you feel a hundred per cent you can get Phoebe to dust off her dance shoes and run you through some steps. She says it's been three years since you helped her practise. It'd make you feel more confident when it's time to dance with Rachel on New Year's Eve.'

'I could practise with you,' he said, opening his eyes and tilting his head towards her.

'You don't want to do that. It tends to be less like dancing and more like struggling.'

He raised his eyebrows.

She laughed. 'You know from your experience with Phoebe there isn't exactly a surplus of teenage boys who want to learn ballroom dancing.'

'I know. It's one of the things I liked most about her doing it.'

She smiled and said, 'If you're tall they make you partner up with a girl but dancing the boy's part. I learnt the girl's part for my exams, but spent most of the time dancing the man's part. Which means I find it difficult not to worry about where we're going, if we're about to crash into anyone else, if we're in time—'

'You like driving.'

'I lead. It's a habit. And it's not my fault if the bloke I'm dancing with needs to be led.' She crossed her arms and shuffled further back into the sofa. 'But don't worry. I'm sure you won't have to fight Rachel round the floor.'

'What do you think of Rachel?'

'Sorry?'

He raised his head and turned so they were facing each other, their eyes on a level. 'Do you think we're well-suited?'

'Um. I'm sorry, but I'm not going to answer that.'

'Why not?'

'Because my opinion's irrelevant. You like her; that's all that matters.'

And if I slag her off and you are sleeping with her, it's too late anyway and you'll hate me, she added to herself.

Charlie removed his glasses and put them on the arm of the sofa. 'But I want your opinion. I value your opinion.'

She sighed. He was going to force it out of her. 'OK, um … I think she's clever and beautiful. And she knows a lot about art and she appreciates your work.'

He narrowed his eyes. 'You haven't answered my question.'

'I told you what I think of her.'

'But do you think we're right for each other?'

'She certainly thinks you're compatible if her behaviour at the wedding is anything to go by. And whatever happened afterwards.'

'What?'

'It's none of my business.'

'Becky!' He stood up. 'I am your business. Tell me what you think!'

Oh, bloody hell. Why had she promised never to lie to him? She bit her lip and looked down, her voice escaping as a whisper. 'No, Charlie. In the long term, I don't think you're meant for each other.'

He crossed his arms. 'Oh? Why not?'

She searched for a response more diplomatic than, 'Because at best I think she's using you to make Virgil jealous and at worst she's using you to suck up to her mother to get control of the family business.'

She rubbed her palms against her knees and considered each word before she spoke. 'I just think that, maybe, you don't have much more in common than art. That's all.'

The weight of the ensuing silence was only surpassed by that of Charlie's stare. His lips disappeared and an ominous vein appeared along his right temple which bulged as his jaw tightened.

'You were right,' he said, his voice sharp and clipped. 'I don't know why I want your opinion. You're hardly a relationship expert: you couldn't even tell your last boyfriend was married, could you?'

As he spat the final accusation at her, Becky's jaw dropped. His words hadn't been simply angry or irritated. She had heard those from him before. No, these had been *spiteful*. That would teach her to bad-mouth his girlfriend.

She swallowed as she got to her feet and pulled on her coat. Keeping her eyes down, she fumbled to fasten the buttons. Fighting his barbed comments with malicious ones of her own wouldn't help. Besides, he had a point.

'True,' she said. 'Very true.' Her voice cracked and she nodded, her gaze still fixed on the floor. She turned away from him and headed for the door.

'Becky,' he called after her.

She sighed and turned back. She knew it. The flu was doing the talking. A lack of sleep, having to breathe through your mouth and getting a sore under your nose were enough to put anyone in a foul mood. And he hadn't been drinking enough, not if all those untouched cups of tea were anything to go by, and probably had a banging headache.

She blinked, waiting for him to speak. A straightforward 'sorry' was unlikely. How would Charlie apologise without apologising this time?

He signalled the pink-and-white striped cake box she had left on the coffee table. 'Tell Ronnie I said thanks for the leftovers.' Waving in her direction as if he were telling a naughty dog to shoo, he added, 'And don't let me keep you, I'm sure you have some urgent cleaning to do.'

Charlie counted to ten after the door slammed and then lashed out, sending the nearest easel to the floor with a kick.

God, she was infuriating! Months pushing him towards Rachel without thinking there was any future in the relationship! And all the while claiming to have his best interests at heart, making him think they were friends, when he was just another part in her grand plan.

He ran his hands through his hair, pulling until it hurt, and gave the sofa a swift kick. In retaliation it jumped back, nudging the side table.

As the table wobbled, his eyes fell on the cake box. Cursing breathlessly, he rubbed his hand across his mouth and bent to pick it up.

Inside was a note: *For Charlie. Handmade with love by Dylan and Becky. Xx.* A shaky smiley face, drawn in crayon, sat underneath. A joint effort by mother and son. Under the note were two triangles of dense, plain sponge cake, covered in white icing and multicoloured sprinkles. He didn't need to taste it to know it would be better than his childhood favourite.

With great care, he put the box back on the table. Holding the note in his shaking fingertips, he ground his teeth and squeezed his eyes shut. When he opened them again, he lifted the note to his lips and sank to his knees.

Not for the first time, Charlie wished his life had a rewind button. Groaning, he slumped forward and let his head drop onto the arm of the sofa.

And if he thought his bed would provide refuge from his guilt, he was wrong.

That night the dream studio was still filled with the muse's early Christmas gifts. But, unlike his previous visits, this time he shivered and watched as his breath created dense clouds of clammy vapour.

The door swung open and the lady came in. As she strode towards Charlie, he understood her previous expression, which he had always seen as inscrutably neutral, had been accepting and friendly. Tonight her eyes were glacial and disapproval radiated from her clenched jaw and stiff posture. She stood in front of him just long enough to fix him with her frigid stare and slap him hard across the face.

When he stopped seeing snow, he found himself sitting on the floor. As he stood up, still shaking, the movement of his feet sent a series of echoes around the building.

She had gone, taking all the paintings with her. Charlie was left alone in the middle of the studio, now empty and sterile, lonelier than a morgue at midnight.

DECEMBER

Chapter 38

When dawn came on Monday, Charlie found it less rosy-fingered and more like another slap in the face. Knowing that trying to paint was pointless, he went for a run.

A couple of weeks had passed since he last completed his normal circuit and the short break in training had taken its toll. Wheezing and fighting a stitch, he decided to cut his route short.

On the way home it began to drizzle. Each damp step ground more guilt into his bones, not helped by the latest playlist he discovered on his phone: a collection of ideal wedding songs, starting with 'Happy Together'.

At home he searched for a distraction and noticed his exercise routine wasn't the only thing he had neglected recently: the house needed a serious clean. Glad to find something to keep him busy, he seized the vacuum cleaner and attacked the carpets, then moved on to the bathrooms and kitchen.

Unfortunately, this burst of industrious activity didn't help either. The smell of bleach and soap made him think of Becky's house and her long-suffering hands.

By lunchtime the house sparkled and the washing machine was singing as it spun. He should tackle the studio next. The dust bunnies out there were starting to resemble tumbleweeds. But he couldn't face it and turned his attention to the garden instead.

The grass was hidden under a carpet of dead leaves which were drying into a broad segment of the colour wheel. He called the gardener who usually came to help in the winter but, as he was busy until later in the week, Charlie went outside and made a start on the operation himself. This kept him occupied for another couple of hours until he was exhausted. He needed to get back to the gym.

He called Mike who was pleased to hear Charlie was alive and delighted to agree to meet him at the gym the next day after his class. Charlie then spent the rest of the day trying to read or watch TV, but his guilt lingered like an itch in a tricky spot on his back, always just out of reach, and he was relieved when it was time to leave for the college.

❧

On Tuesday he went to the Coulson and found Rachel putting a potential lighting supplier through his paces by asking a series of unintelligible questions and demanding lucid answers. While she was polite, she made it plain Charlie's input was not required. If she needed his help, she would call.

He then tried his luck at Sweet's. He discovered immediately that Becky hadn't told Ronnie about the events of Sunday night; Ronnie spoke to him using her normal level of bossy when she told him to come back in the afternoon to help with the Christmas displays. Not wanting to go home, he had lunch at a café before returning to the cake shop and spending the next few hours up to his elbows in red and green fondant. His work was rated as satisfactory but uninspired and he was dismissed until the following day.

At home he checked in with Phoebe who was revising for her last set of exams before university applications and interviews. He found she was cast away on her own island of stress and so, having made sure she was eating, Charlie grabbed his sports bag and headed for the further education college.

His class were their usual jabbering selves, but even Mrs Howard's terrifying attempts at flirtation were unable to spring him out of the dark cell of his memories.

Mike had more success in lifting Charlie's spirits. He always related his and Ronnie's little disagreements with humour and an affectionate appreciation of his girlfriend's crabbiness. But only one part of their conversation held any true interest for Charlie.

They were on the static bikes, pedalling in time with the beat of the ambient music. As usual, Charlie was going faster than Mike, having settled into a steady rhythm quickly.

After ten minutes, Mike slowed and pushed back from the handlebars. He ran the back of his hand over his flushed forehead and asked, 'Do you know if Becky's OK?'

Charlie's foot slipped off the pedal. 'I think so. Why?'

'Ah, it's most likely nothing,' said Mike, flicking away the idea with his hand.

'No, go on.'

'All right. But don't tell her I said anything.' Mike stopped pedalling and dropped his voice. 'I do Becky's accounts. I don't charge her; she gets me photography gigs. Anyway, I know things were pretty tight at the start of November and since then she's only had that one big wedding. I guess she's hanging in until your paintings sell. I'm sure she has it under control.'

Charlie frowned and his pedalling slowed. 'What's "pretty tight"?'

'You know, just enough to cover the mortgage and bills. But please don't say anything. Becky would kill me and I'd have to hope she does a good job because Ronnie would start on me once she'd finished.'

⤚

After a night of dreamless sleep, Charlie spent Wednesday morning not looking at his phone. He filled the rest of the day in much the same way as the one before.

⤚

On Thursday he went out to the studio and sat for an hour staring at the three unfinished paintings. Then he gave up waiting for inspiration to come back through the door and did some portraiture work for his classes.

As daylight faded, he realised how much he had looked forward to movie night. In fact, the last few days had made it clear his pre-July routines were no longer enough.

At dinner, when Phoebe asked him if he was going to Becky's as usual, he still hadn't made up his mind and it took a call from Mike to give him a final push. Ronnie was worried about Becky. She hadn't seen her for a week. When she had spoken to her on the phone, Becky said Dylan had been unwell, but Ronnie suspected something else was up. As she knew Charlie was due to go round to Becky's that night, she had told Mike to call him and order a full report. Submission mandatory.

Chapter 39

After closing the door on Charlie on Sunday, Becky dragged her feet back to the Old Station House. She waited for a moment with her hand resting on the kitchen door, her fingers feeling swollen and rubbery. Then she took a deep breath, pulled a smile onto her face and stepped inside.

She kept the smile on while Phoebe drove them home, singing Dylan's favourite songs to hold it in place. She kept it on during dinnertime, bath time and story time. Then she gave Dylan a longer hug than usual, taking a deep breath of his beautiful soft, clean hair. She kissed him, lowered him into his cot and said night night.

Not one to waste the effort required for a journey up or down the stairs, she scooped up a few toys to take down with her. She made it as far as two steps from the bottom when the aching heaviness which had started in her chest made it to her legs.

She gulped and swayed, sliding down the wall until her knees were up next to her chin. A long, shuddering sigh left her and tears rolled down her cheeks.

With a hollow gnawing in her guts, she blundered through the rest of the evening mechanically. Close to midnight she found herself in bed, unable to remember how she got there.

Dylan woke her at two o'clock. She spent an unproductive hour carrying him up and down the landing, trying to coax him back to sleep, but every time she tried to put him down he wailed and did his best limpet impression. Eventually she lowered him into her bed where his sleep was fitful and he kicked her in the head at regular intervals.

At the doctor's the next day, Becky was told what she expected to hear: her son had a virus and there was nothing she could do but wait it out. Back home, Dylan refused to sleep if he wasn't in his mother's arms and when he was awake he was clingy and tearful, wailing if Becky left the room.

Dylan turned a corner on Tuesday; he started eating and his temperature was constant. But by bedtime that evening, Becky could feel a prickling behind her eyes and the intermittent sore throat she'd had for a week was a permanent fixture.

On Wednesday she woke to find every tube in her head stuffed with goo. Dylan's energy levels were climbing and he was demanding the same exuberance from her, when all she wanted was to lie down in a darkened room.

By Thursday Dylan was better, apart from a runny nose and a lingering cough. In contrast, she couldn't summon the energy to get dressed. She lay on the sofa as much as she could, letting Dylan watch too much television and not caring where he was using his crayons. When Charlie knocked on the door she had been making a start on cleaning Dylan's artwork from the walls, even though standing made her dizzy.

❧

Although it was a frosty night and he had recovered from his recent bout of flu, Charlie had to wipe sweat from his palms before he knocked on Becky's door. His heart pounding, he shuffled his feet as he waited, then knocked again.

A silhouette approached and Becky's voice came through the door. 'Who is it?'

'It's me.'

'I'm in my dressing gown and pyjamas.'

'I think I can cope.'

A deep sigh prefaced the slow unlocking of the door. She didn't wait to show him in, but retreated to the kitchen, leaving him to shut the door behind him. The familiar scent of soap and citrus met him as he followed her. A mop bucket sat by the kitchen door with a scrubbing brush and sponge perched on top of it. He couldn't see any gloves.

The kettle was boiling and she was leaning on the countertop next to it, her back to him. Without turning round, and in a deliberate, level tone, she said, 'How can I help you, Mr Handren?'

Hovering in the kitchen doorway, he put his hands in his pockets. 'I came to see how you are.'

'I'm fine.' She sniffed. 'Don't let me keep you; I'm sure you've noticed I have cleaning to do.'

Glad she couldn't see his face, Charlie flinched at the reminder of his final words to her on Monday. He hadn't thought he could feel any worse, but Becky's voice was like a cold dagger, stabbing at his wounded conscience. She might want him to leave, but he couldn't go before he'd made things right.

'I heard Dylan was unwell.'

'He's on the mend, but your concern is appreciated. Anything else?'

He shivered. 'Why's it so cold in here?

'Boiler packed in on Tuesday.'

'Why didn't you get it fixed?'

'Not all of us are swimming in spare cash.'

'But Dylan—'

'There are fan heaters in the rooms he's in.'

'And the water—'

'The immersion's working. We're fine. I'll take care of it. You should go.'

He opened his mouth to answer when the kettle came to the boil and she set about making tea for one. The elegant tea dance was out of time and clumsy: her hands shook as she picked things up and the order of the process was disjointed and jumbled.

Something was very wrong.

'Becky? You're not OK, are you?'

'I'm fine.'

He crossed the room in three strides and spun her round to face him. Her eyes were red and watery, half covered by droopy lids. He put a hand to her forehead.

'Christ, Becky, you're boiling! How long have you been sick?'

'I'm fine.' She made to escape into the front room but stumbled. Charlie caught her by the tops of her arms and she slumped forward, letting her head rest against his chest. In a small voice, which seemed to come from far away, she said, 'Actually, I don't think I'm very well …'

And then fainted.

Chapter 40

When Becky woke, she had vague memories of being helped to the sofa and told to rest, an instruction she guessed she'd had no trouble following. She must have plummeted to sleep instantly to have no memory of being wrapped in a blanket or a cushion being placed under her head. She rubbed her eyes, hoping to improve her blurred vision. Not that her eyes were her most pressing problem: that was the two brass bands which had taken up residence in her temples and were bashing out obnoxious show tunes.

She shivered, pulled the blanket up to her chin and blinked to focus. On the coffee table in front of her, a mug of tea was waiting. A large box sat next to it and, despite the efforts of the brass bands, the sight of her favourite chocolates made the corners of her mouth twitch upwards. Charlie had been here. With chocolate. He must have put her on the sofa. But where was he now?

She propped herself up on an elbow and twisted towards the kitchen. Beyond the doorway she could see Charlie's back and hear his low voice. He hadn't run away yet.

She was about to lie down when another voice rose in response to Charlie's. She shifted and had just managed to peer round the back of the sofa when a man she had never seen before appeared in the kitchen doorway. Forgetting for a moment she was in her own house, she dropped down onto the cushion and pulled the blanket up over her head.

Cursing her flu-induced stupidity, she closed her eyes and concentrated on the men's voices: they were muttering, but she was pretty sure the stranger was leaving, a suspicion confirmed by the thud of footsteps past the back of the sofa in the direction of the front door. She peeled the blanket down until it was covering the tip of her nose and watched as Charlie opened the front door, shook the visitor's hand, waved him off and clicked the door shut. He was halfway back to the kitchen when he noticed her watching him.

'Hello.' He smiled and sat next to her feet. 'I'll make you some more tea.' He nodded to the mug on the table. 'That one's probably gone cold.'

She licked her dry lips. 'Who was that?'

'Mark. I called him to come and fix your boiler.'

'But I don't have the money—'

'I know. I paid him. I owe you anyway.'

'No you don't.'

'Becky.' He placed a hand on her arm, stopping her getting up. 'How much would I have had to pay anyone else for the work you did on Phoebe's party?'

He had a point. Her goo-riddled brain struggled to come up with a good response. 'But that's all included—'

'Ah!' He raised a finger to silence her. 'It wasn't in the original plan, was it? And, if you like, you can think of it as an advance. I can deduct it from your final commission if it'll make you stop arguing and lie down.'

'I suppose.' She pouted and crossed her arms under the blanket.

'Good. I'm going to make that tea, watch you drink it and then make sure you get to bed. Deal?'

'Deal. Thank you.'

'You're welcome.' He patted her foot, then disappeared into the kitchen.

Becky closed her eyes and let the humming of the kettle carry her back to sleep.

❧

The next morning, Becky didn't wake until 9 a.m.

'Dylan! Dylan!'

'Don't get up! Don't get up!' said Ronnie as she came running into the bedroom. 'He's fine. Everything's fine.'

'Where's Dylan?'

'I got here early, Charlie went home while I sorted Dylan out with breakfast and then Charlie came back and took him to the park. The poor kid was climbing the walls. The fresh air will do him good.'

'Did he find Dylan's hat and warm mittens? Not the wool ones, the thick ones?'

'Yes, yes. And his boots and jacket.' She put her hand on Becky's head. 'Good news. I think you'll live!'

Becky gave her a feeble smile. 'I'm sorry you got dragged into this too.'

'Don't be daft. Charlie was right to call me. I'd have killed him if he hadn't. And I volunteered to come here this morning. I thought he might want to go home and shower, and if you want to get clean too I guessed you'd prefer me on standby in the bathroom in case you faint. Although I'm sure Charlie would have done it; he's turned out to be a proper Florence Nightingale.' She looked up at the ceiling. 'I think I might have been wrong about him.'

'How so?'

'When I got here, he was cleaning crayon off the walls downstairs.' She scratched her neck. 'He might be different from all the others after all.'

Becky nodded. 'I think he carried me up to bed.'

'He was here all night. I'm not sure he slept much, but he says the sofa's comfy.' She put an extra pillow behind Becky's head. 'As my mother would say: "A friend in need is a friend indeed".' She shuddered. 'Oh my God, I've just admitted I was wrong *and* quoted my mother.'

'Perhaps you're coming down with something too.'

'For Mike's sake, let's hope not. You know I'm not the best patient.' She grinned. 'Although the thought of lying up in bed ringing a bell for service does appeal.'

❧

Ronnie brought Becky tea and toast, helped her shower, change, and down to the sofa, where she insisted on making her bed for the day. She was reclining in front of the television, having taken another dose of pills, when Charlie and Dylan came back from the park.

Dylan was much better. The improvement in his health, combined with the excitement of dozens of trips down the slide, had brought a glow back to his cheeks. He made a beeline for the sofa and clambered up and onto Becky, who hugged him while telling him how handsome he was in his bear hat, complete with pom-pom ears.

Charlie looked similarly well. He smiled as Dylan climbed onto Becky, but lifted him off before he could do the invalid any harm. 'How are you feeling?' he asked.

'Pathetic. But a bit better, I think.'

'Temperature's down,' said Ronnie, coming in from the kitchen. She went to stand next to Charlie at the foot of the sofa. 'A few more days with her feet up and she'll be fine.'

Becky opened her mouth in dismay. 'But—'

'We'll hear none of it,' said Ronnie. 'You've knackered yourself. If you don't rest and get completely better then you'll be ill again before Christmas and that's daft when we're here to help. Right, Charlie?' She smacked Charlie on the shoulder using the back of her hand.

'Right.'

'But you both have loads to do.' Becky looked at Charlie. 'You should be painting. You have classes to teach.'

'The paintings are as finished as they're going to get. And I only teach Monday to Wednesday for a couple of hours.'

She turned to Ronnie. 'You've got the pre-Christmas rush.'

'All in the capable hands of the interns. Sure, I need to drop in to check they're not stuffing things up, but I can be here for a while.'

Becky blinked. She felt pleasantly fuzzy and vague, certainly not in any state to mount a defence against a Sweet offensive.

'Becks, relax and do as you're told. We can focus on you for— Christ! What now?' Ronnie glared at her phone as it wailed a tuneless distress signal. 'Bloody interns! I'd better deal with this.' She strutted towards the kitchen, glancing back to bark at Charlie, 'You! Make sure she doesn't get up.'

Charlie gave a mock salute to Ronnie's back then skirted round the arm of the sofa and knelt in front of Becky. He took her hand in both of his and looked into her drooping eyes. 'Becky, you're always telling people to let you help them. Please, this one time, take your own advice. I know you'd manage on your own but you don't have to.'

He stroked her hand as a large, irrepressible yawn closed her eyes. He leant closer and she could smell the clean, creamy scent of shaving foam as he said, 'I'll take that as permission to stay.'

Becky bit her dry bottom lip, not caring if she drew blood. Her neck itched and her fingers burned and twitched, symptoms not of the plague which was causing everyone so much trouble but of her frustration at her own pathetic feebleness.

Charlie raised an eyebrow, clearly waiting for her reply. 'Fine,' she muttered, hating having to give in but unable to think of any way she could reasonably evict Ronnie and Charlie when they were offering to help. 'Fine,' she said again, ignoring the blatant twinkle of triumph in Charlie's eyes to channel her last energy reserves into a small show of defiance. 'But hide my chocolates from Ronnie. I'll want them when I'm better.'

Chapter 41

Becky swallowed her final two pills of the day as Charlie took Dylan up to the bath. Closing her eyes, she listened as Charlie ran the water and passed Dylan his toys, interacting with the toddler's babbling. She lowered her glass to the coffee table and relaxed back into her mound of cushions. Perhaps this was what it was like to have someone around all the time to help out.

The box of chocolates had reappeared on the table shortly after Ronnie's departure. Becky had already managed one, which gave her hope she was on the mend. She popped another into her mouth and sighed. Chocolate should be available on prescription.

She was beginning to get frustrated with the lack of anything half-decent on television when Charlie came back downstairs. He gave her a thumbs up as he dropped onto the sofa. 'Mission accomplished.'

'Thank you.'

She tucked her hair behind her ears. The pills were yet to kick in and she felt lucid enough for a proper chat. 'I expect this is more penance than you were bargaining for when you came here last night.'

'No more than I deserve.' He silenced the television and shifted in his seat so he was facing her.

'Oh I don't know. I'd have liked you to be here on Monday when Dylan was really ill. He was being particularly poolific. It was beyond disgusting.' She wrinkled her nose as she remembered and watched him cringe at the thought of the nappies. Time to bring the conversation back to more tasteful matters. 'Did you like the cake?'

His cringe deepened. 'Phoebe ate it. She said it was great.'

She gave a quick shrug. She knew enough about Charlie's capacity for self-flagellation to expect he wouldn't be able to bring himself to stomach it once he saw the note, although there had been a good while on Sunday night during which she had hoped he would try it and choke. Slowly. 'I mentioned it to my mum and she had a recipe she thought sounded like what you told me about.'

Charlie nodded. 'And thank you for not saying anything to Ronnie about last Sunday.' He picked up the box of chocolates from the table and studied the menu. 'I'd be missing a limb if you had. Or worse.'

'I'm sorry, Charlie.'

'You don't have to apologise. You're sick. I'm happy to help.'

'No, not for that. For July. For being a mean pushy woman who hit you and called you names. Why did you agree to work with me if you remembered all that?'

He popped a chocolate in his mouth and chewed it along with her question. 'Because at that moment, you had a point. And I'm sure you were doing what you had to. It's not like you could have picked me up off the sofa.'

'Maybe not. But I think I'd been saving that slap up for a while and you were unlucky enough to have the face that fit. Same goes for some of the stuff I said.'

Charlie lifted the box off his knees to pass it to her. Becky gripped it, but he didn't let go. He waited until she looked at him to say, 'Maybe I didn't do quite enough to earn a slap back in July, but I deserved one last Sunday.'

He let go of the box. Becky picked out a chocolate and crunched its brittle centre. 'But you were right,' she said. 'I mean, how could I not see he was married? Sometimes I wonder whether, on some level, I knew it was all too romantic but I went with it for once. I was just so impressed he saw me.' She looked at Charlie's sympathetic frown and shrugged. 'And if I can be so wilfully blind, how can I tell other people who is or isn't right for them?'

Charlie pulled off his glasses and tilted them to the light, inspecting the lenses. 'Until recently, I thought Mel leaving was my fault.' This was said to the glasses. He folded the legs carefully and placed them on the coffee table. 'She was so unwell and we'd tried everything ...' He glanced at Becky. 'But I'll leave her to tell you about that, if she wants to.' Sighing, he returned his gaze to the table. 'Her illness was obviously no one's fault, but sometimes seeing her down made me feel so hopeless and so *useless* ...' He shook his head. 'I guess I pulled away when I should have been within reach. And then the week she left, she tried to talk to me, but I was busy finishing some pieces for a big show I had coming up in London. At least, that was my excuse.'

He let his head fall onto the backrest and directed the rest of his speech to the ceiling. 'I told her I was too busy, but I could have made time … I think I knew. She wanted to tell me it wasn't working and I thought if I didn't give her the chance to tell me, then it wouldn't happen. So instead of talking to her, I forced her to leave.' He stopped and rolled his head to look at Becky. 'Or that's what I thought. Six years of "if only": if only I'd spoken to her, if only I'd done this or that. And now Mel says she'd already decided to go, but she wanted to talk to me first. She didn't want to disappear, but after a week of trying to tell me, she couldn't wait any longer.'

He raised his head and put a hand on Becky's foot. He rocked it gently. 'What I'm trying to say … *very* inarticulately … is that you can't put all the blame on yourself. Maybe you did suspect he was married, but he was the one with the wife and kids. It wasn't your job to assume he was lying. And nothing justifies how he reacted to you at that party and not even attempting to contact you afterwards.' He raised an accusatory finger. 'That is unforgiveable.'

He was flushed. She wasn't surprised: this could well be the most he'd ever spoken without interruption.

'And finally,' he said, 'and I will finish soon, I promise …'

Becky took his hand and gave it a gentle shake.

'What I said to you on Sunday wasn't true. You made a mistake in trusting one specific person, sure. But to then say you can't help other people with their relationships because of that one mistake is daft. Think how many brilliant doctors smoke. You may not always follow your own advice, but that doesn't mean it isn't any good.'

Becky exhaled slowly. The pills had begun to take effect at the start of Charlie's speech and she couldn't swear she'd understood all of it. However, he was trying to make her feel better and apologise, in his own, non-apologetic way. She squeezed his hand again.

'You're half asleep. Come on.' He got up and stretched his arms out towards her.

'No, no, no!' she said while doing nothing to fend him off. 'I can walk if you help me. You'll put your back out.'

'I managed it before. Come on.'

Muttering half-hearted protests and warnings, Becky clasped her arms around his neck and let him pick her up. Her heavy head sank against his shoulder as he made steady progress up the stairs. Not entirely conscious, she rubbed her cheek against the soft warm wool of his jumper, breathing in its faint spicy scent.

Without any hint of effort, he lowered her onto the bed and arranged her pillows. He was about to turn off the bedside lamp when she grabbed his outstretched hand.

'Charlie? Will you please check on Dylan before you go?'

'Of course.' He brushed a few strands of hair from her forehead as she closed her eyes. 'And I'll be back tomorrow before Dylan's awake. Call me if you need anything.'

Chapter 42

After a week lounging on the sofa, sleeping off a couple of years of fatigue and letting Charlie and Ronnie take over, Becky felt strong enough to leave the house.

Becky nodded while Charlie tried to persuade her to extend her convalescence, all the while plotting her escape. He didn't want her venturing into town on foot. He couldn't drive her because he had to visit Rachel on Friday morning. She should wait until next week.

He worried too much. Friday was set to be a dry day; if she wrapped up and stayed outside for brief periods there was no reason a short excursion wouldn't do her some good. And ignoring her dwindling bank balance wasn't going to put her back in the black. If she could talk the bank into giving her a mortgage holiday until her commission came in from Charlie's show, with some more belt tightening she should have enough to tide her over for another couple of months.

The next morning Ronnie arrived at nine to take charge of Dylan. Becky's plan was to go to the bank, then to a few shops to get nappies and other essentials. However, after talking to a couple of helpful bank employees, she cut her trip short and was back home less than an hour after she had left.

She slammed the front door. 'Ronnie!' Stripping off her coat, hat and gloves, she strung them up and kicked her boots into the corner before bounding up the stairs.

The world turned grey as she made it to the top. Groaning, she sank to her knees and lowered her head to the floor.

When Ronnie came out of Dylan's room, Becky was curled in a ball on the landing. She crouched and helped Becky to sitting, propping her against the wall. 'You've been to the bank, then?'

Becky tried to raise her head so she could glare at her, but moving did funny things to her vision. She kept her head still and injected some venom into her tone. 'You knew?'

'He already had your account number to pay expenses. And Mike may have given him an idea of how much would cover a couple of months of your mortgage. But,' she said, as Becky growled, 'he'll deduct it from your final commission, which you won't get until well into February or March.'

Becky turned her head just enough so she could fix Ronnie with one squinting eye. Ronnie kept going.

'And it's all your own fault anyway. No one would work for over half a year for free, getting paid everything at the end. You should demand an advance or part payments throughout the project. Mike agrees with me on this one and he knows what he's talking about. Charlie owes you and he's got money to spare.' She nudged Becky. 'Obviously you should give him a hard time about doing it behind your back. But then you and I both know you wouldn't have let him do it if he'd asked you first.'

Becky let her head hang lower.

'And how many times has your policy been "do first, apologise later"?' Ronnie asked. 'He's an observant guy and you can't blame him if he's following your poor example.'

Becky wasn't sure if it was the remnants of the flu making her dizzy or Ronnie's energetic defence of Charlie.

'Anyway, turns out he's a Taurus too. So no point in trying to change his mind now.' She helped Becky to her feet. 'Let's go downstairs and make some tea. And why don't we make something for Charlie too?'

❧

After lunch, Ronnie got Dylan to sleep and installed Becky on the sofa. Charlie was expected any minute. He continued to be expected until he was late and Ronnie couldn't wait any longer. So when he did show up, it was Becky who let him in, causing him to flap apologetically for having forced her to get up.

'Don't worry about it,' she said, leaning against the sofa and watching him take off his coat. 'I was well enough to go to the bank this morning, but I think I overdid it. I had a shock which did unfortunate things to my blood pressure.'

Charlie removed his glasses and used his scarf to clean them. Becky crossed her arms and waited while he put his glasses back on, looked up and cleared his throat. 'You haven't hit me or shouted,' he said.

She raised an eyebrow. 'Do you want me to?'

He shrugged and a shadow of a smile lingered at the corners of his mouth as he pushed his glasses up onto the bridge of his nose. 'No. Are you going to?'

'As long as it's an advance, then no.'

'An advance. Like the boiler repair. Honest.' He held up his hands. 'And I would have told you about it before I did it, but—'

'I would have stopped you. I know, I know.' She sighed. 'I never thought I was so difficult to help.'

'Well, you are.' He looked past her into the kitchen and his smile disappeared. 'You made tea already?'

He sounded disappointed. 'Don't worry, it should still be warm. And there's a treat to go with it. Ronnie made it, so it'll be great.'

He followed her into the kitchen. On the countertop a tray was waiting, laden with two mugs and two plates, each plate holding a right-angled triangle of sponge cake with white icing and multicoloured sprinkles.

Charlie's smile returned.

'Now, although you've done more than enough to help me lately, perhaps you'd be so kind as to carry the tray through to the front room.' She steadied herself by placing a hand on his left bicep and gave the muscle a playful squeeze. 'I may be on the mend, but why risk setting back my recovery when you've spent all that time at the gym?'

Chapter 43

A Christmas miracle came to South Compton rail station on the thirtieth of December when Becky's train arrived a full five minutes ahead of schedule.

She had left Dylan, a warm house and wonderful home cooking to come back to the Comptons and, as Becky stood shivering by the taxi bay, she had to remind herself that the numbness in her toes was for a good cause. Back in July, she had been pleased with her idea of using the New Year's ball to give Charlie's show a boost. But now it was a day away, the prospect was more daunting than inspired.

Virgil having gone AWOL didn't help her flagging confidence either. She hadn't spoken to her date since November, although he had sent her a message to wish her Merry Christmas and confirm he would meet her at the Hall.

Charlie's car came round the corner as the numbness was starting to pass her ankles. 'Sorry I'm late,' he said, taking her case and opening the passenger door for her. 'I would have picked you up at your parents'.'

'You weren't late. This is great, really.'

It was a compromise. Happy to get the train, Becky wouldn't let him make the trek to her parents'. And while Charlie could be persuaded to let Becky make her own way back to the Comptons, he wouldn't hear of her walking the short distance from the station to her house.

They had agreed the arrangement a couple of days after Christmas during a short and difficult phone call. Charlie was attending a noisy soirée with Rachel, apparently the annual shindig of one of the Coulson's most loyal patrons. Straining to hear him over the buzz of conversation, music and laughter, Becky listened to his lecture on the dangers of walking home alone in the dark and sub-zero temperatures. As soon as he paused for breath, she jumped in to agree to let him collect her from the station. Anything to bring the sermon to an end. Besides, she was concerned keeping him on the phone would land him in the doghouse. Towards the end of their conversation she had heard Rachel's voice several times, rising over the background din to call Charlie to heel.

After the sharp chill outside, Becky sniffed as the sudden warmth of the car made her nose run.

'Are you all right?' Charlie asked as he pulled away from the kerb.

'Fine. Well, a bit bereft to be honest. It's weird not having Dylan here. I feel like I've forgotten something.'

'Phoebe would have taken care of him.'

'I know. But she's eighteen and shouldn't have to stay at home on New Year's Eve. Anyway, Dylan had a great

Christmas at my parents'. They didn't have any plans to go out tomorrow night and he's settled there.'

'And your dad's bringing him home on the first, right?'

'Yeah and I know …' She rolled her eyes. 'It's less than two days. I'm being ridiculous. How was your visit to Mel's?'

'Surprisingly OK. Although a few festive drinks definitely helped the conversation along. And you're not ridiculous.' He flashed her a smile, his gaze flicking over to her and back to the road.

'Thanks. Did you and Will get on?'

He shrugged. 'He seems a decent enough bloke. And Mel's happy. That's all that matters.'

'Have they set a date for the wedding?'

'Not yet, but sometime next year.'

The radio crackled as the medley of Christmas classics gave way to the news and weather. The announcer sounded smug to report that the day had met their predictions exactly: clear skies, dry and bitterly cold. Becky smiled as he forecast snow for later that evening. She loved snow. Particularly when she could observe it from a snug, indoor vantage point.

'They've been saying snow's on the way for a week now,' said Charlie as he pulled onto Becky's drive. 'No sign yet though.'

'If they say it enough times they'll be right eventually.' She pointed towards the house. 'Are you coming in? I've got to give you your present.'

'Sure, go ahead. I'll bring your case. And *your* present.' He pointed to a large red bag on the back seat.

She chewed her lip as she opened the front door. The house still smelled of the gingerbread men she and Dylan had made for his grandparents the previous week, but the comforting scent failed to ease her anxiety. She prayed he hadn't bought her anything expensive. After fretting about what to get him for a week, she had printed and framed one of the pictures taken after Clarice and Steve's wedding, showing the bride and groom, Charlie, Dylan and her.

'I know it's not much,' she said as he peeled back the wrapping paper. 'But you could put it up in the studio so you'll have some company while you're painting and it'll be harder to forget us.'

Charlie looked up, his smile fading. 'Why would I forget you?'

'Well, after the show I'm sure you'll be chock-a-block with commissions and stuff.'

'Oh.' He frowned. 'But I can still babysit, right?'

She nodded and forced a smile. 'Do you like it?' She gestured to the picture.

'It's great. Thank you. I'll have to find the right place to hang it.' He set it down on the table and reached for Becky's gift. 'And you'll have to do the same.' He rubbed the back of his neck as she undid the paper. 'I went ahead and got it framed. I hope you like it.'

Becky gasped. The painting showed the water garden with the lilies and the familiar bridge. But this time there were people standing on the bridge, looking down into the water or perhaps over the water at the painter. Although they were indistinct, she could see the woman was dressed in bright blue and holding a small child who was wearing a familiar red sun hat. Unlike the print in her bedroom, with its cool greens and purples, this composition had the warm pink glow of a summer's afternoon. She imagined Dylan's laughter at the bubbling fish and iridescent dragonflies, a breeze stroking her legs and whispering through the trees. Down in the bottom right-hand corner was Charlie's signature, partly obscured by the cream mount within the thick oak frame.

'Charlie, this is … This is brilliant.' She tore her gaze away from the frame to glance at him. 'When did you get time to do this?'

'I started on it when I was finishing the last few pieces for the show. And then I finished it over the past week.'

'It's amazing. And I know where it's going. It's replacing the one in my bedroom.'

He tapped the frame. 'Do you like the mounting? It was Phoebe's idea. I wasn't sure whether you'd prefer it stretched on board or—'

She put the picture on the sofa and wrapped him in a hug. 'I love it,' she whispered. 'It's perfect. Thank you.' She let her chin rest on his shoulder. The skin of his neck was still cool from the outside air but his arms, although they held her loosely, were two warm bands across her back. He must have been helping Ronnie that afternoon because his jumper smelled of cinnamon, sugar and nutmeg. Becky closed her eyes and found herself picturing herself and Charlie on the cosy sofa next to the Station House's crackling open fire, drinking rich hot chocolate and watching snow settling on the windowpanes.

'I'm glad you like it,' he said into her hair.

Becky took a deep breath as she pulled away. Looking at the painting again, and from a distance, it was uncanny how well he had copied Monet's style. It was a shame he wasn't in the picture too. Then again, she supposed in a way he was: the painter was always there, showing the viewer what he could see.

Unable to think of anything else to say that wouldn't come close to gushing, she fell back on a fail-safe. 'Tea?'

'Thought you'd never ask.'

He followed her into the kitchen and leant against the fridge while she boiled and shuffled her way around the room. As she lifted the mugs out of the cupboard she glanced at Charlie's hands. The right one was hidden in his pocket, but the left was by his side, pinned against the fridge. And it was completely bare. The wedding ring had gone. After sixteen years. Wow. What must it be like to be without it?

Not wanting to make fuss about the ring's absence, she got back to the business of making tea and kept her eyes away from him as she asked, 'So am I addressing Mr Handren, eligible bachelor?'

'I don't know about eligible, but Mel filed for the decree absolute a couple of weeks ago. She's still waiting for the final paperwork from the court, but it's all done.'

She nodded and returned the milk to the fridge. 'Speaking of getting things done: did you pick up your tux for tomorrow night?'

'Yes.'

His reply had come through gritted teeth. 'What's wrong with it?' she asked.

'It makes me look ridiculous. But Phoebe says it's fine, so I suppose it'll be all right.'

'I bet you'll look great. Rachel will be pleased.'

Charlie dropped his eyes and replied with a non-committal 'Hmn'.

'What's up, Charlie?'

'You don't understand. You'll be working and can keep a low profile. I have to sit through a fancy dinner with strangers and then get up on stage dressed like a penguin to give a speech!'

Ah. His latest grump was just a case of stage fright. She was relieved it was something relatively simple to deal with, although disappointed his misgivings had nothing to do with Rachel. Becky was still surprised Lady Stone hadn't told Charlie she was attending the event as a guest. A guest accompanied by Virgil. Perhaps Rachel couldn't bear to think about it, much less talk about it.

Giving his tea an extra stir, Becky decided it would be easier not to disillusion Charlie, particularly given that Virgil wasn't one of his favourite people. She didn't want to get into an argument this evening. 'You'll be fine. They'll love your speech, your painting and you,' she said, bringing the teas over to the counter.

'Hmn. Do you have plans for tomorrow?'

'A decent lie-in. Trying not to worry too much. The usual. You?'

'Similar. I'd thought about getting an early night tonight but I don't think I'll sleep much.'

He glared down at his tea as if it were a cup of hemlock he was considering downing in one.

'I doubt I'll sleep well either,' she said. 'The mental lists tend to scroll on their own before a big event. It's difficult to shut them off.' She tapped her nails on her cup and watched his gloomy expression, an idea coming to her. 'Why don't you stay here a while longer? We could see what's on TV or watch a film?'

'Really?' Charlie glanced up and his frown lifted. 'That sounds great. I'll have to get my glasses from—'

'The car.' Becky made a show of rolling her eyes and tutted. 'Honestly. It would save you a lot of trouble if you left a pair here.'

Charlie grinned. 'You know, that's not a bad—'

This time the interruption came from his phone. It shrilled as he took it from his pocket and looked at the screen. 'Sorry. I have to get this. I'll just be a minute.'

Becky nodded and blew on her tea while Charlie retreated to the living room to answer the call. He stopped between the bottom of the stairs and the front door, and rested a hand on the bannister post. While he muttered and nodded, Becky tried to imagine him in the dreaded tuxedo. She prided herself on having a good imagination, but her task was made next to impossible by his sweater. Phoebe had told Becky she was continuing her annual tradition of giving her dad a piece of novelty Christmas clothing, but the teenager's description had failed to do her gift justice. The sweater was bright red and trimmed round the base with large misshapen snowflakes. Charlie had tried to hide this festive detail by tucking the base of the jumper under itself, but it had dropped down at the back, leaving part of the white ring on display. Becky was unable to appreciate the matching decorations on the cuffs because Charlie had rolled the sleeves up to his elbows. This was probably another attempt to hide the pattern, although it had the secondary effect of allowing her to admire his forearms. Unlike her pale skin, which went transparent in winter, Charlie retained his summer runner's tan. He didn't have to worry about being mistaken for a ghost at the ball, a worry which had driven Becky to get the first spray tan of her life the previous day.

Charlie dropped his hand from the bannister and turned towards the front door. The movement made Becky realise she was staring. She shook her head, picked up her own phone and scanned the TV listings. There had to be something worth watching.

Charlie raised his voice to say goodbye to his caller. Still looking at her phone, Becky made her way into the front room. 'Hey. Good news. They're showing *It's A Wonderful Life*. I know we watched it a few weeks ago, but I don't think it's possible to overdose on Jimmy Stewart.'

She smiled and glanced up. Charlie had one arm in his coat sleeve. His expression was pinched, close to pained. 'I'm sorry,' he said. 'I have to go. That was Rachel. She needs me round at her place. Some fiasco with the lighting suppliers for the exhibition. She sounded upset.'

From nowhere, Becky got a new mental image: Charlie and Rachel in front of an open fire. Rachel reclining on the sofa. Charlie sitting on the floor, massaging her bony toes.

She swallowed bile and clenched her fists.

Charlie straightened his coat and grabbed his scarf. Wrapped round his neck, the royal blue band brought out the deep brown of his eyes. It was pristine and the weave was incredibly fine. Becky hadn't noticed it before, but then she had been so worried about his present she couldn't remember if he had been wearing a coat earlier in the evening, let alone a scarf.

She reached out and rubbed the end between her thumb and forefinger, lifting the wispy tassels away from his chest. The touch confirmed her suspicion: cashmere. 'That's a nice scarf. Is it new?'

'A Christmas present from Rachel.'

Of course it was. A perfect colour choice and real cashmere to boot. It probably cost a fortune, while all she'd got him was an amateur photo in a budget frame. Shit. She should have got him a bow tie to go with his ball outfit. But she'd decided against it because it seemed silly to get him something he was likely to only wear once. Dammit. Why couldn't her practical side shut the hell up and take a holiday for once?

She snapped her hand away from the scarf. 'Ah. Of course it is.'

Charlie blinked and looked at her as if she'd spoken in a foreign language. 'Why do you say that?'

She folded her arms across her queasy stomach. 'Oh, nothing. It's ... It's like her: elegant and beautiful.' Tightly wound and cold to the touch too, she thought. But she kept that to herself. 'Right, well, you better get going if she needs you.'

'I'm sorry. You made tea.'

'It's just tea. Another time.' She forced a smile and stepped past him to open the door, her insides turning over as she remembered the exhibition was in little more than a week and the opportunities for her and Charlie to share a drink were slipping away fast.

Outside, the first flakes of snow were falling. A sheer layer of white covered the roof of Charlie's car and a ghostly frozen glow surrounded the street lamp at the end of the drive.

He paused on the doorstep. 'I'm sorry.'

'It's fine. You have work stuff to sort out.'

'At least I know I'll be leaving you in the good company of Jimmy Stewart. And ... I'll see you tomorrow.' His final words were probably meant to be a statement, but sounded more like a question.

'Of course you will.' She patted the top of his arm. 'By this time tomorrow you'll be about to see in the new year having sold the first painting of many and with the woman of your dreams in your arms.' She thought of Charlie's hands on Rachel's clawlike toes again and shivered. 'You'll see.'

'I hope you're right.' He nodded towards the living room. 'You should go in; don't get cold. Goodnight, Becky.'

He turned and made for the car. The icy air wrapped itself around her ankles and she shivered again. Her tummy squirmed and her chest felt tight. She wished Dylan was home. But then he would have been something else for her to worry about and if her guts were acting up already she must be more nervous about the ball than she had thought. Perhaps she should call Lloyd and check he had his side of things under control.

Doubtlessly focussed on racing into Rachel's open arms, Charlie didn't give Becky a second glance as he got into the car and reversed onto the road. Becky gave a parting wave as he accelerated away, leaving her standing alone in the bright frame of the doorway and muttering 'Goodbye, Charlie' to the indifference of the swirling snow.

Chapter 44

The last day of the year began lazily. Becky had a decent lie-in and pottered about in her dressing gown feeling lost without Dylan until lunchtime, when knocking drew her to the front door.

A leering courier, apparently accustomed to finding ladies in their nightwear at midday, brought a large white box out of his van and deposited it on the living room floor.

Having used a knife to slice the box open, she lifted the lid and picked out the envelope lying on top of the mauve tissue paper inside. It contained a black card which carried a brief message in silver script:

Dearest Becky,

A small, belated Christmas gift. Please accept these with my compliments.

I look forward to seeing you in one of them tonight.

Your humble servant,
Lloyd Blake

She peeled back the tissue to uncover three evening gowns. Pinching them out of the box, she draped them over the sofa and stared at them like Goldilocks contemplating bowls of porridge.

The first was a black knee-length dress. It had cap sleeves and dropped to a deep but respectable V at the neck. The skirt was pleated and a thick band of additional fabric pinched the whole structure at the waist.

The second was a fitted, dark green sheath. The shimmering tube of cloth ran all the way to the floor and was designed to hug every lump and bump, leaving them no place to hide.

The last was a ballgown in an off-white fabric, warmed by a faint blush of shimmering pink. Its bodice had wide shoulder bands designed to sit off the shoulder and cling to the top of the arm. The result was a shallow V neckline which skated below the collarbones. This dip was mirrored at the bottom of the bodice, giving the illusion of a cinched waist. Cascading to the floor, the skirt fluted outwards thanks to a number of stiff petticoats. The bodice was plain except for a row of embroidery around the neckline and at the waist. Silver and gold threads formed the delicate and interweaving trails of a dancing procession of stars, each flecked with a few points of bright blue. This same motif was developed on the skirt in a spectacular glittering explosion.

Returning the dresses was not an option. She didn't want to offend Lloyd and, given there was nothing in her wardrobe as suitable, it would be as irrational as it would be ungrateful. Considering the three of them, she dismissed the green as impractical: she was planning to eat and dance. Of the remaining two, Becky's head drew her to the black. It would be flattering and comfy; she had shoes that matched; it was the sensible choice. But her heart drew her to the third dress. This might be her last chance to wear something so flamboyant outside a children's fancy dress party.

She was still undecided when Phoebe arrived at six. The dinner started at eight, but there was a drinks reception from seven. Becky had arranged to meet Virgil there and Phoebe had volunteered to do her hair and make-up before chauffeuring her to the Hall.

Phoebe cast a critical eye over the dresses and was categorical: it had to be the ballgown. Becky responded with a weak protest as Phoebe arranged her hair, a process which involved three electrical appliances, a whole packet of pins and half a can of hairspray. Her stylist then moved on to make-up, another complicated procedure. Becky wriggled with impatience and was told off more than once for fidgeting.

'Remind me. Why can't we do this in front of a mirror?'

'Eyes closed,' Phoebe said, poised to dab another substance onto Becky's eyelid. 'Because we don't want to spoil the big reveal.'

Becky snorted. Phoebe had watched too many makeover shows.

'Now quiet. Almost done.'

When the artist finished her work, she ordered Becky to close her eyes again and steered her to the full-length mirror on the wardrobe door. 'And ... open them!'

Becky blinked. Then stuttered.

'Well?' said Phoebe. 'What do you think?'

Becky lifted a hand towards the mirror. 'Who *is* that?'

The woman in the mirror sparkled. Her soft, glossy curls had been gathered and pinned behind her head. Two spiralling tendrils and some golden wisps framed her face, showcasing her large sapphire eyes. She was lucky enough to have high cheekbones and smooth, flawless skin. And all despite wearing a grey flannel robe.

Phoebe laughed. Becky closed her shiny pink lips and raised her fingers to her new cheekbones. 'How did you do this?'

'Contouring. Jess at school does beauty videos for her YouTube channel. She showed me some stuff and let me borrow her magic kit. Now,' she said, pulling Becky away from the mirror, 'time for the dress.'

'If the law doesn't work out, you should consider beauty school.'

'I'll keep it in mind.' Phoebe moved to the back of the dress and set to work on tightening the complicated corset lacing at the back of the bodice. 'Does my dad think you're working at the ball?' she asked as her fingers looped and pulled.

Becky looked up at the ceiling. 'I'm not sure. I didn't tell him I was.'

'But you didn't tell him you're going with Virgil either?'

Had that last tug been a tad vicious? 'No. But I don't see why he'd care. He'll be busy with Rachel.' Another sharp yank spurred her on to further explanation. 'And I'll be there if he needs help with his speech. I'm not abandoning him.'

'Good.' She threaded the ribbon through another eyelet. 'What's happening with you and Virgil, anyway?'

'Nothing. We're friends.'

'Really?'

'Really.'

'Good.' Phoebe finished her task and came to the front to inspect the results of her work. 'And ... good!' she said, with a note of surprise which Becky tried not to let hurt her feelings.

'You don't think I'm too old to wear this?'

'God, no!' She stooped to help Becky into her silver shoes. 'You sound like Dad. He spent ages fiddling with his bow tie and going on and on about being "too old for this sort of thing".' She stood up, lifted one of Becky's hands for inspection and grinned. 'You used my Christmas present!'

A week staying with her parents, together with the not-so-subtle gift of some expensive hand cream from Phoebe, had given Becky's normally ravaged skin time to heal. Even her finger pads had lost their coarseness. 'Of course I did.'

Phoebe moved onto an inspection of Becky's nails. 'You don't think Dad's too old, do you?'

Becky wondered if she was still talking about the tux, but replied, 'Of course not.'

'I told him he looks good for his age.'

'He looks better than good for his age.'

'Good,' Phoebe said. 'He always says nice things about you too.'

Becky opened her mouth to ask Phoebe to elaborate on her last comment but was silenced by the girl thrusting a silver clutch bag into her hands and spinning her towards the door.

'Enough talking,' Phoebe snapped. 'Let's go. We're late and Dad, um ... I mean *Virgil* will be wondering where you are.'

Chapter 45

Charlie's nerves betrayed him into being perfectly punctual. His taxi arrived at the entrance to Compton Hall at seven precisely, where an equally precise attendant opened its door and gestured for Charlie to enter the building.

He dawdled up the two short flights of stairs leading to the imposing main doors. The three storeys of dark red brick loomed over him and the glass in the rows of tall, white-framed windows shimmered, reflecting the light from the rows of torches lining the path. Originally built in an H-shape, the Hall had lost its two back wings during an eighteenth-century remodel but still conserved the two extending fingers at the front of the building. This meant the main entrance was set back in a courtyard of sorts, walled in on three sides. An optimistic visitor would have seen the arms of the building stretching out to receive him in an embrace; Charlie felt as though he was meandering into the open jaws of a crocodile.

Beyond the doors was the great hall. The floor of the large reception room was black-and-white check and the gleam of the marble tiles suggested they had been cleaned specially for the occasion. Resting on a series of Corinthian columns and accessed via a grand wooden staircase at the end of the room, a first-floor gallery bordered the space. Large gilded frames covered the walls while a series of interlocking plaster ridges divided the ceiling into segments, converging on a central rose which bloomed into an enormous chandelier.

Returning to the great hall from the cloakroom, Charlie took a glass of champagne from a side table and stood behind one of the columns so he could watch the other guests and get his bearings. The rest of the early birds were already huddled in small groups and helping themselves to drinks from trays which weaved among them, held by waiters well-trained in the art of being ubiquitous and invisible.

Rachel was talking to her mother and a couple he didn't recognise. Barbara Stone was as poised and elegant as ever in demure purple velvet. Standing beside her mother, Rachel was wearing a black strapless dress with matching elbow-length gloves. Her hair was sculpted into a smooth cylinder at the back of her head, and an emerald and diamond necklace hung at her neck.

'Beautiful, isn't she?'

An elderly gentleman sporting the most extraordinary white hair Charlie had ever seen had appeared beside him. As thick and stiff as beaten egg white, it had been coaxed into meringue-like waves and crests. Underneath it lurked a matching pair of eyebrows and under them his small, quick eyes flicked between the group in front of them and Charlie.

Charlie nodded and returned his gaze to Rachel.

As he made to walk away, his new companion nudged him with a bony elbow and said, 'Her daughter isn't bad either.' He turned back to wink at Charlie as he made his way over to Barbara Stone. He touched her arm and dipped his head to say something to her in a low voice. Incapable of such subtlety, the lady's head reared up and she stared at Charlie. A few seconds later Rachel was coming towards him, extending her arms in greeting while chiding him for not having found her sooner.

The guests began to arrive in heavy waves. With each new surge Charlie was introduced to the most influential and wealthiest potential patrons. He started to wonder if he had been entered in an artists' version of Crufts and the Stones were hoping to win Best in Show with him as their prize specimen.

❧

Becky arrived ten minutes before dinner. Unfortunately her dream of Compton Hall and its surroundings as a white-coated winter wonderland had been dashed by the arrival of milder temperatures and drizzle. The weather forced her to pinch her skirt up off the damp ground, scurry up the stairs and duck across the threshold. Shivering, she paused by the door to brush a few damp wisps of hair away from her eyes, then headed for the cloakroom.

When she returned to the great hall she used the nearest column as cover while she looked for Virgil. Although the space was packed with the event's full complement of two hundred guests, who were polluting the air with an expensive fog of heavy perfume, she found Charlie straight away. He was flanked by the Stone ladies and, from his pained expression, she guessed he was being involved in schmoozing.

Several ways of getting him out of there occurred to her. Extracting him personally wasn't one of them; her almost-white gown made her a beacon in a dark sea of wine, navy and black outfits. She was weighing up her options when a smooth hand brushed the top of her arm.

'Becky, I'm so sorry I'm late. You look divine.' Virgil pecked her on both cheeks and then stood back to take her in.

'Don't worry. I just got here.'

'Clever girl. Get here too early and you'll be cornered by a gaggle of old bores.' He pointed to the centre of the room. 'Which is exactly what has happened to your Charlie. Aren't you simply aching to charge over there and rescue him?'

Becky lifted her hand to Virgil's sleeve, turning him towards her and his eyes away from Charlie. 'You look handsome as always,' she said, running her fingers over the soft cloth of his jacket. Cut to flatter his slender frame, the impeccable tuxedo had to be a recent purchase. 'What have you been up to? I haven't seen you for ages.'

'Many things. You may remember me mentioning I work for my uncle? The old man's finally loosening his grip on the family business. Plans to retire in the new year. Properly this time. Seems open-heart surgery was the final push he needed. He's planning a cruise with a lady friend, apparently. Anyway, I'm to take over. And that involves endless hours with lawyers.' He shuddered. 'But it'll all be worth it.' A tray bobbed past and Virgil snapped to attention. 'I'm sorry, where are my manners? Would you like a drink?'

'Some water would be lovely, thank you.'

'The finest champagne it is then. Back in a mo.' He patted her on the elbow and set off towards the back of the hall.

Becky sighed. She was already jittery and knew champagne wasn't a good idea, but she daren't draw further attention to herself by calling Virgil back. As the only woman who hadn't got the memo about the navy and black dress code, she was already painfully noticeable.

Her skin prickling under the critical glances of the other guests, she retreated into the shadows of the nearest corner, opened her bag and took out her phone.

～

Charlie was doing his best to appear interested as he was presented to one art collector after another. And, as if being treated like a prize poodle weren't bad enough, Rachel insisted on whispering the net worth of each collector as they approached, something he found deeply unsettling. Praying for a reason to escape, he searched the shadows, looking past the suits and gowns for a familiar figure in black.

After completing two sweeps of the room, his eye was drawn to a shape in the corner. He squinted. The colour of the clothing was wrong, but he doubted anyone else was checking her phone so obsessively. He fumbled in his breast pocket for his glasses and, as Becky came into focus, he relaxed into his first genuine smile of the evening. Glancing at Rachel and the pots of money she was trying to crack, he struggled to think of a polite excuse to abandon them.

His thoughts were alternating between escape and Becky's choice of dress, when Virgil shimmered into view. The handsome young man, wearing his tuxedo like a second skin, extended a skinny wrist and presented Becky with a drink. Charlie frowned. What was going on? They weren't together, were they?

The dinner gong sounded and guests filed into the grand saloon, passing through the double doors under the staircase. Charlie didn't take his eyes off Becky, who was wrapping her arm around Virgil's, ready to go and find their table.

'John!' Charlie jumped as Rachel barked in his ear and dug her satin-covered nails into his arm. She was also watching Becky and Virgil, pursing her lips and wrinkling her nose as if she had been offended by a nasty smell. 'John, dear, we should go into dinner. And remember,' she said as she reached up and pulled his glasses off, 'no glasses. You should have worn contacts like I said.'

As Rachel returned his glasses to his pocket, Virgil and Becky passed by. Her dress was so different and the lacing at the back was … extraordinary. She must have needed help doing that up. She would probably need help unlacing it too.

Virgil and Becky paused in front of the seating plan by the entrance to the saloon and shared a joke. Charlie clenched his fists. If she did need help out of the dress, it looked like bloody Virgil Locke was first in line to volunteer.

At his side, Rachel sniffed. 'I must speak to my mother about this year's guest list.' She tugged at her gloves, grasped Charlie's arm and steered him into the saloon.

Chapter 46

The guests were divided between sixteen circular tables, much to Becky's relief. With twelve of them spaced around the generous circumference, it was unlikely she would be able to hear Charlie and Rachel's conversation, let alone be drawn into it.

The meal passed without incident. Becky enjoyed the food immensely and Virgil was at his witty best, amusing her with more of his outlandish tales. She almost forgot Charlie and Rachel were sitting on the opposite side of the table and the few times she did glance in their direction they were in conversation with the guests within their earshot. By the time dessert arrived, she was already full, but prepared to find space for her mini chocolate cheesecake.

She checked everyone at the table had a plate before picking up her fork. The biscuit base was buttery heaven, and the chocolate was smooth, sweet and beyond divine. She savoured the next bite, closing her eyes and focusing on the flavour. Smiling, she sighed with pleasure.

When she opened her eyes it was a jolt to find Charlie staring at her. It was his penetrating artist's stare; a look both hot and cold. Warm fingers of embarrassment tickled her neck. She dropped her gaze to the table and, when she dared glance up again, Charlie was absorbed in conversation with a couple sitting to his left.

'Are you all right?' asked Virgil. 'Those aren't tears, are they? I know my jokes this evening aren't my best material, but they're not that dire, surely?'

'It's these damn contacts,' said Becky, raising a finger to her lower eyelid and rubbing gently. 'I don't blink enough, my eyes dry out, they hurt, I blink too much to compensate …'

'Here.' He offered her a handkerchief. 'You should see to it or people will begin to think I've upset you.'

Virgil returned to chatting up the blonde sitting the other side of him while Becky dabbed at the corners of her eyes. Turning the cloth over to make sure she hadn't marked it with mascara, she saw three neatly stitched initials: *KVL*. That made sense. Virgil didn't strike her as a handkerchief kind of guy: it must have been his father's.

Tear ducts back under control, Becky decided this would be a good time to find Ronnie and then call her parents. She polished off the rest of her dessert and murmured an excuse in Virgil's direction as she picked up her bag and slipped out of her seat.

Heads turned to follow her as she tried to sneak out of the room. Becky regretted not choosing the first dress and regretted it more when she saw her best friend dressed in comfortable, forgiving black.

Ronnie was standing in the middle of the great hall,

hovering protectively next to the cake: a four-tier cappuccino tower, strewn with golden sugar paste roses and banded in matching silk ribbon. It was installed on its chariot, ready to be wheeled into the saloon. The plan was its grand entrance would grab everyone's attention for the announcement of tea and coffee to be served out in the great hall. Once the guests were out of the saloon, the staff would be able to pack away two-thirds of the tables, leaving space for the dance floor. The stage would also be readied for the band and auction.

Ronnie looked up as Becky approached. 'Wow! You don't even look like yourself!'

'Thanks a lot.'

'You know what I mean. Do a twirl.'

Becky did as she was told. 'Is Mike here?'

'On standby inside to take pictures of the cake. Then he has the pleasure of circulating for the rest of the evening and of course he has to take pictures during the auction.' Two waiters melted away from one of the side tables and appeared beside the trolley. 'Sorry,' said Ronnie, 'but it's time to go.' She looked over Becky's shoulder and smiled. 'Anyway, there's someone else here to see you.'

Charlie had emerged from the saloon. He stood aside as one of the waiters opened the door to let Ronnie and the cake through. Ronnie nodded at Charlie as she flounced past, head held high.

The door swung shut behind her and they were left alone. Although he hadn't relished the prospect of having to wear one, Becky had to admit Charlie could certainly rock a tuxedo. 'Hello.'

He shuffled towards her. 'Hi.'

Becky fiddled with the clasp of her bag. 'I should go and call my parents.'

Charlie stopped two floor tiles away from her, leaving him standing on white, her on black. 'Dylan's fine. You should try to enjoy the party. Given it's one you're not working.'

She nodded, opening and closing her bag. Why hadn't she just told him she was coming as a guest? Though she was sure there had been good reasons, under the weight of Charlie's stare, none of them came to mind.

∽

Charlie noted Becky's discomfort and added it to the list of things that night which were not going as he had imagined. The food had been wonderful, but Rachel insisted on knocking back wine as if it were water and became more boring and spiteful with every sip. She and her friends harped on about a number of subjects Charlie had no interest in, including the other guests and their various social and sartorial faux pas. As Becky had left the table Rachel had made another crack about how staff could now get onto the guest list for one of Compton's most exclusive events. As a few others at the table had joined her in bemoaning this decline in standards he had got to his feet without bothering to excuse himself and made for the exit.

However, while Rachel was irritating, Becky's behaviour had been painful. Sitting opposite her, he'd had an excellent view of how hilarious she found her date. Although she was avoiding alcohol, she found Virgil intoxicating, blushing and giggling as he whispered in her ear. Charlie's

334

palms itched every time Virgil casually brushed his hand against hers. And when Becky lifted a napkin to wipe a stray speck of sauce from Virgil's upper lip, the delicious food in Charlie's mouth turned to ash.

Only a few weeks ago she said she was immune to Virgil's charms. Had she had a change of heart? Had Virgil's disgustingly young, good-looking face and irritatingly eloquent charm won her over?

And if Virgil weren't enough, there had been her reaction to the cheesecake, which had put him in the ridiculous position of feeling jealous of a dessert.

But now he had her all to himself.

He waved a hand towards her dress. 'You look nice.'

Oh, brilliant, he thought. Virgil would certainly be able to do better than that.

Becky shrugged. 'Thanks. And you look great. Positively dapper, dashing, debonair. Any other word of your choice beginning with *D*.'

He gave her a small, nostalgic smile. 'How long have you been thinking about that one?'

'Since I saw you,' she replied and then stuttered, 'This evening. Since I saw you this evening. Obviously.'

'Do you think so?' He winced as he pulled at his lapels. 'You don't think it's ridiculous?'

'Not at all!' She stepped forward to straighten his bow tie. 'In fact, I would go as far to say the tux gives you an air of 007.'

'Which one?'

'Connery, of course.'

～

Becky was delighted when her comment caused Charlie to smile and pull himself up an inch. Whatever the reason for his initial iciness, a thaw was setting in. And just in time. The doors of the saloon opened and guests poured towards them, eager for a sobering drink and some sugary food before they hit the bar hard.

'Here they come,' she said, pulling Charlie aside to save him from being trampled. 'You should get back to your date. And I'd make sure Rachel gets some cake and definitely some coffee.' She smiled. Not all of Rachel's comments had failed to reach her ears during dinner.

'Rachel doesn't like cake.'

And that was the final nail in a coffin which had been pretty firmly shut already. She grasped Charlie's arm and whispered, 'Doesn't like cake?' He shook his head. 'Not even chocolate?'

'I guess not. She didn't touch her dessert.'

Becky gathered up the front of her dress. 'Excuse me,' she said and turned towards the saloon. The urge to run was overwhelming as she pictured a delicate morsel of chocolate heaven being swept into a bin by the catering staff. She made it two steps when a firm hand on her upper arm pulled her back.

'Becky, wait a second. I know you've probably got to deal with a chocolate emergency, but I wanted to say something.'

He was making a joke, but he was biting the inside of his cheek and frowning as if delivering news of a sudden death.

She turned back, nodding to let him know to continue.

'I wanted to say thank you for your Christmas present.'

'You already said thank you.'

'I know, but I was talking to Phoebe about it and, well, I don't think I told you how much I appreciated it.'

'It's OK—'

'No, it's not.' His raised voice and the firmness of his tone made Becky sway back onto her heels. Charlie exhaled loudly and ran a hand over his mouth. 'I find it hard to say … To express …' His fingers splayed, he raised his hand to the centre of his chest and half circled his wrist in short, sharp movements, but still the words didn't come.

Becky frowned as she noted the tension in his knuckles and, without thinking, she covered his hand with her own, stroking his fingers until they relaxed. She dipped her head to catch his eye and curled her lips into what she hoped was a reassuring smile.

Charlie closed his eyes and took a deep breath. When the words finally came, they were barely more than a murmur. 'I love your present. It's the best thing I received this year. In fact, it's the best gift I've been given in a long time. Thank you.'

She was glad he kept his eyes shut long enough for her to close her mouth and blink the surprise out of her eyes. 'You're very welcome.'

Charlie pulled his hand away from hers and ran it through his hair. 'I'll let you get back to your chocolate emergency.'

She had turned away again when he said her name and she glanced back. Charlie was biting his lip and his hands were in his pockets. 'Please don't tell Phoebe what I said. She tries her best with her Christmas gifts …'

Imagining the number of times Charlie must have struggled to feign delight at cartoon snowmen on socks, ties and sweaters, Becky stifled a smile. 'Your secret's safe with me. Now, if you'll excuse me,' she said, bobbing an ironic curtsey as she picked up the front of her dress again, 'I have to see a man about a dessert.'

Chapter 47

When Becky got back to the table, half of Rachel's abandoned dessert had already been eaten.

Lloyd raised his fork to acknowledge her. As Becky returned his greeting, he pushed the seat next to him away from the table and slid the remains of the cheesecake in front of her. Not waiting for a formal invitation, Becky sat, grabbed what had been Charlie's fork and got to work.

Lloyd let her enjoy the cake, contemplating her in silence while dozens of waiting staff cleared tables in a series of well-practised manoeuvres. When the last bite had dissolved away she sipped some water and licked her lips. It was time they put all their cards on the table.

'Thank you for the dresses. Why did you send them?'

'For my sins, I've been working on an extra project since Geoff and Tamara's wedding back in November. I saw some things there that inspired me.'

He winked at her and something about the gesture clicked the last piece of the puzzle into place. The old devil. How had she not put the two of them together before?

'You're Virgil's uncle.'

He held up his hands. 'Technically I'm his great-uncle and only by marriage. But when I first met the boy I saw his potential straight away. Nine years old and already capable of twisting anyone around his little finger. Talent like that needs to be cultivated and given an outlet and, with no children of my own, I thought I might be able to hand my businesses over to the boy one day.'

'And you also take an interest in his personal life?'

'Naturally. I want him to be happy. And while I would have been delighted if he'd had the sense to fall for a gracious lady such as your good self, it appears I have also passed on to him a weakness for a flintier kind of woman.'

Becky ran a finger through the chocolate sauce on the plate and licked it clean. 'And how is your project progressing?'

'Between you and me,' he said, glancing over his shoulder, 'I think it's hit a dead end. The boy will only be satisfied with Barbara's girl and I don't think I can be much use there.'

'I think I can. Would you mind if I had a word with him?'

'Not at all. And perhaps you could talk to him about the job we have in mind for you.'

'A job?'

'You have impressed me. You and your work. And not only what I've seen myself: Kevin told me about what you did at Georgie's wedding. Your skills need to be put to proper use and rewarded appropriately. My nephew is still a young man and it would put my mind at ease if someone like you were working with him.'

'You want me to spy on him?'

'Keep an eye on him. Help him. Be the Mephistopheles to his Faustus but make sure the devil doesn't get near his soul.' He pushed a finger along a spectacular eyebrow. 'My nephew has many fine talents, but he tends to approach situations with hammer and tongs when they need scalpel and tweezers. Your advice and assistance would be invaluable to him.'

Becky mulled this over. She still had no real idea of what it was that Lloyd and Virgil did. Then again, a serious job offer from a wealthy man was not something a modern Mephistopheles would ever knock back without careful thought. 'And would I be wielding this scalpel full-time?'

'Part-time. We thought that might fit better with your other commitments. But of course a generous monthly retainer would be involved. I believe in the value of a steady income.'

She nodded. This was definitely an interesting offer. 'Thank you. I'll talk to Virgil. And about the job too.'

'Thank you, Becky. Now everything is in your capable hands, I plan to enjoy the rest of the evening.' He got up, resting one hand on the table and using the other to gesture towards the stage. 'The band are almost ready; I have been waiting for over thirty years to dance with a particular lady and she is not getting away from me tonight.'

'Are you sure that's wise? What about your health?' She put her hand over his. 'Whatever you might think, open-heart surgery is not a "trifling procedure".'

'My dear lady, I have had over six weeks of excellent rest. I have my doctor's permission to do the deed. I very much doubt he would object to me dancing.'

'If you're sure. But before you go to put your surgeon's work through its paces, there's one more thing I need to know.'

'Yes, my dear?'

She frowned and wrinkled her nose. 'Kevin?'

Lloyd chuckled. 'The boy prefers to use his middle name. He feels "Kevin" is insufficiently intimidating. Personally, I've never got on with "Virgil".' He put a hand on her shoulder and lowered his voice. 'When he's trying to impress women he tells them the name he goes by stems from his mother's devotion to classical literature.' He snorted. 'Utter nonsense. That girl was never one to be found in a library. She was always glued to the idiot box. And as I recall she never missed an episode of *Thunderbirds*.'

Chapter 48

After Lloyd had shuffled out of the saloon, Becky settled into her chair. Chuckling and drumming her fingers on the table, she watched swift hands remove plates and glasses to leave the table empty and Becky in the unusual position of being at a party with nothing to do.

She took the opportunity to appreciate her surroundings properly and finally realised why they hadn't filled her with awe when she had first come in. The large banqueting hall at the South Compton Country Club was a passable copy of the grand saloon, although the original was more opulent. Its intricate ceiling mouldings dripped in an excess of gilding, the windows were dressed with crimson curtains restrained by gold brocade cuffs and the walls were studded with rococo frames holding instantly forgettable paintings.

She was staring up at the central ceiling decoration, a group of celestial figures who seemed thoroughly bored with reclining in the clouds, when she heard footsteps approaching and detected a familiar spice-laden aftershave.

'I got you a piece of the cake,' Virgil said, handing her a plate and then a cup and saucer. 'And tea too.'

She picked up the cup and took a long sip as Virgil sat down. 'Thank you. This is the best date I've ever been on.'

'God, I hope that's not true.'

Several other guests had returned to the room and were filling the air with an escalating buzz. The band tuned up and couples lined the edges of the dance floor, eyeing each other nervously, wondering who would be the first two to tango.

With a flourish, the conductor led the band into their first number: 'Fly Me to the Moon'. Virgil sagged. 'Ugh! Could they have selected anything more turgid?'

Becky chewed her cake. She liked the song but, as it wasn't making Virgil run to the dance floor, she figured this would a good moment for a little chat about Rachel. Trying to work out how to broach the subject, she finished her cake and was washing it down with the last of the tea when Virgil said, 'You know Rachel doesn't like cake? Or she doesn't eat it. I suspect she does like it but her mother told her it was vulgar to eat anything which doesn't necessitate the use of a full set of cutlery.'

He sighed and Becky noted this wasn't the usual sound of despair or weariness but one of affectionate longing; he found her quirks endearing. Blimey. It must be love.

It was funny how a name was capable of having such an impact on the way you viewed someone. Thinking of the man next to her as Kevin, he seemed less confident and polished. But also more approachable and sympathetic.

'Virgil, will you let me give you some advice?'

Now came the look of despair: a man lost at sea without provisions or hope of rescue. 'Absolutely. In fact, if you could tell me what to do, I think I'd prefer it.'

'In that case, take Rachel to one side and tell her. Do it tonight. Tell her you've been following her since New York. Tell her you bought a bloody gallery to make her happy. That it's been crushing you to be around her since she broke it off. That you want to be with her.' She smiled and tapped the back of his hand. 'And then fire her.'

Her final suggestion was met with a rapid intake of breath. 'I was with you up to "fire her".'

Becky brushed crumbs off her fingers and pointed towards the dance floor. Waltzing between the other dancers were Lloyd Blake and Barbara Stone. They were both wearing small smiles of contentment as they glided in perfect harmony, a misstep or a crushed toe an impossibility. 'I think,' said Becky, 'that Mrs Stone is about to join your uncle in retirement. And if the lady is planning to go on a long holiday she can't leave the family business in just anyone's hands. And as Rachel had been in her mother's good books lately I would imagine she already has another job offer coming to her.'

Virgil nodded slowly. She continued. 'Perhaps, if you'd like to be sure before you fire her, you might know someone with some influence over Mrs Stone who could maybe suggest Rachel be given the job of running the family gallery.' She let her gaze wander back over to the dance floor, where Lloyd was spinning a giggling Barbara into a twirl.

When she returned her attention to Virgil, he was grinning like a fox who had found the door to a coop of plump, lazy chickens wide open. 'I think you might be onto something,' he said. Rubbing his hands together, he stood and glanced towards the door. 'And I believe I will take your advice. But, right now …' he paused and extended a hand towards Becky, uncurling his long, smooth fingers, '… I think it's time we danced.'

She guessed Rachel had come back into the room and this was his last chance to needle her. Or, assuming things would go well with Rachel later, he might be viewing this as his last dance with another woman. But whatever his motivation, she wasn't about to say no. Lloyd had promised her a dance but she doubted he would be able to tear himself away from Barbara. This might be her only chance.

'I'd be delighted,' she said, letting him lead her to the dance floor. 'I have to thank you for helping your uncle and me with the auction. And I believe you have to offer me a job?'

'You're welcome. But I think we should leave talk of business until the new year.' He grinned and put a hand on the middle of her back. 'Let's dance.'

❧

Meanwhile, Charlie was in hell.

The auction was getting closer and he could no longer ignore his nerves. It didn't help he had nothing to distract him. He was stuck at the back of the room between Rachel and three middle-aged women he guessed were art buyers. He based his assumption on how Rachel pandered to them, giggling at unfunny jokes and agreeing with opinions which could be described as old-fashioned at best and bigoted at worst. Not having heard their names when Rachel gave him the briefest of introductions, he came to think of them as Carmine, Olive and Sepia, from the colour of their dresses.

And now he was being treated to the sight of Virgil dancing with Becky. Although he saw less dancing and more Virgil putting his hands all over her. He closed his ears to the chatter of the women around him and focused on the one couple who interested him. Their smiles didn't falter once, although Virgil seemed distracted and glanced over in Charlie's direction a few times.

The band changed tempo and dancers stepped on and off the floor. This left Becky and Virgil temporarily exposed in the middle of the space. With the lull in noise from the band, Charlie found his attention being drawn back to the conversation around him.

'I, for one, have never seen her before,' said Carmine.

'You wouldn't have,' said Rachel. 'She would usually be working at an event such as this. But it appears Cinderella has found her way into the ball tonight.'

The three Shades snorted at Rachel's wit.

'So you know her, Rachel dear?' asked Sepia.

'She is currently acting as Mr Handren's agent so, unavoidably, our paths have crossed.'

All eyes turned towards Charlie and he could imagine what they were thinking. Poor man, unable to make sound business choices. Thank goodness he had Rachel to take him in hand.

Reproving looks given, they turned their attention back to Rachel and further gossip.

'However, she is here this evening. And with Mr Locke,' said Sepia.

Rachel sniffed as she pulled at her gloves and flexed her fingers. 'Yes. Although, as I understand it, their being here together is more business than pleasure.'

'How so?' asked Olive.

Charlie dropped any pretence of not listening and joined the others in waiting for Rachel to explain.

'Mr Locke has always had an … *interesting* sense of humour. When he and Ms Watson were negotiating the terms under which the Coulson would host Mr Handren's highly anticipating exhibition, he made dinner with Ms Watson part of the deal.'

The Shades raised their eyebrows in unison and tutted their disapproval. They looked up as Becky and Virgil completed another lap of the floor, chatting and laughing as they went. The Shades sneered at the couple, but Charlie was no longer sure what he was watching. Contrary to his previous impression, the dancers were a respectable distance apart and Virgil's hand was safely stuck to Becky's upper back. Becky was in the driving seat, leading her partner out of corners and avoiding collisions.

'I take it she is unattached?' asked Carmine.

'She has no husband. Although she has a young son,' said Rachel with undisguised relish.

'Divorced?' was the immediate response from Sepia. Her face then shifted to mock sympathy. 'Widowed?'

'No,' said Rachel. 'Never married, as I understand it.'

'My goodness!' came the collective reply.

It fell to Olive to ask the only remaining question, as indecorous as it was. 'Do you know who the father is?'

They held their breath, and Charlie guessed they were hoping for the dirty thrill of greater scandal. Rachel brushed her hair over her shoulder and, staring at the dance floor, said, 'I don't know who the father is. And I doubt she does either.'

That did it. He'd put up with Rachel's drunken bullying all night, but she had stretched his patience to breaking point and he was not about to stand by while she spread malicious, ill-formed nonsense about a woman who was worth ten of her. As she opened her mouth to continue, his hand shot out and grabbed her wrist. She gasped and looked up at him, her eyes wide with surprise. Charlie hoped his own glare told her he was exercising great restraint by squeezing, instead of crushing, every delicate bone in her arm.

'But Rachel,' he said through gritted teeth, 'you do know the father.'

The Shades bristled and snickered at Charlie's sudden intervention. 'She does?' they chorused.

Keeping a firm grip on Rachel's wrist, Charlie turned his attention to the trio. 'Of course she does.' He smiled. 'It's me.' Their stunned expressions were gratifying and took the edge off his anger, but he still thought it best to beat a hasty retreat. 'Now, if you'll excuse me, I have to ask Ms Watson to dance.'

He gave the three witches a curt nod, threw Rachel's wrist aside as if it were soaked in blood and stalked away, leaving Rachel to cover his departure.

Chapter 49

Out on the dance floor, Becky was enjoying herself. Virgil had made her laugh so much she had developed a stitch and had to pull over. While they waited for her to recover, they debated a topic of national, if not international, importance.

'No contest,' said Virgil. '"Nobody Does it Better".'

'Nooo!'

'Come on! You have to agree with me on this one!'

'I agree it's a terrific song. But, ironically enough, it's not the best. The best Bond theme, by a country mile, is—'

'"Live and Let Die".'

They both turned towards the source of the interruption. Charlie was standing a few feet away with his hands in his pockets.

'Exactly,' said Becky.

'Ugh!' said Virgil in mock disgust. 'I don't understand you people.' His gaze danced between Charlie and Becky, and there was a hint of a smile on his lips as he said, 'Well that's left me desperate for a drink.' He moved towards Charlie and put a hand on his back to encourage him towards Becky. 'I'm sure you'll take care of Becky for me, won't you?'

'Excuse me!' Becky crossed her arms and glared at him.

Virgil grinned. 'I think that means you should ask the lady if she would like to dance. I'm getting out of here before I say anything else to annoy her. I'll leave you two to discuss the finer points of sexual politics.' He winked at Becky, turned and said to Charlie, 'Good luck.'

As Virgil sauntered away, Charlie and Becky squared up. He held out his right hand to her. 'Would you do me the honour of this dance?' he asked with a dusting of sarcasm.

She blinked, let him wait a while before she took his hand and, mimicking the overly open vowels of the majority of the people around them, drawled, 'Charmed, I'm sure.'

It took less than a minute for Becky to appreciate Charlie's dance skills. He had helped Phoebe practise her steps for years and, comparing him to Virgil, Becky couldn't help but notice the difference this made. He steered them in the right direction and in time to the music. The hold was also comfortable: he wasn't a lazy partner who dropped the weight of his raised arm into her hand. His other hand was in the middle of her back, resting below the bow at the top of the corset lacing.

After their first complete circuit, she relaxed her shoulders and stopped anticipating collisions. She hummed along to the music, and let her eyes wander beyond their immediate surroundings in time to see Virgil leading Rachel out of the room. She smiled, and this drew Charlie's attention back to her face.

'What's so funny?'

'Hmn? Oh nothing. Something Virgil said.'

'You two are getting on well.'

She looked up at him. His lips had all but disappeared. 'What's bothering you, Charlie?'

'Is it true you agreed to go out with him to get the Coulson for the show?'

Ah. Another cat was out of the bag; something for which Becky guessed she had to thank Rachel. Again.

She ran her tongue over her teeth and glanced up the ceiling while planning her response. 'Yes, that's true. But ...' She raised a finger off his shoulder to stop his eyebrow climbing over the top of his head. 'That makes it sound a lot creepier than it was. I agreed to dinner and I got to choose where and when. I planned to leave it so long he would forget about it, but then I got to know him and it turns out he's one of the good guys.'

Charlie's lips were starting to reappear and his eyebrow was settling.

'But I'm not his type and he's not mine. Like I told you before: I'm immune to good-looking cads.'

'You said "scoundrels".'

'Well those too.'

She bit the inside of her lip. Why was she always having to defend herself? She didn't see anyone else using the dance floor as an alternative to the interrogation chamber.

As the song finished, Lloyd and Barbara completed a dramatic spin and then left the floor arm-in-arm, muttering to each other in a broken, private shorthand. 'I think Barbara's surprising everyone tonight.'

'Barbara,' thought Becky, as she observed Charlie watching the departing couple. On first-name terms with the mother-in-law already.

He snapped his gaze back and caught her staring at him. 'What?'

She flinched. 'What do you mean?'

'You're giving me that look.'

'What look?'

'The "I wonder if I should tell Charlie what I'm thinking" look.'

Oh crap. That was a look?

The band's trumpet player scraped his chair back and ambled to the front of the stage. He swaggered in the spotlight and Becky half expected him to spin the horn on his finger and blow imaginary smoke away from the top of it. Instead, he signalled to the double bass and flautists to begin. Soon the pianist joined them to complete the familiar introduction. Becky beamed as the trumpet player grabbed his solo with both lungs. She put her left hand back in its place on Charlie's shoulder and let him lead her into the dance.

The music swelled in volume and, without breaking their smooth swaying motion, Charlie dropped his mouth closer to Becky's ear. 'So are you going to tell me what you were thinking?'

Lost in "La Vie en Rose", Becky blinked her eyes open. 'Oh, all right.' She examined the ceiling, searching for a good place to begin. It was harder than usual. She was distracted by the music. And by how comfortably her right hand lay in Charlie's left. A perfect fit.

'Becky? It's not highly confidential, is it?'

She lowered her gaze to meet his. The bottom half of Charlie's face was as grave as usual, but she could swear the top half was mocking her. He had nothing less than a twinkle in his eye. A damn twinkle! And what was worse, it suited him.

She narrowed her eyes. 'No, it's not.'

'Highly classified, then? For your eyes only? Burn after reading?'

A society ball was not the place to elbow your dancing partner in the ribs so she squeezed his hand instead. 'Shut up or I won't tell you.'

'I'm sorry.' His tone was serious but the bloody twinkle was still laughing at her. He lowered his lips to her ear again. 'Please carry on. But don't self-destruct after ten seconds.'

To make her reluctance to indulge him clear, she huffed and took a deep breath before beginning. 'The story goes that after many years in an unhappy marriage, Barbara Stone fell in love with a good-looking scoundrel.' She paused to raise an eyebrow and make sure he'd picked up on her purposely irritating choice of words. 'Unfortunately when he disappointed her, her heart turned to solid rock. And she stayed thoroughly miserable until her equally miserable husband had the good grace to die and cheer her up.'

'She's certainly cheerful tonight.'

'Ah. That's because a reunion between her and the old flame appears to be on the cards. And the latest is—'

Charlie twirled her under his arm and the rest of her sentence disappeared into a gasp just as the trumpet soloist stepped aside for the singer to take their place at the microphone. While it wasn't a particularly fast spin, she hadn't seen it coming and she was a little giddy as he pulled her back into hold in time to negotiate a tricky corner. During the manoeuvre, Charlie readjusted his right arm to encircle more of Becky's lower back. They were so close Becky could feel the rise and fall of his chest. If she moved her head slightly, they would be dancing cheek to cheek.

Still feeling light-headed and having forgotten all about local gossip, she closed her eyes. Charlie's breath was slow and steady, a solid rhythm beneath the tickling melody which drifted from the piano keys. She inhaled the lingering hint of his best aftershave and imagined how his closely shaven cheek would be soft and warm …

She snapped her eyes open and her head upright. Fortunately Charlie was looking over her shoulder and didn't seem to have noticed her slip. In an attempt to fight the urge to let her head dip towards his, she started to sing the final lines of the song quietly to herself. She was surprised when Charlie joined in, confirming his vocal talents extended beyond rock versions of Bonnie Tyler's greatest hits.

As the last note faded they joined the rest of the dancers in giving a well-deserved round of applause to the trumpet player who thrilled Becky by spinning the instrument round his finger twice and blowing imaginary smoke away from it.

∽

A few dances later the band skipped off the stage for their break and the auctioneer's rostrum was placed in the centre of the platform. It was nearly time for Charlie's big moment, so he and Becky withdrew to the backstage area where he could practise his speech.

In the dim, narrow space behind the red curtains hanging from the lighting gantry, Charlie marched up and down running through his lines. After a couple of minutes, Becky stepped in before he made either of them dizzy. 'Charlie, Charlie. Stop. It's fine.' She laid a hand on his chest. 'But remember to put your glasses on at some point.'

'Why?'

'Because, as I've already explained, we're not only selling a painting. We're selling...'

'Me.' Charlie lifted his eyes and huffed like a grumpy teenager being reminded to brush his hair. 'I know.'

Becky nodded and used the tip of her finger to part the curtains an inch. Through her spyhole, she watched the auctioneer crawl into place behind the rostrum and the first lot arrive on stage. It was time to take her place out front. 'You'll be great.' She straightened his bow tie. 'And remember the glasses. I know you think it's stupid but, if it makes you feel better about it, this will probably be the last time you have to put up with me pushing you around.'

She made to walk away, but Charlie caught her hand. His lips parted but no words came out. And right then, Becky was back on his doorstep in June, looking into lonely eyes pleading for help.

'Why?' he said. 'Where are you going?'

'Well, with the show coming up, this job will be over. And, if you can believe it, Virgil's offered me a new one.'

Charlie took a sharp intake of breath and released her hand. 'Of course he has.'

'You don't need pushy Becky any more, Charlie. You're all set, so I move on. Like Mary Poppins.'

That got a lopsided smile. 'What, practically perfect in every way?'

'Oh, most definitely.' She rolled her eyes. 'That's *so* me.'

'I didn't mean it, you know. About you being pushy.'

'It doesn't matter.'

'It does. It was just something I said because I kept having to field questions about you and me I wasn't prepared to answer.'

Right, she thought. What in the world did that mean?

A buzzing came from inside Becky's bag. Apologising, she retrieved her phone. A message from Lloyd: it was time for her to get out front.

She looked up. Charlie was staring at the curtains as if they were the fine line between him and a grisly death. Becky brushed his fingers with hers to get his attention. 'It's time, Charlie. I have to go. You'll be fine. I promise.'

'Of course. You should go. Goodbye, Becky. And ...' He put his hands in his pockets and took a step back. 'Thank you. Whatever happens out there, thank you for everything.'

Chapter 50

Becky wriggled her way round to the back of the crowd in front of the stage. She located Lloyd, who nodded as she tiptoed into place beside him.

'Your man's due on any second,' he said. 'Ah! Here it comes.'

Two members of the catering staff carried the painting onto the stage and stood holding it. This was overkill. It was barely one and a half feet square and Becky could have held it above her head with one hand. But, of course, having two people carry it and stand as human easels made it seem so much grander and more valuable.

She couldn't recall having seen this one before. Reminiscent of a fireworks display, it depicted an explosion of colour. The flames reached such great temperatures in places they burned blue, suggesting the coexistence of white cold and heat.

Charlie stepped onto the stage. As he launched into his speech, Lloyd muttered, 'Have you had a chance to talk to Virgil about the job?'

Without taking her eyes off Charlie, she said, 'Not yet. But I think my advice on the other subject has done some good.'

Up on stage, Charlie had put on his glasses. Becky grinned as she heard a murmur of appreciation ripple among the female members of the audience. Perhaps Charlie heard the positive reaction too, because he left them on, even when he received an enthusiastic round of applause and stepped to the edge of the stage.

The auctioneer reminded everyone that Charlie's exhibition would be opening the following Thursday. Obligation fulfilled, he glanced down at the notes he had been passed earlier and, from the resulting height of his eyebrows, Becky knew it was the first time he had bothered to read them. 'Ladies and gentlemen,' he said in a nasal whine. 'We have already had considerable interest in this item. I have several commission bids on the books and can start the bidding at forty thousand pounds.'

Only two people in the room failed to join the collective gasp. Instead, Lloyd and Becky shared a moment of smugness; they, together with Virgil, were responsible for the commission bids.

The next few minutes were glorious as the pre-bids had the desired effect. By the time the gavel fell, the bid was at sixty-four thousand pounds. Becky and Lloyd indulged in a quick hug. The reaction of the other guests was both congratulatory and derisory; such a large charitable donation had to be publically applauded, but there was also a jealous sneer at the inflated amount paid. A tipsy fool and her ex-husband's money were apparently easily parted.

Charlie bounded down from the stage to shake the winner's hand. Becky watched, and although her face hurt from smiling, there was a lump in her throat. The man accepting congratulations from a roomful of strangers had shaken off all traces of his defensive shell. This was the Charlie she sometimes saw on Thursday nights, roaring with laughter at Monty Python or sneakily brushing away a tear as George Bailey's friends rallied round.

Her work was done.

Meanwhile, Mike bobbed and weaved among the well-wishers, firing his camera like a machine gun. When the initial furore had died down, he touched Charlie's elbow to ask him to pose for some formal shots.

Mike was preparing to pull the trigger when Barbara found her way into the frame. She positioned herself between Charlie and the painting's new owner, thus making cropping her from the image impossible and ensuring she would get her share of the credit and a large, full-colour picture of her smiling self in all the local and, if possible, national papers.

As Mike worked, the auction limped to an anticlimactic finish in the wake of its star lot. At ten minutes to midnight, the auctioneer shoved the gavel in his pocket and bowled down the steps towards the bar, abandoning the stage to the band. As they tuned up, a screen was unrolled from the gantry and left to hang in front of the red curtains. It was soon covered with a live image of the Houses of Parliament, projected in preparation for the countdown to midnight and the chimes that would hail the new year.

Tucked away between two stacks of chairs next to the emergency exit, Becky nodded to herself in silent approval of the onstage preparations. However she was less impressed by the cheap confetti cannons being installed around the dance floor and muttered darkly to herself about corner cutting. Where did the money from the ticket sales go? She glanced at her phone. Five minutes to midnight. Another quick glance to the far side of the dance floor confirmed Charlie was still surrounded by a group of adoring older ladies. They took turns to brush imaginary lint from his shoulders while moving around him with unsettling, predatory movements. Being circled by these sharks, Charlie looked more comfortable than Becky would have expected. He smiled and chuckled, probably riding the high from the painting's success.

Confident he was in no immediate danger, Becky fell back into her old habits and scanned the room, revelling in the luxury of only having to search for the people she cared about. Lloyd and Barbara were back on the dance floor. Ronnie was hovering a short distance behind Mike, who was busy earning his admission. That left Virgil and Rachel. Where had they gone?

Three minutes to midnight. The cloud of wealth and maturity surrounding Charlie dispersed as the ladies returned to their official partners in time for the big moment. As the indistinct mass of guests split into pairs, Becky realised she still had work to do: she had to find Rachel for Charlie.

Two minutes to midnight. Becky made a lap of the room, staying close to the wall to ease her progress. She stopped next to Ronnie to see if she had any useful intelligence, but she hadn't seen Rachel either.

One minute to midnight. Standing with her back to the door to the great hall, Becky spotted Charlie in the middle of the dance floor. He was switching his head from side to side, searching for his partner as the clock ticked away the few remaining seconds of the year.

Becky was beginning to despair when she saw them. In the corner of the dance floor nearest to her, Virgil and Rachel were getting a head start on the traditional New Year's kissing. Becky was impressed; whatever Virgil had said or done, it had worked.

But Charlie was still looking for Rachel. She cursed her bad luck; why did he have to be wearing his glasses? He would have to find out about Rachel and Virgil some time, but this was not the ideal moment or the right way. What to do? She dismissed the option of parting Virgil and Rachel; that would take far too long and might be impossible.

Half a minute to go. A distraction. That could work. She made her way to the middle of the room, skating between the dancers as they slowed and turned towards the projected image of the giant clock face. Charlie disappeared from view and she barked an obscenity, causing the stubbornly immobile couple blocking her way to jump aside.

She had him in her sights again and only a few feet away.

The ten-second countdown began.

'Charlie!'

He saw her and shouldered the chanting crowd aside, closing the gap between them in a few seconds.

'Charlie!' she shouted again, desperate to keep his attention. But his gaze wandered over her head, to the corner of the floor where she had last seen Rachel and Virgil wrapping themselves around each other.

Three seconds. Only one idea came to her. She placed her hand gently against his cheek, drawing his eyes to hers and, on the cry of 'one!', she kissed him.

It was over in a second and, as she pulled back, she said, 'Happy New Year!', hoping he could hear her over the first bars of 'Auld Lang Syne'.

But Charlie didn't appear to be listening to her or anything around him. Without taking his eyes away from hers, he grasped her shoulders and drew her into another kiss.

Becky was vaguely aware of the pops of cannons and the soft rain of glitter confetti tickling her bare shoulders. A blush of sound filled her ears, echoing from the outside world into the small circle holding him and her apart. The air above sparkled with the optimistic cooing of happy people, happy to be saying 'farewell' to another year in which they had made lots of mistakes and 'hello' to one in which they would doubtless make a lot more. And maybe, just maybe, they would also do something right.

Her fingers tingled as they brushed through his hair. Somehow her hands had found their way to the back of his neck. His were a solid, warm weight at her waist. And when they finally eased apart, that was where their hands stayed while they smiled and blinked at each other.

It was Becky who broke the spell. She dropped her gaze away from Charlie's, kicking herself for being so stupid. The year was seconds old and she had managed to make her first mistake. She glanced at Charlie, but he was already looking over her head, most likely searching for Rachel and wondering what the hell he'd done. She had to leave. Right now.

'I have to go,' she said, backing away. She flinched as Charlie's smile fell into a frown. 'Enjoy the rest of the evening and congratulations on the painting!'

∽

As Becky slipped through the crowd, Charlie struggled to free himself from the crush. He pushed and jostled his way to the edge of the dance floor, then ran to the door, throwing himself across the threshold.

But the great hall was empty.

With heavy hands, he dragged his glasses off. His fingers were clumsy as he folded one arm, then the other, and lowered them into his pocket.

Drifting back into the saloon, he sank onto the nearest chair and stared down at his empty hands: an abandoned Prince Charming, all alone without so much as a glass slipper.

JANUARY

Chapter 51

Charlie's show was a success before it happened. Eager for stories to fill a slow news day, the national press picked up on the record sale price at the ball auction and were keen to speculate as to how it would influence the exhibition opening a week later. With great satisfaction, Rachel was able to pick and choose who attended the gala evening, building a store of goodwill she planned to take with her to the Stone in March, when she would finally sink her claws into the helm of the family business.

Becky spent New Year's Day busy with the return of Dylan and her parents. Charlie didn't call her, and when he didn't call the next day either she put the kiss down to a New Year's moment of madness which he had already forgotten.

Unfortunately she was finding it a little more difficult to put it behind her and the local press didn't help. The new year edition of the *South Compton Gazette* hit her mat on Friday evening. The section covering the ball included a double-page spread containing several photos, including four in colour. One showed the organising committee at the start of the evening; another was a wide shot of the saloon during dinner; and the third featured Barbara, Charlie and the winner of the auction.

The final picture was taken just after midnight. Mike had found a group of revellers willing to pose with their glasses raised to the camera. In the background was the stage and band. The rest of the photo was populated with smiling faces and people hugging, all covered in a shower of multicoloured confetti. And at the left edge of the photo one of the kissing couples jumped out at her.

She sat back and chewed her lip. The image was blurry. If it hadn't been for her white dress even she might not have noticed them. But if the dress caught Ronnie's eye too she might ask Mike for a closer look at the original. And then the inquisition would call.

Perhaps Ronnie wouldn't see it. Perhaps if she kept quiet then everyone else would too, at least until she'd seen Charlie and had a better idea of what was going on.

❧

Preparations for the exhibition progressed with little for Becky to do but check in on everyone else. Ronnie had finalised her plans for the cake. Phoebe had roped her mum into helping her with publicity and was excited by rumours the regional television news were going to broadcast live from the gallery. Lauren was fully up to date. Becky was unable to reach Rachel, but Virgil told her the Coulson was ready and they had a waiting list for admittance to opening night.

That left Charlie. Speaking to Phoebe on Monday she learnt there was another reason she hadn't heard from him: he was working. According to the teenager, she had barely seen her dad since Friday evening.

'We had dinner as usual and the last time I saw him he was sitting in the study, his feet up, reading the *Gazette*. The next thing I know he's vanished out to the studio and he's hardly come out since.' Phoebe dropped her voice. 'Becky, I think he's sleeping in there. But from how tired he looks I don't think he's sleeping much. At breakfast yesterday he said he was working on an important extra piece for the show and was going to have to put in like, a hundred hours for it to be dry in time. I don't know much else about it, except it's large, about four feet by six. That's one of the reasons it's so much work.'

'Rachel's going to love having to make room for another painting this late in the day, and particularly one that big.'

'That's so what I said. But then he said she would have to bloody well like it because if she refused to include it he would pull the whole show.'

'Wow.' It sounded as if Charlie did need more sleep. 'Drama!'

'I know, right? Anyway, she came over yesterday.'

'Rachel?'

'Yeah. She showed up after lunch and went out to the studio. She must have been here for about half an hour but when she left she looked happy enough, so I guess it's all fine.'

❧

Although she knew he was busy, on Tuesday Becky decided she had put off talking to Charlie long enough. If only to maintain the illusion of professionalism she should talk to him before the show.

She waited until Dylan was immobilised by his favourite television programme and shut herself in the kitchen. She told herself not to be so daft—it was only a New Year's kiss—and dialled his number.

She ran her fingers up and down the countertop while she waited for the call to connect. Eventually there was a click and she heard distant, high-pitched laughter accompanied by muttering and noises that suggested the phone had been retrieved at some cost.

'Hello?'

'Ms Watson! Hello!'

Becky cleared her throat, which was suddenly dry and scratchy. 'Hello, Ms Stone. How are you?'

'Wonderful, thank you. Everyone's so excited about the exhibition.'

'That's great. Great. You must be pleased,' she said, the enthusiasm draining from her voice. 'Can I speak to Char— Um ... I mean ... May I speak to John, please?'

Rachel lowered her voice. 'I'm sure you could, but he's busy at the moment and I know you wouldn't want to disturb him.'

It was true Charlie didn't like distractions when he was working. But apparently it was OK for Rachel to be there, yesterday and today as well, taking his calls and 'disturbing' him.

'Right, right. I'll call another time. Just, if you could tell him I rang, I'd appreciate it.'

'Shall do! Bye!'

Becky opened her mouth to say goodbye but Rachel had already hung up.

She put the phone down on the kitchen counter and started to make tea. Keep calm and make tea: wasn't that what the English did in the face of disaster? No, she corrected herself, this wasn't a disaster; this was good. She now knew what she had wanted to know: it was all a New Year's blip. It was midnight, he couldn't find his date, he'd had a few drinks and so he kissed his sturdiest member of staff after she threw herself at him. It all made sense, said her sensible self: once again, she was just the other woman.

But at the same time, the tiny, timid voice struggled to remind her what she had felt in that supposed moment of madness. For while the details of the kiss were fading as each day passed, she remained certain of what Charlie had put into it: warmth, strength and tenderness. The very best of himself.

Chapter 52

Charlie didn't return Becky's call and life carried on. She and Virgil agreed a date in mid-January to have a proper meeting about working together; she shortlisted nurseries where Dylan could start the following year; and she met with a nervous future groom to see whether she could help with his spring wedding.

With all this and her usual domestic tasks, the time to opening night flew by. She blessed Lloyd's extravagance as she pulled on the black dress he'd sent her as one option for the ball. It fitted well and was as comfortable as she had hoped.

In the second blessing of the evening, Phoebe was late to collect her. As it was, she had no chance to do anything else with her hair but dry it and let it fall over her shoulders, and was still finishing her make-up when the doorbell rang.

The first night of the exhibition started at six and was due to finish at eight. Phoebe had agreed to come and collect Becky and Dylan at seven. That way Becky would only have to keep Dylan amused in a boring, 'don't touch!' building for about forty-five minutes, and Phoebe would be present for the start of proceedings when the press would be in attendance.

Becky stopped humming 'La Vie en Rose', which was starting to become a habit, and ran down the stairs. She shuffled Dylan away from the door and opened it to find Phoebe shivering on the doorstep. It was a foggy, freezing night and there was a harsh breeze in the air. Becky stood aside and waved her in.

'Hi!' Phoebe said as she crossed the threshold. 'We're here!'

She was opening her mouth to ask who 'we' were, when Ronnie scuttled past her. 'Bloody hell, Becks, take your time answering the door why don't you? Not that it's frigging freezing out there or anything.'

The final person to come through the door was a woman with long brown hair and dark eyes. She was familiar, but Becky couldn't place her.

Phoebe stepped forward to supply the missing introduction. 'This is my Aunt Lauren.'

'Lauren? What are you doing here?'

Lauren laughed and gave Becky a hug.

As they pulled apart, Becky corrected herself. 'I mean, when did you get here?'

'Yesterday morning,' Lauren said, blinking her bloodshot eyes. 'Still jet-lagged. It's madness. But when I heard how big this whole thing was getting, I couldn't miss it. And, between you and me ...' She dropped her voice. 'I jumped at the chance to have a good reason for a week away from two teenage boys and their father. I love them but ...' She exhaled noisily, puffing out her cheeks and letting Becky complete the picture.

'It's lovely to finally meet you,' said Becky.

Out of the corner of her eye she watched suspiciously as Phoebe removed Dylan's coat and shoes and picked up his slippers. Meanwhile, Ronnie had disappeared into the kitchen. From the banging and slamming of cupboards, Becky assumed she was trying to make tea.

'How's it going at the gallery?'

'Great,' said Lauren and Phoebe.

'Huh!' said Ronnie, her head appearing through the archway from the kitchen. 'He's been asking after you every five minutes. And Rachel was doing my head in as well. Wherever I went she was right next to me, droning on and on. Everything that woman says is total shite.'

'Hey!' said Becky, covering Dylan's ears.

Ronnie was undeterred. 'When Phoebe said she had a legitimate excuse for leaving we both jumped at the chance of getting out of there.'

Ronnie disappeared back into the kitchen and resumed the clanging. Becky grinned and turned to Lauren. 'So not as thrilling as a night in the West End then?'

'Not exactly. I love my brother, but those people make me want to break things.'

The noise in the kitchen ceased and Ronnie came back into the room holding three tall glasses and a bottle of spirits. 'Don't you have anything that isn't rum?'

'I do apologise. I wasn't expecting you this evening or I'd have the bar fully stocked,' Becky said as she settled further back into the armchair.

'It's all right: I'm driving,' said Lauren, who had taken her brother's usual spot on the sofa. 'And we don't have much time before we have to get back, so I'll come straight to the point.'

She nodded at Phoebe. On cue, the girl jumped to her feet and chased a delighted Dylan to the stairs. As he made progress up to his room, the teenager paused on the bottom step, smiled and said, 'Good luck,' before racing after the toddler.

Not giving Becky time to wonder who Phoebe had been speaking to, Lauren said, 'Now. What is going on with you and my brother?'

Oh my God. Becky blinked as her gaze shuttled between Ronnie and Lauren. Was this what it was like to be on the receiving end of an intervention? She frowned and swallowed. 'What do you mean?'

'He really likes you,' said Lauren. 'Actually, I think he's falling for you, if he's not there already.'

'He hasn't told me that.'

'He hasn't told me either and all of us will die of old age waiting for that to happen. You heard how he proposed to Mel?'

Becky nodded.

'That's Charlie.' Lauren compressed years of exasperation into a dismissive wave of her hand. 'He can put it all up on the wall in ten-foot-high squiggles but getting a few words out of him can be next to impossible.'

Becky reached for the glass Ronnie was offering her. 'What about Rachel?'

Lauren shrugged. 'What about her?'

'It's all about her. All the paintings. She's his muse!'

The intervention party shared another glance and Lauren nodded at her collaborator. Ronnie pulled a rolled-

373

up booklet out of her back pocket. 'The catalogues were only printed at the end of last week.' She held it out to Becky. 'Here, take a look.'

Flicking through, Becky recognised most of the twenty-one canvases. The last-minute painting hadn't made the printed catalogue, although she assumed it would soon be online for all to see. She closed the booklet and read the exhibition title: *The Muse's Eyes*.

Lauren and Ronnie had been watching her. Becky felt as though she should be lying on a black couch and talking about her parents while they wielded clipboards and scribbled notes.

'Did you know Charlie's been getting inspiration from his dreams?' asked Lauren.

Becky nodded again.

'That's where the title of the show comes from. From what I've been able to get out of him, the eyes of the woman in his dreams were her most important feature, the thing that impacted him most. So much so he's used their colour in all the paintings.'

Becky crossed her arms and snorted. This only proved her point. 'That was Rachel's idea, the colour theme thing.'

'Right. But Rachel's eyes aren't blue, are they?'

Becky opened her mouth to respond, then froze. She flicked through the catalogue again. Lauren was right; it was everywhere. She thought back to her afternoon in the gallery with Rachel; the blue flecks, the blue block and, most vividly, the blue cloud on one side of that red line. That frustrated red line. The wedding in November. Charlie and Rachel under the tree. Virgil barging in. But before that. Before that.

They might be on to something.

Lauren pressed on. 'And it's not any old blue. It's the exact colour of your eyes. Or, at least, the exact way Charlie sees them.'

Becky slapped the catalogue shut. 'That can't be right.'

'It is,' Ronnie said, taking a swig of her drink and sitting down next to Lauren.

Becky shook her head. 'But he said it was Rachel in his dreams.' Drowning under so many implications, she reached for Ronnie as if she were a lifebelt. 'You were there when he said it was Rachel.'

'No, he didn't. I said it and he was too embarrassed to put me right.' She shrugged. 'And you can't blame him. To be fair, if you'd been having dreams featuring Charlie half-naked would you be fessing up to it with him sitting right in front of you?'

Becky reviewed what she knew about Charlie's dreams. With this new information she couldn't help but wonder if what he had seen in them came close to some of the things that had featured in hers recently. The most vivid one had come two nights ago. Remembering it made Becky's heart skip out of rhythm, but she found the memories hard to ignore, as if trying not to think about them lodged them more firmly in the front of her conscious mind.

'A-ha!' Ronnie jabbed an accusing finger at Becky's reddening face. 'You so have—'

'Please!' interrupted Lauren. 'Could we not talk about dodgy dreams featuring my brother? Please?'

Ronnie sighed. 'All right.' Turning to Becky, she tapped her nose and leered. 'I'm going to need to know all about that later. But for now, how do you feel about him?'

'I work for him.'

'That's not an answer. Anyway,' said Ronnie, 'that's soon to be irrelevant. When the gallery closes tonight your job is done.'

Becky rubbed her fingers along her brow ridge to ease a throbbing which was threatening to become a headache. Irrelevant, she thought, that's what all this will be soon. So what if she was Charlie's latest muse? How was that different to being someone's mistress? She was still the woman in black, the unseen and uncredited source of solutions and inspiration. He hadn't called her in over a week now he had everything he needed for the show. She had done her job and he could dispose of her services and move on. While she might have been the woman of his dreams, she remained nothing more than an anonymous figure in the background or isolated on one side of a stupid red line.

Looking at Lauren and Ronnie's expectant faces, Becky had another stab at derailing their theories. 'But he kissed Rachel. At the wedding in November.'

Ronnie snorted. 'According to Mike, Charlie tells it more like Lady Stone was blotto and launched herself on him. He was so stunned it was all he could do to stop her falling over while trying to fend her off.'

'But he took her home afterwards and Rachel said—'

'She was out for the count when they got to her place. He carried her indoors and left her on the sofa in the recovery position with the bathroom bin next to her head in case she puked in the night. Nothing happened.'

'But if all that's true why did he take her to the ball?'

Lauren shrugged. 'I think because you kept pushing him towards her and he didn't want to ruin your plans or disappoint you.'

'What? That's crazy!' Becky hadn't craved a drink in years, but now she remembered the glass of rum sitting in her hands and took a long swig, bringing on a fit of coughing.

Lauren wouldn't be deterred. 'Have you seen the new painting?'

'She can't have,' said Ronnie, downing the remains of her drink in one. 'Come on, Becks. Phoebe'll stay here with Dylan. We're going back to town with you.'

'Do I have any say in this?'

'No!' chorused the others.

'And,' said Lauren, putting a consoling arm around Becky's shoulders as they led her out to the car, 'on the way there I want to hear more about this mysterious job you've been offered. After all, contrary to what you're about to see at the gallery, the world doesn't revolve around my stupid brother.'

Chapter 53

Charlie rested his head against the glass. The bright, cold lights of the Coulson were reflected in the dark shop fronts opposite, along with oily ghosts of the exhibition's patrons, milling around inside the fish tank, their mouths opening and closing as they exchanged opinions.

The pavements outside were scrawled with ice and the glass was a cool hand on his furrowed brow. He should be delighted. Everyone kept telling him he must be. Perhaps delight would come when the scraping and crawling in his stomach settled down. It wasn't hunger. Phoebe had made him a plate of pasta for lunch suitable for someone about to run a marathon and he had spent the evening hoovering up trays of finger food while doing his best to make polite chit-chat with the people who would be indirectly funding his daughter's law degree.

'John!'

He pushed away from the glass as Rachel barrelled down on him, followed by Virgil. Those two were inseparable.

Even when they were having independent conversations they contrived to have their fingers, hips or feet touching. But at least this evening Rachel had dropped the irritating habit of shoehorning Virgil's name into every sentence.

'John! Come and meet the Drayslades; dear Amanda and Tim.' She beamed at him as she grabbed his wrist. 'They simply adore everything and want you to talk them through a couple of pieces.' Approaching her targets, she whispered, 'They have deep pockets and fancy themselves collectors. The woman who won the auction at the ball is a *poor* relation.'

The Drayslades turned out to be a pleasant couple, though distractingly horsey in appearance. And if they noticed Charlie's gaze swinging back and forth between them and the door like a metronome, they were polite enough not to comment.

Where was she? The coven had gone to pick her up over forty minutes ago and there were only twenty until the gallery closed. He ran a finger around the inside of his collar. He hated roll-neck sweaters. Phoebe had made him wear the ridiculous thing. Made him look like a bloody turtle.

'We would be keen for you to come up to the house,' said Amanda Drayslade while her husband nodded. 'We're in the process of reconsidering our collection and feel a few specially commissioned Handrens would be just the ticket …'

She drawled on, but her voice became a faint buzz when the door of the gallery slammed open and Ronnie bowled through. Followed by Lauren. Then Becky.

His hand snapped out as a tray of drinks weaved past. Turning his back to the door, he took a gulp of white wine so dry it did little to soothe his parched mouth.

Over the heads of his future patrons he could see the painting which had robbed him of sleep the past five nights. He wasn't entirely happy with his technique and it was beyond derivative. But time had been short and it was a necessary gamble. And if she didn't like what she saw ... At least he would have tried to show her how he felt.

Charlie emptied the glass and threw a final glance at the canvas. All he could do was hope it was eloquent enough to tell Becky the many things he had failed to. Repeatedly.

❧

Once inside the warmth of the gallery, Becky was glad to shed her outer layers. Apparently Ronnie knew her way around; she snatched their coats and disappeared, soon returning clutching a large glass of wine.

Lauren nudged Becky and nodded to the left where Charlie was standing surrounded by a small flock of art aficionados. She squinted to bring him into focus. Like her, he was dressed in black, but Becky suspected Phoebe had taken a hand in creating what she believed would be termed a 'look'. A sharp suit was teamed with a high-neck jumper. He hadn't shaved for a few days and was wearing his glasses.

'Where did you get that?' Lauren asked Ronnie, pinging the rim of the wine glass with her nails.

'Come with me,' said Ronnie, taking Lauren's arm and leading her away.

'Where are you going?' asked Becky.

In response, Ronnie glared at the space past Becky's shoulder and widened her eyes. Becky followed her friend's stare and found herself face-to-face with Charlie. He looked rather handsome, even in a daft turtleneck.

'Hi.'

'Hello.'

'How are you?'

'Fine. You?'

'Yeah, fine. Thanks.'

She rubbed her hands together and wished she had something to hold. Her fingers, taking advantage of their freedom, flew up to Charlie's collar and gave it a tug. 'Nice jumper.'

Charlie laughed. 'I didn't choose it.' He leant forward and whispered, 'I didn't choose anything I'm wearing.'

Becky had already been warm, but something about his tone made her cheeks burn. Flustered, she said, 'Good. That jumper doesn't suit you.'

'I know.'

'And you couldn't have shaved for the big event?'

'I would. But I haven't had time and Phoebe said it would all add to the look so I jumped at the chance to be lazy.' Charlie dug his hands in his pockets. 'You look nice,' he said.

'Thank you.'

'I mean … What I want to say is … That dress is great and … You, you look …' He took a deep breath and stared down at his shoes. 'Beautiful.'

She blinked and opened her lips to respond. But he had caught her off guard and she floundered, an unseen hand tightening its grip around her throat.

'John!' Rachel barked as she sallied over and seized Charlie by the wrist. She gave Becky a quick nod in lieu of a greeting, then used both hands to push him towards a waiting congregation of grey dollars and euros. He looked back and raised his hands by way of an apology.

'Don't leave,' Charlie said, as Virgil added his strength to Rachel's, pulling him into the middle of another circle of cooing and fawning.

Becky raised a hand to cover her mouth as blood thudded and sloshed through her ears. The hand around her throat squeezed. She glanced towards the exit. It was a short walk home. If she could retrieve her coat and slip away ...

Taking a deep, slow breath, she began to sidle towards the door.

'You'll have to push to get near it,' said Ronnie, stepping across her escape route. 'And you'll want to get near it, you being blind without your specs.'

Kicking her best friend in the shins, shoving her to the floor and scrambling out the door would not be the response of a rational person. But it was tempting.

'Get near what?'

'The last-minute painting.' Ronnie jabbed a finger towards the crowd at the back of the room. 'You'd think it was the Mona bloody Lisa the way this lot have been hovering round it. Let's have a little look, shall we?' She clamped the tops of Becky's arms between her hands and steered her friend towards the huddle surrounding Charlie's latest creation. When they reached the back of the group, she gave Becky an encouraging prod in the small of her back.

Becky stepped forward and cast a glance over her shoulder. Ronnie hadn't moved. Her feet were firmly planted and arms folded. There was no going back.

She shouldered her way through to the front. The group appreciating the painting had left a few feet of space around it and, as she got closer, Becky understood why.

It made her Christmas present look like a simple card trick. This illusion was near perfect: it was as if Renoir had attended the art society ball instead of the dance at the Moulin de la Galette. Charlie had used Mike's photos for the details of the moment, and the impressionist's style and composition to bring it to life.

The original painting depicted a bright Parisian park on a Sunday afternoon; Charlie's version showed the dimly lit ballroom of Compton Hall as energetic revellers embraced, laughed and shook hands, celebrating the new year. As in Renoir's painting, the band was a distant blur and most of the dancers were darkly robed shadows. A group of milky-skinned figures sat in the right foreground. Some were sipping champagne and talking, while others gesticulated towards the other side of the canvas, and the viewer couldn't help but search for whatever had attracted their interest.

To the left of centre, the couple were transfixed in a kiss. Her dress was white; he wore black. Their attachment to each other detached them from the bustle of the surroundings as a glimmer of gold and silver sparkled over them, falling softly and silently into their little world.

A nasal bray brought her out of her reverie. Becky closed her mouth and licked her dry lips as she tuned into an energetic argument between the three self-appointed art experts to her right.

'I'm telling you, the title is a reference to these figures in the foreground. A bargain is being struck—'

'No, no, you're wrong. They're mere bystanders. Nothing but filler. It's obviously a nod to this group. It's a play on something from Shakespeare, isn't it?'

'Probably a bastardisation of the bard, yes. But you're both being too literal. The title tells us the piece as a whole is a satirical comment on society.'

'Not society. Artists. It's a blatant jibe at artists who pursue Impressionism for commercial gain …'

They waddled away, still arguing, but Becky had long since stopped listening. She had seen the label next to the painting and knew they were all wrong. Her pedantic literary reflex was screaming 'Marlowe, not Shakespeare, you idiots!' Although that was a minor point. They never stood a chance of guessing the meaning and intention of the painting. How could they hope to understand such a private message? One that was printed on a piece of white card in red letters—the red of fresh blood—congealed into the six words of the painting's title: *Faustus gives to Mephistopheles his soul.*

Becky inched back, keeping her eyes on the canvas as if retreating from a tiger. Mesmerised, she barely heard the grumbling of the other guests as she bumped into them and forced them to shuffle aside.

A few paces from the wall the painting came into sharp focus. She paused and, as she explored its details, was transported back into the midnight scene. The chimes of Big Ben, the tickle of confetti … Charlie's warm smile. As she sank deeper into the memory, ambient sounds of chatter and footsteps faded and the overhead lighting seemed to dim, leaving the couple in the picture alone in a soft glow.

A warm hand brushed the small of her back and, for a moment, she was uncertain if it were real.

'You should sit down.' Charlie had placed a seat behind her. It was angled so she would be facing the painting square on.

'Oh, thanks.' She lowered herself onto the chair and watched as he stepped away to grab another and place it to her right. As he took a seat, the tops of their arms brushed against each other, causing them both to mumble apologies and shift towards the edge of their chairs.

Glancing about, Becky realised they were alone in the semi-darkness: the lights at the front of the gallery had been turned off and only those surrounding the painting in front of them were on. 'Where is everyone?'

'The guests left and everyone else went to Sweet's. Virgil has a couple of bottles of champagne on ice there. Ronnie led the charge.'

They shared a smile and shuffled in their seats until they were sitting staring at the painting in front of them, deliberately not looking at each other, like two strangers on a platform bench.

After a few more awkward seconds, Becky said, 'So your opening's over. I believe it went well.'

'Very well. Everything sold or will sell. Rachel wants to leave things open for a few more days to see if any better offers come in. But you can look forward to a generous commission cheque.'

'After you deduct the advances.'

A mocking glimmer flashed in his eyes as he waved a hand and said, 'Of course.' He shifted in his chair, turning towards her. 'I guess this means your contract has come to an end.'

'Yeah.' She mirrored his movement, twisting to her right so their knees were a few inches apart. 'You're a free man again. No more pushy Becky. Whatever will you do with yourself?'

The sparkle faded from his eyes. 'I don't know,' he said, his voice flat. 'Try to keep working, I guess.'

Her heart sank as his face fell. 'You'll have to try because from what I've seen tonight there'll be no shortage of demand.' She pointed towards the painting. 'And this one seemed popular. How much did it go for?'

Charlie sniffed and pushed the bridge of his glasses back up to the top of his nose. 'The last offer was around seventy-five thousand.'

'*What?*'

He laughed and the happy sound joined the echo of Becky's shrill surprise as it ricocheted around the empty room. She felt light-headed, and she couldn't tell if the cause was shock at such an insane sum of money or the delight on Charlie's face.

'I'm as surprised as you,' he said. 'Rachel's disappointed though. The offer makes it the highest value piece here and vindicates many of her mother's opinions about abstract art.' He swayed towards her and nudged the top of her arm with his. 'What do you think of it?'

Becky raised her hands towards the picture. 'It's … it's … wow! It's …' She was making a windmill motion with one hand and something resembling a chopping action with the other. What was wrong with her?

In an effort to stop her physical, if not mental flailing, she dropped her hands to her knees. 'I mean, it's great. It's just so …'

What she was struggling to say, in a way which didn't sound stupid, was that, not counting Dylan, it was the most beautiful thing she'd ever seen and the best surprise she'd ever had. He was a genius. A frustratingly hard to read, evasive bastard, but a genius nonetheless. Not to mention a hopeless and marvellous romantic.

He brought her struggle to an end by laying his left hand over her right. The simple gesture pulled her focus down to her buzzing fingertips and wiped her mind clear. He smiled as he moved his hand back to his own knee. 'I'm glad you like it.'

She swallowed. He was fixing her with that steady, unwavering stare of his. Under its weight her breath came quickly and she raised her hand to check her buttons were fastened properly, then became more flustered when she remembered her dress didn't have any buttons.

'Who's the lucky buyer?'

'No one. It's not for sale.'

'Oh?' The question had come out as a squeak. A niggling suspicion started to come into focus, making her palms itch. 'How come?'

'It was never on sale.' He kept his eyes fixed on the opposite wall as he said, 'I painted it for you.'

Her stomach flipped. A short laugh escaped her. 'You're kidding.'

'No. It's yours. If you want it.'

She searched his face for the smallest sign of a joke, although she knew he meant it. The unseen hand reappeared at her throat, but this time its squeezing brought tears to her eyes.

Charlie's eyes filled with concern. 'You don't like it?'

'Of course I like it! It's beautiful. I love it … but …' Still at a loss for an appropriate response and fighting tears, she sought refuge in practicalities. 'But where would I keep it? I don't have a wall in my house big enough.

And my contents insurance won't cover it, especially if it's within Dylan's reach. He's often armed with crayons and you know he's not afraid to use them. What if something happened to it?'

'You could keep it in my studio. There's tonnes of room and you could come and see it whenever you liked.'

Becky looked up at the ceiling and sighed. 'And if I don't want it? Will you sell it then?'

A small crease appeared between his eyebrows. 'No,' he said. 'I guess, if you don't want it, I'll scrap it.'

'You wouldn't!'

Charlie turned towards the painting. 'I don't know. Maybe not. But, it's yours. If you want it.'

He glanced at her, then back to the painting. He was wearing the same hangdog expression Becky had first seen back in June. The lost and lonely look she had hoped never to see again. And she certainly never wanted to be its cause.

Her chair shook as Charlie lifted his right foot onto his left knee. He jiggled it in its new resting place for a few seconds then rejected the position, returning the foot to the floor with a graceless thud which made him wince.

Becky's lips twitched. Observing his adorable unease she couldn't believe she'd considered knocking Ronnie over and bolting. Well, Ronnie probably had it coming, but how could she have thought about running away from him again?

She cleared her throat and Charlie straightened, his fidgeting coming to an abrupt end. 'And if I were to keep it ...' She smiled, thinking of the title Charlie had given the picture. 'The painting, of course. What would you want in return?'

'It's a gift.'

'Oh come on! You can't let me have something so valuable for nothing.'

'Well, if you insist …'

'I do.'

'Then I think …' He trailed off as he lifted his hand to brush her hair from her shoulder, his fingers skimming the side of her neck. She watched the movement, marvelling at how quickly her pulse reacted, thudding as if he were sliding a knife along her skin rather than his fingertips. When his hand reached the back of her neck he paused, lifting his gaze slowly until their eyes met. 'Then I believe in the past you've included dinner as part of a bargain.'

Charlie was watching her over the top of his glasses, no frown in sight. His fingers were now stroking the top of her collarbone and it was becoming difficult to think of anything, let alone frame a question.

'Are you asking me out, Charlie?'

'It would appear so.'

She pressed her lips together to prevent a smile escaping, extended her index finger and pushed the bridge of his glasses back to the top of his nose. He didn't flinch, although when he blinked she saw a flicker of surprise in his eyes, then amusement. The smile she'd been suppressing escaped. She had wanted to do that for months, pretty much every time she'd seen him in glasses.

Now unsure of what to do with her hands, she gripped the sides of the chair, pushing her palms against the metal struts until her fingers turned white. 'Do I get to decide where and when?'

'I think I can live with that.'

'Then you're on.'

Bargain made, they shuffled back to the middle of their chairs and faced forward; two strangers back to waiting for their trains. Becky fiddled with the straps on her shoes while Charlie tapped his fingers on his knees and hummed a familiar tune. She let her gaze drift beyond the brightly lit wall immediately in front of them. Staring into the gloom at the back of the gallery, she noticed the canvas sporting the frustrated red line staring right back at her. Enough. It was time to complete what Charlie had started.

She put a hand on top of his, bringing the tapping and humming to a stop. 'What about now?'

'Huh?'

She stood up and spun round to face him, making the skirt of her dress fan out and swirl around her legs. 'Dinner. Now. There's a French place near Tyler's that stays open late. And I think they may have after-dinner dancing.' She held out her hand. 'So, are you hungry?'

Charlie got to his feet. He watched Becky's beautiful blue eyes glittering silver under the cool spotlights. His stomach bulged from his late lunch and nervous snacking. The last thing he needed was more food.

'Absolutely starving,' he said, smiling and taking her hand.

AUGUST

Becky and Dylan stood on the bridge looking down at their reflections in the water below. The little boy gripped the green metal rail and bounced on his toes as a dragonfly buzzed past, dipping to skim the surface of the pool. He was eager to run through the rest of the garden. There was so much space to explore. But they had to wait until they were told they could move. They didn't want to ruin the picture.

Phoebe stepped onto the bridge to give the all-clear. Becky loosened her grip on Dylan's hand and he sped away from her, giggling. Phoebe ran after him, falling into the familiar game.

Charlie had suggested making the trip in May to see the glory of the wisteria, but Becky didn't see the point in going if the water lilies wouldn't be in bloom. Besides, by making the trip in the summer, Phoebe would have finished her exams and could enjoy the holiday before getting back to London for her internship.

Becky rested her arms on the side of the bridge and closed her eyes. Dylan's and Phoebe's laughter tripped over the rising hush of the dusk and she heard boards creak as the space next to her was taken.

When she opened her eyes, Charlie was busy putting the lens cap back on the camera. He glanced up over the top of his glasses and caught her watching him. Putting his arm around her waist, he leant to kiss her cheek. She smiled. Pulling away, she took his hand and led him in the direction of their children.

They stepped off the bridge together. Charlie put his left arm around Becky's shoulders and dropped his head to kiss her hair. Now he woke every morning to find her next to him, Charlie never needed to dream of his muse again.

As they followed the laughter deeper into the garden, the setting sun sent a last warm breath over the garden, tinting the light a gentle pink.

THE END

Also by Claire Huston

The Only Exception
(Love in the Comptons Book 2)

Lucinda Green knows something is missing from her life. But what? Her catering business is enjoying modest success and she loves her cosy house, even if she does have to share it with her irritating ex-fiancé.

Whatever's making her unsettled and edgy, Lucinda's certain that a lack of romance isn't the problem. How could it be when she doesn't believe in true love?

But Lucinda's beliefs are shaken by a series of electric encounters with Alex Fraser, a newly notorious actor who gradually proves himself to be infuriatingly funny and smart, as well as handsome.

Not that any of that matters. Because Lucinda doesn't believe in all that 'The One' nonsense. That's the rule.

But doesn't every rule have an exception?

Elle's A to Z of Love

Haileybrook, a beautiful village in the peaceful Cotswolds countryside, is most people's idea of heaven on earth.

Born and raised in this small slice of paradise, Elle Bea can't wait to leave.

It should be easy, but every time she packs her bags for exotic adventures, old loves and loyalties pull her back.

Will Elle be forced to forget her dreams of far-flung places and epic romance, or can she grab one last chance to have it all?

An uplifting, romantic story about friends, family and the relationships that make a place a home.

Acknowledgements

Thank you:

Everyone who has ever said anything kind about my writing and, in particular, has listened politely while I've wittered on about this book. Special thanks to my Mum, my husband, and Liz who have suffered me more than most.

My first readers for your time and insightful comments: Charlotte, Daniel, the Venerable Jo, Lila, Liz and Victoria.

My RNA NWS reader and all those involved in organising such a wonderful scheme for new writers. Extra thanks to the members of the RNA Birmingham Chapter for your encouragement and friendship.

My brilliant editor, Alison May, and my eagle-eyed proofreader, Imogen Howson.

Sarah Houldcroft for all her hard work publishing this book and responding so patiently to my many questions. Gail Bradley for the cover design.

Rachel Gilbey for her sterling work in organising my blog tour. Thank you to the book bloggers who took part and, more widely, to all the bloggers who have supported and encouraged me over the past few years. You're all marvellous.

Writing acknowledgements is surprisingly difficult. If you feel I've missed you out, I can only apologise. Please let me know and I'll mention you first next time!

About the author

Claire Huston lives in Warwickshire with her husband and two children. She writes uplifting modern love stories about characters who are meant for each other but sometimes need a little help to realise it.

A keen amateur baker, she enjoys making cakes, biscuits and brownies almost as much as eating them. You can find recipes for all the cakes mentioned in *Art and Soul* at www.clairehuston.co.uk along with over 100 other recipes. This is also where she talks about and reviews books.

You can also find her on:

Instagram:	@clairehuston_author
Twitter:	@ClaraVal
Facebook:	clairehustonauthor
Pinterest:	claire_huston